Blessings From the Father

Blessings From the Father

Michelle Larks

www.urbanchristianonline.com

Urban Books, LLC
78 East Industry Court
Deer Park, NY 11729

ISBN 13: 978-1-60162-841-1
ISBN 10: 1-60162-841-2

First Printing August 2012
Printed in the United States of America

10 9 8 7 6 5 4 3 2 1

Distributed by Kensington Corp.
Submit Wholesale Orders to:
Kensington Publishing Corp.
C/O Penguin Group (USA) Inc.
Attention: Order Processing
405 Murray Hill Parkway
East Rutherford, NJ 07073-2316
Phone: 1-800-526-0275
Fax: 1-800-227-9604

Blessings From the Father

A Novel

by

Michelle Larks

This book is dedicated to my Mom, Jean Harris;
Remember one day at a time!

And to my daughters, Mikeisha and Genesse,
I love you!

Acknowledgments

I give praises with my hands uplifted to God, from whom all blessings flow. My faith continues to deepen as He shows me grace and mercy. This book is the eleventh one I've written. I never imagined when I was a small girl, and my Daddy took me to the library to check out books, that one day I'd have written not one but eleven books.

I'd like to thank my family, all of you for loving me, all parts, the good and bad. And, thank you for giving me the space that I need when I morph into my main character, and immerse myself in her life and thoughts. We had a new baby in the family this year, my great-niece. Her name is Kennedi and I along with the rest of my family welcome her into our lives.

I'd also like to give a shout-out to my girlfriends. I am so heartened when we talk; even though months may elapse between those talks, we converse like we had just talked yesterday.

I'd like to thank the many libraries and booksellers for stocking my books. I'd also like to thank book clubs for reading my books. I hope they've generated a lively discussion.

Thanks to my agent Tee C Royal. To my editor Joy-lynn Jossel, thank you for being patient with me. I managed to write this book through many adversities.

If I've forgotten anyone, please forgive me. I'd also like to thank the readers who've supported me over

Acknowledgments

the years, and have bought every book I've written. I appreciate my Facebook friends who stop by my page from time to time and leave their comments.

Most of all, to the man who has been there with me on this writing journey from day one, I say thank you to my husband, Fred.

Prologue

Rosemary Green knelt on aching, arthritic knees inside the closet inside her bedroom. The small, boxlike enclosure was her refuge in times of storms. She called the closet her prayer warrior room. Rosemary's shaking hands were clasped together tightly across her bosom. Tears trickled from the corners of her eyes as she poured her troubles out to God. Then, Rosemary raised her arms upward and whispered fervently, "Father, forgive me for the sins I committed years ago. Please, Father, I beg of you, don't let the sins of the parents be visited upon the children."

She stayed in the closet for over an hour, beseeching the Lord to give her guidance and to watch over her children, her daughter, Cassandra, and especially her granddaughter, Mariah.

Rosemary departed the closet and walked gingerly to her bed. She sat down and sighed, glad that the pressure was off her knees. She took deep breaths until finally her spirit was settled. She pushed off her face tendrils of spongy hair that had escaped from the untidy bun. Then Rosemary picked up her Bible and opened it to Exodus, 20:5.

Thou shalt not bow down thyself unto them, nor serve them: for I, the Lord thy God, am a jealous God, visiting the iniquity of the fathers upon his children unto the third and fourth generation of them that hate me.

Rosemary squeezed her eyes shut. "Lord, I was a sinner then. I didn't know right from wrong. I thought I had to control the situation when all along you were in control. I was wrong, so wrong, please forgive me. Please let Mari forgive me." Rosemary rocked back and forth on the bed. She smiled remembering her counseling sessions with Reverend Dudley. Rosemary quickly turned to the book of Deuteronomy, 24:16.

The fathers shall not be put to death for the children, neither shall the children be put to death for the fathers: every man shall be put to death for his own sin.

Rosemary was raised in a strict Southern Baptist church in Florida. Her childhood minister emphasized scriptures from the Old Testament scripture, which left the young girl fearing instead of trusting in God. Only after she and Mariah joined Christian Friendship Church did Rosemary develop a relationship with God. She knew tough days lay ahead and she was going to have to draw on the strength of her relationship with God to see her through the crisis. It was a storm that had been lying dormant for years. The storm was now gathering steam and threatened the very fabric of her relationship with her precious granddaughter.

Rosemary bowed her head, folded her hands together, and prayed more. Later, she went into the bathroom and washed her face. After she patted her face with a faded pink towel, Rosemary went downstairs to prepare dinner for herself and Mariah. Rosemary vowed to rely on her faith and wait on the Lord to guide her path. In times of trouble He promised to never leave us alone and that would become Rosemary's mantra. She nodded and whispered to herself as she put the pots and pans on top of the stove, "I'll be just fine, because He promised never to leave me alone."

Chapter One

William Cook, the lawyer and executor of Mariah Green's late father's estate, picked up a batch of documents. He folded them in half, then placed them inside a legal-sized brown folding envelope. Attorney Cook then handed the packet to the slightly dazed young woman sitting in the brown wooden chair in front of his desk. "Ms. Green, this concludes all business related to your father, Harold's, estate. Included in the packet are the keys to the house, your father's business and rental properties, as well as four motor vehicles. There is also a passbook for your savings account, which include proceeds from the insurance claims for Harold and his wife, Dorothy. In the envelope are keys to the safe deposit boxes. Please feel free to call me if you have any further questions." He made a notation on a pad of paper inside an opened folder on his desk. He closed the folder and then looked up at Mariah and smiled.

Mariah's hand began trembling when the attorney placed the envelope inside her hand. "Thank you," she murmured shakily. Her doe-shaped inky black eyes dropped momentarily and then she looked directly into the lawyer's caring eyes. "I think that's it for now. I appreciate your help in getting my father's will probated as well as your guidance during this entire process." She nervously jiggled her left leg. Mariah suppressed an irrational urge to flee the office, and run outdoors to a bench that sat outside the office to read the papers herself.

For the past couple of hours, she had listened intently as the attorney explained the documents, and followed his instructions when he bade her to sign documents. Mariah placed the envelope inside her shoulder bag, zipped the purse shut, and then stood up. The attorney did likewise, removing his tall, lanky form from his gray swivel chair. He thrust out his hand. "If I can be of any further assistance to you, feel free to call me, Ms. Green. I know you're new to the Hammond area." He dropped her hand. "What are you planning to do with the properties, if I may ask?"

"I haven't quite decided yet," Mariah answered shrugging her shoulders. "Finding out my father's identity and then learning he is deceased and leaving me all his worldly possessions has been overwhelming to say the least. My brain needs time to process all of this."

"I understand." He walked her to his office door and opened it. "You still have my card, don't you?"

"Yes, I do and I'll call you if I have any questions or if any problems arise," Mariah promised. She was tall, almost eye level, with the six-foot-tall lawyer, courtesy of her three-inch heels. She wore black rayon pants and a pale pink short-sleeved oxford shirt. The temperature in late July was hot and muggy. The breeze off Lake Michigan gave little relief against the waves of heat that encompassed the Midwest region.

The two exchanged farewells. When Mariah exited the office, she picked up her step and sped down the brown paneled hallway to the glass double doors and out the building. Her legs shook as she headed for the gleaming green painted bench. Mariah checked the bench for debris and then she sat down. She took her purse strap off her shoulder and set it on the bench and pulled out the envelope. Mariah quickly removed the papers and read.

When Mariah finished perusing the document, her eyes widened. She could hardly believe that she was the owner of a two-story house, formerly a boarding house, located in Hammond, Indiana, along with many other rental and commercial properties. Mariah would be twenty-nine years old in a couple of months. She had been raised by Rosemary Green, her maternal grandmother, whom she lovingly called Granny. The pair resided in the Altgeld Garden housing project on the far south side of Chicago.

Mariah's emotions were elevated as her eyes misted. She hadn't ever met her father, Harold. She felt saddened when she learned that he lived less than ten miles from where she was raised. Mariah was rendered speechless momentarily when she received the call from Attorney Cook's law firm, notifying her that she had inherited property from her deceased father.

When she was a child, Mariah had plied her grandmother with a million questions about her father. But no answers were ever forthcoming; Rosemary said she didn't know who Mariah's father was. Rosemary suffered from hypertension and asthma. Her asthma medication, in the form of an inhaler, was never far from her reach. As Mariah became older, she noticed how her grandmother's breathing became labored if Mariah pressed Rosemary regarding her father. Or Rosemary would rub her brow and complain she could feel a headache coming on. So eventually Mariah left the subject alone. When Mariah became old enough to work, she requested a copy of her birth certificate from her grandmother and was stunned to see that the box notating her father's name was blank.

Mariah's mother, Cassandra, had been a drug addict most of her daughter's life, leaving Rosemary to raise her only grandchild. Cassandra was a fleeting presence, flitting in and out of her daughter's life like a ghost.

Years would elapse between visits from Cassandra. Mariah had gotten up her courage when she was thirteen and asked Cassandra about the identity of her father. Cassandra seemed to shrink within herself and her eyes darted about the room, landing anywhere but on her daughter. She simply replied mysteriously that it was sometimes best to let sleeping dogs lie. Then, after an awkward period of silence between mother and daughter, Cassandra jumped out of the chair she'd been sitting in and sped from Rosemary's house. Mariah didn't see her mother for another six months. Mariah always felt that her mother, out of spite, refused to divulge the information to her.

After scanning the documents again, Mariah folded and placed them back inside her purse. She walked two blocks to the parking lot, where she'd parked her beat-up, silver-colored Ford Focus, and got inside the vehicle. Instead of returning to Chicago, Mariah decided to visit her father's house. She'd driven by it what seemed a million times since she received the notification of her inheritance. The trip was a short drive from the lawyer's office and within fifteen minutes, Mariah pulled up to the curb and gazed at her newly acquired property. The building was a white-frame, two-story house. The roof looked like it needed cleaning, but overall the house seemed to be in immaculate condition. The lawn behind a shimmery silver chain link fence had been recently mowed, and the wooden stairs leading to the wraparound porch were sturdy.

Mariah reached across the seat and took the keys out of the envelope that Attorney Cook had given her. Then she opened the car door and swung her legs outside the door. She slammed the door shut and then walked to the front of the house. Mariah pushed the gate open, and walked to the back of the building. Two huge oak trees were planted in the backyard and promised shade from the sun's rays in the summer. There was also a small coach house in the rear of the property, which Mariah thought would be perfect for Rosemary. The backyard was large.

She returned to the front of the house and walked up four stairs to the door. Mariah put the key in the slot, turned it, and pushed the door open.

There was a door immediately to Mariah's left; she pulled it open to find a cedar closet. She closed the door, took a few steps forward, and paused in front of an oak staircase that led to the second level. Mariah walked into the living room. She stopped and her eyes scanned the room. There was a large bay window framed by two smaller ones. A mantled fireplace was built into one of the walls. There were an old-fashioned sofa and two chairs, surrounded by two end tables and a cocktail table. The top borders of the living and dining rooms were trimmed by dark, old-fashioned woodwork.

An old television set console was used to house photographs of her father and his wife. The walls were painted white. Mariah's eyes were drawn to an oil painting over the mantle of a couple from a bygone era. She knew automatically the pair was Harold and Dorothy. Mariah walked over to the painting and stared at it for a few moments. She knew she didn't resemble Cassandra very much, although Rosemary swore the two women shared the same smile and complexion. When Mariah looked at the picture, she knew from whom she had inherited her thick, dark hair, widow's peak, and upturned nose. Harold couldn't deny Mariah parentage if he wanted to. She bore an uncanny resemblance to him. Whereas his coloring was a walnut color, Mariah's complexion was deep Hershey's brown like her mother.

Mariah stifled a sigh; she was dismayed to see that Harold appeared old enough to be her grandfather. She often had fantasies of a handsome, dashing young man coming to claim her and rescue her from Cassie. The idea of an older man just didn't sit well with her. She couldn't image her erratic mother being intimate with someone so old.

There were dozens of pictures of the couple scattered about the room. Mariah picked up one of the frames and noted that she also inherited her height from her father. She set the picture down and continued inspecting the house. There was a room off the kitchen that appeared to be a den, and a kitchen, dining room, and powder room on the first floor.

Mariah finally went upstairs. There was a wood-burning fireplace in the master bedroom along with an attached bathroom. There were three bathrooms, a sitting room, and a door that led to the attic on the second floor. Three of the bedrooms were a good size and the other two smaller.

She continued roaming the house and discovered a finished basement with additional rooms on the lower level. An hour later, Mariah returned to the living room and sat on the camel-colored sofa. She could hardly believe her good fortune. It was more house than she would ever need. Mariah also wondered why her father hadn't ever bothered to come see her. She knew from Attorney Cook that her father's wife had preceded her father in death by six months. The couple didn't have any children, so Harold left all his worldly goods to his only child, Mariah.

There were so many questions Mariah feared she'd never get the answers to. Her cell phone rang. She pulled the phone out of her purse. "Hi, Rocki," she said after looking at the caller ID.

"Hello to you too. How are you feeling, Mari?" Rocki asked. She was one of Mariah's best friends, and though her birth name was Raquel Mitchell, she'd been nicknamed Rocki since childhood.

"Girl, I feel so strange, and I'm trying hard not to trip. You wouldn't believe the house my father left me. It's huge. Right about now, I just feel overwhelmed by so many emotions." Mariah's words spewed quickly from her mouth, leaving her breathless.

"Don't look a gift horse in the mouth," Rocki advised her friend. "I'm happy for you. I know how you've always wanted a daddy. You may not have known him, but he left you a beautiful legacy. Now you just have to figure out what you're going to do with it."

"That's true." Mariah nodded. "It would make sense for me to sell everything and save the money. I could probably buy myself two new houses from the sale of his house alone. But, I've been thinking about keeping it. I have a feeling that Cassandra won't be leaving me any legacies." Mariah's lips twisted into a wry grin.

"I think you should think long and hard over the matter before you decide what to do," Raquel suggested helpfully. "You don't have to make any decisions right at this minute. What does Granny think you should do?"

"You know what, she hasn't said much, short of offering her condolences in one breath and then congratulating me in the next one. I feel like Granny is holding back, and I don't know why. She's never been shy about expressing her thoughts."

Raquel's gaze drifted to one of her clients. She had pushed the dryer bonnet up, indicating her hair was dry. "Look, I've got to go. It's Friday and you know how busy the shop gets today. How about me and Sonni go to Hammond with you tomorrow? So we can see everything. You know I'm nosy. I ain't ashamed. I'm dying to see your inheritance."

"That sounds good. I have the keys to the place, so I can give you both the two-cent tour. Maybe I can get Granny to come too. I suppose I can treat you all to lunch, courtesy of Harold Ellison."

"Aren't you the big spender?" Rocki giggled. "I'll call Sonni and see what she's up to. Maybe we'll stop by to see you later. Gotta run."

Mariah pressed the end button on her cell phone and sat motionlessly. She leaned back on the sofa and closed her eyes. She spoke aloud to her father. "Harold Ellison, why didn't you ever come to see me? I don't understand that at all. Were you ashamed of me? Were you married when I was born? Granny struggled for many years trying to provide for us. I began working when I was sixteen. Most importantly, what made you decide to leave this house and everything else to me? Don't you have other relatives? I can't believe you lived this close to me and never once inquired about or attempted to take care of me, when it's obvious you had the means to."

Shadows danced on the wall as daylight faded and Mariah rose from the couch. She put on her jacket and decided to head back to Chicago. She took a last look at the house and then opened the door, locked it, and walked to her car.

During her junior and senior years of high school, Rosemary insisted her granddaughter receive some formal education or training after high school. Mariah was a B-average student and didn't particularly wish to attend college. Rosemary was like a bulldog on the subject and Mariah eventually attended Olive-Harvey College the fall semester after her high school graduation. Mysteriously Rosemary provided the funds for Mariah to attend college, just as she had pulled out all stops to ensure Mariah was dressed lavishly for her senior prom.

When Mariah questioned Rosemary as to where the money came from, Rosemary smiled and said she had a little something set aside. Two years later, Mariah received an associate's degree in child development, preschool education. Mariah especially enjoyed a few of the electives she had taken: child, family, and community relations, along with consumer economics, and a class on the national government.

She later took a grant writing course and after receiving government funding, Mariah opened an office in Altgeld Garden and became a community activist as well as an advocate for abused young women and children in the housing project. Mariah had found her calling in life and truly enjoyed what she considered her life's mission. She learned early on that she couldn't always make a difference in all of her clients' lives, but when she did, a sense of accomplishment filled her soul.

As time elapsed and Mariah began to make progress with community issues, her achievements had been written up in several local newspapers. The teen pregnancy rate had dropped and more girls were participating in child parenting classes. Mariah was never more proud than when the elite *Chicago Tribune* newspaper wrote a piece profiling her work. Rosemary cut the articles out of the paper and pasted them in a scrapbook.

Rosemary worked at a local elementary school in the cafeteria. She had a strong sense of self, along with a strong work ethic, and she willed that trait to her granddaughter. Rosemary was determined her granddaughter would not share the same fate as her daughter.

Rosemary and Mariah were long-time members of Christian Friendship Church. Until Mariah received her driver's license, she and Rosemary took public transportation to the church. Mariah followed Rosemary's lead and worked in the Sunday School department. It was there that Mariah discovered her love for children and found her niche: teaching.

As Mariah drove home, she wondered if God had another plan for her. Maybe He was leading her to Hammond. Perhaps there was work to be done farther up Interstate 94. Her future, which had always seemed so clear, had suddenly become a little cloudy.

Thirty minutes later, Mariah had parked her car in the housing parking lot and walked inside her home. After she opened the door, popping sounds of grease frying and the aroma of catfish greeted her at the door.

Mariah's eyes scanned the gray-colored cinderblock walls, and the run-down furniture that hadn't been replaced in years. The house was always clean, warm, and cozy. Still it had an old-timey feel to it.

As she sniffed the air, Mariah knew that her granny had prepared her favorite Friday night meal: fried catfish, spaghetti, and there was probably a bowl of creamy coleslaw chilling in the refrigerator. Rosemary stood at the stove, holding a long-handled meat turner in her hand. She quickly turned over the fish. She glanced at Mariah, smiled, and said, "How was your day, dear?"

"I don't even know how to explain all the emotions I felt today, Granny," Mariah answered her grandmother after she hung her jacket on the coat rack.

"Well, that's to be expected." Rosemary nodded her head. Her black hair, threaded with strands of gray, was pulled into a bun. She wore a shapeless blue dress that covered her bulky shape. Rosemary's complexion was dark like her daughter's and granddaughter's. Her figure had expanded over the years, but the twinkling in her eyes and the will to see her granddaughter succeed hadn't ever diminished. Rosemary's husband, Joseph, was a soldier in the Vietnam War and had been declared MIA. His body had never been recovered.

The couple had moved to the housing project when it was newly built, before it became a haven for criminal activity. They lived there for five years before Uncle Sam sent Joseph his induction papers.

Rosemary remained in Altgeld Garden. She swore she wouldn't let some knuckleheaded boys run her away from the home she shared with her late husband. The gangbangers pretty much left Rosemary alone since she'd fed most of them in the school cafeteria and had been a mother figure to more than a few of them.

Rosemary was able to make ends meet from the wages from her job and the monthly stipend she received from the Veterans Administration. Other than her daughter's drug addiction, Rosemary was content with her life.

A coworker at the school mentioned to Rosemary how she enjoyed the wonderful minister and choir of Christian Friendship Church. She absolutely glowed when she told Rosemary how she was moved by the preaching and teaching of Reverend Lawrence Dudley. She invited Rosemary to visit the church. Several weeks later, Rosemary, with Mariah in tow, paid a visit to the church. Before long, she and Mariah joined the church membership. The two had been members of the church for over twenty years.

"Is there anything I can do to help?" Mariah asked her grandmother. She sat at the kitchen table with her hands folded.

"You can set the table," Rosemary directed her granddaughter. "The fish will be done in a few minutes. There's nothing that tastes better in the world than eating freshly fried catfish hot out of the skillet."

"Sure." Mariah walked to the cabinet and had removed two plates and set them on the table when the doorbell rang. "Are you expecting anyone?" she asked Rosemary.

"No, but that don't mean anything." Rosemary turned the jet off under the pot of spaghetti.

Mariah walked to the front door, she peeped out the hole, and a smile curved along her lips. She opened it and Raquel and Sonyell walked inside the house.

"Now, you didn't think we were going to miss out on the latest happenings with our best friend and Granny's cooking did you?" Raquel smiled. She was a plus-sized redbone-colored woman with slightly slanted eyes on a cute face. She changed her hairstyles regularly. This week, she sported an auburn weave that fell midway down her back. Raquel was the comedian of the group. She was loud and bubbly, and obnoxious at times. She spoke sometimes without a care of another person's feelings. She was a party girl. Still, Mariah and Sonyell knew that Raquel had their backs. Raquel was the oldest of the trio of friends, by four months.

"I assumed Granny would fix your favorite Friday dinner to celebrate your good fortune. And you know, I love me some Granny catfish," Sonyell chimed in. She was petite sized and her figure was pencil thin. She had a café au lait complexion with dark brown eyes, and reddish brown hair she wore styled in a bob. Sonyell possessed a bright, dazzling smile.

The young women followed Mariah into the kitchen. They walked over to Rosemary and greeted her with a warm hug.

"You got enough food for these two interlopers?" Mariah asked her grandmother mockingly.

"Inter-what?" Rosemary squinted at Mariah. "If you're asking if I have enough for these two"—she pointed a fork at Raquel and Sonyell—"of course I do. What would our Friday fish fry be without my honorary granddaughters?"

"Thank you, Granny." Raquel sniffed and rubbed her stomach. "I can hardly wait to chow down. It smells good up in here." She placed a plastic bag on the table and opened it. "I bought a strawberry cheesecake for dessert." She took the box out of the bag and placed it inside the refrigerator.

"And I bought a bottle of champagne to celebrate Mariah's good fortune," Sonyell added. "It isn't every day that we have an heiress in our midst."

"Oh, stop already," Mariah added playfully, "I'm still the same Mariah that I was a month ago."

"Yeah, right," Sonni said after she placed a bottle of bubbly inside the freezer.

"The food is ready," Rosemary announced after she took a loaf of browned Italian bread out of the oven. "Fix your plates."

A few minutes later, the women sat at the table with bowed heads. Rosemary blessed the food. "Father, above, thank you for allowing us to wake this morning to see another day clothed in our right minds. Thank you for bringing us safely to and from work today. We thank you for providing food for the nourishment of our bodies. Amen."

"Amen," the young women echoed.

"Make sure you get as much as you want," Rosemary told the women. "I made plenty of food. Sonni, there's enough for you to take a plate home with you for Sasha." She took napkins from the holder sitting in the middle of the table and passed them around the table.

"We forgot the hot sauce." Raquel popped up from her chair and removed the bottle from the cabinet.

Soon everyone had prepared their plates, and partook in the meal. The only sounds in the room were the clink of forks upon the plates, and the slurping of Pepsi-Cola.

Sonyell was the first one to finish eating. She pushed her chair away from the table and burped loudly. She covered her mouth and said, "I swear you put your foot in that, Granny. The food was great as always."

"Yes, it was," Raquel echoed as she got up, walked to the stove, and put another piece of fish on her plate. She ladled a few spoonfuls of spaghetti onto the dish and sat back down.

Sonyell passed her friend the hot sauce. She looked across the table at Mariah. "So, Mari, when do we get to see the house?"

"I suggested earlier we go to Hammond in the morning and check it out," Raquel added after she ingested a forkful of pasta. "What do you have planned tomorrow, Sonni? We could do breakfast and then go to Indiana?"

"I don't have anything planned," Sonyell answered. "So you can count me in. This is so exciting." She rubbed her hands together.

"Great," Mariah said. She glanced at her grandmother. "Granny, I'd love for you to join us tomorrow. I want you to see the place too."

Rosemary nodded her head, looking pleased. "Sure, I'd love to."

The women chatted. Later Rosemary excused herself. She said she had a few telephone calls to make. Rosemary departed from the room and walked upstairs to her bedroom.

Sonyell stood up and took the champagne from the freezer. Then she removed three wine goblets from the cabinet, opened the bottle, and poured champagne for each of the women.

When she sat down, she held up her glass and said, "I'd like to propose a toast to Mari's good fortune. We all grew up here in the ghetto, and it's not every day that someone leaves here with an inheritance."

Raquel quipped, "Shoot, usually when someone dies in our world, we pass the hat to take up a collection to pay for a funeral."

The friends burst out laughing gaily.

"I heard that," Sonyell added, raising her glass.

Then Sonyell continued speaking. "Mari, I'm so happy for you. At least your daddy came through, even though it was at the end of his life. I know you will do wonderful things with the money your father has left you."

"Here, here," Raquel said. The friends touched their glasses together and sipped the ice-cold liquor.

"Thank you, ladies," Mariah replied. "I appreciate you for being there for me and always having my back. He left me a little something, something, so I'm going to break off a little bit to you. Oh, he also left me a gas guzzler, a Lincoln Town Car, a Toyota SUV, and two other autos. I'll probably sell the Lincoln."

"Thanks, Mari, you don't have to do that," Sonyell murmured. She sipped from her glass.

"I know that," Mariah replied emotionally. "It's what I want to do. You're like family to me, and I want to share my good fortune with you."

"Speak for yourself," Raquel admonished Sonyell, bucking her eyes. "You know I'm not turning down anything."

"Well, you do have a point there." Sonyell's eyes darted to Raquel.

"I also plan to buy more college bonds for Sasha," Mariah said, looking at Sonyell. "You know I had planned on contributing to her college education anyway. When the time comes, my goddaughter will be ahead of the game."

"That's really nice of you." Sonyell swallowed hard. "She's only ten, but time is passing so fast, before I'm ready Sasha will be starting on a new phase of her life." Sonyell had found herself pregnant with Sasha a few months after her nineteenth birthday. Sasha's father, Michael, was in currently serving a ten-year stint in jail, for accessory to grand robbery. Since his early teenage years, he'd been in jail more than he'd been out. Michael would be released from prison in December before Christmas.

Sonyell was devastated when she learned she was pregnant shortly after his conviction. Had it not been for Mariah and Raquel pitching in when needed, Sonyell would not have graduated from high school, much less attended college. Granny often took care of Sasha, so the girls could complete their homework and study for tests.

"When some people get a little something, they try to put on airs," Raquel interjected, snapping her fingers in the air. "They forget where they come from and act like they don't know anybody. I'm sure you'll do the right thing."

"So, are you thinking about opening a day care center?" Sonyell asked. "I know that's always been one of your dreams."

"I don't know." Mariah bit her lower lip indecisively. "I've been thinking about how the property could best be used. I would like to use the house to help others, especially women. I have been thinking along the lines of a day care, or a halfway home for women reentering society at the completion of their prison terms. I would also like to focus on teenage girls. So, I just need to brainstorm more."

"We're here if you need us," Raquel volunteered. She sipped from her glass of champagne.

Sonyell nodded and then she looked at the clock on the wall. "I hate to break up the party, but I've got to go. Sasha is at Michael's mother's house and I need to pick her up." She took her car keys out of her purse and her cell phone sounded. She pulled it out of her purse and pressed talk. "Hi, Sasha, what's up?"

Sonyell listened for a minute and then she said, "Let me speak to your grandmother." She waited for Sasha to give the telephone to her grandmother. "Hi, Miss Nedra. Sasha tells me she wants to spend the night with you. Are you sure it's all right? I was just leaving Mariah's house to pick her up."

The older woman assured Sonyell that Sasha's spending the night with her was fine. She went on to say that she planned on keeping her other granddaughters, and Sasha was welcome to join them. Nedra informed Sasha that the girls would be at her house until noon, so Sonyell could sleep in the following morning if she wanted to.

"Great. Please put Sasha back on the telephone." She waited for daughter to return. "I talked to your grandmother and she said that you can stay the night. I will pick you up tomorrow around noon, so be ready."

"Thanks, Mommy. Granny keeps pajamas and a change of clothes here for me. Tell Auntie Mari and Auntie Rocki I said hi. Love you, Mommy."

"I will. I love you too, baby. Have fun." Sonyell smiled like she could see her daughter's face. She ended the call.

"I guess I'm free the rest of the evening. Sasha, as you could probably tell, is spending the night with Miss Nedra. So what y'all got planned for later? At least I don't have to go home and cook."

"Like you were going to cook anyway. We all know that you were going to fix a plate from the leftovers on the stove," Raquel teased her friend. "It's Friday. Who cooks on a Friday?"

"Okay, I'm busted." Sonyell held up her hands. "What do you want to do?"

"How about a game of gin rummy?" Mariah suggested as she stood up and walked to the cabinet and took a deck of cards out of the drawer.

"Bring it on." Sonyell laughed as she rubbed her hands together. "I feel like giving someone a good beat down."

Raquel took the plates off the table and took them to the sink. "Let's clean up in here first, and then I'll show you what a real beat down feels like, Sonni." She reached under the sink and removed the dishpan and turned on the hot water faucet. She squirted drops of Dawn dishwashing liquid into the pan and quickly washed the dishes as Mariah brought them over to the sink.

Sonyell put the fish in a bowl and covered it with aluminum foil and did likewise with the spaghetti. She put the food inside the refrigerator.

Twenty minutes later, Raquel turned the portable stereo on the kitchen counter to V103, so they could listen to old school R&B music while they played cards. Mariah dealt the first hand. The friends laughed, talked, and played cards until the doorbell rang.

"Are you expecting anyone else, Mari?" Sonni asked.

"Not really," Mariah replied grimly. "I just hope that's not who I think it is." She looked fearfully at the door.

Chapter Two

Mariah exhaled loudly as she rose from her chair and walked to the front door. She stared out the peephole and saw Cassandra. Mariah quickly unlocked and opened the door. With an inexpressive look on her face, Mariah said, "Cassie, come in." She stepped back to allow Cassie entrance to the house. "We haven't seen you in a long time. How have you been doing?"

When Cassie stepped over the threshold, Mariah's nose twitched and she flinched from the odor emanating from Cassandra's body. Mariah changed her mind about kissing her mother.

Cassie strolled to the living room and plopped on the sofa. Mariah sat in the chair across from the sofa. Her eyes roamed the room and landed everywhere except on her daughter. "I'm okay, just a little short of cash," she mumbled and looked downward. She looked up at Mariah, and said, "I came by to see if you or Momma could loan me a few dollars."

Mariah's heart rate dropped a notch as she took in her mother's haggard appearance. Cassie looked and smelled like she hadn't bathed in weeks. Her micro braids were hanging loosely from her scalp. She wore a soiled red sweatshirt, and the sleeves didn't cover her thin wrists. He jeans were tattered and not because that was the latest fashion style. Mariah's eyes traveled from the top of Cassie's head to the thick soles of the dingy, run-down tennis shoes on her feet.

Cassie's eyes were blurry and her nose was running. She rubbed her shirtsleeve across her face. Mariah stood up and walked into the kitchen. Sonyell and Raquel had become quiet and looked at their friend questioningly. Mariah shook her head and returned with a napkin for her mother. She handed it to Cassie and returned to her seat. Cassie wiped her nose; then she balled up the napkin in her hand. "So what do you think, Mari, can you spare me a few dollars?" She looked at her daughter hopefully.

Mariah was averse to giving Cassie any money. She knew from past experience, her mother would just shoot it up into her arm. Mariah tried to change the subject. "Are you hungry? Granny fried catfish. You're welcome to stay for dinner."

"No, I'm not hungry." Cassie's legs jiggled impatiently. She pushed a braid out of her face.

Rosemary walked slowly down the narrow staircase. "I thought I heard the doorbell ring." Her eyes filled with sadness as she looked at her daughter. "Come give me a hug." She held out her arms to Cassie.

Cassie stood up and walked over to Rosemary. Rosemary engulfed Cassie in her arms as Cassie's arms dangled at her sides. Then, mother and daughter sat on the sofa. Mariah watched their interaction from the chair.

Raquel and Sonyell walked into the room. They greeted Cassandra, shot Mariah sympathetic looks, and informed Mariah that they were going home.

"I'll call you later," Sonyell said. Then she and Raquel departed.

"So, can I get some money?" Cassie asked her mother impatiently after Mariah locked the door.

"I don't have any money." Rosemary shrugged her shoulders. "I don't get paid until next week."

Cassie sucked her lips and rolled her eyes at Rosemary. Then she looked at Mariah. "What about you? You got any money?"

"I may have a couple of dollars. I don't keep much money on me," Mariah answered as she stood up and walked upstairs to her bedroom. She had five dollars in her wallet. She removed it and returned downstairs. Mariah gave the money to Cassie.

Cassie turned up her nose. She waved the bill in the air and asked, "Is this all you got? I can't hardly get nothing with this."

"I'm sorry, like I said," Mariah repeated after she sat back on the chair, "I don't keep money on me."

"Hmm," Cassie mumbled as she stuck the money in her jeans pocket.

"Why don't you spend the night with me and Mariah?" Rosemary suggested anxiously. "You look like you could use a good meal and a bath."

"Whatcha trying to say, Momma?" Cassie rolled her eyes at her mother.

"I'm not trying to say anything, Cassandra," Rosemary said soothingly. "You look like you've lost weight since the last time I saw you. I made dinner and I'd like to spend time with you."

"I've been good." Cassie folded her trembling hands together.

"Why don't you stay and have dinner?" Rosemary pleaded. "Sonni bought a cheesecake. It looked good."

"I really got to go." Cassie stood up. "One of my friends drove me over here and he's waiting on me. Maybe next time." She walked toward the door.

Rosemary stood up and walked over to Cassie. Her voice was full of anguish when she asked her daughter, "Where are you living now, Cassie? Are you still living in the Garden?"

Cassie turned around. "You know me," she said with a dimpled smile. "I'm like the wind: here, there, and everywhere." She wiped her dripping nose again. "Hey, I gotta go. I'll see you next time." She opened the door, waved, and slipped out of the house.

Rosemary twisted the lock and returned to the living room. She sat heavily on the sofa. Her face was bowed and her arms were clasped around her body.

Mariah stood up, walked to Rosemary, and patted her shoulder. "I'm sorry, Granny. I know how seeing Cassie upsets you."

Rosemary lifted her head. "You would think I would be used to Cassie's behavior by now. But I guess I'm not." She tried smiling and her lips twitched into a grimace.

Mariah nodded her head. Rosemary's life hadn't been easy. Mostly because of her worries regarding Cassie's drug addiction. Since she was a young child, Mariah tried to do everything in her power to make her grandmother's life happier. Most of the time, she succeeded. Whenever Cassie visited, Rosemary would become sad and withdrawn for a couple of days afterward. Rosemary was fearful that Cassie committed crimes to support her habit, along with prostitution. Actually Rosemary was partially incorrect; Cassie wasn't shy about selling her body for drugs. She had been living with a man for over ten years and he helped support her habit.

"I wish Cassie were stronger and could get herself together." Mariah sighed as she rubbed her grandmother's arm.

"Me too." Rosemary exhaled loudly as she wiped a tear from her eye. "I think I'm going to pass on going with you and the girls tomorrow. I would just be in the way. You should go with your friends and enjoy yourself. Though your father wasn't around when you were growing up, I do approve of the way he's taken care of you in death."

"Granny," Mariah protested. Her mouth dropped and her eyes widened in disbelief. "You would never be in the way. You've taken care of me my entire life. And now I'm in a position to do something for you. You've worked your entire life and have never taken a vacation. I don't even think we ever went to one of the better stores to shop until I finished school and started working. We never went to the movies when I was a kid. You always washed and styled our hair on Saturday nights, so we'd look presentable for church. You sewed our clothes and now it's time for me to give back to you. I didn't mention this to anyone before, because I was still trying to process everything that happened. But my fa . . . father"—she stuttered a bit—"left me quite a bit of money. I mean a lot." Her hand fluttered in the air. "His will has finally been probated and I can do what I want with the money now."

Rosemary twisted her hands together. She turned and looked at her granddaughter's face. "I did what I had to do, Mari, and everything I've done was out of love for you. You don't need to spend any of your money on me. Maybe you can go back to school and get your degree, if there's enough money for that."

Mariah chuckled. "I could get a PhD if I wanted to, Granny. He left me enough money for that and more. I received possession of his house and other properties he owned."

Rosemary blinked rapidly, as her hand flew to her throat. "I thought you were talking about a house and perhaps twenty thousand dollars, like most folks leave their kin. You mean he left you more than that?"

"Yes, ma'am." Mariah nodded, grinning. "That's why I want you to go with me and the girls in the morning.

Please, Granny, please come with us tomorrow?" Mariah cajoled her grandmother. She threw her arms around Rosemary's neck. "Pretty please with sugar on top?"

Rosemary blinked back tears. She bobbed her head. "Okay, I guess so. Let's get an early start. I have a meeting at church tomorrow afternoon."

Mariah kissed Rosemary's cheek loudly. "Thank you. I think you're going to be in for a pleasant surprise."

A few minutes later, Rosemary stood up. "I'm going upstairs. I guess I'll turn in for the night. I'll see you in the morning."

Mariah nodded. She stood and turned off the light in the kitchen and downstairs. Then she went upstairs to her bedroom. She sat on the bed, reached for the remote control on her nightstand, and turned on the small television. She lay across the bed; her head was filled with thoughts of everything that transpired that day. With a smile on her face and praises to God on her lips, Mariah fell asleep.

She awoke around eight o'clock Saturday morning. She had showered and dressed and could hear Rosemary puttering in the kitchen. Mariah rushed downstairs. "Granny, I forgot to tell you last night that I'm treating everyone to breakfast. So don't bother making anything."

"Okay." Rosemary nodded. She sat in the kitchen with a cup of coffee in one hand and thumbed through the newspaper with her other one.

Mariah glanced at her watch on her wrist. "Rocki is driving. She should be here shortly. I just need to do my hair; I should be ready shortly."

Rosemary couldn't help but notice how her granddaughter was filled with nervous energy. The corners of her lips curved into a smile, and she turned her attention back to the newspaper.

Twenty minutes later the doorbell sounded. Rosemary opened the door for Sonyell and Raquel. "Good morning, girls. Would you like coffee?" She walked back to the table, took her cup to the sink, rinsed it, and put it in the drain.

"I have a cup in the car," Sonyell replied. She walked to Rosemary and kissed her cheek.

"Thanks, Granny, I'm good," Raquel replied as she sat at the kitchen table across from Rosemary.

Mariah ran down the stairs. "I'm ready. I'm so excited. I can hardly wait for you to see my inheritance," she exclaimed with a wide smile that covered her face from ear to ear.

The women left several minutes later and shared breakfast at a local restaurant. Forty minutes later they were on the expressway en route to Hammond, each eagerly looking forward to behold the blessing bestowed on Mariah by a father she'd never known.

Chapter Three

Before long, Mariah excitedly instructed Raquel to make a left turn onto Hohman Avenue. Raquel made two more right turns, and per Mariah's direction, pulled into the driveway of the house. Slamming sounds could be heard as the women closed the car doors.

"Oh, my God," Sonni squealed as her eyes roamed the property. "This place is huge. We could all move into here."

Rocki shaded her eyes from the sun. "It is. You didn't tell us it was this big. It looks like a mansion."

"I'll show you the backyard first and then we can go inside," Mariah stated.

They walked to the rear of the house. Rosemary admired the flowers and the vegetable garden. "I bet you girls wouldn't know what to do with this."

"You're right," Mariah conceded, holding up her hands. "I definitely don't have a green thumb."

They returned to the front of the house. Mariah took her keys out of her purse.

"The area looks good," Rosemary observed as she looked up and down the street at the spacious, multi-colored brick-and-frame homes. Huge trees lined the street along with privacy fences.

"Do you think you'll move here?" Sonyell asked Mariah.

"I haven't decided yet. My father has more properties. I haven't had a chance to look at them all yet. You know I'd like to move Granny out of the Garden." She glanced quickly at her grandmother. Rosemary studied the house.

Mariah opened the door and the women walked inside and stopped inside the foyer.

"Wow," Rocki exclaimed as her eyes roamed the area. "This place looks like something from the old days. Look at that woodwork. They don't make houses like this anymore. My great-grandmother had a house like this on the west side."

"I thought the same thing, it's an old-style house," Mariah admitted as they walked to the living room. All eyes were on Rosemary as she walked to the fireplace and stood in front of the painting. Her face paled.

Mariah didn't miss her grandmother's reaction. "What's wrong, Granny? Do you know them?"

"I just felt a little dizzy for a minute," Rosemary answered, wiping her moist forehead.

Mariah rushed to Rosemary's side and took her arm. "Well, sit down then. Are you all right?"

Rosemary sat on the sofa. "I'm fine. I just need to catch my breath for a minute," she replied shakily.

"Did you take your medicine this morning?" Mariah asked her grandmother solicitously. Her voice vibrated with concern as she bent over Rosemary.

"Of course I did," Rosemary shot back defensively. "You girls go on and look at this house. I'm going to sit for a few minutes." Rosemary took a tissue out of her purse and mopped her forehead. "I'm all right. Go ahead and look around. I'll join you after I catch my breath."

Mariah took a step away from Rosemary hesitatingly. "Okay. Call me if you need anything."

"Mariah, I'm not a child," Rosemary chided her granddaughter. She made a shooing motion with her hand. "Now, go."

The three women went upstairs, while Rosemary sat on the sofa. Her chest was heaving as she stared at the picture over the mantle. She thought that Mariah was the spitting image of her father. After her breathing settled, Rosemary stood and walked around the living room. Her eyes gobbled up the pictures of Mariah's father and his wife. She wandered into the kitchen.

Meanwhile upstairs, Mariah, Raquel, and Sonyell had just left the master bedroom.

"Not only did you get a house, it's furnished, too. It doesn't get any better than this," Sonyell commented.

"You ain't never lied," Raquel chimed in wonderingly. Her arm swept the room. "Girl, what are you going to do with all this room? It's not like you're married or have children."

"You're right, this is too much house for me alone, but it might be the ideal spot for a transition home for mothers leaving the prison system, and their children. What do you think?" She looked at Sonyell then at Raquel.

"Well, it's big enough that's for sure." Raquel nodded her head in agreement.

"If you turned the house into a transition home, would you have to live here?" Sonni turned to Mariah. Her mind processed information like a computer as she considered what Mariah possibly planned to do.

"I don't think it would be mandatory, but that is something I'd have to look into," Mariah answered as she bit her lip.

"Let's look around some more," Rocki said, heading for the bedroom door. "I am excited. There are so many things you could do with this place."

The friends walked downstairs. Rosemary joined them as they toured the rest of the house.

Within forty-five minutes, all four women had visited every nook and cranny in the house from top to bottom. They were seated at the dining room table discussing what Mariah's next move should be.

"You know, this is the house my father lived in. As I mentioned he owned other rental properties. The lawyer gave me the list of the houses, and I plan to go look at each of them. I want to meet his tenants and see when the rental agreements end. If I see something I like, maybe I'll end up moving to another property. The more I think about it, this is too much house for one person."

"That sounds like a good idea. Now, if you need some help managing your properties, keep in mind I'm available," Sonyell volunteered. "Don't forget that I majored in business administration in college. And, I have a—"

Mariah nodded her head and finished Sonyell's sentence. "An MBA. Like you would ever let us forget." She shook her head from side to side. "I may just take you up on that," Mariah added. "Outside of the rental properties that Harold Ellison owned, his other business holdings include commercial property. He owned a laundromat, two drycleaners, a beauty and barber shop, and a nice building that houses a doctor's office. So his holdings were varied."

"Mari, are you a millionaire?" Raquel gasped. Her mouth dropped open.

"Something like that," Mariah replied modestly. Her eyes dropped to the table. "This whole process with the will and all seems like a dream. I keep pinching myself to make sure what's happening is real."

"Can I touch you?" Sonyell reached out and touched Mariah's hand. "I've never known a millionaire and now my best friend is one."

"Wow, this is simply unbelievable." Raquel remarked as her eyes wandered around the room. "Who would have thought?"

"Since we're all here, I have a few bequeathals of my own to make." Mariah's eyes shone. "If you guys are open to the suggestion, I thought it might be nice if we all moved to Hammond. I just need to check on the status of the houses and see what's available. I'd like to gift a house to each of you, and pay for Sasha's college education."

"Oh, my God." Sonyell's hands flew to her face as tears trickled from her eyes. "Are you serious? I can't believe it. Mari, thank you so much." She jumped from her chair, flew around the table, and hugged Mariah.

Raquel swallowed hard; her eyes were shining brightly. "Wow, I'm speechless and you know I always have a comeback. I've never received anything so generous in my life. Thank you, sis. I don't have any ties to Chicago per se. My family can come visit me here. I would love to move to Hammond. If I can help in any of your business ventures let me know."

Rosemary moistened her lips. "I'm like the girls: I don't know what to say. I am content with my life. I can certainly stay in the Garden. I don't know that I want to uproot myself from the only home I've known."

"Oh, no, you're not, Granny." Mariah shook her head and peered at her grandmother. "You're the closest thing to a mother to me. Sonni and Rocki are my sisters by another mother. Granny, I want you to stay with me. I'm almost one hundred percent sure that I will convert this house to a transition home, or group home for teenage girls. If you feel like you still want to work, Granny, then you can cook. Personally, I'd like you to just sit back and enjoy the rest of your life."

Rosemary looked down, then up at Mariah. She smiled from ear to ear. "That sounds like a plan. Count me in. But why a transition home, Mariah?"

"I guess because I've always had a strained relationship with Cassie. And I'd like to help other young girls in similar circumstances. Daughters struggling with the negative choices their mothers have made."

"The Lord will surely bless you, darling," Rosemary said. "Maybe you could use some of the money and send Cassie to rehab?" she asked her granddaughter. Her eyes shone hopefully.

Mariah exhaled loudly. "If only it were that easy. Cassie has to want to change to stop taking drugs, and from what I've seen, she isn't quite ready."

"Maybe she needs help making that decision, and you're in a position to help her. Maybe we could talk to her, and see what she thinks." Rosemary looked at her granddaughter pleadingly.

Mariah shook her head. Her lips tightened. "Humph. She was just hitting us up for money last night. If she catches wind that I've got money and a lot of it, what do you think would happen then? She's going to wonder where we got the money from and then she's going to want her share. We all know she would use it to score more drugs."

"But, she's never been to a real good place for rehab, just a few state-run outpatient programs. Maybe a private program would make a difference. Please think about it, Mariah. It wouldn't be fair for you to help everyone else and not your own momma." Rosemary pleaded her case earnestly.

"Granny, Cassie has never been a mother to me. She's been more of an irritant, and embarrassment. You've been a mother to me," Mariah retorted.

"But, I'm not your mother," Rosemary said softly. "Cassie can't help herself. After her daddy died, she changed. Then she fell in with the wrong crowd and became wild. I don't think she ever really got over his death. She's sick, baby, and she needs help."

Raquel and Sonyell nodded their agreement thoughtfully.

"I'll think about it," Mariah said weakly. "Why don't we go look at more of the properties and then we can head back to Chicago. Oh, before you ask, Granny, I do plan on making a hefty donation to the church."

Good," Rosemary said approvingly. "Now, you got me excited. I'm ready to go."

The women gathered their belongings and headed to the car. Mariah was bursting with pride. Happy that God had given her the means to help her beloved grandmother as well as her friends. She looked forward to seeing the rental and commercial properties. She programmed the first address in the car's GPS unit.

Several hours later, the women had stopped by most of Mariah's properties. They were thrilled for their friend. Sonyell and Raquel felt blessed that Mariah planned to include them in her future plans. Raquel had her eye on one of the smaller houses, while Sonyell envisioned raising Sasha in a three-bedroom, gray painted frame house not far from the house Raquel planned to occupy. The two friends also saw other properties they liked. Mariah promised to look at the lease agreements ASAP.

Conversation among the friends on the drive back to Chicago was gay. There was a constant chatter from everyone except Rosemary. Due to the excitement of the day, none of the women noticed that Rosemary wasn't participating in the conversation. She wore a troubled expression on her face as she stared out of the car window.

Chapter Four

A week later Mariah made an appointment with Rosalind, Reverend Dudley's secretary. Rosalind promptly penciled in Mariah for two o'clock on Thursday afternoon. Mariah drove to the Christian Friendship Church, and stepped out of her car amid a gray sky and drizzly rain. Mariah put up her umbrella and rushed into the church.

After Mariah removed her coat and sat on the sofa across from Rosalind's desk, the two women exchanged pleasantries. Within fifteen minutes, after an intercom call from Reverend Dudley, Rosalind escorted Mariah to the minister's office.

"Hello," Reverend Dudley said as he stood to greet Mariah with a smile. "How have you and Rosemary being doing?"

"We've both been doing fine," Mariah replied as she crossed her right leg over her left knee. "Thank you for seeing me on such short notice."

"No problem," Reverend Dudley replied. "I had a cancellation this afternoon, so the timing was great. What can I do for you?"

"Well, I recently came into a large inheritance and I wanted to donate a portion to the church. I wanted to talk with you to see how the money could best be used," Mariah explained earnestly.

"Praise the Lord," Reverend Dudley exclaimed with a twinkle in his eyes. "What brought about this turn of events?"

He listened intently and nodded at the appropriate places while Mariah explained about the legacy from her father.

"That is an intriguing tale. I am happy for you, Mariah. I know life hasn't always been easy for you and Rosemary. We never know where our blessings may come from." Reverend Dudley leaned back against the back of his burgundy leather chair.

"I agree, but still something doesn't seem quite right to me," Mariah confessed as she leaned forward in her chair.

"What do you mean by that?" the minister asked her with a puzzled look on his face.

"The whole situation seems surreal to me. A man who I've never known—just learned his name not quite six months ago from an attorney—has left me his entire fortune. If it wasn't for Attorney Cook's call, I don't think I would have ever known his name. I'm still trying to process all the information," Mariah confessed unhappily.

"You know, we don't always understand why things in life happen the way they do, but know that whatever happens is part of God's plan. It wasn't meant for you to know your father in this lifetime. He obviously knew of you and maybe the gift or legacy he left you is his way of atoning for not being a part of your life."

Mariah looked downward, then back up at Reverend Dudley. "I guess you're right," she said doubtfully. "I mean, I saw a picture of him and his wife at his house, and I can't figure out what my mother could have seen in him to have a child with him. He's old enough to be my grandfather," Mariah sputtered.

Reverend Dudley nodded his head gravely. "I see. Have you tried talking to your mother or Rosemary about him?"

"I have with Cassie—I mean, my mother—once, and hit a brick wall. My mother is a difficult person. We rarely have conversations unless she's hitting me up for money. She spoke so cryptically of the matter of my father that I never dared ask her again. I've asked my granny many times about him over the years, but she claimed that she didn't know who my father was." Mariah stared out the window behind Reverend Dudley. "The whole situation seems strange." She shrugged her shoulders.

"If it is meant for you to know about your parentage, God will answer all your questions. The truth will be revealed in time," Reverend Dudley advised her. He spoke earnestly with a caring expression on his face.

"Reverend Dudley, I have a question for you. I'm almost embarrassed to ask you, but how does one love a parent who doesn't seem to love or care about you? As the years have gone by, I realize on some level that I detest my mother because of the lack of attention she has paid to me. I know on another level that she doesn't love me. When I was smaller, Granny would tell me to read Ephesians 6:2. I know it by heart."

She closed her eyes, moistened her lips, and recited, "'Honor thy mother and father which is the first commandment with promise.' When I think of my mother, verse four comes to mind, and I would substitute father with mother: "'And ye, fathers, provoke not your children to wrath but bring them up in the nurture and admonition of the Lord.'" A tear slipped from her eye.

"I'm sorry you feel that way," Reverend Dudley consoled Mariah. "I have talked to Rosemary over the years regarding Cassie and I truly think that whatever is going on is something within Cassie that she has not come to terms with. Rosemary has told me how Cassie's personality changed after her father passed.

People rebound from tragedy differently, while others never recover for various reasons. I would advise you to stay prayerful. I am certain all that you need to know will be revealed in time. Don't give up on your mother; she may not know it but there will come a time when she needs you. Just believe God is our Savior, and our Redeemer, and that He can fix all things."

Mariah brushed away the tear from her eye. "I guess so," she replied dolefully. She put a smile on her face. "Anyway, on a more pleasant note, I plan to make a donation to the church in the amount of half a million dollars. I would like to donate two lump sum payments, one this year and the other one next year."

Reverend Dudley was stunned silent for a minute. "I didn't expect such a generous gift, Mariah. I think I can speak on behalf of the church when I say thank you. Bless you."

"It is my pleasure, Reverend Dudley. I guess as a child I would play the 'what if' game. For instance, if I had a million dollars, what I would do with it. I never imagined that I would actually be in a position to do that in real life." Mariah beamed.

"Do you have any suggestions as to how the money should be spent? Do you have any specific ministries in mind? Or would you like to leave it to the discretion of the official board?"

"I know I'd like to do something for the Sunday School ministry. Perhaps buy new Bibles and new teaching materials. I think the rest could be used at the discretion of the board."

"Would you like to participate in the disbursement of the funds?"

Mariah nodded. "I hadn't thought about it, but, yes, I think I would."

"Great. I'll have Rosalind set up another meeting and see if we can come to a meeting of the minds. If you're donating that much to the church, then your father must have left you a hefty inheritance?" Reverend Dudley probed gently.

"He did. Not only did he leave me money, but residential and commercial properties, too. I plan to share the proceeds with my friends and of course Granny. I'm almost one hundred percent sure that I will move to Hammond, Indiana. That's where my father lived."

"I hope you continue to attend our church," Reverend Dudley remarked.

"For sure. Although I've wondered if God has a plan for me in Hammond."

"I understand, take your time and heed God's voice." Reverend Dudley nodded. "Now, what about your mother? What do you plan to do for her?"

"Because my mother has been such a thorn in my side all of my life, I haven't really considered doing anything for her. Granny thinks I should consider using part of the money for therapy for my mother. I told her I would think about it."

"With money comes great responsibility. You must use it wisely and knowing you as I do, there is no doubt in my mind that you will. I agree with Rosemary, you should try to help your mother."

A grimace crossed Mariah's face. "I can't promise that I will but I will certainly give it consideration."

"You know what the Lord said about forgiveness don't you?"

"I sure do. Matthew 18:22 says, 'Jesus saith until him. I say not unto thee, Until seven times: but, Until seventy times seven.' Truthfully I think my mother had exceeded those times. " Mariah tittered nervously.

"That can be said of a lot of people whom we are close to." Reverend Dudley laughed. "But on a more serious note, maybe helping her will effect a change. Sometimes we have to be the bigger person and reach out to those in need. Drug addicts definitely fall under the category of those in need. I will tell you as I've told others that an addiction is an illness, so try to be patient with her."

"You're right and I know that but because we don't have a relationship, it's hard for me to be forgiving with her."

"Be that as it may, God still provided for your needs through Rosemary. You were brought up in a Christian home. And, most of all you've accepted Jesus Christ as your personal savior. Now, it's time for you to put into practice all that you've been taught. You know what, Mariah? I know that you are up to the task."

"You have more faith in me than I have in myself," Mariah said. She swallowed. "Maybe it's time for me to grow up and try to make amends with my mother again."

"Meditate on it. I'm sure God will steer you in the right path." Reverend Dudley glanced at his watch. "I don't mean to rush you, but I do have another appointment. Think about what we've talked about. I have a meeting scheduled with the board on Friday and will talk it over with them. Keep God's teaching in your heart and share your blessings, in turn you become a blessings for another person in need."

Mariah stood up and thrust her hand out to the minister. "Thank you, Reverend Dudley, for seeing me and the advice. I will certainly give serious thought to what you've said."

Reverend Dudley rose from his seat and shook Mariah's hand warmly. "If you need someone to talk to, you know that I'm here for you."

"Again thanks," Mariah replied.

Reverend Dudley walked her to the door. "Don't forget to set up another appointment with Rosalind for next week."

"I will. Have a blessed day, Reverend Dudley." Mariah smiled.

"It has already been." The minister smiled. He greeted his next appointment and they disappeared into his office.

Mariah made an appointment with Rosalind. Soon she was back in her car and driving home. After she parked her car in the residential parking lot, Mariah sat inside. Her thoughts were centered on her conversation with Reverend Dudley.

A teeny part of her wanted to try to forge a relationship with Cassandra. After all, Cassandra had given birth to her, as Granny so often reminded Mariah.

The other part of Mariah, the one that had been burnt too many times, was averse to subject herself to further rejection.

She bowed her head and scrunched her eyes together tightly. "Lord, show me the way," she whispered. "Help me to do the right thing by Granny and Cassie. I know you can make a way out of no way, and with me and Cassie there is nothing, no feelings, no relationship, we are a big fat zero, nothing. Guide me, Jesus, help me find the way. You have given me such blessings and sometime I don't know if I am worthy.

"I don't know so many things. Why my father didn't come around and why he left me so much money. I feel like I'm about to embark on a journey and I know you will be there to catch me if I fall. Lord, I am excited about the wonderful things I can do in your name, I just ask that you guide and keep me on the right path. Amen."

Mariah opened her eyes, grabbed her purse, and exited her car. She rushed into the house she shared with Rosemary, exhilarated about the positive changes that lay ahead in her life.

Chapter Five

On the second Sunday in September, Mariah squirted a few drops of perfume over her body. She pulled a lock of hair across her forehead and smiled in satisfaction at her image in the mirror. Mariah nodded approvingly at her appearance. She had on a black suit, along with a lemon-colored blouse, and stylish patent leather pumps on her feet. She grabbed her Bible and purse and hurried downstairs, where Rosemary waited for her. They left to attend the morning church service.

After Sunday School ended, the women slid into their usual seats in the middle section of the sanctuary. Mariah looked around the sanctuary until she caught sight of Sonyell, Sasha, and Raquel. Mariah flashed a smile at her friends.

As the service progressed, the church members sang the second verse of the congregational hymn, "Sweet Hour of Prayer." Hands were raised in the air, and choruses of "amen" rented the air at the conclusion of the song.

The microphone cracked briefly before Reverend Calvin Nixon adjusted it, and prayed. Later the choir director rose and stood in front of the adult choir. He lifted his arms to signal the choir to rise. Nichole Singleton moved the congregation to tears when she sang the A selection, "Long As I Got King Jesus." At the end of the song, her voice caressed the words, "I don't need nobody else." Quite a few members stood, clapped their hands, and sang along with the choir during the stirring rendition of the B selection, "Victory Shall Be Mine."

After the choir finished singing the offering was collected. Reverend Dudley rose from his chair and walked to the pulpit. He adjusted the microphone and said, "Good morning, church. Let us rejoice in being able to praise God another Sunday morning."

The membership responded with "hallelujah's" and "amen."

Reverend Dudley bowed his head. "Gracious Father, thank you for waking us up this morning and allowing us to see another day. Bless everyone assembled in your house this morning. Bless the sick and shut in. As Sister Singleton sang, long as I got King Jesus, I don't need nobody else. Truer words were never spoken. These blessings I ask in the Father's name. Amen." He sipped from a glass of water.

"The Lord placed it upon my heart to speak of two matters today: selflessness and charity today. The two often go hand in hand. The dictionary defines selflessness as being concerned with the needs of others instead of one's own. Charity is defined as benevolent goodwill toward or love of humanity, along with generosity and helpfulness, especially toward the needy or suffering. The greatest example of selflessness for Christians is God sending His only Son here on earth to die for our sins. That single act alone is the greatest sacrifice ever made. It is a blueprint of how we should lead our own lives; incorporating selflessness, sacrifice, and charity as part of our regular routine or daily lives."

Reverend Dudley's eyes roamed the sanctuary. "I charge each of you practice this edict, which I call SSC: selflessness, sacrifice, and charity. Make a concerted effort to put your fellow man first. By that, I mean help your sister and brother when you can. Assistance doesn't always come in the form of finances, but instead it can be accomplished with use of our time.

"How many of you have relatives in a nursing home?" Quite a few hands were raised.

"Then stop by and visit them. Visit the elderly person next door or two doors down from your relatives. You will be surprised at how much joy you will bring that person in addition to satisfaction to yourself. Call, text, or e-mail your niece or nephew; find out what's going on in their lives. Visit your local Boys & Girls Club; volunteer at your child's school, a hospital, or library. I'm not asking you to make it a full-time job, maybe an hour or two a month. Let's do what we can to be more charitable and incorporate the selflessness trait. Those SSCs are pleasing in God's sight. And at the end of the day our goal is to attain entrance into heaven. So let us do humanitarian acts while we're on this earth. Doing so will help us reach our ultimate goal, heaven. Can I get an amen?"

The organist played a riff to emphasize Reverend Dudley's request. Church members waved their church programs in the air.

"I ask that you open your Bibles and read along with me the first scripture taken from the Book of Luke, 6:38." Reverend Dudley and the church members read together, "'Give and it shall be given to unto you; good measure, pressed down, and shaken together and running over, shall men give unto your boson. For with the same measure that ye mete withal it shall be measured to you again.'"

"Now, I ask that you turn to I Timothy, 6:17-19. 'Charge them that are rich in this world, that they be not high-minded, nor trust in uncertain riches, but in the living God, who giveth us richly all things to enjoy;

That they do good, that they be rich in good works, ready to distribute, willing to communicate.'"

Rosemary's heart swelled with pride because she knew that Mariah would do all those things Reverend Dudley described in the scriptures and more. She waved her hand and shouted, "Amen!"

Mariah bowed her head, closed her eyes, and prayed briefly. *Lord, help me to do those things and more. Guide me, Father. These blessings I ask in Jesus' name.* She returned her undivided attention to her minister.

Reverend Dudley continued his sermon, firmly emphasizing examples of selflessness and charitable acts. Ninety minutes later the sermon was concluded. The doors of the church were opened. Reverend Dudley invited those without a church home to join Christian Friendship Church.

After Rosalind led the new members to her office, Revered Dudley returned to the pulpit. "I have a special announcement to make. One of our members, who wishes to remain anonymous, made a hefty donation to our church. We are not going to divulge the member's name, but abide by their wish. The member knows who he or she is. I just want to say thank you from your Christian Friendship Family."

The membership clapped loudly along shouting heartfelt hallelujahs. Mariah fought mightily to keep a grin off her face, as she clapped along with her church family.

Reverend Dudley continued, "Because of this generous bequeathal we will be able to keep several of our ministries funded. Every ministry will receive a stipend. In this uncertain financial time, God is still in the blessing business. And one thing I know about God, He always steps in right on time." Reverend Dudley paused to let his message sink in. "So to our donor,

I say God Bless and continue your wonderful works.
Know that that your gift is appreciated and the work
you do is pleasing in God's sight. So please join me as I
give a round of applause for our generous donor."

The members rose from the pews, they smiled at
Reverend Dudley, and clapped along with him for a
long while. The service wound down and at the conclusion of the benediction, there was a buzz in the air as
members tried to figure out who the donor was.

Rosemary turned and winked at Mariah. The women
removed their coats from the back of the pew and made
their way toward Sonyell and Raquel.

"Well, well," Mariah drawled when she saw Raquel.
"Look who the Lord sent to His house today." She
hugged Raquel. "I am so happy you came to church
today."

Raquel was dressed conservatively in a navy blue suit
with a cream-colored blouse. "You know me." Raquel
shrugged. "I'm a CE churchgoer. I come to church on
Christmas and Easter. I have to say, I enjoyed the service. Your minister is a good speaker. I'm glad I came."

"Praise God," Sonyell said dramatically. "Miracles
do happen. You know, I was shocked when Rocki
called me this morning and asked me to pick her up for
church."

Raquel's voice dropped. "Well, I had to support a
sister, even an anonymous one."

The friends and Rosemary shared a hearty laugh.

"Let's find Sasha and get out of here," Mariah told
her friends, "I guess I'll treat everyone to lunch."

After chatting with church members for twenty minutes, the group departed and did just that.

The following week, Mariah decided to definitely
use her father's residence as a transition home for
mothers leaving prison with daughters. With the help

of Attorney Cook, she began step one of the process. Mariah hoped within a year to see the fruits of her labor mature. Mariah was floating on cloud nine; life was progressing greatly. She had found her purpose in life.

Chapter Six

By the end of September, Mariah's plans were becoming finalized. She decided to move into a slightly smaller, yet sizeable house next door to her father's residence. Doing so would allow her to have easy access to the transitional home, and oversee the renovations. The owner had passed away recently and Mariah put a bid on the property and won the bid. Like her father's house, the neighboring house had a coach house for Rosemary. Mariah planned to reside in her father's house until she could close on the new house. The owner's will was in the process of being probated. So Mariah would reside in the "big house" as Sonyell and Raquel called Mariah's father's house for a short time.

Mariah kept the center operational in Altgeld Garden. She promoted her second-in-command, Ciara Davidson, to managing director. Ciara would oversee the day-to-day activities. Mariah planned to put in an appearance at the facility once or twice a week.

Since Sonyell had majored in business management in college and minored in accounting, Mariah hired her as her business manager. Sonyell's primary function would be to learn the inner workings of the businesses. She would with present management to ensure the businesses continued to turn a profit. Raquel, a hairdresser by trade, would manage the beauty and barber shops. The girls were ecstatic about their new duties and felt like they had won the lottery.

Mariah and her friends planned to move into their new homes within two weeks. Mariah would move into her home first, with the friends moving the following weekend. That way they could help each other. Mariah had stopped at a U-Haul storage facility on the way home from the center, and picked up packing boxes. She planned to keep some of the furniture from her father's house but was anxious to imprint her own brand upon it. The Salvation Army in Hammond was scheduled to pick up donations during the week.

"Granny," Mariah yelled as she set the boxes on the floor, "are you home? I picked up more boxes so we could finish packing. Moving day is right around the corner."

Rosemary didn't reply. Mariah glanced at her watch and noted her grandmother should be home any minute. She picked up a couple of boxes and walked upstairs to her bedroom. Mariah had just taped several boxes shut when she heard the front door open and close. She could hear Rosemary walking up the stairs. Mariah looked up as Rosemary entered her bedroom and smiled.

"How was your day, Granny?" she asked as she put a stack of books into one of the boxes.

"Not bad. How was yours?" Rosemary replied. She pulled her jacket off and fanned herself with one hand. "Today was such a nice day. I just hope we have a few more like this before the hawk hits Chicago."

"I'm sure we will," Mariah agreed. "I brought more boxes." She waved her hand at the stack and then turned her attention back to her grandmother. "I noticed you haven't done any packing. Why not?"

"Mari," Rosemary began hesitantly, "I need to talk to you about the move." She sighed heavily. "I don't think I'm going to come with you."

"What do you mean?" Mariah's eyebrows rose questioningly. "Of course, you're coming with me, Granny." She dropped the box on the floor.

"My place is here in the Garden. I don't know any other life, I'm older. The changes you want to make are better for younger people, like you, Sonni, and Rocki." Rosemary's eyes dropped to the floor.

"Granny, I don't believe you." Mariah's voice rose hysterically. "Of course, you're coming with me. I can't do anything without you being there." She flung her hand. "You've been with me my entire life. It's time for you to take it easy and enjoy life."

Rosemary shook her head sadly. "Those are your plans not mine. I've prayed and given thought to moving with you to Hammond. But, my place is here in Chicago. I've lived here since I moved from Florida and it's home. And someone has to be here for Cassie."

Mariah opened her mouth then closed it. She said, "I already thought about Cassie. I plan to look into some rehabilitation centers for her. Like you said, maybe she can go to a really good one that will help her straighten out her life. You can't put your life on hold for Cassie."

"Cassie is my child as much as you are," Rosemary reminded her granddaughter. "I can't leave Cassie." Rosemary's voice was strong and brooked no argument.

Mariah felt a sinking feeling in the pit of her stomach. She stared at Rosemary with disbelief flashing in her eyes. "Granny." Her hand fluttered to her throat. "I just assumed you were coming with me. You never said you weren't." Mariah's voice trailed off. She sat down on her bed and dropped her face into her hands.

Rosemary walked to the bed and sat down next to her granddaughter. She put her arm around Mariah's shoulders. "I should have said something to you earlier. Like I said, I thought long and hard about coming with you. But I can't leave my child without one of us being here if she needs us."

Mariah thought how Cassie always seemed to disrupt her life. She was at a point in her life when she could make life easier for her beloved Granny and once again Cassie was coming between them. A teardrop slipped between her fingers.

"Now, Mari, don't be like that, baby. I have my life to live just like you have yours. Why you're right up the expressway; I promise to come spend some weekends with you. I know this will be a change for you. But, you need a chance to live your life; meet a nice young man and give me some great grandchildren. I'm not getting any younger you know." Rosemary tried to lighten the mood, but Mariah wasn't having it.

Mariah stood up. She said with a voice that resonated with resignation, "If that's how you feel, then I have no choice but to go along with your wishes. I am disappointed though. It seems I can never be happy and as always it's Cassie's fault."

Rosemary grabbed Mariah's hands and forced her to sit back down. She turned Mariah's face toward her. "I don't want you to feel like that. Your mother has issues. I've always told you that. She has demons that she just can't overcome. Despite everything she has done—stolen from us, lied, and God knows what else—she is still my child, my only child. As Jesus preached, I will love her unconditionally. It would be good if you could do the same."

"I try to, but it's hard. I still remember the taunts I received from kids in school, teasing me about how my mother is a crackhead. It was hard for me. As I imagine it has been for you. But that doesn't mean you have to put your life on hold, either," Mariah said petulantly.

"What makes you think I'm putting my life on hold? I have a job that, I might add, I enjoy, and my friends live here." Rosemary gestured toward the window. "I wanted a better life for you, more than what I had. And thanks to your father, you will have better and you will go out and make your mark on the world, just the way I knew you would."

"How can I do all those things without you?" Mariah whispered. She looked at Rosemary with tear-stained eyes.

"The same way you always have," Rosemary said gently. "I can do all things through Him. And you will, Mari, I promise you will. I'm sorry you had to endure hardships as a child because of the things you mother did. But, you know the saying, that which doesn't kill you makes you stronger. I know you were never sympathetic to Cassie as a child. Some children reject their drug-addicted parents, or are protective of them and love them to death. All I ever wanted you to do was accept Cassie for who she is and try to help her. Pray as I do every night that she will turn her life around."

"That's where we differ. I accept Cassie for what she is: a crackhead. In my own way I have feelings for her. I understand without her I wouldn't be alive, but she's never done anything for me, nothing."

"How could she? She's never been in a position where she could."

"Why not? Why wasn't I ever more important to her than drugs? Why weren't you?" Mariah retorted. Her voice rose.

"I don't know. . . ." Rosemary shook her head helplessly. "I just know things went bad for her, and Cassie was never the same. In her own way she loves you. I know that, but she just can't express it." Rosemary tried hard to justify her daughter's actions.

"It doesn't matter at this point." Mariah stood up. "I'm going out for a bit. I need some air." She looked sadly at Rosemary, picked up her cell phone from her nightstand, grabbed her purse, and departed from the room.

Rosemary trailed behind her. "I'm sorry. . . ."

Mariah rushed downstairs. She stomped out the door, locked it, and walked rapidly to her car. Her emotions boiled with rage when she thought of Cassandra. Mariah put the car in drive and sped from the parking lot. The car tires squealed and burned rubber as she exited the parking lot.

Fifteen minutes later, she pressed Sonyell's doorbell.

Sasha peered through the peephole, then opened the door. She enveloped Mariah in a bear hug. "Hi, Auntie Mari, come on in." She gestured inside the house. "Mommy didn't tell me you were coming over." Sasha took Mariah by the hand and led her into the apartment. They walked to the living room after Sasha locked the door.

"It was a spur-of-the-moment decision," Mariah informed the young girl after they sat together on the sofa. Mariah turned to Sasha and asked, "How are you doing, and how is school?"

Sasha seemed to look older and taller each time Mariah saw her. Whereas Sonyell was short, Sasha was tall like her father. Her complexion was a medium brown. She had heavily lidded eyes. She wore braces and bemoaned how she was too fat. She wore her shoulder-length dark hair in an elaborate cornrow style that Raquel had concocted.

"School is great. I like my teacher and I'm thinking about going out for the cheerleading or pep squad." Sasha replied.

Sonyell walked into the room carrying a dish towel in her hand. "I thought I heard your voice. How are you, Mari?"

"I'm okay," Mariah replied tersely.

"I just finished making dinner, would you like to join us?" Sonyell couldn't help but notice the painful look on her friend's face, though Mariah was trying to mask it for Sasha.

"I'm not really hungry. I wanted to talk to you, if you have a few minutes to spare." Mariah glanced over at Sasha and back to Sonyell. "Is this a good time?"

"Sasha, I know you have some spelling words to study. Don't you have a test tomorrow?" Sonyell turned and asked her daughter.

Sasha dipped her head up and down.

"Why don't you go over the list while I talk to Auntie Mari." Sonyell sat in the chair across from the sofa.

"Okay," the girl replied as she stood up and walked toward her bedroom. She turned and asked her mother, "Can I have a snack?"

"No, we'll be eating dinner soon," Sonyell replied definitely. "I need to talk to Mari for a little while."

Sasha crinkled her nose. "Okay, talk to you later, Aunt Mari."

"I'll come see you before I leave." Mariah watched the young girl as she exited the room. "She is getting so big. She looks just like her daddy."

"That she does, and yes, she is getting big. It seems like just yesterday, I came from the hospital, and didn't have a clue as to how to raise a child. Now enough about me. What's happening with you?"

Mariah pushed a strand of hair off her face and sighed heavily. "I don't know where to begin. It seems like some parts of my life are falling apart."

"What do you mean?" Sonyell asked. She stared at Mariah quizzically, giving her friend her undivided attention.

"It's Granny, she doesn't want to move to Hammond with me. She says it's because of Cassie. And that really bothers me. Also, I feel like she's keeping something from me."

"Something like what?" Sonyell's left eyebrow arched upward.

"I don't know. . . ." Mariah said with frustration in her voice. "I just know something isn't right. You were there when she said she would move to Hammond with us. Then today, just up out of the blue, she tells me that she isn't going."

"Did she say why?" Sonyell asked sympathetically.

Mariah leaned forward in her seat and explained Rosemary's reasons for not moving and how they related to Cassie.

Sonyell listened attentively. When her friend finished speaking, she bit her lower lip, and said carefully, "Maybe, Granny is being honest. Cassie does come by to see you two occasionally, not often. Maybe, she would sink even further in her drug usage if she thought your grandmother abandoned her."

"I really feel like Cassie has always messed up things for me, one way or another. Granny not moving with me is another example of Cassie messing up things for me." Mariah's voice cracked. "Cassie never liked me, even as a child. Maybe she's jealous of my and Granny's relationship. I don't know."

"Whatever your grandmother's motives, you've got to accept them. She has lived in the Garden her entire life. You know how some older people are; they don't like change."

"I hear you, but I don't accept it." Mariah's eyes fell to the floor. "Something just isn't right. Who in their right mind would want to live in a housing project if they could do better?"

"Maybe an older person?" Sonyell shrugged her shoulders. "I don't know what to tell you, but, Granny has never lied to you. I can't think of any reason for her to start now. I think she's happy with her life and doesn't want to change it."

"Maybe," Mariah said stubbornly. "I just feel hurt and I can't imagine not living in the same house with her."

"Okay, so you don't want to cut the apron strings yet." Sonyell rubbed her chin.

"That's not it," Mariah protested. She shook her head from side to side.

Sonyell held out her hand. "Just listen to yourself. You have this great life in front of you, you're planning to make a difference in the world, and just because one part of it isn't going the way you planned, you're complaining. I'm with Granny; you have too much time on your hands. You need a man, girl, and then you won't be so concerned about what you grandmother is doing. You need to get a life."

"You're a fine one to talk," Mariah responded crossly, and folded her arms across her chest defensively. "I haven't seen you in any relationships since Michael. And he's been in jail more than he's been out."

"Now, that wasn't fair." Sonyell shook her head. "That was just hitting below the belt. Mike and I have a child together and that makes a big difference. He's doing him, paying the consequences, and I'm doing me. You know I love him. Mike will be out of prison by the end of the year. If things don't work out between us, or he finds himself locked up again, then it's a wrap."

"Wow, you've never once implied that you planned to let Mike go if things don't work out. I'm surprised." Mariah's eyes widened.

"With Sasha getting older, I have to think about her and who I am exposing her to, even if he is her father. Maybe it's time for a change for me too. I am firm though this time. If things don't work out this time, I am done with him."

"Well, good for you then." Mariah bobbed her head approvingly. "It would be nice to see you in a relationship with a man who is actually in the same city with you."

"It's time," Sonyell admitted. "Now, back to your problem. Where your grandmother lives is really her choice. Maybe she's not ready to leave Altgeld now."

"Maybe," Mariah conceded. "I'm just so frustrated." Mariah smacked one of her hands inside the other.

"That's why you need a man," Sonyell announced triumphantly. "You have too much energy and need to burn off some of it," Sonyell teased her friend.

"I don't know about all of that." Mariah waved her hand in the air. "You know I decided to be celibate after my last disastrous relationship with Jameer. I swore off men for a while."

"That was two years ago. It's time for you to open yourself up to new possibilities. And, as for Granny, she may realize after you leave the nest how much she misses you. Maybe she'll end up moving to Indiana."

"As long as Cassie stays in her drug-infested world, that's not happening," Mariah predicted glumly.

"Cassie is her child. I'm sure she's as hurt as you are by the situation."

"I know that, and you raise good points," Mariah conceded. She rose from the sofa. "I know you need to finish dinner. I'm sorry I took up your time with Sasha with my problem."

Sonyell stood up too. "Now, you know talking to you is no problem. That's what friends are for. I think you need to cool off and try to look at the situation from Granny's viewpoint and give it time. You are more than welcome to join me and Sasha for dinner. I made more than enough."

"No, you go ahead and enjoy your mother-daughter time. I know you've been putting in a lot of overtime at work. I'll call you later. I'm going to tell Sasha good-bye, and then head out."

Sonyell rubbed Mariah's arm. "Give thought to what I said. And don't forget, I'm here if you need me."

"Thanks, Sonni." Mariah walked to Sasha's room and told her goddaughter good-bye. She left minutes later and entered her car.

Mariah started the car, and sat indecisively inside it for a few minutes. She didn't feel like going home just yet. Her feelings were too raw, and she didn't feel like facing Rosemary just yet. She put the car in reverse and backed up. She drove to Interstate 94. Maybe she would stay in Hammond overnight or for a few days, and let Rosemary see what life felt like without her company for a day or two.

Chapter Seven

By the time Mariah had exited I-94 Expressway at Calumet Avenue, she was already regretting her decision to stay overnight in Hammond. As she stopped at a red light on 165th Street, Mariah looked around to get her bearings. The streets were deserted and the streetlights glowed dimly under the dark, cloudy sky. She immediately surmised there was a big difference between traveling at night and in daylight.

Mariah was heading north on Hohman Avenue when her car experienced a mechanical problem. The car made a loud sound. She glanced in her rearview mirror. Mariah sighed with relief when she saw there weren't any cars behind her that might have hit her car. She had just about made it to the curb when car died. Mariah stomped on the brake, and quickly put on her blinkers. She struggled to shift the car into the parking gear. Mariah pulled the knob to open the hood. She hopped from the car and peered inside. She glanced at the battery, but not being mechanically inclined, Mariah had no idea what the problem could be. She returned to the inside of the car.

Mariah sat indecisively for a few minutes. She regretted not renewing her AAA membership. Then Rosemary invaded her thoughts; her grandmother had often stressed the importance of Mariah subscribing to a towing service since the young woman often traveled alone. Mariah chewed her lower lip as she twisted a strand of hair, trying to contemplate her next move.

A loud rat-a-tat at the window startled Mariah out of her musing and she jumped. She looked outside to see a man holding his hands up. Mariah lowered the window a few inches.

"Do you need help?" the man asked carefully. He looked to be around thirty years old. He was dressed casually in neatly pressed dark denim jeans with a lightweight white pullover sweater. He also wore a black leather jacket, and had a baseball cap pulled over sandy-colored locked hair. He had parked his white Ford pickup truck in front of Mariah's car.

Warning bells chimed in Mariah's brain. She exhaled loudly, then said, "Yes, I do need help. My car stopped and I don't have a clue as to what could be wrong."

"My name is Carson Palmer," he introduced himself. "You looked like you're stranded and could some help. The hood of your car being up is a dead giveaway. I just want to help. I don't mean you any harm."

Mariah looked out the car window at him doubtfully.

He held his palms out. "Is it okay if I take a look under the hood of your car?"

"Sure. My name is Mariah Green," she introduced herself. She watched Carson walk to the front of the car, and fiddle under the hood. Mariah pulled her cell phone out of her purse and called Sonyell. She quickly filled her friend in on what was going on. "I need you to stay on the phone with me at least until I can find out if he can fix it."

"Be careful," Sonyell warned her friend. "You don't know him from Jack. See, if you had gone back home instead of being hardheaded, your car wouldn't have broke down so far from home."

"You're right, but it's too late now. I just want to get going. Now is not the time to fuss at me." Mariah tried to defend her decision.

"You know that there are crazies out there. I'm still helping Sasha with her homework. I'm going to put you on speaker and set the phone down. Make sure your doors are locked."

"Okay." Mariah put the phone on the passenger seat, and looked in the back seat for a jacket. The temperature had fallen and there was a distinct chill in the air. She shivered then put the jacket on.

A few minutes later, although it seemed like an eternity to Mariah, Carson walked to Mariah's car door. She pressed a button and the window slithered down a few inches. "What's the verdict?" she asked apprehensively.

"I'm not a mechanic by trade, but I think your engine has locked up," Carson said ominously.

"So, what does that mean? What can I do to fix it? Do I need oil? I kept putting off getting my oil changed and other things came up. Do you think that has anything to do with my problem?" Mariah babbled.

"That could definitely be the cause of the problem." Carson nodded. "Especially if you haven't had an oil change for a while. Unfortunately, your car isn't drivable. You need to call a tow truck and have it towed to your mechanic or home."

Just then the siren from a police car screamed in the air. A black-and-white vehicle with flashing lights pulled behind Mariah. The officer exited his vehicle and walked to Mariah's car.

"Miss, do you know you're parked in a no parking zone? What's the problem?"

Carson quickly explained Mariah's dilemma.

"Okay, it would be better if you could move it down the street. If the vehicle isn't drivable, try to have it towed as soon as possible."

"I could push her farther up the street," Carson volunteered.

The officer dipped his head and returned to his car and departed. Mariah and Carson watched him pull away from the curb and merge into traffic.

"So do you have a towing service?" Carson asked Mariah.

"I don't. I think my best bet would be to call a tow truck. I know it's going to cost me an arm and leg this time of the night."

"I have a buddy who has a tow truck company. I could have him meet us here. I'm sure he will allow you to keep your arms and legs. I can wait with you until he gets here." Carson pointed to a pickup truck.

"If you could that would be wonderful," Mariah said feeling relieved. She wasn't quite out the woods yet. She sensed Carson was on the up and up and didn't feel threatened by him. "I hope I'm not keeping you from any plans you may have made."

"No problem, I'm good. After I push your car up the street, I'm going to go to my truck and call Alex. When I'm done talking to him, I'll come back and give you his ETA."

"Thank you, Carson, I don't know what I would have done had you not come along."

"I'm going to push you up the block and then I'll call Alex." He nodded and went to his truck. Ten minutes later Carson had pushed Mariah away from the no parking zone and returned to his truck.

Mariah picked up her cell phone and said, "Sonni, are you still there?"

Sonyell replied, "Of course I am. I felt relieved when the police came. I was going to ask you for his license plate number. If something had happened to you, I would have a point of reference. So you're waiting on his friend to come. Are you going to stay in Hammond tonight?"

"I feel safe with him. I think he's my Good Samaritan. Yes, I'm going to stay in Hammond tonight. I'll have his friend tow my car to my dad's house. Luckily my dad had a SUV, so I'll drive that tomorrow."

"I don't understand why you aren't driving it anyway. You know your car is on its last leg. Carson sounds sexy. Is he fine?"

"Like I was looking at him. Girl, I was concerned about my car," Mariah replied nonchalantly.

"Please, there isn't anything wrong with your eyes. So again I'm going to ask you to give me the 411, is he fine? Tell me how he looks."

Mariah twisted a strand of hair nervously. "Well, not that I was looking that hard. But, yeah, he is fine. He's tall, I'd say about six feet five, kind of thin but muscular, like he plays basketball, and, Sonni, he has the prettiest green eyes. He has thick eyebrows, he's butter colored, and he looks more European rather than African. And, girl, he has a Kirk Douglas cleft in his chin. But, he's definitely not my physical type." Mariah pooh-poohed the thought. Truthfully he took her breath away.

"For someone who wasn't looking that hard, you seem to have taken more than one look. I knew it, with that baritone voice and all," Sonyell told her friend.

Just then Carson returned to Mariah's car. "I spoke to Alex, he will be here as soon as he can. He lives in Griffith, which isn't that far from here. So, I'll wait with you for him and, hopefully, we'll have you at your destination in no time."

"Again, thank you, Carson, you've been a big help," Mariah thanked him graciously.

"Glad to have been of service. I have sisters and I'd like to think if one of them got stranded, someone would help them. Say, how far are you from your destination?" Carson looked at Mariah curiously.

"Not too far, I'd say about five miles," Mariah calculated the distance.

"Good. Your limbs are safe then. I'll be in my truck; holler if you need anything."

"I will," Mariah replied. She watched Carson return to his vehicle.

"Hmmm, I can hardly wait to meet him. If you're not interested, I bet Rocki would be. You know she's on the prowl."

"Yes, twenty-four seven, 365 days a year."

The friends laughed.

"Are you going to call Granny? I know you didn't tell her where you were going. You know she's probably going crazy about now."

"I'll think about when I get my dad's. Right now, I just want to get out of this car and inside the house, so I can stretch my legs. I'm starving, I didn't have dinner, and you know I don't know where the restaurants are located in this city."

"Look, it's time you stop calling the house your dad's. Say 'my house.' Anyway, maybe Mr. Carson can suggest a few eating places," Sonyell said slyly.

"Look, I don't have the time or energy to devote to a man right now. I have too many things on my plate."

"Ain't nothing wrong with a little loving," Sonyell advised. "You're so uptight anyway. A man would help you to relax."

"Well, we know that's not going to happen, since I'm practicing celibacy," Mariah retorted haughtily.

Sonyell shook her head. "It's easy to practice that when there isn't a man in the picture. We'll see how your self-control is with a man around."

Mariah and Sonni talked for a while.

A vehicle turned the corner with flashing red lights. "Sonni, I've got to go. I'll call you again when I arrive home."

"Okay."

The women disconnected the call and Mariah watched as Carson exited his vehicle, and walked to the tow truck that was parking in front of her car. She hoped he would take a credit card, because she didn't have any cash on her.

A few minutes later, Carson and Alex walked to the car. Mariah let her window down.

"Mariah, this is my friend Alex Morales. He will tow your car; he just needs the address of where you need the car towed to."

Alex appeared to be of African American and Hispanic descent. He was portly with a mop of dark ringlets on his head. "Hello, Ms. Mariah." He stuck out his hand. "Yeah, I just need to know where you're going and I'll have you there in no time. Carson says you aren't going very far."

"Hello, Mr. Morales," Mariah replied as she placed her hand inside Alex's. "How much will the tow cost? Also, I don't have cash. Do you accept credit cards?"

"What is the address that the car will be towed to?" Alex inquired. He began filling out a service request form.

Mariah told him her address.

"That will be fifty-five dollars. And, no, I don't accept credit cards, cash only," Alex informed Mariah.

"In that case I'll need to stop at an ATM," Mariah said.

"That's not a problem. Would you like to ride in the truck with me?" Alex asked.

"No, she'll ride with me," Carson interjected. He looked at Mariah. "I mean if that's all right with you."

"I'll ride with Carson," Mariah decided. She covered her mouth to stifle a yawn. "Sorry, it's been a long day."

"I'll get the car loaded on the flatbed and then we can be on our way." Alex headed to his tow truck.

Mariah put on her jacket and grabbed her purse. She prayed that Carson and Alex weren't running a game. She put her hand inside her purse and pressed the speed dial for Sonyell's number. She didn't intend on talking to her—didn't want to insult the men. She just wanted Sonyell to at least have the capability to be listening in if something went down.

She walked with Carson to his pickup truck. He opened the door like a gentleman and closed it after she got in. He got inside.

"What's the name of your bank? Perhaps there's an ATM nearby."

"I bank at Chase," Mariah replied after she put on her seat belt.

"There's an ATM about a block away at a 7-Eleven store. We can go there and then to your place."

"I am truly indebted to you tonight." Mariah thanked him as Carson started the truck. Five minutes later he pulled into the 7-Eleven parking lot.

"I'll be right back," Mariah said as she placed her hands on the side of the truck to open the door.

Carson jumped out of the truck. "Let me," he said. Carson walked to the passenger side and opened the door for Mariah. Then he waited outside the store for her to return.

She went to the ATM and withdrew $120. Then she bought snacks to eat later on. When she returned outside, Carson opened the door for her, and Mariah entered the truck. They chatted and it didn't take long before the trio arrived at Mariah's house. Sonyell had certainly given Mariah food for thought during their conversation.

As Mariah exited the truck, she was filled with apprehension. What would she do if Carson put the moves on her? Or asked her for her telephone number? She felt comfortable with him, though she had just met him. There was an undeniable attraction between the two. The question in her mind was should she or shouldn't she act upon it?

Chapter Eight

Sonyell's landline telephone rang shrilly. She rose from the chair in the dining room and went toward the kitchen to answer the call. She looked at Sasha, warning, "I'll be right back. I want the last two math problems finished when I return, young lady."

"I'm tired, Mommy," Sasha whined.

"You're almost done; just finish those two problems, then we can call it a night."

Sonyell walked rapidly into the kitchen, and removed the receiver of the gold wall phone. "Hello," she said.

"You have a collect call from Marion Correctional Facility," an automated tone informed her. "Do you accept the call?"

"Yes," Sonyell said, as she smoothed her bangs off her forehead. A frown in the middle of her forehead marred her pretty face.

"Hey, baby girl, what's up?" Michael asked Sonyell. "How's Sasha?"

"We're both fine, Mike. She's finishing her homework. How are you doing?"

"I'm good. I haven't talked to you all week."

"I know," Sonyell replied. "You weren't on lockdown or anything, were you?" Her stomach muscles clenched sporadically.

"Naw, they're starting to process my release papers, and waiting to get phone time in this joint some days ain't a joke."

"Hmm." Sonyell removed her earring from her ear with her free hand. "I guess the time is right around the corner. Now, if you could just act right, and keep your nose out of trouble, it would be all good."

"I promise, things are going to be different this time," Michael responded ardently. "Sasha is growing up and I don't want her memories of me to be of me just behind bars. You and my moms have both told me that she's at the age where she needs me, and I promise I'm going to be there for her."

"I hope so." Sonyell sighed. "Unfortunately, I've heard that before."

"I'm going to straighten up and fly right," Michael asserted. "Hey, have you talked to my moms?"

"Yeah, I did last night. Miss Nedra is fine. I saw her at church Sunday."

"She told me that your minister works with people with criminal records and helps them find jobs. I told her I'd talk to him."

A thrill of hope enveloped Sonyell's body. In all the times Michael had been locked up, and released, he had never spoken of finding a job when he got out.

"She's right. Reverend Dudley has some city and state connections. He's been working hard to help men and women find jobs once they are released. I went to see him last week, and got some information from him on how the program works. I'll bring it up so you can look it over when I visit in two weeks."

"So, you still plan on moving to Hammond?" Michael asked. He knew his time on the phone was growing short.

"Yes. Mari is moving this weekend, and Rocki and I will be moving into our houses the following weekend. I am really excited about moving to a new place, with a new job; it's like a fresh start," Sonyell gushed.

"Do you think Mari might have something I can do?" Michael mused aloud. He turned and looked behind him. The line to use the telephone behind Michael had grown by leaps and bounds. The natives were getting restless.

"I don't know. . . ." Sonyell said doubtfully as she twisted the telephone cord. "I can talk to her about it."

"It would look good on my papers if I can secure work before or right after I'm released."

"I agree." She nodded her head. "I'll see what she says, and tell you the next time I talk to you."

"I got to go, baby girl. Tell Sasha I said hi, and I love her, and ditto that for you. Thanks, Sonni, for hanging in there with me. I promise things are going to be different this time."

"Love you too, babe. I'll talk to you next time."

They hung up the telephones.

Sonyell stood in the kitchen wonderingly for a few moments. She then rushed back to the dining room. Sasha's head was resting on her arms atop the table. Sonyell picked up her homework and noted her daughter had completed her math homework. The answers were correct. She gently pulled her daughter's shoulder. "Come on, sleepyhead, let's get you ready for bed."

Sasha stood up and rubbed her eyes. "Was that my daddy on the phone?" she asked her mother.

Sonyell nodded as they walked down the hallway to the bedrooms, which were across the hall from each other. "He said to tell you hi and that he loves you."

"I can hardly wait for my daddy to come home," Sasha said enthusiastically. She walked into her bedroom and took her pajamas from a hook inside the closet. Then she walked to the bathroom.

"Don't forget to brush your teeth," Sonyell reminded her daughter.

After Sasha closed the bathroom door, Sonyell walked to her bedroom. The house was overcrowded with boxes and her bedroom was no exception. She was looking forward to the move. She and Sasha felt like they'd been invaded by brown boxes.

Sonyell took an outfit out of her closet to wear to work the following day. She eyed the olive green suit critically and decided it needed pressing. She laid the suit and blouse on the bed. Then, she sat down. She closed her eyes and prayed. "Lord, please let Michael get it right this time. Anybody can change it they want to, and especially if they have you in their corner. I want so much for things to go right for us this time. Sasha is growing up and she needs her father. Father, please put it on his heart to get his life together. These blessings I pray in your Son's name. Amen."

Sonyell went back into the dining room and looked at her cell phone. She debated calling Mariah, but she knew if Mariah needed her that she would call.

She laid the cell phone back on the table, when it chimed, indicating she had an incoming call. Sonyell glanced at the caller ID unit and saw that it was Rocki. She pressed the accept call button. "Hey, girl, what's happening?" Sonyell walked back to her bedroom.

"Nothing much. My feet are aching. I had a busy day at the shop. Tuesday is my last day at work and then I'm going to finish packing next week."

"Good. I'm just about done. I have a few things to pack on the day of the move. Other than that, I'm moving right along. You may want to come over one day next week before you pack up your tools, and hook a sista and her daughter up."

"I think I can manage that. Did you talk to Mari today? I called her, but she didn't call me back. She must have been busy. Mari usually calls me in the evening."

Raquel was sitting in her living room on the sofa. She picked up the remote control for the television, and channel surfed.

"I did." Sonyell brought Rocki up to date on the falling-out between Mariah and Rosemary.

"That's too bad. I know Mari must be torn up," Raquel commented as she turned to BET.

"You're right, she didn't take it well at all. I started to call Mrs. Green and ask her if she would reconsider. But, then I thought I should stay out of it," Sonyell confided to Raquel.

"You're right, just stay out of it. Personally, if it was me, I wouldn't want my grandmother living with me. She would just cramp my style." Raquel crinkled her nose.

Sonyell laughed. "That's true, but we know Mari isn't nearly the social creature you are."

"Maybe without Mrs. Green hovering in the background, she will be," Raquel threw in.

"Somehow I doubt that, but I guess one can hope. Mari's car broke down and a nice brother came to her rescue. He sounded fine over the phone."

"He did? Dang, some sistas get all the breaks. I wonder if he has a brother or a good friend," Raquel said. Her telephone receiver was nestled against her neck. She filed her nails with an emery board as she talked. "Did she tell you how he looked?"

"She did and he sounds like a keeper, after she learns some more vital information. She had me on the line with her, until she felt comfortable with him. She should be at her house by now. I'm going to call her when I get off the phone with you."

"You're right about the vitals. Is he married, or does he have any children, does he have his own place, and most of all is he gainfully employed. We don't want her hooking up with a street entrepreneur."

"You're right, and I don't think Mari would have let him wait with her until a tow truck came if he wasn't an okay brother."

Raquel stopped filing her nails. "Yeah, you're right about that. Our girl is cautious if nothing else."

"Mommy, I'm done," Sasha yelled as she came out of the bathroom. She looked pretty in pink pajamas.

"Okay, Sasha, give me a minute." Sonyell looked over at her daughter. She returned her attention to the telephone. "Rocki, I've got to go. I'll call you back if I have time; if not I'll talk to you tomorrow."

"Have a good evening. Tell Sasha I said hey, and I'll talk to you."

The call ended. Sonyell went into Sasha's bedroom. She tied a wrap scarf around Sasha's head. Mother and daughter sat on the side of the bed and talked for a few minutes. Later, Sasha said her prayers. Then she got under the covers. Sonyell kissed her daughter good night, turned off the light, and walked to her bedroom.

She removed her outer garments then went to the bathroom to shower. Afterward, she brushed her teeth and returned to her bedroom. She turned the radio to a soft jazz station, and pulled out her Bible to study her daily devotional. Later, she asked God to forgive her for her sins, and thanked Him for the blessings He had bestowed upon her.

Sonyell stood up and dropped to her knees. She clasped her hands together and closed her eyes. She prayed, "Lord, please be with my Mikey tonight. I hope he's trying as hard as he can to get himself together. But if he doesn't then he's history. Lord, I want so much for us—Sasha, him, and me—to be a real family." Every night since Michael's sentencing, sitting in the courtroom and learning her lover's fate, Sonyell said a special nightly prayer for Michael.

Unbeknownst to Sonyell, Sasha had sneaked out of bed and watched her mother pray on more than one occasion. And tonight was no exception. The young girl's eyes filled with tears as she listened to her mother implore God. Sasha scampered ever so quietly back to her room on the dark, carpeted floor, and returned to her bedroom.

As she lay under the comforter, Sasha's mind wandered back to a conversation she'd had with her grandmother, Miss Nedra, about her mother's nightly prayer. The young girl also opened up to her grandmother regarding her feelings about her father being incarcerated. Miss Nedra bade the girl to always love her father. And she told her how Michael meant well, but he just couldn't always control his impulses and deliver on his promises. Miss Nedra told the young girl that her father had been talking to a doctor inside the prison about his behavior, and that her father seemed to be doing better. She also told Sasha not to worry because her mother was strong. If need be, Sonyell could function as mother and father if Michael couldn't get himself together.

Lastly, Miss Nedra told her youngest grandchild not to even worry because she had a Heavenly Father who would always be with and for her. She explained to the girl how God sent angels to help us to through the rough patches of life. Miss Nedra promised Sasha that she would always be there to help guide her. Sasha closed her eyes and said her prayers again. Then, as she fell asleep, a smile filled her lips.

A half hour later, Sonyell walked from her room to her daughter's bedroom. She pulled the comforter over Sasha's arms and kissed her daughter's cheek. When Sonyell returned to her bedroom, she sat on the side of the bed. Then, she glanced at the clock on her nightstand. Sonyell wondered why Mariah hadn't called her. She arose from the bed and took her phone off the charger that sat on her dresser. Mariah quickly dialed Mariah's telephone number. Her body tensed and she held her breath waiting for Mariah to answer the phone.

Chapter Nine

Mariah waved good-bye to Alex. He tooted his horn lightly as he drove down the street. She was just getting ready to tell Carson good night when her cell phone sounded. She pulled it out of her purse, which sat under the glider on the porch. "Excuse me," she told Carson, "this is one of my friends. I have to take this call." Mariah walked to the other end of the porch.

Though the night was chilly, the stars twinkled in the clear sky, like blinking lights on a Christmas tree. A full moon showered the couple with a dim light, like a candle.

"Girl, what's going on? Is he still there?" Sonyell queried her friend.

"Yes, he is," Mariah responded. "He's getting ready to leave now. I'll call you back in a few minutes."

"You'd better. Don't have me get Sasha up and we drive out to Hammond to check on you," Sonyell warned her friend before they ended the call.

Mariah pressed the disconnect button and dropped her cell phone in her jacket pocket. She walked back to the other side of the porch where Carson was sitting. He stood up. "I know you must be tired. Before I go I wanted to ask you if you are related to man who owned his house. Mr. Ellison? When you told me his address, I thought I recognized it."

Mariah's body trembled. "Uh, yeah, I am. Did you know him?" She couldn't prevent her voice from cracking.

"Yes, Mr. Ellison was a mentor and friend to me. He passed not too long ago, and his wife a short time before he did. So how are you related to him?" Carson's eyes raked over Mariah's body. Then understanding dawned in his eyes. "You look like Mr. Ellison; are you his daughter?"

Mariah couldn't trust herself to speak. She nodded her head.

"Wow, it's a small world. Imagine me running into Mr. Ellison's daughter. He mentored me when I was a boy. He volunteered at the Boys & Girls Club in Hammond."

"Did he really?" Mariah tried but couldn't keep bitterness from seeping into her voice.

"Yeah, he did a lot of good things for the community, especially for African Americans. He is still sorely missed." Carson couldn't help but notice the look of distress on Mariah's face.

"That's good." Her voice became tight. "Maybe I will learn something of the man. I never knew him and still don't."

"He was a good guy. Everyone who knew him respected him. He did a lot for many people. He helped me start my business. In fact he was my silent partner. When he passed, he left me his share."

"If he was such a good guy, then I wonder why he never did anything for me," Mariah said sadly. She spoke her thoughts aloud before she could catch herself.

"I can't answer that, but I can tell you he was a good guy. He told me bits and pieces about his background, which I would be glad to share with you."

"I would definitely be interested in hearing that story one day," Mariah said. She yawned, covered her mouth, uncovered it, and then said to Carson, "I'm really tired. It's been a long day. I really need to get some rest. I have a lot of tasks planned for tomorrow." She fumbled in her pocket for the keys to the house. Mariah felt them and pulled them out.

"I understand. Look, if you need any help with anything, feel free to call me." He fumbled in his pocket for a business card and came up empty.

"If there is anything I can do for you, Carson, let me know. I appreciate all your help tonight. I don't know what I would have done had you not stopped to help me."

"Oh, I'm sure you would have figured something out. I do have a request of you, though."

"What might that be?" Mariah looked at him and then down at her feet. She couldn't mistake the look of interest in his green eyes.

"How about going to dinner with me over the weekend? I think that would even up the score between us." Carson looked at Mariah hopefully.

"Not this weekend. I'm moving from Chicago to the house"—she gestured behind her—"this weekend."

"All the better to have brunch or dinner with me on Sunday. You will still be in the process of unpacking, so going out for a meal will give you a break. If not this weekend what about the following one?" Carson extended his hands as he pleaded his case.

"Hmmm." Mariah narrowed her eyes. "Let me think about it. I may be too tired to get dressed and go out to eat."

"Fair enough," Carson conceded. He pulled out a piece of paper and a pen. He wrote down the name of his business and telephone number. "In case you lost my number. I've written it down again. let me know what you decide. I'll be looking forward to your call." he handed the paper to Mariah.

Her hands closed around the piece of paper. "Okay." Mariah exhaled loudly. "I guess so, but let's say tentatively this Sunday, unless something comes up."

"You got a deal." Carson held out his hand and Mariah took it. He clasped her hand warmly.

Electrical sparks seemed to course up her arm. They weren't unpleasant at all.

A smile filled Mariah's face as she watched Carson lock the gate behind him. "Uh, Mariah," he said.

"Yes, Carson," she replied. Her eyes were twinkling.

"Two more things: can I get your digits, and is it okay if I come by Saturday to help you move?" He took his cell phone out of his pocket and looked at Mariah pleadingly.

Mariah recited her cell phone while Carson programmed the number into his phone.

"You really don't have to come here on Saturday. I have movers; everything is under control," Mariah told him.

"You never know what might come up. You might need my help again." Carson smiled engagingly at Mariah. His grin warmed her heart. She beamed his way.

"I guess so." She turned to unlock the front door, and then turned back around. "Hey, Carson," she said.

Carson faced her. "Yes?"

"You aren't married or anything, are you?" She gazed at him with a penetrating stare.

"No, I'm not married or anything." Carson shook his head with a serious expression. "I'm not that kind of man. Give me time and you'll find out. Have a good evening, Mariah Green. It was a pleasure meeting you. I have a feeling we're going to become good friends."

Mariah blushed and waved at Carson. She watched him get inside his truck, which was parked in the rear of the driveway. He waited for her to go inside the house. Then he honked his horn and drove off.

Mariah flipped on the light switch after she walked into the foyer. She set her bag from the store on the dining room table and walked to the living room. Mariah turned on the table light and sat on the sofa.

The contemporary living room and dining room set she had ordered had been delivered yesterday. She also bought a wall-mounted flat-screen television. She requested that the delivery men remove the television console from the room. She left the picture of Harold and his wife over the fireplace.

She looked at her father and his wife and shook her head. "How could you work with boys and girls and not do anything for me? I don't understand you at all." She picked the remote off the cocktail table and turned on the television. She decided to sleep downstairs for the night. Mariah didn't have any nightclothes so she would have to wing it and sleep in her clothing and hope she didn't look too disheveled in the morning.

Mariah checked her phone for missed calls and saw that Rosemary had called a couple of times. She decided to call her back in the morning. Mariah didn't want to turn the heat on, so she ventured upstairs to get a comforter and blanket out of the linen closet.

When she opened the closet door, she saw a pair of pajamas, with the price tag still attached, folded on the shelf. Mariah had forgotten to put it with the other clothes she had donated to the Salvation Army. Based on photographs Mariah had seen of Dorothy, she appeared to be plus sized. Mariah held up the pajamas; they were a little large for her. Still Mariah was glad that she wouldn't have to sleep in her clothes. She quickly shucked her clothing off and put on the PJs.

After she put on the nightclothes, Mariah went back downstairs and set the burglar alarm. She had bought a bag of Goldfish Crackers and a bottle of 7 Up. She eagerly tore open the bag and munched on the snack. She took a pad of paper out of her purse and added grocery shopping to her to-do list. When she finished eating, Mariah relaxed her body against the back of the sofa, and thought about her day. She focused on Rosemary declining to move to Hammond, and then meeting Carson. She had to admit she felt a spark of attraction between them. He was very handsome, a pretty boy turned man. She had sworn off pretty boys a long time ago. They were way too much work. She wondered if he was interested in her for herself, or because of the money he must have known that she had inherited. "Only time will tell," she told herself.

Mariah looked at the grandfather clock in the corner of the room. She noted it was nearly ten o'clock. She picked up her cordless phone off the end table and dialed Sonyell's number.

"What took you so long to call? I was getting ready to put on my clothes, get Sasha to the car, and drive out there," Sonyell scolded her friend after she answered the telephone.

"I talked to Carson for a little while. I was starving, so I ate the snacks I bought. I changed clothes and made a bed on my new leather sofa. Thank God, it was delivered today. So I'm just getting around to calling you."

"Good. I really was worried, Mari. I'm glad everything turned out okay. You really took a chance depending on a stranger for help. He could have been a crazy."

"He turned out to be a godsend. Can you believe he actually knew my father? You know I'm going to pick his brain."

"Hmm, is that so? Do you plan on seeing him again?" Sonyell tried to keep the excitement out of her voice. She sat upright in the bed.

"Well, we have a date of sorts on Sunday."

"You don't waste time." Sonyell cackled. "What do you mean by a date of sorts? Either you do or you don't."

"I guess we do," Mariah said wonderingly. "We definitely do."

"Cool beans. It's about time you got out and tested the waters again." Sonyell lay back in the bed.

"I don't know about this, Sonni. He knows that Harold Ellison is my father. He spotted the resemblance. How do I know that he likes me for me and not for the money I inherited?"

"You don't. You're a smart woman, you'll figure it out. I've got to go. I have to go to work early in the morning. Since I gave my month's notice, they have found a million things for me to do before I leave. I'll talk to you tomorrow. Oh, did you call Granny?" Sonyell turned off the light on her nightstand.

"No, I didn't. I thought it was too late, that she was probably asleep. I'll call her in the morning."

"You know that you're wrong. She called here earlier looking for you. I told her I would have you call her. Now, would you please do that?"

"I'll think about it. Good night, Sonni. Thanks for having my back."

"That's what sista/friends are for. Sleep tight."

The women hung up. Mariah held the cordless phone in her hand indecisively for a few minutes. Then she dialed Rosemary's number.

The older woman didn't sound like she been asleep. "Mari, I've been sick with worry. Why didn't you call me sooner? Where are you?" Rosemary asked tensely.

"I'm all right. I decided to stay in Hammond tonight. I had car trouble. I just got here a little while ago."

"Praise God, you're okay. I'm sorry you're upset with me for not moving with you. But, I feel my decision is the right one for both of us."

"I think I would feel better if you moved out the projects. Why won't you at least let me buy you a house? You could stay in Chicago, but just not in the projects."

"I don't want you to spend your money on me, Mari. I am independent and I want to stay that way as long as I can. Now if something changes, then we'll talk about it at a later date. Can we call a truce?" Rosemary voice was full of trepidation. She clutched the telephone receiver tightly in her hand.

"Do I really have a choice?" Mariah sighed. "I guess so." She shifted her body on the couch.

"Thank you, baby," Rosemary said, relief evident in her voice. "I want you to enjoy your life and enjoy the new projects you are about to embark on. I know with God's help, you are going to make a difference in the lives of people in Hammond the way you have in the Garden."

"I plan to. I know you have to go to work tomorrow. So I'm going to let you go. If I decide to stay here tomorrow I'll let you know."

"Fair enough. I love you, Mari. I only want the best things in life for you and Cassie. I hope you'll still consider finding a good rehabilitation facility for her. Don't let your anger about the things she didn't do for you while you were growing up cloud your judgment. Praise the Father that you are in a position to help her. Maybe she might turn her life around."

"We'll see. Good night, Granny."

"Good night, Ms. Mari, sleep tight. I love you."

"Love you too, Granny, you have a good night."

After the call ended, Mariah clicked the phone off and held it next to her chest. Then she put it back inside the base. She got up and turned the light on in the dining room. The light switch had a dimmer. She set the lighting low. Then she returned to the living room, lay on the couch, and turned off the table lamp. Before she fell asleep, she thanked her Heavenly Father for the many blessings He had bestowed on her. She made a mental note to get her old car repaired and donate it to charity. She planned to ask Carson if he could recommend a good mechanic. Mariah had a feeling he could.

A smile filled Mariah's face after she fell asleep. A pair of green eyes and the person they belonged to made for a pleasant dream for the young woman. Mariah admitted to herself that she looked forward to talking to Carson Palmer again. She really hoped he used the digits. If he didn't perhaps she would call him herself. Though the day had been rocky, there had been a light at the end of the rainbow and the rainbow came in the guise of Carson Palmer.

Chapter Ten

Mariah had been on pins and needles the remaining days leading up to her moving date. By eight o'clock Saturday morning her stress level had rapidly accelerated. The weatherman had predicted rain in Hammond. When Mariah returned home Thursday evening after work, she resumed packing. As the day elapsed and Friday was upon her, Mariah reflected on how drastically her life was about to change and prayed that God would be with her every step of the way. Her mind like a needle on a vinyl record was stuck on the same melody: *Granny won't be living with me anymore.* Every time that thought crossed Mariah's mind, her inhalations seemed to slow down and get stuck in her throat. The thought of not seeing Granny every day caused a sensation to trickle through Mariah's body. Like a giant finger poked her in the middle of her back, that was sending her reeling into uncharted waters.

She had just put the last pieces of her clothing inside a box. Mariah left her room and walked into the bathroom. She verified that she'd removed all her personal belongings. She opened the medicine chest, and scanned it quickly. Nothing.

She had returned to her bedroom when the doorbell rang. When Mariah opened the door, Sonyell and Raquel stood at there with cups of coffee, bagels, croissants, and a fruit tray for breakfast. After they went into the kitchen, Sonyell removed the food from the bags. Rosemary came down the stairs; she was dressed in a blue sweat suit.

"I see you girls brought breakfast. I planned to fix my grandbaby her last morning meal at this house. Since today is the M day." Rosemary brought her shaking hands up to her midsection and clutched them together.

"I'm afraid we don't have time for that," Mariah informed her grandmother. "The movers will be here soon. Let's just eat what the girls bought. I'll come visit you one morning next week before you go to work, and you can spoil me rotten, like you did when I was a child." She swallowed tears and then ran from the kitchen upstairs to her bedroom.

Rosemary looked toward the staircase; matching tears to Mariah's sprang into her eyes. Everyone looked at other in amazement. Raquel's mouth formed a perfect O, while Sonyell's eyes widened dramatically. Sasha looked dismayed. "Is Aunt Mari all right?" she asked Sonyell fearfully. Her knuckles appeared to be glued to her mouth.

"I guess I'd better go up and see her. Let us know when the mover gets here," Rosemary finally said with a grim look on her face. She marched up the stairs while everyone watched her ascent. A chorus of babbling ensued in the kitchen between Sonyell and Raquel after Rosemary arrived upstairs.

Mariah stood at the window wiping tears from her eyes; she turned toward the door when Rosemary came into the room.

Rosemary walked over to her granddaughter and the women hugged each other tightly, for a long time. Rosemary led Mariah to the bed.

"Come on now, you're too old for this," she tried to tease Mariah. "You're moving about fifteen miles away and you're blubbering like you're moving to Africa or someplace."

"Granny, it just doesn't feel right, you not moving with me," Mariah blurted out.

"It might not feel right today, but give it some time. You knew you had to leave the nest one day, and that day is today." Rosemary nodded her head, while she wiped a tear from Mariah's cheek.

"I want you to come with me," Mariah said stubbornly like she was a ten-year-old child.

"We've had this discussion. You're twenty-nine years old, Mariah. It's time you stand on your own two feet. I feel like a mother bird, pushing her baby out of the nest." Rosemary tsked.

"I know you're right, I'm just afraid," Mariah mumbled.

Rosemary took her granddaughter's hand. "You have nothing to be afraid of. Once you make up your mind to do something, you do it and do it well. I don't live that far from you. I promise I'm going to come and stay with you next weekend."

The doorbell rang.

"That's probably the movers," Rosemary said matter-of-factly. She stood up. "Mari, I love you so much. God has good things in store for you. Now it's time for you to embrace all the blessings He's going to send your way. You will be fine. I'm going to miss you like the dickens, but I know it's the right thing for me to do, to stay here and you move to Indiana. Now, go wipe your face, and then join us downstairs so we can get this party on the road."

Mariah swallowed hard. She hugged Rosemary again and went to the bathroom. She ran a towel over her face, while Rosemary went to her bedroom and got her purse. She wiped a few tears from her own face.

When she went downstairs, Mariah was instructing the men on what tasks needed to be completed.

"What do you need us to do?" Sonyell asked, with her hands on her hips.

"Not too much. If you just put my television and a few of the boxes in my bedroom in your car, that would be a big help. The boxes contain my cosmetics and books, those kinds of things," Mariah told her friends.

An hour and a half later, Mariah went to upstairs to her now empty bedroom. For sentimental reasons she decided to keep her bedroom set. She planned to store it at the new house. She was astounded at how small the room seemed. She planned to take her granny shopping and buy new furniture for Rosemary's house the upcoming week. Mariah took one last peep inside the closet. She walked to Rosemary's room and removed her purse from Rosemary's closet. She had put it there while the movers were removing the possessions from her room. Mariah put the strap on her shoulder and joined the women downstairs.

"Is there anything else?" a mover asked Mariah.

She shook her head and looked around the kitchen and into the living room. "That's it."

"Okay, then. We'll be on our way. See you in Hammond." He departed the room and went out the door.

Sonyell grabbed one of Mariah's arms and Raquel the other one. She said, "Let's get out of here before she changes her mind."

Rosemary threw back her head and laughed. "I know that's right."

After the friends went outside, Rosemary pulled the door shut and locked it.

"Mommy, can I ride with Aunt Mari?" Sasha asked her mother hopefully.

"If it's all right with Mari, then you can," Sonyell answered.

"Can I, Aunt Mari?" the young girl asked Mariah hopefully.

"I'm going to ride with Sonni and Rocki," Rosemary informed her granddaughter. She knew that Sasha's constant chatter would keep Mariah's mind occupied. Mariah wouldn't have time to dwell on Rosemary not moving with her.

"Of course you can," Mariah told Sasha while she and the girl walked to Mariah's silver Toyota 4Runner.

"I like Aunt Mari's new truck," Sasha said as she got inside the vehicle.

Rosemary and Sonyell entered Raquel's midnight-blue Chevy TrailBlazer.

Mariah and Sasha chatted during the drive. The day was sunny and bright. Traffic slowed down due to an accident ten minutes into the trip. By the time Mariah exited the expressway, pricks of excitement danced in her stomach. Quiet as it was kept, she was truly excited about the move. Before long Mariah parked in front of her new lodgings. Raquel pulled in behind her.

The moving truck had not arrived yet.

The women exited the car and walked up the stairs leading to the entrance of the house. Sasha asked if she stay on the porch and swing on the glider.

"You can for a minute," Sonyell informed her daughter. "It's cold outside. But, you're going to help Aunt Mari get situated. So don't get too comfortable."

Mariah opened the door and the women followed her inside.

"Wow, you did a lot of shopping," Sonyell noted as she looked at the stacks of boxes piled neatly in the living and dining room.

"Well, I thought the room needed lighter colors after the painter finished painting the exterior of the house." Mariah beamed. "Come see what I did with the kitchen."

Rosemary, Sonyell, and Raquel followed Mariah into the kitchen.

"I like it. The marble countertops and new appliances are great. Have you done anything upstairs?" Raquel asked.

"Not yet. I want to do some remodeling up there, particularly in the attic. Luckily there's a bedroom down here, and I'm going to bunk there temporarily. I plan to talk to construction crews next week and take some bids."

"Listen to her," Raquel commented. "I swear she sounds so professional. I need to go to the little girls' room; I'll be right back." Raquel departed from the kitchen and to the powder room.

Beep! Beep! sounded from outside.

"That must be the movers," Mariah exclaimed excitedly. She flew out of the house.

Rosemary and Sonyell chuckled. Then they followed their friend outside.

Mariah directed the truck driver to the driveway leading to the rear of the house. She turned to Rosemary and said, "I kept some of my dad's things and put them in the coach house. You know I've been going through his and his wife's things in my spare time."

"Hmm, have you found anything interesting?" Rosemary inquired. She too was caught up in the excitement.

"Not yet. I had the coach house painted. It can be used by the director of the transitional home when the time comes," Mariah answered. The women followed her into the small dwelling.

"It's so quaint, I love it," Sonyell proclaimed upon entering the house.

They took a quick tour and then returned to the main house.

By afternoon, the movers had completed their work. Mariah had special ordered a dining set, and other furniture. She had visited the new house several times. Mariah had decided to order furniture for it now instead of later. That would be one less chore she would have to do later down the road. Plus, it wasn't like she had to move far from where she was staying.

The store called that morning to say the set had come in. She asked the movers if they would pick it and for a fee they agreed.

Sasha said, "I'm hungry, do you have anything to eat, Aunt Mari?"

"Oh no," Mariah moaned, "I forget to order food." She smacked her forehead and twisted her lips.

"Not to worry," Raquel interjected. "I made a pan of lasagna last night, and brought Italian bread."

"I made a salad. I also stopped by the Chicken Shack last night and bought wings and pop. So you're good for now. I suggest you go grocery shopping tomorrow," Sonyell admonished her friend playfully.

"You're right," Mariah said chastened. She looked downward, then up. "I didn't even think about buying groceries. I'm so used to Granny having dinner ready when I come home."

The doorbell sounded. Mariah said, "I wonder who that could be." She walked to the front door and peered out the peephole. "Reverend Dudley," she cried out after she opened the door. "I didn't expect to see you today. Please come in." She stood aside so he could enter the house.

"A little bird told me you were moving today. She also requested"—his eyes darted toward Rosemary and he smiled—"that I come and bless your new house."

"You guys think of everything," she told her grandmother and friends. She turned back to Reverend Dudley. "I would be so appreciative if you would bless my house. We're going to eat shortly. Reverend Dudley, you are more than welcome to join us."

Mariah took Reverend Dudley on a quick tour. When the two returned to the living room, everyone stood and joined hands. They closed their eyes.

Reverend Dudley said, "Father above, thank you for the many blessings you have bestowed upon Mariah. We know that your faithful servant will continue to do great works in your name. Father, we ask that you bless this house and the many endeavors Mariah is about to embark on. Keep her safe from harm and danger. Let your light shine upon her. These blessings I ask in your Son's name. Amen."

Mariah shook Reverend Dudley's hand. "Thank you, Pastor. This is a great start to my move. As I mentioned earlier we are about to eat. Would you join us?"

Reverend Dudley looked at his wrist. "I'd love to, Mariah, but I have an appointment in an hour. I need to start back to the city. The house is beautiful. I know you're going to enjoy living here. I'll see you at church tomorrow, Rosemary." He nodded at her. "I'm sure you're going to be busy the rest of the day and probably tired. I'll see you next Sunday, Mariah."

Mariah and Rosemary walked outside with the pastor. Meanwhile, Sonyell and Raquel walked to Raquel's car. With Sasha's help they removed beverages and snacks from the vehicle. They took them inside to the kitchen where they warmed up the food.

Before long the five of them sat in Mariah's kitchen, eating to their hearts' content. Mariah wiped her hands on a napkin. "At least it didn't rain, as the weatherman predicted. I think the move went well." She balled the napkin up and laid it back on the table. She pushed her chair back, picked up a can of Pepsi, and sipped from it.

"So what are your plans for this week, Mari?" Sonyell asked after Sasha asked if she could watch television. The girl departed for the living room.

"Like I said earlier, I'm going to meet with some local contractors within the next couple of months and take bids, so I can get a feel for prices. I'd like to get started on the upstairs renovations as soon as I get word from the planning committee. I met with Sister Cunningham from church two weeks ago. She wrote a grant for federal funding. She's also helping me cut through the red tape for the city, so I can get licensing for the transitional home."

"You are not wasting any time," Raquel commented after she took a sip of Arizona iced tea.

"There is so much that needs to be done that I am staying busy," Mariah replied. "The ideas just keep coming."

"Well, don't bite off more than you can chew," Sonyell advised her friend. "The transitional house alone is going to take up a lot of your time. Did you find a psychologist to work with you?"

"I did. I talked to Sister Zora at church. She gave me a couple of recommendations. She volunteered to help, too. She's going to help me interview candidates when the time comes. I meant to ask you guys if you want to spend the night? I have plenty of room."

"Sure," Sonyell said. "We don't have any nightclothes. Maybe we can run by Wal-Mart if you know where one is, and pick up some things."

"Ditto for me, I don't have a hot date tonight," Raquel said mournfully.

"What about you, Granny?" Mariah stole a look at her grandmother.

"Well, I would, but I promised Alma that I would go with her to visit her mother this afternoon. She's been dying to see your house, I've bragged on it so much. She's going to come and pick me up from here, if that's okay with you?" Rosemary asked Mariah tentatively.

"Sure. I'll have to rely on my crew to help me unpack my meager possessions and unpack the new stuff that I bought. I'll come and see you one day next week."

"Thanks. I'm going to call Alma now. She'll be tickled pink." Rosemary left the room and went to the living room to make the call.

"You'll have to tell us about your adventure last night," Raquel said to Mariah. "Sonni gave me an overview. I want all the details."

The doorbell rang. "Hold that thought," Mariah told her friend as she walked to the front door.

Chapter Eleven

"Carson," she exclaimed as her eyes widened. Her hand fluttered to her throat. Truthfully she was happy to see him.

"Hello, Mariah." He smiled, showing his bright white teeth. "Alex and I"—he gestured behind him—"came by to see if we could do anything to help with your move."

"Hi, Alex. Well, come on in." Mariah waved the men inside.

When they entered the house, Mariah introduced Carson to her grandmother first. "Granny, this is Carson Palmer." She pointed at Carson. "He was the man who helped me when my car stopped. And this is his friend Alex. He towed my car here."

"Pleased to meet you both," Rosemary greeted the men. She looked at Carson and said, "Thank you for taking care of my girl the other night. God bless you."

"The pleasure was all mine." Carson smiled at Rosemary, then at Mariah.

Sonyell and Raquel came out of the kitchen when they heard male voices.

Mariah introduced them. "These are my best friends, Sonni and Rocki. That's Sonni's daughter Sasha on the couch." Sasha looked up and waved at the men. Then she returned her attention to the television.

The men and women shook hands. Then Carson and Alex sat at the table.

"We just finished eating. Would you like something to eat or drink?" Mariah offered.

"Water if you have it," Carson requested. Alex asked for tea.

Mariah led everyone to the dining room. Raquel went into the kitchen to get the drinks. She returned shortly and sat across the table from Alex, so she could get her look-see on.

"The house really looks different," Carson commented. "Different in a good way, I always thought it was too dark in here."

"So, you knew Mariah's father?" Rosemary asked Carson casually. Her body tensed.

"Yes, ma'am. I did." Carson nodded. "Mr. Ellison was a good guy. I've known him since I was a teenager. I told Mariah that he was my mentor."

While Carson and Rosemary conversed, Raquel and Alex were giving each other the eyes. They both liked what they saw. Raquel tore her eyes away from Alex and looked at Carson. "So, Carson, tell us a little about yourself."

"I was born and raised in Hammond. My parents live here. I have three older sisters, and a younger sister. Two of my sisters live in Indiana, and the other two live in South Holland. They didn't venture too far from the family fold. I have two daughters and I own a construction company."

Mariah was surprised to hear Carson say that he had children. As a rule, she avoided dating men with children. She shunned baby momma drama.

"Two daughters?" Raquel's perfectly arched eyebrows rose. "You aren't married are you?"

Everyone's head swiveled toward Carson.

He took a sip of water, set the glass back on the table, and answered easily, "No, I'm divorced. I married my high school sweetheart too young, and things didn't work out. "

"Does she live in Hammond too?" Sonyell chimed in. She looked at Mariah and could tell by her friend's expression she wasn't happy about Carson's revelation.

"No, she lives in Whiting. It's located north of here, closer to the east side of the city."

"How old are your daughters?" Rosemary asked.

"My oldest, Aaliyah, is twelve, and my baby girl, Ashanti, will be ten in two months." A bead of sweat broke out on Carson's brow. He felt like he was on the hot seat. Carson didn't miss the chagrin that filled Mariah's face.

"Are you a good father? Do you take care of them the way a daddy should?" Rosemary asked the young man curiously. She didn't miss the look of pleasure in his eyes when he observed her granddaughter. Rosemary also caught Mariah peeking at Carson when someone at the table held his attention.

"I do." Carson nodded. "My ex-wife and I share joint custody. That's one of the reasons we live near each other. The girls spend a month with me then the following month with their mother. I take them to school when they're with me. I am a member of the PTA. They are close to my family, too. I have nieces and nephews around their ages." His eyes lit up when he talked about his girls.

"You have to give him big props for that. There are way too many deadbeat dads out there not taking care of their kids." Sonyell voiced her opinion. She wished she could say the same for Michael.

Raquel's onyx eyes swept over Alex. "What about you, big guy? Are you married? Do you have children."

Alex held up his big, meaty hands. "I plead no to both of the above. I've never been married and I don't have any children. I can vouch for Carson. He is an excellent father and his girls are crazy about him." Alex tried to help a brother out. He didn't envy his buddy at that moment, having to answer all those questions.

Rosemary's cell phone chimed. She clicked it on, rose from her seat, and walked to the hallway to answer the call. When she was done, she returned to the room. Rosemary said to Mariah, "That was Alma. I'm going to go outside to wait for her. It was nice meeting both of you." She went outdoors.

"You don't have no baby momma drama going on, do you? Your ex isn't a psycho is she?" Raquel asked Carson bluntly.

Mariah held her breath waiting for Carson's answer.

His lips turned downward into a slash. "We did initially on her part. We've worked through it though." He looked at Mariah pleadingly.

The young people talked. Ten minutes later Rosemary came back inside with her friend Alma. Rosemary started the tour in the living room. Alma squinted at the picture of Harold and his wife. "He looks familiar. Don't you think he looks like—"

"Shh," Rosemary hissed at Alma as Mariah walked into the room.

Alma's mouth dropped open. She then recovered and said, "Hey, baby. Give me some love." She held her arms out.

Alma hugged Mariah. She gushed, "This house is huge. I'm so happy for your blessings from your father."

"Thank you, Miss Alma. I'm sure Granny can't wait to show you the whole house."

"I can't," Rosemary said, relieved. "Come on, Alma."

The women walked to the kitchen. Mariah returned to the dining room. Her friends and the men were deep in conversation. Apparently Raquel had completed her interrogation of Carson.

"Do you know how Mari's father was able to acquire all the property he owned? I find it amazing that a black man would own so many diverse businesses," Sonyell said.

Carson nodded. "I can answer that. He and an army buddy settled here after they completed their stint in 'Nam. They were able to tap into the G.I. Bill. He and his friend Walter went into business together. Walter never married and didn't have any children, so all the business holdings reverted to Mr. Ellison after Walter's death. He was able to capitalize on the extra assets and expanded his empire. The rest, as they say, is history. He always felt real estate was the best form of asset to have."

Mariah soaked up the information. Rosemary and Alma returned from the tour, and took their leave. Mariah walked them to Alma's car. "Granny, I promise to be a big girl." Her nose crinkled. "I'm going to miss you, and especially your excellent cooking." She looked forlornly at her grandmother.

"Maybe I can hook you up with a few meals. Let me know when you're coming, and I'll prepare a care package for you," Rosemary said.

Grandmother and granddaughter hugged. Then Rosemary and Alma were on their way back to Chicago. Mariah went back inside the house and sat at the dining room table.

"Rocki, I need your car keys. I want to make a Wal-Mart run before it gets too late." Sonyell held out her hand.

"I could drive you," Alex volunteered. "I mean all of you."

"Sure, let's go. We probably need to stop at the grocery store and get food for breakfast in the morning," Sonyell said.

"There is a Wal-Mart store next to the Food 4 Less grocery store on 169th Street," Alex informed the group. He and the ladies stood up, collected Sasha, and left Mariah alone with Carson.

"Why don't we go to the living room?" Mariah suggested. Carson followed her to the living room and sat on the butter-colored leather recliner, while Mariah sat on the matching sofa.

"You'll have to take me on a tour. It sure looks different, at least down here," Carson observed as his eyes roamed the room.

"I forgot you said that you'd been to this house before. Did you visit here often?" Mariah couldn't stop herself from asking Carson. She leaned forward in her seat.

"Yes. Mr. and Mrs. Ellison hosted an annual barbeque in the backyard for the kids at the Boys & Girls Club."

"That's good." Mariah settled back against the back of the sofa.

"I hope you don't hold it against me, Mariah, that I have children. They are a big part of my life."

"I don't know, Carson. I haven't had much luck dating men with children. In fact I've crossed daddies off my list." Mariah crossed one shapely leg over the other one.

"Really, it's no different from daddy drama, at least that's what me and my buddies call it. I certainly wouldn't hold it against you if you had a child."

"But, I don't," Mariah whispered softly. "How long have you been divorced?"

Carson closed his eyes and then opened them. "Five years. Lola and I married when I was eighteen and she was seventeen. We got pregnant her junior year of high school. I loved her and did the right thing by marrying her. As we grew older, we grew apart, and found out we didn't have much in common. We separated for a while, got back together, and tried having another baby to save the marriage, but that didn't work."

"It usually doesn't. Anyway, who am I to judge you? It's just not my preference to date a baby daddy."

"You just weren't hanging with the right brother. I promise you that," Carson proclaimed.

"We'll see about that," Mariah said seriously.

"Oh, come on, lighten up on a brother," Carson said as he held up his hands. "So tell me a little about yourself. What makes Ms. Mariah happy? What makes you tick?"

"I'm twenty-nine years old, my birthday was in April. I've never been married, I don't have any children, and I've never been in a serious relationship."

"What do you do for a living?" Carson asked.

"Well, I wear a number of hats. I run a nonprofit organization for women and teen girls in Altgeld Garden. Up until today, I've lived with my grandmother," Mariah answered. She looked downward to avoid Carson's probing eyes. Her hands trembled so she tucked them at her side.

"Is your mother deceased?"

"No, not really." Mariah became flustered. "I didn't mean that the way it sounded. My mother lives in Chicago, and she has been a drug addict for most of my life."

"That had to be tough. I'm sorry."

"You don't have anything to be sorry about; my mother made her own choices. She just didn't think about the consequences it would have on me," Mariah said bitterly.

"Most addicts don't. It's part of the illness," Carson opined.

"That's what I lot of people say and I disagree. An addiction is just pure selfishness, and if a person really wanted to beat that addiction, they would do everything in their power to do just that."

"I don't think it's that easy, but you're entitled to your opinion, like I am."

"Unless you've walked in my shoes, which I'm sure you haven't, then it's just an opinion and not reality. Trust me, I've been there and done that."

"You're not the only one who has had to endure the rigors of being the child of an addict," Carson said. "I've walked in those shoes too."

Mariah's eyes widened. "Really? Who?"

"My dad, he developed an alcoholic addiction after losing his job. That was years ago and luckily he was able to get help and eventually get himself clean."

Mariah felt foolish. Her eyes dropped. "I'm sorry for coming off sounding so sanctimonious. I do tend to forget I'm not the only one who has experienced the lows of being a child of an addicted parent."

"Apology accepted. I think we have more in common than you think," Carson added.

The couple continued to talk, and before long, Sonyell, Raquel, Sasha, and Alex returned.

"I thought you had gotten lost," Mariah commented when they were inside the house.

"No, Alex took us on a tour of sorts in Hammond. We got him to take us by our houses, and, of course, Wal-Mart. The grocery store was crowded with it being Saturday evening," Raquel said.

"I guess we're going to head out." Carson stood up. "Ladies, it was nice meeting you. Mariah, I'll see you tomorrow at seven."

"Yeah, it was a cool meeting you. Welcome to Hammond," Alex said. "I'm sure you're going to like living here. Hammond is a nice town."

The pair talked while Mariah, Carson, and Sonyell continued to chat a few more minutes. When the conversation ended, Sonyell turned to her daughter and said, "Sasha, why don't you help me put up the groceries? Then you can get ready for bed."

"Mommy, it's not that late," Sasha complained. "Why do I have to get ready for bed so early?"

Sonyell looked pointedly toward the kitchen. "It's not up for discussion. Now, young lady. Carson, it was a pleasure meeting you. I hope we'll be seeing a lot of you in the future."

"That's my hope too." Carson's eyes darted to Mariah.

Mariah shrugged her shoulders helplessly.

Sonyell and Sasha walked into the kitchen.

"Well, I know you have things to do. If you need me or Alex to help with anything, just let me know. I'm looking forward to our date tomorrow evening." Carson's voice seemed to caress the word "date."

A shiver crawled up Mariah's spine. She didn't trust herself to speak and merely nodded.

The pair walked outside. Alex and Raquel stood near the glider engrossed in animated conversation.

Alex whispered in Raquel's ear. She threw back her head and laughed. After telling Mariah good night, he and Carson departed.

Mariah and Raquel waved at the men, and then went back inside the house.

***

Sasha had cleared the dining room table. She was now taking a bath in the Jacuzzi tub upstairs. Sonyell had loaded the dishwasher. She walked into the living room and found her friends sitting on the sofa. "Looks like both y'all got your groove on," she teased her friends.

Mariah looked down and flexed her fingernails. "I don't know what you talking 'bout," she said innocently.

"Well, I do and Alex has potential," Raquel said bluntly. "It's not like Hammond's got a nightlife like Chicago. So if I can find someone to spend time with, I'm game."

"You're always game." Sonyell shook her head.

"Hey, I always say, don't knock it until you try it. If you weren't so Ms. Devoted To Your Baby Daddy, we could hook a sista up." Then Raquel turned her attention to Mariah. "So, Ms. Mari, Carson is one fine man. Let me say that again, super fine. Now what you gonna do with all that man?"

"That's what I want to know," Sonyell chimed in. She and Raquel exchanged high fives.

Mariah opened her mouth and closed it. "Hold that thought." She went to the kitchen and returned with a bottle of wine and three goblets in hand. "Now, what were you saying?"

Chapter Twelve

After leaving Mariah's house, Alex and Carson decided to stop at Pepi's Mexican Restaurant for a beer before calling it a night. The crowd was sparse. Old school R&B music flowed from the speakers. The Temptations song "Papa Was a Rollin' Stone" wafted in the air. The men sat at the bar. Within a few minutes the bartender wiped the area dry in front of them. He set two bottles of Heineken on top of the bar. Carson took a ten dollar bill out of his wallet and laid it on the bar.

Alex held up his bottle. "Here's to looking out for a brother. I tell you Rocki is a real firecracker. It bet it won't be a dull day once she moves to Hammond."

Carson clinked bottles with Alex's. "Yeah, I can see the potential there." He laughed.

"I can see you have eyes for Mariah. Sonni is real easy on the eyes, too. Too bad she isn't available." Alex turned up the bottle and took a deep gulp. He set the bottle back on the bar.

"You're right." Carson nodded enthusiastically. "I am feeling Mariah. Fate brought us together that night." He smiled smugly and rested his folded arms on top of the bar.

"You know I'm all for love and the pain and pleasure it could bring, but Lola, remember her," Alex said candidly, "your hot-tempered Latina ex-wife. She is never going to let you be. You and I both know that," Alex told his buddy candidly. "She has always managed to mess up your relationships."

"I'll admit," Carson replied nonchalantly, "that she's caused me grief in the relationship department in the past. But, maybe, I just hadn't found the right woman who would give me incentive to put my foot down and get Lola off my back. Who knows? Perhaps Mariah is the one. Only time will tell."

"Ms. Lady didn't seem too happy to find out you had children and an ex. I don't know, bro. . . ."

"She just has to get to know me; as my mother says, to know me is to love me," Carson retorted.

Alex snickered. "And Lola did just that. She came, she loved, and never left."

Carson was a little stung by Alex's comments, but he knew they were true. His cell phone chimed, indicating he had a text message. Carson scanned the message quickly: Cn u call me shanti refuses to go to bed til she tlks to u. Carson stood up and told his friend, "I'll be back in a moment."

Alex could tell from Carson's beleaguered expression that Lola had sent him a text. "I rest my case." He held up his hand and motioned for the bartender to bring him a refill.

Carson walked outside, and quickly dialed a number, but not his ex-wife's. "Hey, Ali, how are you and your sister doing?"

"We're good, Daddy. How are you?" Aaliyah asked her father. She and her sister were lying on their stomachs on the floor in the den, watching an episode of *Everybody Hates Chris* on Nick at Nite.

"Just checking. What's your sister doing?"

"Eating some popcorn and laughing at Chris. We're watching TV." The girl laughed and Carson could hear Ashanti's high-pitched laughter in the background.

"Be good. Let me speak to Shanti," Carson requested. He told his youngest daughter he loved her, made a kissing sound, and told her good night.

The younger girl handed the cell phone back to her sister. He then told Ali the same thing. Carson told the girls he would see them Monday morning when he took them to school.

Carson's lips tightened when he closed the phone. He returned to the bar and sat beside Alex.

"Is everything all right on the Western Front?" Alex asked his friend curiously.

"Everything is fine. One thing I've learned is that you have to stay one step ahead in the game and be mentally prepared for anything."

"Come again?"

"Lola texted me saying Shanti wouldn't go to sleep until she talked to me. In reality, Lola wanted to talk to me. I bought Ali a cell phone a few months ago, and told her it's for her and her sister to call me when they need me."

Alex guffawed. "Oh, you busted Lola, did you? The Queen Bee is not going to be pleased with your move." He took a swig of beer.

Carson picked up his bottle and did likewise. "She'll learn to live with it."

"So tell me . . ." Alex's expression became serious. "Are you digging Mariah because you know sister's got a lot of money? We all know Mr. E was loaded."

A look of disdain crossed Carson's face. "We've known each other since we were in fifth grade, and you have the audacity to ask me that question? I haven't even known Mariah that long, but I like what I see. She seems to be good people, and I'd like to know her better. Mr. E was good to me, actually, both of us. If I can help his daughter out why not? She doesn't know a soul here."

"Hey, you don't have to convince me. You're right, I do know you. I was just messing with you," Alex apologized. He looked chastened.

"I know the fact that she has money might come between us. Still, I'm hoping she'll get to know me and know that I would never date a woman for money. I'm not that hard up. And I respect women too much for that."

"My bad, you know my mouth is faster than my brain sometimes."

"You're right about that. Look, I think I'm going to call it a night. I'm going to church with my moms in the morning; I haven't been in a few weeks. If you miss going to church one Sunday, she says you're backsliding." Carson threw another five on the bar. "I'll holler at you later, man."

"Take it easy, bro, and thanks for hooking a brother up. Rocki gave me her digits and I think I'm going use them soon. I'ma finish this bottle, then I'm gonna head home too."

"I heard that. It's been a long day and I have a million things to do tomorrow. Later."

Carson walked out of the restaurant to his truck. As he drove home he couldn't help but wonder what Mariah really thought of him. He knew that he was impressed with her. Carson hoped the feeling was mutual.

Had Carson been a fly on the wall he would have learned the answer to that burning question and more.

When Mariah returned to the living room, she told her friends, "Who says I have to do anything? Carson and I are friends, nothing more." Mariah opened the wine with the corkscrew and poured a small amount into each goblet.

"Stop fronting, Mari," Raquel told her friend skeptically. "If you hadn't seen him first, I wouldn't mind jumping his bones myself. Don't act like you're immune to his looks and charm."

Mariah couldn't believe what her friend had said. She also didn't like Raquel's comment that she would sleep with Carson. The green-eyed monster had reared its ugly head.

Sonyell could tell by Mariah's drawn expression that her friend didn't appreciate Raquel's comment. "Well, it's a good thing he didn't see you first, or he'd have found out how nasty you can be at times. I think it's a good thing that Carson is interested in Mari. I just told her she needs to settle down with a man."

"I'm not nasty. I'm a woman with needs, and when I feel the need I do what I can to scratch that itch. That's more than I can say about either one of you," Raquel shot back.

"Whoa, let's not let things get out of hand here. We're celebrating Mari's moving." Sonyell took the high road with Raquel. Both she and Mari knew their friend could be impulsive. She also had a tendency to speak her mind without realizing how negatively her words could impact others.

"No harm," Mariah said, following Sonyell's lead. "And here I was ready to confess my deepest desires to my friends, and let you in on how I really feel about Carson Palmer." She smiled mysteriously and then sipped her wine.

"I'm going to check on Sasha, and then I'll be back. Don't spill the beans until I return," Sonyell warned Mariah.

"I wouldn't dream of it," Mariah reassured Sonyell.

"Look, if I was out of line by saying I would jump Carson's bones, I was keeping it real. He's a fine man. But I also remember our rule, no messing around with each other's men, so I would never act upon it." Raquel tried to apologize in her inept way.

"Don't think I don't know. We played that game back in eighth grade. You haven't slipped since then. So don't even try it now," Mariah joked.

Raquel realized Mariah was serious and regretted her comments.

Sonyell returned ten minutes later. "Sasha is asleep. I pulled the door up, so now we can share grown-up talk." She sat on the recliner. "I think I'm going to sleep here tonight."

"My old bedroom set is set up in the guest bedroom. I had to bring something from home with me. You're welcome to sleep there. I can bunk out with Sasha. She doesn't take up much room."

Sonyell settled into the buttery chair. "So, tell us for real, Mari, what do you think of Carson?" Sonyell questioned her friend.

"So far Mr. Palmer is like a breath of fresh air after all my past failed relationships. I enjoy his conversation. He seems caring. We know he's gallant because he helped me out the other night. He's definitely easy on the eyes. But . . ."

"But what?" Raquel interjected. "Shoot, he sounds like a winner to me. He owns his own business. What more do you need?" She stared at her friend incredulously.

"Let her talk," Sonyell urged Raquel.

"Well, he's divorced and has not one"—she held up her fingers—"but two daughters. You know my second rule."

"We do." Raquel rolled her eyes and nodded. "Never to get involved with a man with children."

"And who can forget your first one: never—I repeat, never—get involved with a married man," Sonyell said wryly.

"I have issues with children, not so much the kids themselves, but those exes who will be there 'til death do us part. I also had a feeling Carson wasn't being quite honest with us when he said his ex is a thing of the past."

"I have to agree with you." Raquel shook her head. "Who in their right mind would give all that up?"

The women laughed. Mariah said soberly, "I don't know. I like him, but I don't want to deal with the drama."

"Maybe it won't be any," Sonyell suggested. She crossed her legs comfortably.

"Humph, don't believe that. It never seems to work that way, especially where children are concerned. Some women will never give up. Can you really blame her?" Raquel said. "I'm sorry."

"I'd like to add my opinion." Sonyell held up her hand. "It takes a real woman to stand her ground and let another woman know that her man is hands off bounds." She looked at Raquel. "And, that includes you, Rocki. If you love a man, then you fight for him with all your might. Eventually the competition will get the message."

Raquel looked up and shook her head. She replied dryly, "And this from the woman whose man is in the joint more than he's out. You know you can do better than Michael. What are you afraid of?"

"I am not afraid of anything or anyone. I do get tired of you mouthing off about Michael. He has issues, I admit, but I believe a person can change if he or she wants to. I see signs of change in Michael. He is my daughter's father and I owe it to her and to me to establish a life with him, if he's changed."

"How many times have we heard that?" Raquel threw in. "Just how many chances are you going to give him? You're a college-educated sister, with a fabulous job. You own a home and you want to settle for a con? I don't understand you."

"Maybe my situation is not for you to understand," Sonyell said hotly. A glint of annoyance filled her face. "Nobody made you the know all, be all of relationships. You've just had more relationships than the two of us put together." She snickered as she pointed to herself and Mariah. "What have you accomplished with the men in your life? Sometimes you change men like you do like sheets. Don't criticize my life and I'll do the same for you."

"Now that was low," Raquel volleyed back. "I'm just trying to find Mr. Right. I have to take my time and sample all the goodies."

Michael was a bone of contention between Raquel and Sonyell. Sonyell stayed on the defensive regarding her man. Not only to Raquel but to some of her family members as well. Raquel always felt Michael was beneath Sonyell, whereas Mariah was more accepting of her friend's situation. She had a feeling this time, that if Michael reverted to his criminal ways, then Sonyell would probably move on. Sasha was growing up, and Sonyell was concerned about the example she was setting for her daughter.

"You know I only want the best for you," Raquel finally said awkwardly. "I didn't mean any harm. I'm sorry."

"Apology accepted. You do you and let me do me, and we'll be fine." Sonyell changed the subject. "Did you like Alex? Or were you just toying with a brother?"

"He's not Carson, by any stretch of the imagination. He seems to be a good guy, he makes me laugh. I plan on seeing him again. In fact," Raquel said slyly, "I asked him to help us move next weekend. You can never have enough manpower. I also gave him my number."

"You really don't waste any time do you?" Sonyell said half jokingly.

"Don't you two ever listen to me when I say life is short? You got to go for what you want."

"Remind us never to get in your way." Sonyell shook her head.

"You two don't count. But on the real, I like him. I'm not trying to settle down or anything. We'll see what comes of it."

"Good. Then I'd say today was a good day." Sonyell nodded and raised her glass. "We got Mari moved to Hammond. She's ready to embark on new career goals, and she found a man to boot. Life doesn't get any better."

The friends changed into their nightclothes and talked into the wee hours of the night. Mariah was the last to fall asleep. Her last conscious thought was, *Raquel had better stay away from Carson.* Shivers tingled up and down her spine as she speculated on her date with Carson the following evening.

Chapter Thirteen

Church services were coming to a conclusion at the St. Mark AME Church located on Field Street in Hammond. As Carson and the ushers, clad in uniform dark suits with white shirts and blouses, opened the exit doors to the church, the congregation sang in harmony "God Be With You." After the organist struck the final chord, the members streamed out of the church.

Carson whispered to his mother that he planned to stay late and speak to Reverend Cambridge. After that he would stop by his parents' house. The ushers busily collected the hymnals left on the church pews, and put them back into their slots on the back of the pews. Carson dimmed the lights in the sanctuary. He glanced at his watch and hurried to his minister's office.

Reverend Cambridge, a brown-skinned, burly man with salt-and-pepper gray hair and the same colored beard had just finished changing from his robe to his suit. He was tying his tie when Carson knocked on the door.

"Come in," Reverend Cambridge said. He sat down at his untidy desk after he and Carson shook hands.

"Thanks for seeing me," Carson said after he sat in the chair across from the minister. "Pastor, I wanted to talk to you. Brother Ellison's daughter has moved to Hammond. She is on a mission to learn about her father. I feel torn because a part of me wants to tell her everything I know. As fate or maybe divine intervention would have it, she had car issues. I was able to help her get home. We ended up talking. She moved to Hammond to Brother Ellison's house yesterday," Carson explained.

"You've learned a lot in a short period of time, haven't you, brother?" Reverend Cambridge observed after wiping his glasses with a white handkerchief. He planted the glasses back on his nose. The minister smirked as he gave Carson a knowing look.

"I guess so; opportunity presented itself and I rose to the occasion," Carson said. He sheepishly shrugged his shoulders.

"What type of woman did Brother Ellison's daughter appear to be? Or were you able to tell in that short period of time?" The minister leaned forward and placed his arms on his desk.

"She is very attractive. She looks very much like Brother Ellison. She is bitter that he didn't spend time with her while she was growing up. From what I can tell, her family hasn't told her about the events surrounding her birth."

"That's unfortunate. Still events unfold in life in God's time, not in our own. Praise God that Brother Ellison put some mechanisms in place that will help explain his actions. I just hope his daughter is receptive. What is her name?"

"Mariah Green." Carson's tongue seemed to caress Mariah's name.

His soft tone of voice didn't go unnoticed by his minister. "You seem impressed with her. Or is 'smitten' the word I should use?" Reverend Cambridge grinned as he teased Carson.

"I, ah, liked what I saw. She doesn't seem to have let her inheritance influence her. By that I mean she didn't seem snobbish. I met several of her childhood friends.

She and her friends all seem firmly rooted. I would say we shared a vibe," Carson admitted.

"That kind of puts you in an awkward position, son. As Harold's story comes to light, Mariah might feel you deceived her. I would suggest you tread lightly," Reverend Cambridge cautioned Carson. He folded his hands together in a triangle.

"Oh, I will." Carson nodded. "She's been hurt badly by what she perceives as her father's defection. I can tell she puts up walls. I feel other than her grandmother and friends, Mariah doesn't let people get too close. Complicating matters is her mother's drug addiction. One can't help but feel Mariah's anguish and be moved by it. If, and I think it will, our friendship progresses, I plan to invite her here to worship here with us at St. Mark."

"That sounds like a good idea. I just hope that her faith in God is strong enough, that she can understand Harold's actions in time."

"I think if she weighs the good against the bad, Harold will come out okay. But, I don't know her well enough to say that with certainty." Carson held out his hands.

"God in His infinite wisdom brought the two of you together, so I have a feeling you will be the vehicle God uses to enlighten Mariah about her father. I will pray for God to give you guidance. Who knows what might come of this new friendship?" Reverend Cambridge commented lightly, though his eyes twinkled.

"Well, it's time for me to go. I don't want to take up too much of your time. I plan to stop by my parents' house, visit my girls, and then Mariah and I are having dinner." Carson rose from his seat.

"Is that so?" The minister's eyebrow arched upward. "Be careful, son." The minister's face and tone became stern. "This matter has to be handled gently and with sensitivity."

"I will, Pastor," Carson promised. "Have a blessed week and I will keep you posted on Mariah."

"Thank you. You too have a blessed week and enjoy your date." Reverend Cambridge rose from his seat. He and Carson exchanged farewells.

Carson departed. After he entered his black Cadillac STS, he fastened the seat belt. Carson decided to pick up his daughters and take them to his parents' house. The family hadn't seen his daughters in a while. He couldn't keep a smile from filling his face as his thoughts traveled to Mariah.

In anticipation of her date with Carson, Mariah had suffered a bout of indecision. She had changed her outfit several times. At 7:30 P.M., Mariah and Carson were seated inside a cozy leather booth at Freddy's Steak House. The restaurant was located at 165th Street and Kennedy Avenue.

The waitress had taken their orders and left a basket of warm bread at the table, along with glasses of water.

"Are you sure you don't want anything to drink?" Carson asked Mariah. He wore khakis and a polo pullover with a lightweight sports jacket. His locks were held together with a thick rubber band and Mariah thought he was the most handsome man she had ever laid eyes on. His green eyes enthralled her.

Mariah, not to be outdone, looked very attractive as well. Raquel had hooked up her hair before departing to Chicago. Mariah had finally settled on a pair of dark leggings, with a belted, tomato-red oversized top. It brought out reddish tones in her dark skin. She wore multiple bangles on her wrists along with a tiny gold watch. Her feet were encased by short black leather boots. Mariah wore a black leather cap pulled over her head. She loved caps. Mariah had an extensive collection of them.

"No, I'm good. I'm not much of a drinker," Mariah confessed. "My girls and I tend to imbibe on special occasions and yesterday was one of those days. That's my quota for a while." Her eyes stole around the restaurant.

"I'm not a heavy drinker myself. I like to have a beer every now and then, but with girls in the house I try to set a good example." Carson commented, "You look lovely."

"Thank you, Carson." Mariah dipped her eyes. She then sipped from the glass of water and placed the glass on her left side.

The waitress returned to the table with French onion soup for Carson and a Caesar salad for Mariah.

Carson blessed the food. They chatted easily and dined until the waitress brought their entrees. Mariah had chosen salmon with rice pilaf and steamed broccoli. Carson had a T-bone steak, with a baked potato and asparagus.

Mariah had just eaten a piece of salmon when she asked Carson if he was a Christian.

He wiped his mouth on his napkin, laid it back on his lap, and answered, "Yes, I am. I was raised in an AME church. I still attend my childhood church here in Hammond. What about you?"

"I definitely am. I think I told you that I attend Christian Friendship Baptist Church in the city. My minister, Reverend Dudley, stopped by yesterday to bless the house. I teach a children's Sunday School class. How do you serve?"

"I am a member of the usher board and head of the beautification committee," Carson answered. He cut a piece of steak and placed it inside his mouth.

"What is that exactly? The beautification committee?" Mariah asked with a puzzled expression on her face.

"My group helps with church repairs, cleaning up the inside and outside of the church. We mow the lawn in the summer, and shovel in the winter. We paint and do whatever is necessary to keep the Lord's house in order."

"That's cool," Mariah replied enthusiastically. "It's kind of like one of those behind-the-scenes ministries."

"Exactly. Most people want to sing in the choir, whether they can carry a note or not, or be seen walking down the aisle. My family has served on the usher board, and I didn't want to break tradition. Truthfully, I'm more a low-key person, so that committee was another way for me to serve the Father."

"You continue to surprise me. I haven't met many men who admit to going to church. Or if they do"—she crinkled her nose—"it's not for the right reasons. Most of the time they want to hook up with a sista."

"Oh, I told you" —Carson put down his knife and fork—"to stick with me. There are more surprises in store for you. I should also tell you that Mr. Ellison also attended my church."

Mariah dropped her fork. It clattered as it fell on her plate. Her smile turned to a frown. "Is that right?" She was clearly flustered; her hand fluttered to her throat. Mariah swallowed and deftly changed the subject. "Speaking of church and trying to do all things pleasing in His sight, this might be a good time to mention that I am practicing celibacy," Mariah told Carson after sipping water.

Carson nearly choked on the water he just swallowed. "Is that so? How long have you have you been celibate? And, yes, this is a good time to mention that."

"Truthfully" —Mariah dipped her head—"a little over a year. I had a bad experience with the last guy I dated. It became a physical relationship and I was looking for more. So after I manage to shed him like a bad haircut, I decided to treat my body like the temple it is."

"Okay," Carson quipped. "I can't say I've met many women who practice that theory."

"I'm sure there are some of us out there. So if you can't hang, Mr. Palmer, then we will need to keep this relationship on a friendship basis."

"I've never been one to shy away from challenges and keeping my body in check will definitely be a challenge."

"Just so you don't view me as a challenge and try to change my mind," Mariah declared ardently. "Like the old song my granny sings, 'I Shall Not Be Moved.' That is my position and I am sticking to it." She thumped on the top of the table for emphasis.

Carson held up his hands. "Gotcha. Just don't get an attitude if I slip up accidently. You know a man likes to show affection for the woman he is interested in."

"There are ways to show affection other than sexually. You seem to be smart, I'm sure you can think of some of them," Mariah teased him.

"You're right, but I'm still a man. Seriously, I respect your position, and I'll try, no, do my best, not to defile that lovely temple."

"Deal?" Mariah held out her hand to shake Carson's. She sighed and thought, *that hurdle is over. Thank you, Lord.*

Instead, he took her hand in his and kissed it. "Deal." He smiled wickedly.

They continued to enjoy the meal, the ambiance, and getting to know each other. Mariah hadn't enjoyed herself with a man in a long time.

"So, my father attended your church. What type of member was he? Did he tithe? I suspect he did. Did he attend church most Sundays? What was his ministry?" The questions flew from Mariah's mouth.

"Whoa." Carson held up his hand. "Let's see, the answers are as follows: He was a faithful member. He rarely missed church. And, yes, he did tithe. He also donated money and his time equally as needed. Officially he was a member of the finance committee. But truthfully, he served wherever there was a need to be filled. My minister, Reverend Cambridge, was very fond of Mr. and Mrs. Ellison."

"Somehow, I'm not surprised. I figured he was a big shot in church. I saw the many awards from the church as well as business-related ones," Mariah commented.

"That's true, he was especially proud of the ones from the church. Reverend Cambridge believes in giving credit where credit is due. There were times he planned to borrow from Mr. Ellison, and Mr. Ellison would tell him that the monies were gifts. Mr. Ellison was a charter member of the church."

"Hmm, that's interesting. My father sounds like a saint, if we don't include how he wasn't a part of my life," Mariah stated bitterly.

"Oh, no, I don't want to give you that impression. He was a man with flaws like most humans. He did a lot of good with his money. Mr. Ellison admitted to me that there were parts of his life he wasn't very proud of," Carson told Mariah.

"It sounds like you knew him quite well," Mariah commented as her eyes probed Carson's.

The couple's heads turned toward the entrance of the dining room when they heard a female voice yell, "Carson, is that you?"

Their eyes turned toward the sound. A woman walked hurriedly to the table.

"Hey, Tiffany. What are you doing here?" he said to the pretty, young woman as he rose from his seat. She turned her head and he kissed her cheek.

"I might ask you the same." She looked point blank at Mariah.

"This is my friend Mariah. Mariah, this is my youngest sister, Tiffany," he introduced the women.

"Hello, Tiffany." Mariah offered her hand.

The women checked each other out as they shook hands.

"Nice to meet you. Do you live in Hammond? I don't remember seeing you around," Tiffany observed. She slid into the booth next to her brother.

"No, you wouldn't," Mariah explained. "I literally just moved to Hammond."

Tiffany glanced back at the waiting area. One of her friends waved her hand, indicating their table was available. She turned back to Carson. "I'm having dinner with some of my friends. It looks like our seats are ready. I'll talk you later, big brother," she told Carson. She looked at Mariah with her head tilted. "It was nice meeting you, Mariah."

"Same here," Mariah answered. She and Carson watched Tiffany walk back to her friends.

Tiffany's gaze wandered back to Carson and Mariah as she talked to her friends.

"Your sister seems nice," Mariah said. She watched Carson watching his sister.

"I wouldn't say all of that." Carson shook his head. "If anything she's a pest. But, I love her. Now, where were we? Tell me about this transitional house you plan to open." He gave Mariah his undivided attention.

A twinkle sparkled in Mariah's eyes. "Growing up in the projects gave me a lot of insight into people, the good, bad, and ugly. There seems to a growing epidemic of mothers inside prisons. A good many of them don't have the people skills to reenter society. They need help trying to enter the work world. I'd like to provide short-term housing, with counseling sessions and parenting classes, to get them ready to reenter society." Mariah had a fervent expression on her face as she explained her plans.

"That's a tall order," Carson noted after he took a sip of water. "Somehow I have the feeling you'll accomplish that and more. What made you decide on prison mothers? Surely there are other social programs you could have pursued?"

"I guess not having a real mother"—she made quote marks with her fingers—"has just made me sensitive to the needs of female children. My mother has always been an embarrassment to me. I remember as a child, if I saw her in the Garden, I'd go out of my way to avoid her. I want to help girls who find themselves in similar circumstances."

"What have you done so far?" Carson asked after he chewed the last bit of steak. He leaned back and placed his arm across the top of the booth.

"I've applied for licensing and grants," Mariah answered with a smile, warming to her favorite subject. "I think it will be a win-win situation for Hammond and prospective clients. The project will create jobs in this tough economy. If all goes well, we should be up and operational in a year to eighteen months. One of my church members is a grant writer and she wrote an awesome proposal. So I have a lot on my plate right now. I am also hiring a construction company to work on renovating my father's house if I get approval. That's where I plan to house the facility. I know you mentioned you own a construction company. I'd like to work with someone local, so if you're interested in submitting a bid, I can give you an application."

"Wow! You plan to take Hammond by storm," Carson said admiringly. "I think what you're doing is great. Of course I'd like to submit a proposal. What is your vision?"

Mariah leaned forward in her seat and gave him an overview of the house renovation.

As Mariah continued talking, her happiness and dedication to the project became contagious. Carson was receptive to her plans and reacted enthusiastically.

Before long the waitress returned and removed their dishes from the table. "Can I get you anything else? How about dessert?"

"No, I'm stuffed, but I would love a cup of espresso," Mariah answered as she patted her tummy.

"I'd like a cup of decaf," Carson replied. "Are you sure you don't want anything else?"

"I'm positive. I can't eat another bite." Mariah shook her head

"I know dinner is your treat, but I'd love to pick up the check. This evening has been special. I feel comfortable with you, like we've known each other forever."

"Same here." Mariah smiled. "You can't pick up the tab, at least not this time. It's my repayment for helping me out the other night."

"I appreciate it. You know I would have helped you whether I had dinner with you or not. I have enjoyed myself tonight. You are deep, Mariah, and compassionate. I find that a great combination in a woman." He nodded approvingly. Then he smiled so brightly that Mariah's knees felt weak.

"Thank you, Carson. I've enjoyed myself as well."
She stood up. "I have to go to the ladies' room. I'll be
right back."

Carson stood up and watched her retreating figure.
A smile played across his face. He was pleased with the
way the evening had progressed.

A few minutes later, Mariah returned to the table. "I
took care of the bill when I left the ladies' room. I need
to get going. I have a million things to do tomorrow,
and need to do some prep work."

Carson exited the booth. "I'm sorry the evening has
to come to end. Maybe we can do this again? My treat?"

Mariah knew Raquel would tell her to play coy, and
how that would keep a man coming back for more. But
Mariah had no interest in indulging in games. She liked
Carson, enjoyed his company, and wanted to see more
of him. "I think I would like that," she said simply.

"I'd like to call you during the week. Is that okay?
And we'll take it from there. I don't want to rush things.
I want us to spend time to get to know each other."

"That sounds like a plan." Mariah said demurely.
Her lips curved into a brilliant smile.

The couple departed and within twenty minutes,
Carson had pulled inside Mariah's driveway.

"While you're here, why don't you come in and I can
give you an application," Mariah suggested.

Carson nodded. He got out of the truck, opened
Mariah's door, and followed her inside the house.

She sped upstairs to her office and returned downstairs with a binder detailing the project.

Carson took it and tucked it beneath his arm. Mariah
walked him to the door.

Before he exited, Carson leaned forward, he held out
his hand, and then leaned forward and kissed Mariah's
cheek. "Thank you for a great evening. I can hardly wait
to do this again."

"Thank you. I had a good time. Have a good week; we'll talk," Mariah promised.

After Carson departed, she went upstairs and changed into a lounging outfit. She went into her home office, put a CD into the player, booted up her PC, and began checking her e-mails.

Later she fixed herself a cup of cocoa and sat in the living room with a new book she'd purchased. Mariah read, but she wasn't really reading. In her mind, she analyzed her date with Carson, over and over, until she fell asleep

Chapter Fourteen

Rosemary had been home all afternoon, relaxing after attending the eleven o'clock church service. The church was hosting a musical that evening and she debated attending because of the inclement weather. She had prepared Sunday dinner and had fixed enough food to feed a small army. She didn't realize until the food was actually simmering in the pots that she had prepared enough for herself, Mariah, Sonyell, Sasha, and Raquel. Rosemary chuckled to herself at the oversight. She decided to freeze the leftovers. Sooner rather than later, she knew that Mariah would want one of her granny's home-cooked meals. Mariah wasn't much of a cook. Rosemary's granddaughter could do many things well, but cooking wasn't on her list of accomplishments.

She bent over, opened the oven door, and checked to see if the pan of cornbread she'd put inside had browned. It had, so Rosemary removed the pan from the oven and turned the appliance off. She turned the pot down that contained the collard greens. Last, she turned over the candied yams with a spatula, and turned the pan off. The macaroni and cheese cooled on the countertop.

Rosemary turned on the water and rinsed her hands. She tore a paper towel from the roll on the wall rack, and then walked into the living room. Rosemary turned off the CD player and sat on the couch. She took her Bible off the coffee table and thumbed through it, rereading the scriptures from the earlier church service.

There was a rat-a-tat at the door. Rosemary stood on stiff knees to answer it. She opened the door. "Cassie," she said. Her eyes lit up. "Come in." She took her daughter's thin arm and led her into the house.

"I was just cooking," Rosemary informed her daughter. "Give me a minute to turn off the pots and then we can have a good visit. I'd love for you to stay and have dinner with me. I made enough." She left the room and went into the kitchen.

Cassie sat on the edge of the chair and fidgeted while she waited for Rosemary to return. She squinted as she looked around and took in her surroundings with red, bleary eyes.

Rosemary came back into the living room and returned the sofa.

"Look like you got new furniture, Ma. What happened? Where did you get the money from? You always said you'd keep the house the way it was when Daddy died." She looked around the room disapprovingly. She tuned and stared at her mother intently.

"Uh, yes, Mari came into a little money. So she, uh, bought new furniture," Rosemary stammered. She clasped her shaking hands together and rested them on her lap.

"So, where is she?" Cassie peered into the kitchen and then looked upstairs. "You two are like Frick and Frack. Where you see one, you see the other." Cassie scratched her arm as she giggled at her little joke.

Rosemary licked her lips, and paused before answering the question. She knew if she told her daughter where Mariah lived, Cassie would shoot over to Hammond in a minute to get a share of Mariah's legacy. Unfortunately, anything she got from Mariah would be used to replenish her stash of drugs.

"So, where is she?" Cassie asked again. She focused her attention on her mother, and then scratched her arm.

"I was going to wait for Mari to tell you herself. She moved and got her own place."

"Her own place where?" Cassie wanted to know.

"Well, she moved to Indiana. Hammond."

Cassie did a double take and stared at her mother. "I know you didn't say Hammond, Indiana." Her thin hand fluttered in the air. "Why would she want to go there? It's nothing there."

"She's working there now. So she decided to move there."

"Really?" Cassie snorted. "That doesn't make much sense. It would take wild horses to separate that girl from you. Are you telling me the truth, Ma? What's really going on?" Cassie's gazed held her mother. Cassie seemed to have built-in radar, and knew when Rosemary was being evasive with her.

"Yes, I'm telling you the truth. She moved yesterday," Rosemary added.

Cassie stood up and walked upstairs. She returned a few minutes later. "She is really gone. I don't believe it." Cassie slouched down on the couch.

"Well, you didn't think she was going to stay here the rest of her life, did you? Mariah is a grown woman. It's time for her to show a little independence and move out," Rosemary said staunchly. She had a sinking feeling in the pit of her stomach. Cassie could become manipulative and make her reveal information she didn't care to share.

"Hmmm." The lids on Cassie's eyes drooped. "Well, maybe I'll have to pay her a visit and find out what's really going on. I know you and Mariah think I don't know what's going on, because I stay high all the time.

But I hear things and when I hear them"—she pointed to her head—"they stay up there. It just don't make no sense to me that Mariah would leave her job. We both know how proud she was of that little group she started," Cassie said sarcastically.

"Just because a person work in one place don't mean they're going to work at the same place their entire life. At least not in this day and age. Mariah is young, so she moved. Her new job is a promotion."

Cassie pursed her lips together tightly and looked at her mother skeptically. "You almost sound convincing, Momma Dearest, but I know you're lying. I been hearing things, and I heard Mariah came into some money." She shook her head. "Do you really think Mariah would get money, and I wouldn't get my fair share?" She lifted her arms and spread them out along the top of the couch.

A look of horror shot in Rosemary's eyes and her body trembled. "Uh, Mari won the lottery so she decided to fix up the house." Rosemary glanced up. *Forgive me for lying, Lord.* She then looked at Cassie with a steely glare. "Why can't you just leave her alone, Cassie? Let Mariah live her life the way she sees fit. She's done a lot of good in the world. She don't need you around pulling her down."

A cold look came into Cassie's eyes. "Now that wasn't a nice thing to say." Venom dripped from her voice. "I brought her into this world. I feel I should get a little something for that. I didn't even want to have her. Who would want a child that—"

"Shut your mouth," Rosemary barked at her daughter. "A baby is a gift from God, and it would behoove you to remember that." She pointed her finger at Cassie.

"To me it could go either way: be a gift from God or from the devil. And we know it wasn't nothing holy about the way Mariah was conceived, now don't we?"

Fear struck in Rosemary's heart. She told her daughter coldly, "Don't talk like that. Mariah has been a blessing to me her entire life. She's a good girl, and I don't want you to do or say anything to hurt her."

"See that's always been your problem. You screwed up my life by making me have Mariah. Then to make up for what you did, you treated her like she was your child. And you threw me away like yesterday's news." Cassandra pointed her finger at her mother.

Rosemary shook her head sorrowfully. "You know that's not true. I've always been there for you, until you turned to the streets and drugs. If you would just get yourself cleaned up, life could be so much better for you. You need Jesus in your life and let Him lead you to a good rehabilitation center." She leaned forward in her seat and held out her hand, and said, "Let us help you, Cassie. Let me and Mariah help you. She loves you because you're her mother, but she just doesn't know how to deal with your addiction. Please let us help you," she begged passionately.

Cassie threw her head back and laughed with ugly, harsh tones. "Help me? You're going to need help when Mariah learns the truth about what happened twenty-eight years ago. Just wait until she finds out the part you played in the lies. I bet Daddy is still turning over in his grave," Cassie spat at her mother.

Rosemary's body heaved with unshed tears. She felt mortified. "I did what I thought was best at the time. And I'm not going to sit by and let you mess up Mariah's life any more than you have." She stood up and walked to the door. "I think you'd better leave now." Rosemary opened it.

Cassie stood up and shook her head. "Same old Ma."
She walked to the door. "I'll go for now, but if I find out
you've been lying to me, and I know you have, I'm going to tell Mariah everything about her precious grandmother," she spat.

Rosemary recoiled from her daughter's body. She
stared at Cassie fearfully like Cassie was the devil himself.

"In fact, if Mariah has come into money like I heard
she did, then you'd better make sure I get my cut. Or I
will make you and her life miserable. Did you get that,
old lady? I'll be back, and you'd better have something
for me." Cassie shot a sinister smile at her mother and
walked out the door.

Rosemary slammed the door with all her might.
She walked to the sofa and sat heavily on it and put
her hands over her face. Her shoulders heaved as she
cried. She couldn't believe what had just transpired.
She knew her daughter was sly and cunning. She had
to be to survive on the streets. Never in a million years
did Rosemary imagine those traits would be turned
against her. She tried to help Cassie in her own way.
She gave her food and money when she could. And for
her daughter to turn on her like that was a shock to her
system.

Rosemary's breathing became shallow. She felt light-
headed as she went into the kitchen and picked up her
inhaler. She pressed the pump, and the medication
shot into her mouth. After what seemed a long time,
Rosemary's breathing returned to normal. She went
into the bathroom and splashed cold water on her face.
Rosemary returned to the living room and sat down.
Her mind raced a mile a minute as she tried to figure
out how to diffuse the situation. There was no doubt in
Rosemary's mind that her daughter would make good

on her promise to tell Mariah what really happened regarding her conception those years ago.

Rosemary didn't have a lot of money. She knew if her daughter got a whiff of how much money Mariah had, she would blackmail Rosemary over and over. Rosemary wasn't ready to tell Mariah the truth of her beginnings just yet. Rosemary planned to tell her in the future after she settled down and had a family.

She rocked in her seat, closed her eyes, clasped her hands together, and implored the Lord to help her. "Father, I know the way I handled the situation wasn't the best way to do things. I hurt Cassie in the process, and she may hurt Mariah. I can't allow that to happen. Lord, please stop by here and guide me. I need your help. Help me, Jesus. I can't fight this battle alone. Please show me the way." Her voice cracked as tears streamed down her eyes.

Rosemary sat on the sofa and prayed for a long time. With shaking hands, she picked her Bible up off the cocktail table and opened it to Psalm 32 and read aloud the first five chapters. "'Blessed is he whose transgression is forgiven, whose sin is covered. Blessed is the man unto whom the Lord imputeth not iniquity and in whose spirit there is no guile. When I kept silence, my bones waxed old through my roaring all day long. For day and night thy hand was heavy upon me: my moisture is turned into the drought of summer. Selah. I acknowledged my sin unto thee, and mine iniquity have I not hid, I said, I will confess my transgressions until the Lord; and thou forgavest the iniquity of my sin. Selah.'"

Reverend Dudley gently suggested many years ago that she read that scripture. Rosemary had sought counseling on how to handle the events regarding Mariah's conception. Rosemary read the scripture and it had given her comfort when she needed forgiveness for her sins. Now she knew the text by heart and it had become part of her daily prayers. Reverend Dudley also advised Rosemary to tell Mariah everything that happened.

Rosemary heart rate accelerated at the thought. She decided not to return to church for the musical. She needed time to decide how to proceed with Cassie's threat. Rosemary felt betrayed, like a viper had struck her heart. Dinner was long forgotten as she sat in the living room, as daylight grew dim. "What should I do, Lord?" she beseeched her Father above. "What should I do?" A few hours later she picked up the phone to warn Mariah about Cassie.

Chapter Fifteen

The doorbell chimed rousing Mariah from her nap. She smiled to herself, thinking maybe Carson had forgotten something and returned. Mariah opened the door and gasped. Her stomach somersaulted. She couldn't believe who was standing on the other side of the door.

Mariah's legs felt weak. "Cassie, what are you doing here?" she asked. Her eyes scanned up and down the street. Praying no one had sighted the motley-looking woman standing at her doorway, Mariah sighed with relief to see that none of her neighbors were outdoors. Then she frowned when she saw a hooptie parked slanted in her driveway. Black waves of smoke belched from the rear of the vehicle.

"Well, daughter, aren't you going to invite me in?" Cassie turned her face, and put her finger on her left cheek.

Mariah's senses kicked in. She definitely didn't want Cassie inside the house. If she saw the surroundings, the luxury they projected, she would never leave. She would have her hand in Mariah's pocket constantly. Mariah pulled the door shut behind her.

"No, we can talk on the porch. Why don't we sit on the glider?"

Mother and daughter sat next to each other. Each studied the each other warily.

"How did you know where to find me?" Mariah turned and asked Cassie uncomfortably.

"You know me." Cassie smiled mysteriously. She looked like a cat who had just sipped a bowl of cream. "I have my sources. A little birdie told me you came into some money, and I know you want to share it with your mommy."

Mariah's eyes bucked. "Who told you that?" Her hand grasped the side of the glider.

"Does it really matter? I just came to get my share and then I'll be on my way," Cassie said casually. She pulled a loose thread from the knee of her dingy black pants.

"Did Granny tell you?" Mariah asked fearfully.

"No, she didn't." Cassie snorted. "Wild horses couldn't drag that information from Momma. We had a nice little chat today. She did tell me that you won the lottery, got a new job, and moved here."

Mariah's body relaxed. She was grateful that Rosemary had not revealed to her mother what had really occurred. "I did come into some money, that's true. But you know how that goes. A big chunk of the money went toward taxes. So I don't have a lot left."

Cassie's fist came down hard on the armrest on her side of the glider. It made a clanking noise and startled Mariah. Her body jerked.

Cassie reared her head back and hissed, "Girl, don't play with me. I'm not a fool. Momma got new furniture and you're living in this big, fine house. So I know you got some serious dough. I just want what's coming to me."

"What makes you think you have anything coming?" Mariah asked snidely. "You were never a mother to me. You either treated me like crap or ignored me. If anyone has anything coming that would be Granny and not you."

"See you always placed Momma on a pedestal. Those who are up high are always headed for a fall. You're right. I might not have been the best mother in the world, but I still gave you life and for that you owe me," Cassie announced with a malicious gleam in her eyes.

"All those years of shooting drugs in your veins must have addled your brain. I don't owe you jack," Mariah said coldly. She had a note of finality in her tone. "You were never a mother to me. I can't believe you had the audacity to come here today, acting like you were. In fact, I think you need to leave." She tried to stand up but her legs were shaking too badly. Her teeth chattered and she realized that she had feared Cassie her entire life.

"Is that what they teach you in that church you go to?" Cassie shot back at Mariah. "I thought being a Christian was about being forgiving. Here you are acting and treating me like I ain't nothing. See that's what I hate about church folks: they are so hypocritical. I'm your mother, not Rosemary Green." She thumped her chest. "Me, Cassandra Green."

"Where were you when I needed a mother, Cassandra Green?" Mariah hissed at Cassandra. Her eyes flattened into slits. "Did you take me to school my first day? When I had my tonsils removed, did you come to the hospital? No. You didn't come to any of my graduations. You are an embarrassment to me. I've been ashamed to be your daughter my whole life. All the kids in school used to whisper behind my back about my mother, the crackhead. I'd see you sitting on the bench at the bus stop, zonked out from drugs. Spittle would run down your chin; you looked disgusting. So don't ever tell me I owe you anything. I have nothing for you, just like you gave me when I was born and then while I was growing up. So if you'll excuse me"—she glared at Cassie—"I have things to do."

At that moment, as she had most of her life, Mariah felt deep-seated revulsion for the woman who had given her life. She was filled with a hot rage; her breathing was shallow. How dare Cassie come to her door with her hand out to replenish her drug supply?

"Bravo, what a performance. You need to go to Hollywood." Cassie clapped her hands. The driver honked the horn.

Cassie stood up. "I suggest you call Momma so you two can put your heads together and come up with something to give me. I am not going to be left out of whatever is going on. I deserve something for the hell my life has been since you were born. So you two talk it over. I'll either come back here and get it from you, or from Momma. Your choice." Cassie rose from the glider and strolled to the car.

She got inside the old white Ford Escort and blew Mariah a kiss as the driver steered the car slowly down the street.

Mariah dropped her head inside her hands. She heard someone walking up the stairs. She prayed Cassie hadn't returned. She couldn't deal with her again. She took a deep breath and looked up to see Carson walking toward her. Care and concern glimmered in his eyes.

"Mariah, are you okay?" he asked as he sat on the glider next to her. "You must have dropped your wallet in my truck. So I came back to return it. I saw you talking to that woman, and it didn't look like you were having a pleasant conversation." Carson looked at her questioningly.

She looked at Carson with a wild look in her eyes. "That was my dear old mother, Cassie. She had the nerve to come here and try to extort money from me," Mariah told Carson bitterly in a leaden voice. Then she looked away from him. She had never felt so humiliated in her life.

"I'm sorry. . . ." Carson's voice faltered, then gained strength. "You know what they say about inheriting money: it brings relatives and friends out of the woodwork. I guess it goes with the territory."

"You know, if my mother had been there for me at least part of my life, I wouldn't mind helping her. But, she pretty much ignored me. As I told you my grandmother raised me. She has a lot of nerve coming here. Cassie is acting like there's a big secret that she and my grandmother know that I don't. Being around her makes me physically ill. I feel like I'm going to be sick." Mariah stood up and rushed inside the house.

Carson sat on the glider indecisively. He wasn't sure if he should run after Mariah, or give her time to collect herself. He decided on the latter.

Finally Mariah came back outside. Carson handed Mariah her wallet. "Here you go. I know that had to be tough. Your mother looked like she's in bad shape. Maybe you can get her to agree to go to rehab."

Mariah waved her hand dismissively. "Actually, this was one of Cassie's good days. She was coherent enough to tell me what she wanted, and that's not usually the case." She shrugged her shoulders as she shook her head.

"Maybe you need to see a counselor and sort out your feelings. You looked really bummed out," Carson suggested.

"I don't need to see anyone," Mariah yelled, furious with Carson. "My mother is a heavy burden that I have to bear. And, she made some references about my grandmother that got under my skin. Cassie has also been a prime manipulator. Like a leopard she'll never change her spots."

"You know with God, all things are possible. So never say never," Carson said soothingly.

"That rule would apply to anyone except Cassie. She's been a thorn in my side since I was little. I never understood why she hates me. But, she does." Warm waves of mortification colored Mariah's cheeks. "I apologize for dumping all of this negativity on you. I've had enough of my mother for one day. I also need to call my grandmother and find out why she told Cassie where I live."

"Are you sure your grandmother told her? You don't know that for sure?" Carson tried to be the voice of reason in the volatile situation.

"Humph, how else would Cassie know to come here? To this house?" Her hand arced in the air. She looked at him skeptically. "Cassie has a way of worming information out of people. I know somehow or another, she got Granny to tell her where I live. I appreciate you bringing me my wallet. I probably wouldn't have discovered it was missing until the morning."

"I would have brought it back to you before then," Carson replied as he stood up. He knew he had worn out his welcome. "You have a good evening and try not to let what happened ruin your evening. We all have our crosses to bear, no one is immune. Maybe you should turn this burden over to the Lord and pray for guidance."

"Do I really have a choice?" Mariah twisted her lips together. "I'll talk to you. Have a good evening," she said dismissively with her arms folded across her chest.

Carson knew he could have taken her actions personally, but he knew she was shaken by her mother's actions. "You too. I meant what I said. Try not to let your mother coming here get you down."

"I'll try to take your advice, but it's a little late for that. Cassie has had years of practice and knows what buttons to push to get under my skin."

Carson squeezed her arm and then he departed.

Mariah walked inside the house. She went into the kitchen and turned on the hot water faucet. She filled the kettle with water to boil for tea. She picked up the telephone and scrolled through caller ID. She noted both Sonni and Rocki had called in addition to her grandmother. She pressed the message button and listened to voice mail. When she heard Rosemary's voice, her stomach lurched.

"Hi, baby, it's me, Granny. I just wanted to tell you that Cassie came over and she implied she planned to get in touch with you. She must have heard through the grapevine that you've come into money. I told her you'd won the lottery and moved to Indiana. She was upstairs in your room for a minute. She claimed she went up there to see if you had actually moved. So I wanted to warn you that she might try to get in touch with you. I hope she doesn't but at least you know. Call me when you get a chance."

Mariah angrily pushed the delete button. Then she sighed. Carson was right. She had left a few papers on the desk in her old room and knowing Cassie as she did, Mariah was sure she'd riffled through some of the papers. "Lord, I just can't escape that woman and I live in another state," she muttered. "Father, you have blessed me tremendously over the past months, and I am so grateful. I vowed that I would do good things with the money and share it with others.

"Right now the money seems a burden. Granny wouldn't move to Indiana with me. And my worst nightmare, Cassie, had the audacity to show up here. I can't believe she demanded I give her money. She also implied something isn't right with Granny. Lord, I try to do the right things. I tithe. I really love contributing to the Sunday School ministry. Why can't you perform a divine intervention and get Cassie out of my life? Life would be perfect except for her.

"I don't understand why I had to be born to a mother who's a drug addict. Why did I have to miss out on a real mother-daughter relationship?" She snorted bitterly. "In fact I didn't have a relationship with either of my parents. I know you said in the Word to honor your mother and father, but what if they're not worthy of honoring? What do you do then?" She exhaled loudly as she waited for the water to boil.

Mariah paced the length of the living room as she continued her pity party. The shrill whistle of the tea-kettle broke her out of her reverie. She opened the cabinet and took out a cup, and removed a box of orange tea, and a bag from the box. Mariah poured water into the cup, and sat at the kitchen table. She dipped the teabag inside the water until the liquid turned a bright orange color. She rose from the chair and rummaged through the pantry until she saw a box of sugar. She was grateful Sonyell had picked up groceries for her. She knew her friend had purchased the tea and sugar.

After she sat back down and drank the cup of tea, Mariah felt calmer. She resumed her talk with her Heavenly Father. "Lord, forgive me for being selfish. If Cassie's coming here was a test, then I surely failed it. I know if no one else on earth has my back, that you do. I just have to remember that when things don't go the way I think they should. There are always negatives in life. I just have to deal with them better. I have truly been blessed. Thanks to your generosity, I am in a position to help those in need as the Good Book states.

"As I count my blessings today, I have met a man who is a Christian. He appears to really like me. My best friends are moving to Hammond this upcoming weekend. So I won't be alone. I don't know what you the future holds, but I must trust and have faith that whatever happens is your will and not mine. So forgive me, Father, for being immature and folding at the first sight of trouble. Tomorrow is a new day, and I can't wait to see what blessings will come my way."

Later that night with the television turned low, Mariah returned to the living room and resumed reading her book. She had talked to Sonyell and Raquel on three-way earlier. The women were looking forward to the move over the weekend. Afterward, Mariah headed to her bedroom and prepared for the night. She tossed and turned most of the night, trying to figure out what Cassie implied about Rosemary. She wondered what other tidbits Carson knew about her father. It was the longest night. She was glad when daylight finally broke. Yesterday was over and done. Today was another opportunity to start anew.

Chapter Sixteen

Time sped and the winter season was quickly approaching. Light snowflakes were falling in the Midwest on Thanksgiving Day. Originally Sonyell and Raquel planned to join Mariah and Rosemary at Mariah's house after dining with their families. Sonyell decided to spend the weekend in Marion, Illinois to visit Michael in prison. Instead Raquel opted to go to Michigan with her family to visit her grandparents. Mariah, too changed her plans. She decided to have dinner with her grandmother at Rosmary's home.

Sonyell's and Raquel's moves to Indiana had gone without a hitch. The two women were comfortably settled in their new houses. All three new houses were beginning to feel like home.

After Cassie's disastrous visit to Hammond, Mariah had given Rosemary $1,000 and asked her to give Cassie twenty dollars a week. So far Cassie hadn't made any more impromptu visits to Indiana. For that Mariah was grateful.

Mariah had presented Reverend Dudley with a check for $250,000 two weeks ago. The two had previously decided the bulk of the money would be allocated for building improvements and to further the homeless ministry. A nice percentage of the funds were allocated to the Sunday School ministry, The rest would be distributed to other ministries.

Raquel, with Mariah's blessing, had renovated the hair salon. She'd added a day spa complete with manicures, pedicures, and massage offerings. Though Raquel managed the salon and barber shop, she still set up her own space in the salon and did brisk business.

Mariah had visited several local high schools and offered internship opportunities for junior and senior students at the beauty and barber shops. The salon offered ten dollar wash and sets on Wednesdays to women who resided in senior complexes. The barber shop offered similar haircuts to senior men. Business was thriving and the local newspaper had written an article on Mariah.

Though she was initially averse to doing so, Mariah acknowledged her father publically where business matters were concerned. Sonyell had audited the various businesses that Mr. Ellison had owned. She made recommendations for the businesses to run more efficiently. A few were sold. Mariah hired Carson's company to make minor repairs in the apartment buildings that she now owned. Mariah wasn't sure how she and Carson would get along from a business perspective. As it turned out, her worrying was for naught. She was impressed by his business acumen. Being a local Hammond businessman, he helped her when she ran into local roadblocks.

Their romance was also blossoming. All was well in Mariah's world.

Raquel's involvement with Alex was short-lived. She crossed the border back into Chicago for excitement. Michael would be released from prison the following month. Sonyell thrived in her position as Mariah's business manager. She proved to have a sharp, analytic mind. Mariah felt blessed to have her and Carson on her team. The three were a force to be reckoned with. At Carson's urging, Mariah joined several business organizations.

Mariah stood in her bedroom in front of the dresser mirror and fussed with her hair. She pulled a few tight twists loose. She wore a burnt-orange two-piece pantsuit with a cream-colored shell with gold accessories. She glanced at the clock on her nightstand. It was nearly three o'clock. She needed to get going to make it to Rosemary's house by three-thirty. Originally Rosemary was going to have dinner at Mariah's house, but this changed when Sonni and Rocki changed their plans. Either way it went, Mariah was running late. She removed two bags from the kitchen, grabbed her purse, put it on her shoulder, and hurried out of the door.

Thirty minutes later, she opened the door to Rosemary's house with her key. Appetizing aromas teased her sense of smell.

"Is that you, Mariah?" Rosemary called from the kitchen. She paused washing dishes.

"Yes, it is," Mariah answered as she walked into the kitchen. The room was warm and cozy. She walked to the sink and kissed Rosemary. She set a case of soda on the floor. "It sure smells good in here. Do you need me to taste anything?" Mariah asked her grandmother hopefully.

Rosemary shook her head and smiled. "No, not really. I think I got this cooking thing down pat. I just took the turkey out of the oven. You can see if my stuffing is up to par."

Mariah rubbed her hands together and grinned at Rosemary. She had stopped by a local baker the previous day and purchased a red velvet cake and sweet potato pies. She took the desserts out of the bag and put them on the counter. Mariah then took a saucer out of the cabinet, walked to the stove, pealed a corner of the foil back, and put a small bit of stuffing on the plate.

She blew on it, and gobbled it down as Rosemary watched her with an amused twinkle in her eye.

"It's so good, Granny. The stuffing doesn't even need cranberry sauce. You haven't lost your touch. Is there anything I can do?" Mariah put the saucer in the dishpan.

"You can set the table. The food is just about done. I suppose you're hungry?"

"Yes, I am," Mariah responded as she took plates and glasses out of the cabinet. Before long the table had been set. The two women sat at the table and bowed their heads.

"Father, God, we come to you content to see another Thanksgiving Day. You have blessed Mariah so abundantly this year, Lord. She in turn has shared her blessing with her family, friends, and even strangers. Continue to guide her to do the right thing. Bless us for the food we're about to receive. All blessings in your name. Amen," Rosemary said and opened her eyes.

The women passed the bowls and platter between them and within minutes began to partake in the meal. They conversed about local happenings while they ate.

Thirty minutes later, Mariah wiped her mouth and hands with a napkin and pushed her chair away from the table. "That was so good, Granny. I can't eat another bite."

"Yes, I agree with you, the meal was good. It's time you learned to cook more. Who knows, you may have to cook for Carson's daughters one day." Rosemary took a sip of iced tea as she waited for Mariah to reply.

"Uh, I hope not. I'm not a homemaker," Mariah protested haughtily, like cooking was beneath her. "I always wanted a career. My life is simply amazing."

"There's nothing wrong with doing both. Would you cut me a piece of pie?" Rosemary asked.

Mariah stood up, walked to the counter, and cut a slice of potato pie. She put it on a saucer and handed it to her grandmother.

"You aren't going to have dessert now?" Rosemary cut a tiny portion of the pie, and put it into her mouth.

"No, not right now. I'm too stuffed. Plus, I've got save room for dessert at Carson's parents' house." Mariah rubbed her tummy. "I hear you about doing both. Although I don't know, I hear a lot of women complain about how tiring and stressful trying to be Superwoman is."

"Anything worth having comes with work and stress. Nobody promised life would be easy," Rosemary responded sagely. "I'm glad you and Carson are hitting it off. It's time for you to settle down. You're not getting any younger."

Mariah sat upright in her chair. "I'm not even thirty yet. There's plenty of time for me to settle down." She crinkled her nose.

"Sometimes love only comes around once in a lifetime, and good men are so hard to find. There was only one man for me in this life and that was your grandfather." Rosemary sighed. She had finished eating the pie and put the saucer on top of her dinner plate.

"Is that why you never remarried? Because Gramps was the one?" Mariah asked as she stirred the sugar in her iced tea.

"Partially. Cassie was a handful even as a child. She was always a bundle of nervous energy. Then there was you; there just wasn't enough time. Now, I'm in my sixties and that part of my life has passed by."

Mariah shook her head. "It's not like you're that old. I bet there's still some romantic life left in you." Mariah folded her arms across her chest.

"No, I'm good. I cook at the school during the week and teach Sunday School on the Sabbath day. Alma and I go to the movies or shopping, so by and large life is good." Rosemary switched gears. "So how do you feel about meeting Carson's folks? Are you nervous?" She put Mariah's empty plate on top of hers and gathered the eating utensils.

"Just a little bit." Mariah's voice trailed off as she looked away from Rosemary.

"I don't see why." Rosemary shook her head as she squirted dishwashing liquid into the plastic dishpan. "You're gorgeous and independent. You have a kind, loving heart, everything a man looks for in a wife."

"Now, don't you think you could be a wee bit biased, Granny?" She held up two fingers close to each other. "You know my rule is never to date a man with children. But Carson is such a good man, I bypassed my rule. I've enjoyed the time we've spent getting to know each other. The only dark spot I can find is that his ex-wife calls a little too much for my taste. Even though they've been divorced for a while, I think she's not ready to let go. Plus they have children, so she'll always be around."

Rosemary looked at Mariah. "Haven't you been listening to me? Once again, that same rule applies as before: nothing worth having ever comes easy. You're doing the right thing by giving the relationship time. Y'all would make some beautiful babies. After marriage, that is."

The doorbell rang. Mariah glanced at her watch. "I wonder who that is. Are you expecting anyone else?" Although Mariah asked the question, she knew it couldn't be anyone else except for Cassie at the door. Her stomach churned like she had acid reflux.

"It's probably Cassie," Rosemary said guiltily. "I invited her over for dinner." She wiped her wet hands on a dish towel. "I'll get it."

Mariah's good mood deflated like a balloon. After her last encounter with Cassie, she hoped she wouldn't have to see her mother for a long time. She watched her grandmother walk into the living room, peer out the peephole, and open the door.

Rosemary kissed Cassie's cheek when her daughter stepped over the threshold. "I'm glad you could make it." She beamed at Cassie.

"Well, I ain't staying long." Cassie slipped out of a down jacket, opened the closet door, and hung the jacket on a wire hanger. She actually looked presentable. She wore a green sweater that clung to her thin frame. She had a pair of wrinkled jeans and a pair of scuffled Timberland boots. Her eyes were clear though.

Mother and daughter walked into the kitchen.

"Cassie." Mariah bowed her head grudgingly.

"Mariah," Cassie said in return. She sat on one of the kitchen chairs.

"I tell you I feel so blessed today." Rosemary grinned from ear to ear. "Both of my girls are here." She looked at Cassie. "Can I fix you something to eat?"

"Just a little stuffing and turkey," Cassie replied. She looked down and folded her hands in her lap as Rosemary bustled about the kitchen fixing her plate. Rosemary closed her eyes and thanked God for her daughter and granddaughter's presence on the holiday.

Mariah watched her mother wolf down the food with her hands. She couldn't prevent herself from asking Cassie, "Did Granny fix you enough food? Do you want more?"

Cassie cut her eye at Mariah and answered, "If I want more, I know how to ask." She made a sucking sound with her lips.

"Sorry, I was just asking. You seem to be hungry." Mariah shrugged her shoulders.

After Cassie finished eating, she pushed her chair back, and said, "That was good, Ma. I forgot how well you can cook. That's one thing I miss."

"Thank you," Rosemary replied modestly. "So what you been doing with yourself, Cassie? I hope you been staying out of trouble."

"I been good, since you been giving me money. I been real good." Cassie smirked at Mariah.

Mariah rolled her eyes and commented, "I hope you haven't been spending all of it up your arm."

"Whatever I been doing with it," Cassie said tersely, "is my business. I don't remember you saying what I have to spend it on. I'm taking care of myself and you would do well to keep your nose out of my business."

"What business?" Mariah snorted. "To my knowledge you don't have any."

"Girls," Rosemary interrupted the two with a distressed expression on her face. "Can't we just have a nice visit without any arguing? It's Thanksgiving Day. We have so much to be thankful for. We're all gathered together as a family. It's been a long time since we've been together."

"Sorry," Mariah mumbled toward her mother. "I didn't mean that the way it sounded."

"Thank you." Cassie wiped her hands on a napkin. "I been all right. Nothing is new with me; same ol', same ol'."

"Good." Rosemary nodded at her approvingly. "I hope you've been giving some thought to what we talked about the last time you were here, going into rehab."

"I thought about it, and I'm not going to do it. There is nothing wrong with me. I have my life under control. Everything is fine," Cassie replied. She refused to make eye contact with Rosemary or Mariah.

"You must be more delusional than I thought you were," Mariah remarked. "There is nothing about your life that screams control. You are so out of control that you don't even realize how sad your life is."

"If there's anything wrong with my life, then it's your fault and Momma's," Cassie spit out. Her voice rose as she glared at Mariah. "And, you need to keep your nose out of my business. I can take care of myself."

"Please." Mariah shook her head. "Your business is hanging around the bus stop trying to score your next hit. You wouldn't know the meaning of business or taking care of yourself if it hit you in the head."

"You've always placed Momma on this pedestal haven't you?" Cassie asked her daughter. "Well guess what? Momma is not perfect. Why don't you ask her what happened when you were born? What part she played in all this? She always comes across as the innocent, long-suffering mother. But you'd better believe me, she is the root of all my problems."

Rosemary looked stricken with each word that came out of her daughter's mouth. She tried to speak, but couldn't find her voice.

"How dare you criticize Granny?" Mariah shouted. "She's been nothing but good to you. She raised your child, me." Mariah pointed to her chest. "She's loved and stood by you when anybody else would have given up on you." She pointed a trembling finger in Cassie's direction. "You've lied and stolen from us and you have the nerve to criticize someone. You need to lay down the pipe, get some help, and get yourself together."

"You need to wake up and see things for what they really are." Cassie stood up and pounded on the table. "You are so blind." The napkin on her lap fluttered to the floor. "I think I've overstayed my welcome. I don't know why I came here anyway. Coming here just never seems to work out." Cassie stalked to the living room as Rosemary watched her with tearstained eyes. Mariah glowered at her with twisted lips.

Cassie removed her coat from the closet and put it on. She opened the front door, stomped outside, and slammed the door behind her.

Rosemary bowed her head sorrowfully.

"That's an addict for you. Their problems are always someone else's fault and not their own." Mariah turned to her grandmother and said, "I don't understand how she had the nerve to blame her problems on you and me."

"Me either." Rosemary shook her head sadly. "That's just Cassie being Cassie." Her hands shook.

"She sounds like she has mad beef with both of us. I think I liked her better when she ignored me." Mariah sighed. Then she looked at Rosemary. "Granny, you don't look good. Are you sure you're all right?" Anxiety shone in her eyes.

"I do feel a little shaky," Rosemary admitted. She stood up. "I'm going upstairs to lie down for a while."

"Can I get you something? You have been taking your medication haven't you?"

Rosemary nodded her head. "I'll be fine. I just need rest for a minute."

"Okay, I'll wash the dishes. Do you need me to stay here with you?" Mariah stood up and began clearing the table.

"No, I just need to lie down for a minute," Rosemary said. She started walking toward the staircase. "Try not to be so hard on Cassie, she's just mixed up."

"It's Thanksgiving and I'm not going to let Cassie spoil the day for me. Go ahead and get some rest. Let me know if you need anything."

"I will." Rosemary walked heavily upstairs to her bedroom. After she removed her shoes, she lay on the bed and closed her eyes. "Lord knows I've got to do something to fix things before this situation gets out of control. Cassie is becoming more unpredictable. I should have come clean with Mariah years ago and told her the truth regarding her birth. She has been through so much, and I just didn't want to be hurt anymore. Lord, did I sacrifice my daughter's love and respect for my granddaughter's happiness?

"People always say how they wish they could turn back the hands of time. I know that I can't but I so wish that I could. Father, help me to make things right. Help me to get my two girls together. In the name of Jesus I pray."

While Rosemary poured her heart out to God, a troubled Mariah washed dishes and tidied the kitchen. Though she tried to put down Cassie's ranting as dope talk, Mariah had a feeling that there was some truth to Cassie's ramblings. She was disturbed and vowed to get to the bottom of things.

Chapter Seventeen

At the correctional facility located in Marion, Sonyell and Sasha were dressed in holiday colors. Sonyell wore a form-fitting red top with black slacks, while Sasha looked pretty in a gold sweater and black skirt. Mother and daughter were nearing the end of their visit with Michael. Many families were gathered in the common area to spend Thanksgiving Day with their loved ones. Michael's brother, Marvin, his wife, Ashley, and their daughters accompanied Sonyell and Sasha on the visit. Conversation in the visiting area was nonstop. Voices rose and fell intermittently with loud crescendos.

Michael dipped his head and said in his deep bass voice, "Just think I'll be home back in Chi town in three weeks. I can't hardly wait." He rubbed his hands together.

Sasha was glued to her father's side. She'd given him her undivided attention during their two-hour visit. "I'll be so glad when you come home, Daddy," she said shyly.

Michael leaned over and pulled one of his daughter's braids. He grabbed Sonyell's hand. "Spending time with my two favorite girls will be the best Christmas present in the world." He dropped Sonyell's hand and made a circle with his hands.

Michael's brother and his wife were sitting on the other side of the room. They allowed the family private time.

"Sasha, why don't you go sit with your Uncle Marvin for a minute? I need to speak to your dad privately before we leave," Sonyell asked her daughter

"Do I have to?" Sasha lips drooped as she whined.

Sonyell gave her daughter a look that brooked no argument. Sasha stood up and looked at her father pleadingly. He shook his head, and the girl walked away from the table.

"So, do you have a definite release date?" Sonyell asked Michael. Her eyes watched Sasha sit down with her uncle, his wife, and their children. Soon she was chatting with her cousins. Occasionally her eyes landed back on Michael.

"December fifteenth. My paperwork is all done and being processed. I would like to have a job lined up by the time I get out of here. Did you have a chance to take to Mari?"

"You know I have my doubts about you working for Mari." Sonyell licked her lips.

"I don't know why." Michael's eyes narrowed. "It's hard for a con. We both know my record is pretty bad. In times like this it helps to have friends with a hookup."

"Before I talk to Mari, I need proof that you've changed. I know you've talked a good game. But, I still need to see you and verify for myself that you've changed before I ask a friend for favors."

Michael looked askance toward Sonyell. "I guess I can understand that. But the difference is that I'm older. I'm actually getting out a little early for good behavior, not to mention the overcrowding of the jails. I've completed my GED. Heck, I've even been going to church here on Sundays. Sonni, I want to try to do right by you and Sasha." Michael grabbed her hands and held them tightly.

Sonyell was moved by Michael's words. Still she wore a stoic expression on her face. She'd heard this before, especially when Michael was being released from prison. His good intentions usually lasted a month or two.

"I can see you don't believe me, and if you don't feel comfortable asking Mari to help me, then so be it. There are some things I may have to do on my own. Being in here"—Michael's hand swept the space between the couple—"has shown me the error of my ways. I've talked to therapists and they've explained to me how I ended up the way I have."

"And, what did they say?" Sonyell lifted her eyebrow as she leaned forward in her chair.

"My environment played a big part in my life choices," Michael answered knowingly.

"If that's the case, then how come your brother Marvin went to college, got married, and has his slice of the American dream? After all, you two were raised in the same house by the same mother."

"Well, Ms. College Girl." He smiled. "All of us are not the same. You know I was never into school the way you and Marvin were. My brother was a straight-up nerd. Some of us are cut out for school and some of us aren't. They explained all of that to me during the sessions. All I can say is that I was young and dumb and I made some bad choices. You've been there for me. Now it's my turn to do what I can to make life better for you and Sasha." There were no signs of deception and Michael's demeanor reflected sincerity.

Sonyell tried not to get her hopes up. She had been down this road a time or two. She was acutely aware of how Michael could be charming when he choose to. Sonyell was grateful that his criminal activity consisted of mostly robbery and auto theft. He'd dealt drugs at one time. Michael had never gone as far as to commit murder.

"Babe, this time I completed a HVAC course. You know that I've never taken any classes while I was locked up before. I was always plotting my next criminal move because that's where I thought the money was. But now, I'm getting older and Sasha is growing up. She needs a father. I want to be the best I can for her. I don't want her to visit me in the joint the rest of my life. That's why I'm a changed man. I have two reasons in the world to change my ways: you and my baby girl." Michael spoke earnestly and with his hand over his heart.

"Well, like you, I don't want Sasha to question me in the future as to why I stuck by a man in prison." Sonyell dipped her head toward Michael. "So I hope you've really changed. I don't plan to go down this road with you again. You'll either get it together this time or we're through. I've loved you since we were in eighth grade. My family and friends think I'm crazy for standing by you."

"I know, Sonni. If I could undo parts of my past, I would in a heartbeat but I can't. I can only move forward and I know my actions will speak louder than words. I want us to get married." He placed his hand over his heart.

Sonyell's eyes widened. She and Michael had spoken of marriage back in high school, even after she became pregnant and had Sasha. But it never happened. Michael was always in jail and Sonyell refused to get married while he was incarcerated.

"I just hope you can live up to my and Sasha's expectations." Sonyell pointed to their daughter. "It's too soon to talk of marriage, but if you are sincere and prove to be the man I thought you were years ago, I'd be proud to be your wife."

Just then Sasha walked up. She looked at her mother and yelled, "Married? Are you and my daddy getting married?" She clasped her hands together.

"Slow your roll, little girl, we'll see." Sonyell smiled. She pulled Sasha's hand and guided her daughter to the chair next to hers.

Sasha looked at her father solemnly. "Grandma Nedra said you have demons and that's why you go to jail so much. Are your demons gone, Daddy?"

"Yes, they are." Michael smiled at his daughter. "You can tell my momma that I'm a changed man."

Sonyell looked at her daughter and Michael soberly. *If only it were that simple,* she thought. *I hope so. I hope to God that Michael is sincere and a changed man.* A shiver passed through her body and she tried to hold her fears at bay.

Marvin and his family returned to the table shortly after Sasha did. The family conversed a while longer. Then Marvin announced they were ready to go. "That drive from Chicago wore me out. We left for Marion early this morning after I got off work. We're staying here for the weekend, so we'll be back."

"Thanks for bringing my family here to see me for the holiday, bro," Michael said appreciatively to his brother.

"I hadn't been here in a minute to see you, so I figured I'd better get a visit in. We're all excited about your coming home. We just want you to do right and stay on the outside for a while," Marvin scolded his brother.

"No doubt." Michael nodded. "I was just telling Sonni, I've learned the error of my ways and I'm going to do right by her and Sasha."

"I hope so, man. Momma ain't getting no younger. It would be nice if she could see her baby boy doing right."

"I hear you," Michael said good-naturedly. "I hate to see you go, but knowing you'll be here for the weekend is a real treat."

"Momma," Sasha said glancing at Sasha, "where is Daddy going to stay when he gets out of here?"

"Wow." Sonyell raked her fingers through her hair. "We hadn't really talked about that. I guess we'll talk about it some more over the weekend."

"Wouldn't he stay with us? I mean he is my daddy," Sasha replied. She tugged her snowflake earring.

"We'll see," Sonyell replied vaguely. "There are still some decisions we have to make."

Marvin stood up. "We're going head out so we can check into the hotel." He held his hand out and the brothers shook hands. Ashley and the couple's daughters, Whitney and Jasmine, hugged Michael and told him good-bye. The family headed for the exit.

Sonyell stood up. "I guess we'd better be heading out too. Come on, Sasha, you will see your dad Saturday."

Sasha stood up reluctantly. "I wish we didn't have to go."

"By this time next month, we'll see each other on the regular. So do what your mom says," Michael instructed Sasha.

He stood and hugged Sasha for a long time. He whispered in her ear. She nodded at him admiringly. Then he turned to Sonyell. "I know your mind is going to go into overdrive, but I promise you, babe, everything is going to be fine. You just wait and see." He took her into his arms and held her tightly. He gave her a chaste kiss since Sasha was with them.

Sonyell took her daughter's hand. They walked toward the exit. Mother and daughter turned to wave to Michael before they left. Michael blew them a kiss in return.

Sonyell held Sasha's hand as they stood in line to be processed out. She closed her eyes and prayed with all her being that things would work out this time. She wanted her daughter to have both parents actively in her life. Sonyell sighed heavily and opened her eyes; she knew only time would tell. Sonyell and Sasha rushed to catch up with Marvin and his family.

Chapter Eighteen

Mariah walked upstairs to the second floor of Rosemary's house. She was surprised to see Rosemary up reading her Bible. "Unless you need me to do something, Granny, I'm going to head back to Hammond."

"No, child. You go on back and enjoy your visit with Carson's family." Rosemary closed the Bible and placed it on her nightstand.

"If you want to, you could spend the night with me. Carson invited you to dinner too," Mariah reminded her grandmother. She glanced at her reflection in the mirror, and fluffed her hair.

"No, I'm actually going to try to catch some sales tomorrow and do Christmas shopping," Rosemary told Mariah.

"There are stores in Hammond too. We could spend the weekend together."

"I'm sure you have better things to do than spend time with an old lady," Rosemary teased her granddaughter. "Seriously, I already made plans with Alma. I'm sure Carson will find something for you two to do over the holiday weekend. This is your first time meeting his family, so why don't you go ahead. If things continue to go well with you and him, I'll meet his family at a later date."

"Be that way," Mariah pouted. "I'm going to meet a bunch of strangers for the first time. I could use someone on my side. I absolutely detest meeting the parents and family en masse. All eyes will be on me."

"Carson will be there. I'm sure he'll take good care of you." Rosemary laughed.

"I'm glad to see you're in better spirits. I thought for sure Cassie had ruined your day."

"I try not to give Cassie that much control over my life. I was a little upset. I read my Bible and prayed. Now I feel better."

"That's good. Well, I'm going to head out and get the deed over with."

Rosemary rose from the bed. "I'll go downstairs with you."

They walked downstairs. Mariah had prepared a doggie bag to take with her. She put on her coat and kissed Rosemary good-bye. "I'll call you when I get in."

"Okay, just relax and be yourself. I'm sure things will go fine."

Mariah crossed her fingers. "I hope so."

She departed and within fifteen minutes, she was driving on the Bishop Ford Expressway headed to Indiana. Thirty minutes later, she exited at Kennedy Avenue and soon she parked the car down the street from the Palmer household.

Before she exited the car, she picked up a bag containing a sweet potato pie from the back seat. She laid it on the passenger seat. Mariah wrapped her scarf around her neck; then she gathered her purse and the bag. She closed the car door, pressed the remote, and locked the car. By the time she put her foot on the first step, the door flew open, and Carson came out to greet her.

"How are you doing?" Carson kissed Mariah lightly on her lips. "I've been peeping out the window for the past half hour looking for you."

"I'm good." She smiled at him. "I enjoyed my time with Granny—well, that is, until Cassie showed up— but all in all my day was good."

Carson took her free hand. "Great! My family is looking forward to meeting you."

The couple walked inside the Christmas light–lit, two-story black-and-white frame house. A wreath was perched on the front door. An older tall man with peanut-colored skin dressed in a green and orange print dashiki opened the door. His face creased into a bright smile. As the couple stepped over the threshold into the foyer, Mariah heard a babble of voices. Then conversation ceased, as eyes in the nearby vicinity traveled to Mariah and Carson.

Carson smiled at his father and said, "Poppy, this is my friend Mariah Green."

Mr. Palmer extended his hand and said in a dignified melodic voice, "Ms. Green, welcome to my humble abode."

Mariah dipped her head and said shyly, "Please call me Mariah. I'd like to thank you and your wife for inviting me to share your holiday."

An attractive, pleasing plump light-skinned woman dressed in a cranberry-covered two-piece pantsuit hurried into the foyer. She wiped her hands on a dish towel and slung it over her shoulder. She stepped in front of Mariah. "Hello, my name is Helen Palmer. You must be Mariah." Her eyes traveled the length of Mariah's body from head to toe.

"Yes, ma'am. I am Mariah. I was just thanking your husband and you too for inviting me today."

"You are quite welcome," Helen responded. She turned to her son. "Carson, take her coat and then introduce her to the rest of the family. When you're done, then bring her to the dining room so she can eat."

After Carson hung Mariah's coat in the closet, he put his arm across her shoulders. He led her to the dining room. An older couple sat on the love seat. "Mariah,

these are my grandparents, Winston and Suzette Palmer. They are my father's parents. Gram and Granddaddy, this is my friend Mariah."

The older man stood up gallantly. "Pleased to meet
you, young lady. We've heard nothing but good things
about you from Carson." A fuzz of white hair covered
his head.

"You're a pretty young lady," Suzette observed in a
quivery voice.

"Thank you, the pleasure is mine," Mariah replied.
She had a feeling Carson's grandparents would be the
only relatives who wouldn't give her a hard time that
evening.

The elderly couple asked Mariah a few background
questions; then Carson whisked her off to meet other
relatives.

They walked downstairs to the basement. Carson
introduced Mariah to his aunts and uncles. Some were
listening to Christmas music, while others played spir-
ited games of bid whist and dominoes. Children were
playing a Wii game on a big-screen television.

Mariah and Carson returned upstairs and strode into
the dining room. Carson's sisters looked expectantly at
their brother for an introduction.

He pointed each sister out. "That's Michelle; she's
the oldest. Then, Veronica—we call her Ronnie—Nadia, and you remember my sister Tiffany."

The sisters were very attractive women who strongly
resembled their brother. They were perfectly coifed
and dressed in expensive clothing.

Carson's sisters scrutinized Mariah carefully. The
women exchanged greetings. Carson pulled out a chair
at the dining room table and Mariah sat down.

"Say, are you hungry? My mom makes a mean caramel cake," Carson told Mariah.

Though she wasn't hungry, Mariah nodded her head.

"What would you like to drink?" Carson inquired solicitously.

"Water would be good," Mariah answered moistening her lips. Her heart sank as she watched Carson go into the kitchen. She took a deep breath and smiled at his sisters, who stared openly at her.

"Did you have a good holiday? I had dinner earlier with my grandmother and mother," Mariah volunteered.

"Yes, we had a good time." Michelle nodded. "We always spend holidays together. We rotate the holidays between our houses. Usually we have Christmas dinner here with our folks, but with Nadia being pregnant this year, we'll have the holiday at her house."

"That sounds good. So, Nadia." Mariah turned her attention to the obviously pregnant woman. "When is your due date? Are you having a girl or boy?"

"My date is December thirty-first, so I'm almost done. My husband, Rodney, and I chose not to learn the baby's sex ahead of time. We wanted to be surprised. It's out first baby, so we're excited."

"Do you have children?" Michelle asked Mariah.

"Good gracious no. No, just a goddaughter, my best friend Sonyell's daughter. Sasha is ten years old." Mariah's hand fluttered to her throat. She felt as if she were babbling.

"You sound like you don't want children," Veronica said in a mocking tone. "You know that Carson has two daughters, don't you?"

"Yes, Carson has told me about his daughters." Mariah thrust her chin up. "I guess I want children eventually, just not now."

The sisters' eyebrows rose as they glanced at one another.

Carson's Uncle David walked into the dining room. He said casually to Mariah, "Aren't you Harold Ellison's girl?"

"Yes, I'm his daughter," Mariah said in a prickly tone of voice. She folded her trembling hands together. The last name she expected to hear was her father's.

"I thought so, you look like him. You could have knocked me and the fellas over with a feather when we heard Harold had a daughter. A bunch of us used to go on a yearly fishing trip with him. He never mentioned having any children."

"Is that so?" Mariah looked up at him with her head tilted to the side. She didn't want to admit to Carson's family that she had never known her father.

It seemed like an era had passed before Carson returned from the kitchen, though it had only been several minutes. He handed Mariah a bottle of water and sat in the seat next to her. "Sorry it took me so long. I brought some ice from the freezer in the garage for my mom." He looked at his sisters. "I hope my sisters have been on their best behavior and not giving you a hard time."

The sisters rolled their eyes at him before Veronica replied sweetly, "Of course we have. We've just been chatting with Mariah, trying to get to know her better."

"Yeah, I was telling Mariah how me and the guys were surprised to know that Harold had a daughter. He had never mentioned having any children. And she wasn't ever around him. . . ." David commented.

The room became silent.

Then Carson said in a hearty tone of voice, "Well, you know how that goes sometimes, Uncle Dave. Let me tell you, though, Mariah is definitely her father's daughter. She's put her stamp on the community. Mariah is doing great things for Hammond, much like Mr. Ellison did."

Mrs. Palmer strolled into the room and heard the tail end of the conversation. Veronica stood so her mother could sit in her seat. She said to her brother-in-law, "David, would you bring some folding chairs from the basement? We seem to have run of seats."

David made a hasty retreat out of the room.

"So, Mariah, tell us about yourself? Do you have any sisters or brothers? How do you like living in Hammond so far? I love your idea for a senior hairstyle day. You've shaken up Hammond. I guess you have an entrepreneurial spirit like your dad?" Questions and comments spilled from Mrs. Palmer's lips.

"No, I don't have any siblings; I am an only child. So far I love living in Hammond. I was raised in Altgeld Garden, so Hammond is a refreshing change. I think the idea of hair care for seniors has gone over well. I guess I've always wanted to own my own business; I just didn't have the necessary funds. Thanks to my father, I am able to make some of my dreams come true."

"What a blessing." The corners of Mrs. Palmer's lips curved into a smile. "Do you have a church home or are you attending a church here in Hammond?"

"I belong to Christian Friendship Church in Chicago. I've been going there since I was a child. I work with the Sunday School ministry."

"Great. My sister, Vivian, attends Christian Friendship," Mrs. Palmer exclaimed. "I've worshipped there many times with my sister and her family. If I can do anything to help with your business endeavors, don't hesitate to call me. I own a catering business, and have done business with many business owners in the area and beyond."

"Thank you, I'll keep that in mind," Mariah replied. "I am always looking for opportunities to network. I have joined several business organizations and made good business contacts." She took a sip of water and set the bottle on the table. "What are your professions?" she asked the sisters.

"I am the assistant principal at Morton High School," Michelle said proudly. "In fact, I met with your business manager and several of our students participate in your internship program for hair stylists and barbers. I find your suggestions to be refreshing and look forward to any new ideas you may have to motivate our young people." Michelle nodded giving Mariah her sign of approval.

"I am a housewife," Veronica announced primly. "I have a degree in library science. Before my children were born, I worked as a librarian at one of branch libraries here in Hammond. I volunteer at a local hospital a few days a week. I love reading, so becoming a librarian was a no-brainer for me."

"I am a bookkeeper. I freelance and work from home," Nadia added to the conversation. "I also help keep Carson on track with his business. I am a CPA."

"I work for Carson. I'm a carpenter," Tiffany admitted with an impish grin. "I was always a tomboy. I loved helping my dad when he repaired broken items when I was a child. I like working with my hands. So I became the first female on the crew. It helps when your brother is the owner." She grinned at Carson.

"You all have varied skill sets. That is so interesting. And not all of you took the traditional career path." Mariah couldn't help but be impressed by the sisters.

"Luckily, our parents instilled in us a good work ethic. They encouraged us to go into field that would make us happy. It was easy for us to find our niches in life," Michelle said.

The women continued chatting. Carson entered the doorway of the room and found Mariah deep in conversation with his sisters. His mother would interject comments now and then. He felt good that Mariah seemed to mesh with his family.

He glanced at his watch and returned to the living room to peep out the window. *Lola should have dropped off the girls at least an hour ago.* Carson hoped against hope that Lola would stay in the car and allow the girls to walk to the front door unaided. That hope was short-lived as Carson watched his ex-wife and his daughters walk on the path leading to the house. Carson reluctantly opened the door.

Chapter Nineteen

Mariah and Carson's sisters heard the front door open and then close. Their eyes traveled to the dining room entrance. Tiffany looked at her sisters and shook her head. She gave Mariah an apologetic look.

Carson strolled into the dining room holding the hands of his two daughters. Mariah caught her breath. The youngest girl was the mirror image of Carson. She had thick, wavy hair, with a gap between her two upper teeth. Her green eyes were a testament to her paternity.

The older girl was breathtakingly beautiful. She smiled at her aunts. Then her gaze fell on Mariah. She looked Mariah up and down; her nose twitched in the air. She turned to her father and asked in Spanish, "Who is she?"

"Now, Ali, we will not have that," Carson firmly chastised her daughter. "Please speak in English. She's a friend of mine. Please act like you were taught manners. I want you and Ashanti to meet Ms. Green."

Mariah rose from her seat self-consciously and pushed a lock off her face. She pasted a smile on her face.

As he introduced the girls to Mariah, Carson's ex-wife, Lola, stepped into the room. Gazing at her it was obvious to Mariah whom Carson's oldest daughter had inherited her looks from. Lola was model thin. She looked as if she wore a size zero. Her shiny raven-colored hair cascaded over her shoulders. Deep dimples were carved into her high cheekbones.

"*Hola,* everyone," she said boisterously as she slipped off her black sable coat. Lola handed it to Carson. Carson sighed as he put the coat over his arm. Then, he walked to the closet and hung up the coat. He quickly returned to Mariah's side.

The smile on Lola's face faded as her gaze fell on Mariah. Then she shrugged her shoulders and walked over to Carson, Mariah, and her daughters.

"I don't believe I've had the pleasure. My name is Lola Palmer. I am Carson's ex-wife. Who are you?" Her dark eyes seemed to probe into Mariah's soul.

"My name is Mariah." She thrust out her hand. "I am a friend of Carson's. Your daughters are simply beautiful." *I will not let this woman intimidate me.*

All conversation seemed ceased in the house. Carson's relatives' attention was glued on Mariah and Lola. The family members knew that Lola considered herself a diva to the max.

"Yes, they are." Lola smiled down at her daughters. She ignored Mariah's hand.

Carson clasped his hand around Mariah's waist. He told Lola smoothly, "Mariah is a very good friend of mine."

The light in Lola's eyes dimmed at bit. Her lips turned down upon hearing Carson declare Mariah as a good friend. Lola had known Carson since she was fourteen years old. She was aware that her ex-husband didn't invite just anyone into the inner sanctum of his parents' home.

Lola sashayed to the other end of the table. She began talking with her ex-sisters-in-law.

Tiffany gestured to Mariah to join her in the kitchen, while Carson and his daughters chatted. The two women walked into the kitchen and stood by the sink.

"In my brother's defense, Carson didn't invite Lola to dinner. She can be a bit overbearing. If you stand your ground with her, she tends to leave you alone. But at any sign of weakness, she will walk all over you."

Mariah smirked and waved her hand. "Carson and I are just friends. Lola has nothing to fear from me."

"Are you kidding me?" Tiffany exclaimed incredulously. "You are the first woman Carson has brought home since his divorce from Lola. You feel me?" Tiffany nodded her head.

Carson walked into the room. "Tiff, are you telling Mariah all my secrets?" He scolded his sister.

"Sorry, I just wanted to give Mariah a heads-up about Lola. You know how she can be." Tiffany smiled guiltily at her brother. Then, she went back into the dining room.

"I wish you had told me your ex was coming," Mariah remarked unhappily. "I wasn't quite ready for meeting your folks, your daughters, and her."

"Trust me, Lola's being here wasn't planned," Carson apologized. "I was going to pick up the girls myself. Then Lola volunteered to bring them since she's going to her parents' house. They don't live too far from here."

"I guess I'll forgive you this time." Mariah exhaled loudly. "Next time, just give me notice if there's a possibility she'll be around."

"I promise." Carson pulled her into his arms. He leaned down and lightly kissed her lips. "Everyone seems to like you. I know you were worried about that. The only people I was concerned about were my parents. Although at the end of the day, who I choose to see is my choice. Anyway, I can tell they approve of you."

"Hmmm, Granny likes you too." Mariah snuggled against Carson. Then she pulled away from him. "I guess we should be getting back, before someone wanders in to check on us."

Carson grabbed her hand and they returned to the dining room.

Lola finally left the house thirty minutes later. She stared suspiciously at Mariah when she thought Mariah wasn't looking at her.

As the evening progressed, Mariah felt more comfortable with Carson's family. She loved the way the family interacted with one another. Carson was a caring father, solicitous of his daughters' feelings. Ashanti was warm with Mariah. The younger girl's personality was much like her father's, while Aaliyah was aloof.

The men retired to the rec room to watch the basketball game. The women sat around the dining room table talking. Mariah confided in Carson's mother and sisters her plans for opening the transitional home. The Palmer women were impressed by the young woman and offered to help in any way they could.

Mariah could not help but feel the love in the room. There were family dynamics present that she wished had been present with herself, Rosemary, and Cassie. She knew Rosemary would have enjoyed being with the Palmer family that evening.

Finally at eight o'clock, Mariah excused herself and decided to go home. She walked to the rec room and gestured to Carson.

They stood in the hallway. "I'm going to go home," she informed him.

"Do you have to leave now?" Carson asked as they walked upstairs and to the foyer.

"Yes. I might go back to the city tomorrow and go Christmas shopping with Granny."

"You're welcome to hang out with me and the girls tomorrow," Carson offered as he removed Mariah's coat from the closet.

"I know. But I think I need to come around them a little bit more before I intrude on your time with them."

"Fair enough." Carson held up his hands in a conceding manner. He held Mariah's coat, and she slipped it on. Carson was at her side as she bid everyone farewell. She thanked Mrs. Palmer for having her to dinner.

"It was my pleasure," the older woman preened. "We enjoyed having you. Thank you for bringing the pie. It tasted wonderful. Don't be a stranger, and you don't have to wait on Carson to bring you here, feel free to stop by anytime," Helen told Mariah warmly.

"Thank you so much, Mrs. Palmer. I may take you up on that." Mariah grinned.

Ashanti walked to Mariah. "It was nice meeting you, Ms. Mari. I hope to see you again." She smiled shyly at Mariah.

"It was nice meeting you and your sister," Mariah responded. She looked at Aaliyah. The young girl looked past Mariah.

Carson grabbed his jacket out of the closet. "I'll walk you to the car."

The pair walked outside and down the block to Mariah's car. Carson took the keys from Mariah's hand. He unlocked and opened the car door. Mariah got inside the car. She started the car, and rolled the window down. "I had a great time. Your family is awesome. I'll call you when I get home," she promised.

Carson leaned into the open window and kissed Mariah. "Please do."

She shifted the car into drive and pulled off. She glanced back and Carson stood in on the stairway waving at her. She tooted her horn.

Before long Mariah arrived home. She parked the SUV in the driveway, and walked inside the house. She took off her coat and hung it in the closet. After she turned on the lights in the living room, Mariah kicked her shoes off, and tucked her legs on the sofa. She then mulled over the day's events.

Her cell phone rang interrupting her thoughts. "Hello," she said after pulling the phone from the bottom of her purse.

"Hey, Mari. How was your day?" Sonyell asked.

"Good and bad," Mariah answered truthfully.

"Tell me the bad first, then the good," Sonyell prompted Mariah. She crossed her legs as she reclined in the bed. Sasha was having fun with her cousins in Marvin and Ashley's hotel suite.

"Well, you know, I went to Granny's house and everything was going well, except Granny didn't mention that she'd invited Cassie to dinner. Things went well for about five minutes and then Cassie started with her usual sob story. You know the drill, how Granny puts me before her. Things went downhill after that and Cassie ended up storming out."

"That's too bad," Sonyell stated. "I know your grandmother wants all of you to get along." Sonyell picked the remote control from the nightstand, and powered on the television.

"That wasn't the worst. Cassie has been hinting about a mystery surrounding my birth, and she acts like she has the goods on Granny or something," Mariah admitted. "She's been doing that for a while."

"You didn't tell me about that," Sonyell exclaimed. She dropped the remote control on the bed.

"I didn't mention it because I assumed it was because Cassie was high. But now I'm not sure," Mariah said indecisively.

"Talk to your grandmother again, that's all you can do," Sonyell opined. She picked up the remote and channel surfed.

"You're right, but sometimes I'm scared to. I know whatever happened had to be bad."

"I'm going to repeat this again, talk to your grandmother. She is the only one who can clear the matter up."

"Okay, I will, when the time is right," Mariah promised. "You know I went to Carson's parents' house for dinner, right?"

"Yes, I know. How did that go?" Sonyell inquired nosily.

"Pretty good. His family was nice, although I know his sisters were giving me the once-over. Of course they asked me fifty million questions. That wasn't the bad part. His ex-wife, who, I might add, is drop-dead gorgeous, dropped his daughters off at his parents' house. If looks could kill, I would be dead." Mariah flexed her hand.

"She was that bad?" Sonyell asked in an incredulous tone of voice. Her eyes widened.

"I tried to play it off. But yes, she was pretty bad. His oldest daughter was very wary of me. She was a clone of her mother."

"What about the youngest girl? How was she?" Sonyell craved details.

"She was a sweetie. I really liked her. She reminds me a lot of Carson. She even looks like him."

"Well, one out of two isn't bad," Sonyell quipped. "Suppose neither one of them liked you?" She smoothed her top down which had risen up.

"You have a point there. Carson invited me to hang with him and the girls."

"What did you tell him?" Sonyell took a can of Pepsi from the nightstand and sipped.

"I told him I didn't want to intrude on their father-daughter time. I think I need to be around them a little longer"

"Go with your instinct." Sonyell set the can down on the nightstand. "But if the relationship is going to move forward, then you need to get to know his daughters."

"You're right." Mariah sighed. "I could tell Carson wants me to spend time with all of them."

"You got yourself a package deal, girl. I'm so proud of you," Sonyell teased her friend. "You are a true case of never say never."

"Yeah, I guess so. Enough about me; how is Michael?" Mariah changed the subject.

"He's good. Making all the promises he usually does when he's about to be released. Oh, I forgot, he wanted me to find out if there is something he can do, as in work for you?"

"Is he going to live with you and Sasha?" Mariah asked. "Doesn't he have to stay in the city and not cross state lines?"

"If he had been released on parole then that would have been the case. But, he's served his sentence. He just wants to find a job."

"I hadn't thought about it," Mariah responded. "Let me think about it."

"I don't want you to feel obligated. However way you decide is fine with me."

"Where's Sasha? I know it's too early for her to be asleep."

"She's spending the night with Marvin and Ashley. Their room has an adjoining suite for the girls. So Ashley invited Sasha to stay with the girls."

"I know Sasha is enjoying that. So do you think Michael is ready to make a change this time? Is he a reformed man?"

"You know Michael." Sonyell exhaled loudly. "He has the best intentions in the world for about two weeks after his release date. Then things change quickly. Sasha is older and she is already asking Michael hard questions. That's why I don't want you to feel obligated to help him. Let's just wait and see how he's acting by week three."

"Girl, you know you're not any good." Mariah laughed. "Seriously though, I can put out some feelers. I have a few associates who own their own businesses. I can do some checking."

"Miss Nedra has been talking to Reverend Dudley. Maybe he might be able to come up with something."

"You didn't answer me, Sonni. Is Michael going to live with you?"

Sonyell tittered nervously. "I really haven't decided. Sasha asked me the same question. My heart wants to say yes, but my head says wait until week three is up."

"That sounds reasonable to me."

"I guess we both have some hard decisions to make. Like you talking to Granny."

"I guess we do. I also sense Ms. Lola, that's Carson's ex, still has feelings for him. You know I don't want to have to deal with baby momma drama."

"Don't let Satan steal your happiness. You better claim that man, because he has surely claimed you. I think he just wants to see how well you get along with his daughters. So be cautious, but still take the time to get to know them. Girl, you'd better claim that fine man God has sent to you."

The friends shared peals of laughter.

"I'm going to let you go. Did you talk to Rocki?" Mariah asked Sonyell.

"I did this morning; she texted me this afternoon. She planned to hit the clubs with her cousins. I'm sure she's out having a good time right about now."

"I talked to her this morning too. Okay, sista, I'm going to call Granny and then I am going to settle in for the night. Oh, I found some journals belonging to my father. When I get the time, I plan to read them."

"Good idea. Where did you find them and how many did you find?"

"In the corner of the attic in a trunk. I think there are about twenty or more volumes. A part of me wants to read them. And, the other part doesn't. Silly, huh?" Mariah snickered nervously.

"No, not silly, just overly cautious like you tend to be. You know everything you want to know about your dad can be found in those books. Don't you?"

"Yeah. I've just been so busy I haven't had time to read them. I will get around to doing that soon."

"Okay. Have a good night."

"You too, Sonni. I love you."

"Love you too, Mari."

The friends ended the call.

Mariah laid her head against the back of the sofa. Then she sat up, swung her legs off the sofa, put her shoes on her feet, and went upstairs to the attic. She walked to a corner of the room and opened a black and gold antique steamer trunk. Mariah bent over and she removed a few journals from the trunk. She opened one journal to see the time frame of the book. It took her a few minutes before she removed two black leather-bound journals, labeled volumes 1 and 2.

She closed the trunk, turned off the lights, and returned to the living room. She laid the books on an end table and picked up the remote control. She clicked the television on and stared at the journals. "I wonder what secrets you hold," she said aloud. Then she stared at the television until it stared back at her.

Chapter Twenty

On Tuesday, a week before Christmas, Mariah sat at her desk in her office at work. She was looking over the final version of the paperwork to be submitted to the city of Hammond for the transitional home. Attorney Cook had faxed the papers to her that morning. The office was silent save for Mariah flipping the pages as she read. When she was done, a rush of adrenaline surged through her body. She was another step closer to realizing her dream. Mariah picked up the telephone and called the lawyer. After they exchanged greetings, Mariah effusively exclaimed, "William, good job. I am quite pleased. I just hope we hear something favorable from Hammond in the not too distant future."

"Thank you, Mariah. These matters take time, but I am sure we will hear something one way or the other within sixty days or so. We may have to make modifications to our proposal, but I know the transaction will eventually be approved."

"That sounds good. I know the process takes time. I am impatient to get the project started." Mariah tapped an ink pen on the desk.

"Just be patient." Attorney Cook chuckled. "I planned to call you anyway to tell you that the attorney handling the estate of the house next door to yours called this morning to inform me the court finally approved the sale of the property. You should be able to close on the house next month after the first of the year."

"That's more good news," Mariah cried happily. "Don't get me wrong, I enjoy staying in my father's house, but it's too big for me. I am so ready to move into my own house."

"I understand. Is there anything else I can do for you?"

"I can't think of anything else at this minute. I will call you back if anything else comes up. William, have a great holiday," Mariah told him happily.

"You too, Mariah. Merry Christmas."

The telephone call ended.

Mariah pushed the button on the phone connecting her to Sonyell's office. Then she disconnected the call. She remembered today was the day Michael was to be released from prison and Sonyell had taken the day off. Mariah quickly dialed Carson's number. She told him the good news.

"That's great news. A celebration is in order. How about going out to dinner tonight?"

"I had actually planned to do some Christmas shopping. I've decided to have the holiday dinner at my house. I figured if the weather becomes inclement, everyone can spend the night there."

"Do you want company? I should probably ask what kind of shopping you're doing first," Carson teased her.

"Well, you may want to pass on joining me. I'm planning on going to Carson Pirie Scott to buy gifts for Granny, Sonni, and Rocki. Then I'm going to head over to Best Buy to get a Wii system for Sasha. I wanted to ask you about buying gifts for your girls. What do you think?"

"I guess so. Best Buy sounds like fun, and Carson not so much fun. I plan on finishing up around here at five o'clock. I can pick you up around five-thirty and after shopping we can have dinner. I have a taste for Mexican food. How about Pepi?"

"That sounds like a plan. I have an idea of what I'm buying everyone, so shopping shouldn't take long. The timing will just depend on the crowd."

"Sounds like a plan. Uh, Mari, are you buying something for your mother? Do you plan on inviting her to dinner on Christmas?"

"I . . . I don't know," Mariah replied guiltily. "I guess so. I will never hear the end of it from Granny if I don't get her anything. I'll have to think about it some more. I still have flashbacks of the disaster on Thanksgiving."

"You should be patient, and most of all remember the scripture, be forgiving. Obviously something in the past has caused her destructive behavior. Once you figure that out, and confront her with it, maybe she'll get help. Who knows, maybe your relationship will get better."

"I doubt that." Mariah snorted. "I asked Granny again if there was anything she wanted to tell me about my father and mother, and she said no. But, I know she's keeping something from me. I guess she'll tell me in her own time. I don't want to pressure her too much considering her medical conditions: asthma and hypertension."

"Okay, babe, I've got to run. I'll see you later."

"Talk to you later." Mariah pressed a button and ended the call. She sat back in her chair and felt a sense of contentment. Life was certainly grand. Her plan was making progress, even if it was baby steps. Her relationship with Carson was deepening. The only problem was Lola. She seemed to have no sense of boundary where Carson was concerned.

The couple had gone to a movie a couple of weeks ago, when Carson's cell phone vibrated. He excused himself and went to the lobby to return the call. One of the toilets in Lola's condominium had backed up and she wanted Carson to come over and look at it. Carson ended up sending Alex over to the house, much to Lola's chagrin.

Lola had dropped over at Carson's house unexpectedly a couple of times, causing Carson to cancel his and Mariah's plans. Mariah had made her displeasure known to Carson, and asked why he didn't put a stop to Lola shenanigans. Mariah was tired of Lola calling Carson at the hint of any trouble.

Carson had looked into Mariah's eyes and said his daughters were the reasons why. Mariah mustered up the courage to ask Carson if he thought Lola was still in love with him. He hesitated before he finally responded that he didn't think so. He further explained how Lola was territorial and she didn't want to let go. Carson reassured Mariah that he didn't love Lola in a romantic way, but he had feelings for his ex as the mother of his children.

He further explained about his ex-wife's competitive and jealous nature. That's what had broken up the marriage. In the past, Lola had run off a few women Carson had dated along with Aaliyah's help. Carson pleaded with Mariah to be patient with him; he planned on changing how he responded to Lola's requests. Mariah told him that she would.

Mariah closed eyes. Her body was relaxed as the smooth jazz sounds from the radio serenaded her. She opened her eyes and turned her attention back to her work, looking forward to her date with Carson.

That evening after filling Carson's truck with bags after a shopping spree at Carson Pirie Scott on Indianapolis Boulevard, Carson and Mariah feasted on tacos and chicken fajitas at Pepi's Restaurant.

"That was good," Mariah proclaimed. "I haven't had Mexican food in a while." She wiped her hands on a napkin and sipped from a glass of 7 Up.

"I agree." Carson nodded after he swallowed his last bite of tacos. "So are you done shopping yet?"

"I have one more gift to get and that's yours. I haven't quite run across your gift yet," Mariah told him.

"You don't have to go to any trouble you know. I'm an easy kind of guy."

"I know. I just don't know what to get you. It's one of those situations where when I see it I'll know it's for you. Know what I mean?"

The young waitress returned to the table. "Can I get you anything else?" she asked politely with a smile on her face.

Mariah returned her smile and shook her head.

"We're good for now," Carson replied.

"Then I'll bring the check shortly. Let me know if you need anything else." She left the table.

"Now let's see, where we were? Oh, I remember, I guess I know what you mean," Carson agreed.

"I am not a shopper by nature, but I do enjoy Christmas shopping. It's something about the music, and smiles on children's faces, that puts me in the spirit. That along with the birth of Christ," she added quickly.

"I understand; same here. Say, I noticed you don't have any lights or decorations around your house. Do you want me to stop by and put some up for you tomorrow?"

"Sure. I meant to ask you earlier, but got caught up on working with William on the proposal for the city of Hammond. Growing up in the projects, there's only so much you could do on the outside of the house. Granny and I always put up a tree and decorated the living room. I noticed the lights on your parents' house on Thanksgiving Day."

"Yeah, I guess having children makes a difference. When I was growing up, we always put up our tree on

Thanksgiving night or the Thanksgiving weekend. So I've gotten into the habit of doing it then."

"I hear you, traditions are nice. So is Christmas your favorite holiday?" she asked him.

"It is. What is yours?"

"Thanksgiving," Mariah answered promptly. "I love the foods, even preparing some of them." She wrinkled her nose. "My favorite hot holiday is the Fourth of July. The temperature for Memorial Day can be cool. I love warm weather, and unless it rains, the Fourth is always nice. Sonni, Rocki, and I would go downtown to the lake sometime to see the fireworks."

The waitress brought the check to the table and set the leather folder containing the check in front of Carson. "Enjoy your evening, and happy holidays."

"Thank you," Carson replied. He took his wallet out of his jacket pocket and pulled out his American Express card. He checked the figures and added a nice tip to the total.

After his card was processed, he told Mariah, "I hate to rush you, but I have an early appointment in the morning. So I need to get you home."

"I understand," Mariah replied. She stood up and put on her coat. Soon the two left the restaurant and were at Mariah's house in no time.

Carson walked her to the door and opened it. Mariah disengaged the burglar alarm.

Carson brought Mariah's shopping bags inside the house. "I will be glad when you move next door. Sometime I worry about you being in this house alone. It's a big house," he commented as his eyes scanned around the room.

"If it wasn't for the alarm system, I would be worried too. I'm fine."

"That you are," Carson agreed in a husky voice. "I'd better be getting on my way." He pulled her into his arms and kissed her passionately.

"See you tomorrow," Mariah said emotionally. "Carson, I just want to say that I appreciate all you have done for me. You've enriched my life. I feel like I'm a better person for having known you. Thank you."

"I love doing things for you," Carson began. "You are a phenomenal woman. I feel the same way; my life seems complete. We'll see where this thing goes. So far, my lovely, you're batting a thousand."

Mariah hugged him. When they parted, she pointed to the door and said, "Go, I'll see you tomorrow."

"Pleasant dreams," Carson said as he walked to the door.

"Back at you."

Mariah smiled to herself as she locked the door. She walked to the window and watched Carson as he pulled away from the curb. Then she walked to her bedroom. She knelt down, closed her eyes, raised her hands, and said, "Father, Carson is a good man. Thank you for bringing him into my life. Forgive me for my sins today. Continue to guide me, and help me to hear your voice clearly. Today was a good day, Father. I rejoice and I am glad. God, bless and take care of Granny, Sonni, Rocki, and Sasha. Lord, also bless Carson, and his family. Amen."

Mariah showered and put on her bedclothes. She opened the Daily Devotional and read the message for today, along with the Biblical verses.

She sighed audibly as she caught sight of the journals on her nightstand. Mariah took a deep breath. Her hand shook slightly as she picked up volume 1. She opened it and read the first entry.

My name is Harold Wayne Ellison. I was born on August 23 in Gainesville, Florida. I never knew my mother or father. My earliest memories are being in a large room full of cots. I was raised in an orphanage. I never found a trace of my parents. Perhaps they perished together, and that's how I ended up where I did. Maybe my ma was an unwed mother. Those were questions that I never got an answer to. I always worked, even as child. We had chores at the orphanage, and from the time a child could walk, they were put to work. I don't remember anyone explaining to me about having any goals. In my heart I knew that one day, I would grow up and leave that place. Me and the other kids were farmed out like slaves for lack of a better term to help people in the area. The orphanage got the money and it seemed like all we kids got is a heap of misery. Some of the homes were nice and some not so nice. Most of the time, we worked for white families. I saw the differences in how Whites and Blacks lived. We were called Negroes back then. I knew that I wanted better for myself and that's what I strived for my entire life: better. On many levels I attained my goals, but others I failed miserably.

Mariah was mesmerized after she read that entry. She quickly closed the book. She knew if she continued reading she would be up the rest of the night, and that wouldn't do for the career woman that she was. She glanced at the clock on the mantle and saw that it was nearly ten o'clock. She hadn't talked to Sonyell all evening, nor had her friend returned the text message Mariah had sent her earlier. Mariah hoped Michael's homecoming celebration was a joyous one. Still she was bothered that Sonyell hadn't called.

Mariah clutched the cell phone in her hand. Then she decided not to call to Sonyell. She and Michael had many issues to work out. Knowing Sonyell as Mariah did, she assumed that's what the couple was doing at that minute.

Chapter Twenty-one

Michael nuzzled against Sonyell's chest. "Baby, I am so glad to be home," he said. Michael's voice was slightly slurred. The two were sitting on the sofa in her house. Sasha had finally gone to bed. The young girl was ecstatic that her parents were finally together. It was her fervent hope that she would have a mommy and daddy who lived in the same household.

The odor of liquor on Michael's breath turned Sonyell's stomach. She firmly pushed him away. "You know this is not a good start, don't you?" she asked Michael, barely masking the disgust she felt from her voice.

"I don't know what you mean." Michael looked at her puzzled. He pulled her toward him again.

"I mean you aren't supposed to be drinking are you?" Sonyell scooted away from him.

"Remember, I'm not on parole. I am a free man, so I can darn well do as I please." Michael shot Sonyell a look that begged her not to nag him. His voice was even as he said, "I haven't been outside for a long time. So what if I had a few drinks with my friends? It's not a big deal; it's not like I'm drunk or anything."

"You're not setting a good example for Sasha. I rarely drink around her. You have to remember that you're a parent now and what you do around our daughter influences her." Sonyell's lips were tight as she glowered at him.

"Okay, I messed up," Michael replied in a petulant tone, as he raised his hands. "I'll talk to her tomorrow and tell her that I was celebrating being out of the joint. I'll explain this isn't an everyday thing." He stroked Sonyell's hair.

"Thank you, I'd appreciate that." Sonyell moistened her lips. "Uh, Michael, you can spend the night here, but you can't sleep in my bed. Once again, I don't think it sets a good example for Sasha. It's not like we're married." She peered at Michael with a nervous look on her face.

"Woman, are you crazy or something?" Michael's voice rose. He eyes widened as he stared at her in disbelief. "Do you know how long it's been since I been with you?"

Sonyell put her finger across her lips, and shook her head warningly. "Keep your voice down. Sasha is asleep. I don't want her to wake up and hear us arguing. I know it's been a long time. I don't even know that I want to have sex with you. I'm still thinking about it."

"Why wouldn't you want to make love to me? Is there another man you haven't told me about?" Michael asked her. His eyes shone with hurt.

"Of course not. Don't be silly." Sonyell twisted her lips. "Mike, you've spent so much time in jail that you don't realize how hard it is to raise a child alone. Especially a female child. I try to live a decorous life because I don't want Sasha to repeat the mistakes that I've made. I certainly don't want her to become an unwed mother at an early age. What kind of signal am I giving her if I allow you to come and lay up in here?" She spoke patiently to Michael trying to explain her position.

"I bet Mari has been influencing you," Michael muttered harshly. "Didn't you tell me she's been celibate?

Hon, our situation is not like Mari's at all. I'm Sasha's father. Seeing me here would be the most natural thing in the world."

Michael's hand wandered to Sonyell's thigh. She quickly pushed it away.

Sonyell held up her left hand. "Hello? We are not married. Sasha and I go to church and I talk to her about waiting until marriage before she has sex. So how can I possibly have sex with you under these circumstances? I certainly wouldn't be practicing what I preach, now would I?"

Michael rubbed his chin. "I guess I kind of see what you mean, but, baby, I think you're being unrealistic. Why wouldn't you put her on the pill to stop her from getting pregnant? You know like I do that most teenagers are going to do 'it.' It's simply a matter of time."

"Oh, Michael." Sonyell shook her head dismally. "That would probably work if she hadn't been taught different. I hear what you're saying, but I want her life to mirror mine. I want her to wait to have sex. I'm hoping she'll wait until marriage."

"I guess. . . ." Michael replied doubtfully. He looked down. Then he looked at Sonyell and his eyes brightened. "Are you saying that you want to get married? Heck, we can do that. I ain't got a problem with it." He took her hand in his.

"No, that's not what I'm saying," Sonyell said impatiently and snatched her hand away from his. "We certainly won't be married anytime soon." Her eyes narrowed. "I mean we've got to see how long you can stay out of prison before we make any long-term plans."

"Dang it, girl, I thought you wanted to marry me. Are you sure you're not seeing another man? Where is all of this coming from?" Michael looked at Sonyell with a confused look on his face.

"It's coming from a single parent, like a good many African American women. I love you, Mike, and I have for a long time. But we haven't spent enough time together, at least for extended period of time. You've been gone for a good portion of Sasha's childhood. I think we need to take things slow and see if we're the same people who fell in love with each other. You've got to step to me correctly." Sonyell gently punched his arm. "And that means getting a job, spending time with me and your daughter, and no sex until I have a ring on it," she stated resolutely.

Michael looked at her with a panicked look on his face. He shook his head dumbfounded, and raised his hands. "I don't know, Sonyell. This is not what I envisioned for my first night home. Shoot, I planned to rock your world. I mean, it's been a long time for both of us. Hasn't it?" He looked at her suspiciously.

Sonyell bit her bottom lip apprehensively. "It has, but what if it hadn't? I have been alone for a long time, going to school, raising our child. I've been there for you, too. I've come to visit you, put money on your account at least for your birthday. But today is a new day, Mike. I want you to be the man you promised me you would be before you started all that foolishness, a life of crime."

Michael studied Sonyell for a long while. "I can take many things, Sonni. I did my bid, I paid for my mistakes; as the man says, I paid my debt to society. But, I if I find out that you've been with another man then it's over," he informed Sonyell coldly.

"Like you've been one hundred percent faithful over the years." She sniffed, and waved her hand dismissively. "Don't think I don't know about other women visiting you over the years. What were they, your pen pals? But I felt secure knowing that I had your child and to me that made me better than them. I was one up on them. I'm not going to say I wasn't tempted because I was. I was eighteen when you first went to prison. I'm twenty-nine now and you think I wasn't tempted?"

Michael looked like he'd been sucker-punched. "Those women came to see me years ago, before you got pregnant. I don't know what to say. I know it's been hard on you too. You pulled your weight and raised our daughter to be a beautiful young girl. The thought of you being with another man drives me crazy," he said ominously.

"Then don't think about it," Sonyell told him. Her voice rang with passion. "Think about where we go from here. Focus on finding a job and helping me take care of your daughter. I love you and I shiver just thinking about being with you, but I can't. Not just yet."

Michael looked at Sonyell long and hard. He stood up; his high was gone. Suddenly he felt clearheaded. "Okay, I hear you and I will think about everything you've said. You've made your feelings clear. I'm going to go to my mom's for tonight. Tell Sasha I'll see her in the morning." He grabbed his jacket and put it on.

A tremor of guilt surged through Sonyell's body. Her head knew she was doing the right thing, but her heart was another matter. She watched Michael zip up his jacket and followed him to the front door. "Where are you going? How will you get back to the city?" she asked him.

"I'm a man, I'll figure it out," he grumbled. He opened the door. Then he turned to Sonyell, he pulled her into his arms, and kissed her with a passion that nearly made her swoon. "I love you, Sonni. I'll think about all you said. I'll talk to you tomorrow. Tell my baby girl I love her."

Michael closed the door behind him. Sonyell was tempted to run after him and tell him to come back. But she was scared that if she did that Michael would never man up. She realized that she had given him an abundance of food for thought. She prayed he would be up to the task.

She locked the door and returned to the sofa and sat down. She put her hands over her face. *Lord, did I do the right thing? How come doing the right thing feels so wrong?*

Sonyell contemplated her actions. She was tempted to call Raquel. Of the three friends, Raquel had the most experience with men. In her head, Sonyell could see Raquel mocking her. She had always called Michael a loser. So Sonyell knew that Raquel would have little patience with her fears. She turned out the light in the living room, made a hasty retreat to her bedroom, and quickly called Mariah.

"What's up, girl? How was Michael's homecoming celebration?" Mariah asked her friend after they exchanged hellos.

"Miss Nedra prepared a feast. All of Michael's relatives put in an appearance. Everything was going well until Shorty Man and GQ stopped by. They had liquor, Michael had a few drinks, and, needless to say, I was not impressed."

"Did he stay at his mom's house? Where is he now?" Mariah asked.

"I made the mistake of bringing him home with me. I think I just wanted to show off a little with the house and my accomplishments and bring him into my world. The only thing he had on his mind was jumping my bones."

"And you're surprised by that? You know he hasn't had any in a long time," Mariah teased Sonyell.

"True enough, but I couldn't do it. I thought the reason was because Sasha is in the house. And that was a big part of it. But, as I began explaining to him how I felt, I discovered I don't want to make love again without a ring on it."

"Oh, my. I'm shocked," Mariah exclaimed flabbergasted. "I mean that's the route I've chosen and, girl, sometimes it's so hard for me to be with Carson. All that manliness and virility around me, and I just can't do the thing. It's not easy. Thank God he understands my position. But, it's different with you and Michael because you have a history and share a child."

"That's pretty much what he said too, in his mission to try to convince me to give him some. But, I stood my ground. And he ended up leaving in a huff." Sonyell rubbed her eyes.

"You didn't discuss it with him before he came home did you?" Mariah asked.

"No, I didn't. I wanted to but the timing was never right. Now, I wish I had."

"Well, give him time. Mikey loves him some Sonni. He'll come around."

"Mari, I'm scared." Sonyell gulped. Her body began shaking uncontrollably. She used her free arm and wrapped it around her body.

"Scared of what?"

"I'm scared Michael won't be able to turn his life around. Then, I'm scared that he might be able to. I don't know what's wrong with me." She ran her hand nervously across her brow.

"I think if you're patient and give Michael time, he'll come around. He isn't a bad person. He fell in with the wrong crowd and made bad decisions. He's paid the price, and I believe he'll get it together."

"You're not just saying that to make me feel better are you?"

"No, I think it's good you're standing your ground. Michael was one of those fine, bad boys. It's time for him to grow up, if that's what he wants to do. If you slip up, I won't be mad at you. But you can't send mixed signals. Michael will pick up on it, and he'll have you back in the palm of his hand like he did back in the day."

"Yeah, you're probably right. I'm trying hard to do the right thing for Sasha's sake. I've been trying to teach her about the importance of not having sex at an early age. God knows I don't want her to end up like me." Sonyell leaned against the back of her bed and closed her eyes.

"You turned out okay, but you're right. Outside of the Biblical connotations, there are too many diseases floating around. I know you want to do the right thing for her. I understand and support you one hundred percent."

"Thanks, Mari, I needed to hear that. I thought about calling Raquel on a three-way, but I could just hear her saying, 'girl, are you crazy?' She would never understand why I feel so strongly about not having sex with Michael."

Mariah laughed. "You're right about that."

"I told Michael in no uncertain terms, sex is a no-go, not without a ring on it."

"Hmm, listen to you." Mariah chortled. "I didn't think you'd be able to stick to your guns with Michael up close and personal. You are full of surprises."

"In his own clumsy way, he proposed to me." Deep inside, Sonyell was thrilled and petrified at the same time.

"Get outta here. What did you say?" Mariah was all ears, soaking up the information.

"Humph. I think he popped the question to get me vulnerable so he could get the goodies," Sonyell replied candidly. "I told him we needed to take things slow and see how the relationship progresses. It seems like he's been in jail forever. I don't want to rush into something I might regret later."

Mariah nodded. She wholeheartedly agreed. "That was the right call. You have to give it time and see if Mr. Michael Fletcher has truly changed." She unwrapped a stick of gum and popped the gum in her mouth.

"Do you know, he had the nerve to accuse me of stepping out on him," Sonyell informed her friend, incensed. "He also implied if he found out that I had been messing that our relationship is over." Sonyell's eyes widened with disbelief at the thought.

"Girl, you must have really had him going for Michael to make those threats," Mariah commented.

"You got that right," Sonyell agreed. "I had to remind a brother of the women who came to visit him back in the day. You know men; in his mind that didn't count."

The doorbell chimed at Sonyell house. She glanced at the door. "Mari, hold on. Someone is at the door. It's probably Michael. I'll be right back."

"Take your time," Mariah told her friend. She checked a text message as she waited for Sonyell to see who was at the door.

After Sonyell opened the door, she nearly fainted. Her heart skipped a few beats. Two policemen stood on the front stairs along with Michael.

"Officers?" she asked nervously. She gripped her trembling hands together. "Is there a problem?"

The younger police man doffed his hat and said, "Ma'am, we found this gentleman loitering around your house. We asked him for his ID and asked him if he resided at the premises. He stated he didn't have his ID on him, and stated he's your boyfriend. We just want to make sure he is who he says he is."

Sonyell could see the look of rage on Michael's face. His face was red and the vein on the side of his neck pulsated rapidly. She prayed he would keep his anger in check. Sonyell's voice squeaked as she answered, "Yes, Officers, he is my boyfriend. He went outside for a smoke. No harm was done."

"Okay then, ma'am. We had to check his explanation. Better than safe than sorry. You two have a good night." The officers departed.

Michael walked into the house. He slammed his hand inside his fist. "Why do I feel like my rights have been violated?" he said with attitude.

"Michael where is your ID?" Sonyell asked him angrily. She folded her arms across her chest. "When you don't carry ID, you're looking for trouble."

"I accidently left my wallet at my mom's house. It's not like I was breaking the law or anything. I was outside smoking like you said. I was trying to figure out how I was going to get home." Michael paced the small area like a caged animal. Tension rose from his body.

Sonyell walked to him, and patted his arm. "I'm sorry you had to go through that. I know that must have brought flashbacks."

"Yeah, it did. It's not like I was picking your lock or something. I heard Indiana po-po ain't nobody to mess around with." Michael exhaled loudly and then went to sit in the living room. Sonyell followed him.

"Actually, I'm glad they checked with me. It's good to know the police are earning their keep. Why don't you stay here tonight? I'll drive you to the city before I go to work in the morning," Sonyell offered trying to ease Michael's shattered ego.

Michael ran his hand over his head. "I guess so. I guess that means I'm bunking on the couch huh?"

"Well, I do have a spare bedroom. You can stay there, but, no sneaking into my room in the middle of the night," she informed Michael in no uncertain terms.

"Lead the way, lady," he said humbly. Michael knew realistically the officers were doing their job. His head was plaited in corn-rows. He wore dark jeans and a dark hoodie. Most of all he was a black man. He could see how the officers could mistakenly think that he was trying to break into Sonyell's house. He followed Sonyell to the other side of the house.

"In there." She pointed to her third bedroom. "Oops, I forgot Mari is on the phone. Give me a minute and I'll give you a towel and soap so you can freshen up. I don't have any nightclothes for you to sleep in."

"Okay." Michael went inside the room and sat heavily on the bed. The night had not gone like he planned. He'd assumed he would be spending the night in Sonyell's bed. In his mind pajamas weren't needed.

Sonyell hurried to her bedroom and explained to Mariah what happened. After the call was completed, she went to the linen closet and removed towels, a bar of soap, and a spare toothbrush that she kept for guests.

When she went back into the guest bedroom, Michael was still sitting on the bed, his head dropped between his hands. "Here you go," she told him. "I found an extra-extra-large T-shirt. Perhaps you could sleep in it."

Michael stood up. "Sorry for what happened," he mumbled. "If I hadn't got upset about you turning me down, none of that would have happened. I hope none of your neighbors peeped that action." He pulled his hoodie off and laid it on the bed.

"I am not concerned about what people think. The police didn't take anyone out of the house. No one was arrested."

Michael glanced at the door, and Sasha was standing at the entrance. "What's up, baby girl?" he asked her.

"Is everything all right?" she asked tentatively. Sasha rocked from side to side. "I heard the doorbell ring and then I heard the police talking."

Sonyell walked over to her daughter. "Everything is fine. There was simply a misunderstanding."

"I was scared my daddy was going back to jail." She peered shyly at Michael.

Michael walked to the girl and knelt down by her. "Of course I ain't going back to jail. I have too much on the outside, right here inside this house, to ever think about going back and being locked up. I'm sorry the doorbell woke you up."

He stood up and hugged Sasha. "How about I tuck you back in bed?" He looked at Sonyell for confirmation. She nodded.

"I would love that, Daddy," Sasha said gravely as she held out her hand to her father.

Tears sprang to Sonyell's eyes as she watched father and daughter go inside Sasha's bedroom. She closed her eyes. "See, Lord, that's what I'm talking about. I want my daughter to feel secure and know that her father is there for her every night, to talk to, and to tuck her into bed and listen to her prayers. But will it happen?" Sonyell was besieged with doubts. She'd been there and done that.

Chapter Twenty-two

On Christmas morning, Mariah's eyes flew open like a child's. She turned and glanced at the clock; it was 6:00 A.M. She stretched her arms over her head and then burrowed back under the ecru-colored comforter. Mariah tried to go back to sleep, but sleep eluded her. She rose from the bed, put on her robe, and peeked out the window. A dusty covering of snow lined the sidewalk and street. Snowflakes twinkled on the branches of the trees. The scene outdoors looked like a Christmas card. Mariah smiled with contentment.

She tiptoed to her closet, opened the door, and removed two large garbage bags. She sneaked downstairs and laid the presents around the elaborately decorated, brightly lit giant Douglas fir tree. She sat on the sofa with her legs crossed and admired the tree. She looked up to see Sonyell and Raquel walking down the stairs with similar bags. Mariah giggled.

"Girl, what you doing?" Raquel asked. She and Sonyell stopped dead in their tracks when they spied Mariah.

"The same thing as y'all: playing Santa Claus," she informed her friends as she glanced at their hands. "The bags are a dead giveaway."

"Well, we've had plenty of practice. We've been doing this for a while," Raquel remarked as she set her bags on the floor. "Since Sasha was a baby. Thank God, we still don't have toys to assemble. I still have nightmares of us trying to put together her Barbie dream house."

"True. Remember how we ended up calling Marvin to come over around midnight? He ended up coming over to help us finish putting it together," Sonyell added, as the friends chuckled.

"And, here we are ten years later." Raquel shook her head. "Still playing Santa Claus." The women quickly spread the gifts around the tree.

Sonyell said, "I'm going to run upstairs and get my camera. The tree is simply beautiful. You and Carson did a great job decorating it," she complimented Mariah.

"Well, he did most of the work. It was fun though." Mariah beamed. "While you're getting the camera, I'll put on coffee. I have a feeling Miss Sasha will be up early. We had the hardest time getting her to bed last night, she was so excited. I want to thank both of you for spending the night with me. Sonni, even though you said it didn't matter, I know you preferred to be at your house with Michael."

Raquel grinned as she sat on the sofa. "Girl, there's no place I'd rather be."

"We visited my family earlier on Christmas Eve. Sasha, Mike, and I spent most of the day with Michael's family. He had family members visiting from out of town. So, I know he's in good hands. I know he's enjoying himself with his family. We've been together through thick and thin. So where else would I be?" Sonyell started walking toward the stairway. "I'll be right back."

When she returned a few minutes later, Mariah and Raquel were sitting in the kitchen. "Sasha was still asleep. I estimate we have another fifteen to thirty minutes before she will be up."

"We had fun last night, watching movies, eating of course, and just catching up," Raquel told the women.

"I really got a blast out of Sasha looking under the tree for her gifts. I thought we were going to have to pry that girl away from the tree."

"Yes, we did." Mariah took cups out of the cupboard for the coffee.

"So are you excited about Carson bringing his girls to dinner?" Sonyell asked Mariah. "That's a big step."

"Definitely. I've gone skating and bowling with Carson and the girls a few times. Aaliyah is still standoffish, but Ashanti is a little darling. She is such a sweet girl. She greets me with a hug. Aaliyah barely acknowledges my presence. Carson has to literally make her speak to me. Ashanti more than makes up for Aaliyah's behavior."

"Today is going to be interesting. Michael will be joining us for dinner, along with Carson and his girls. And you even invited Cassie. The evening will be interesting to say the least," Raquel commented as she rubbed her hands together.

"Let's not forget your new friend will be at dinner too," Sonyell reminded her friend.

"Yes, that's true. I couldn't let you all have all the fun. I met Louis at a networking event in Chicago last month, and we've been kicking it. I'm not in love like you two. Louis and I are having fun."

"I'm not in love," Mariah tried to protest halfheartedly.

"Girl, save it," Raquel sputtered as she held up her hand. "I know what time it is for both of you. Seriously though, I'm a little jealous. But I am happy for both of you. I must say, Michael is doing better than I expected. It's been what? A week and he hasn't landed back in jail yet."

"Now, you know that wasn't a nice thing to say. He had a job interview last week. Reverend Dudley set it up for him, with a steel mill here in Indiana. The company receives a subsidy for hiring ex-cons. His interview went well. So we're staying prayerful. Mariah was going to find something for him to do. But, I didn't want her on the hook if things didn't work out." Sonyell gave her friends an update.

Mariah stood up and checked the coffee maker. The aroma of hazelnut filled the room. She quickly prepared three mugs of coffee and set them on the table in front of her friends. With a cup of coffee in hand, she sat down and joined the women.

"So does that mean that he's going to move to Indiana?" Raquel asked. She sipped her coffee and set the mug on the table.

"I think so. It will really depend on where he ends up working."

Raquel shook her head. "And he's staying with you. I thought you said that was a no-no and you didn't want to give Sasha the wrong impression."

"He is living in my house, staying in the spare bedroom. Since he hasn't started working yet, this is a good time for him to spend time with Sasha."

"And, is he creeping in Mommy's bed, when the chickie is asleep?" Raquel couldn't help but ask.

"No, I'm firm on that. There is no hanky-panky going on," Sonyell stated decisively.

Raquel shook her head and sucked her teeth. "I swear I don't understand either of you. Especially you, Sonyell; it's not you haven't given it up to him before. Dang, he just got out of prison. I bet his hormones are raging like a teenage boy's."

"That's his problem, and not mine." Sonyell sniffed. She was becoming upset by the conversation.

"If he's getting it from someone else, then I'd say that's your problem," Raquel proclaimed. She stood up, walked to the counter, and poured herself another mug of coffee. "Do either of you want a refill?"

Mariah and Sonyell shook their heads.

"And you, Mariah, I don't understand you at all. Any other woman would have sampled the goods by now." Raquel looked at her friends wide-eyed, like they were creatures from another planet.

"See, that's why you need Jesus. You need to spend more time in church to cool off your hot behind," Mariah teased her friend. "Carson is okay with my celibacy. So, you need to get out of my video."

"Ditto that." Sonyell chortled.

Sasha ran into the kitchen in a pair of new red and green pajamas. "Mommy, come look. Santa Claus has been here," she shouted excitedly. "You should see all the presents he left here. It looks like the trees at the stores." She ran over to her mother, grabbed her hands, and pulled her away from the table. "Come on, Aunt Mari and Aunt Rocki, what are you waiting for?"

They made an exodus for the living room. They women sat on the sofa, while Sasha scampered under the tree. "Can I pass out presents?" she begged Mariah.

"We should really wait for Granny," she said.

"I'm up," Rosemary said. Her hair was wrapped in pink foam rollers. She wore a red satin lounging outfit that Mariah had given her as a pre-Christmas gift. She walked into the room and sat on a chair. "I knew the little one wouldn't sleep long. I've been up for a little while."

Sasha became more excited. "Can I pass out the presents now, Aunt Mari?"

"Yes, you can do the honors," Mariah told the girl.

For the next hour, Sasha went back and forth, passing out gifts to the women. Mariah had given her grandmother a new coat and several outfits, along with a new pair of boots and a designer purse. Rosemary kept saying, "This is too much." Still her face was filled with pleasure.

Mariah gave her friends designer bags with hats and scarf sets. She also gave them iPhones and mini computers.

Rosemary gave Mariah a lace tablecloth for her dining room table with matching accessories. Raquel and Sonyell gave Mariah a gift certificate to a spa in Lake Geneva. Sonyell also gave Mariah several hats, since she knew her friend loved hats. Everyone was pleased with their gifts. But none more so than Sasha. The young girl was in seventh heaven. When Sasha opened the box containing the Wii system she screamed with pleasure. She ran to Sonyell and showed it to her.

Raquel gave Sasha a couple of Wii games and an iPod. Sonyell and Michael bought their daughter new outfits and computer games. Mariah also gave Sasha a small Coach purse, and an American Girl doll, complete with accessories. Rosemary gave Sasha a children's Bible.

Sasha hugged and kissed the women with great enthusiasm. "This is the best Christmas I've ever had." She held up a green velvet dress. "Mommy, can I wear this today for dinner?"

"You sure can." Sonyell nodded.

Sasha sat down on the floor near the tree, and reexamined her gifts.

"There's nothing like children to bring about the real meaning of Christmas, the excitement and laughter. I just love to see their faces when they open a new gift." Raquel sighed. "I think we outdid ourselves this year."

"I would have to agree with you," Sonyell agreed. "Although, methinks Aunt Mari went a tad overboard this year. This is probably the last year we'll be able to get away with her believing in Santa Claus. Sasha asked me many times if there was really a Santa Claus. I just want her to enjoy that myth one last year."

"Shoot, we're lucky she believed this year. As far as going overboard, my motto is you can't take it with you. So why not spend it on the ones you love?"

"I second that. I love the Coach bag you got for me," Raquel said, unzipping her purse. "By the way, I got a spa visit for Sonyell too. So I figured when you have some downtime, Mari, we can all go to Wisconsin for a weekend."

"Sounds like a plan to me," Sonyell said approvingly.

"I'm going to fix breakfast," Rosemary said. She stood up and walked to Mariah. "Thank you, baby. I love my gifts."

"You are welcome, Granny. I am trying to give back for what you did for me when I was a child."

"You know you don't have to," Rosemary protested.

"I know, but I want to." She stood up and kissed her grandmother.

Raquel picked up the remote control off the coffee table and turned on the television to a music station. Christmas songs were playing.

Several hours later, the trio of friends napped after hooking up the Wii system to the television in the den. While Sasha checked out her games, Rosemary headed to the kitchen to finish dinner that she began preparing the day before.

Sasha walked into the kitchen. "Can I have a cookie, Granny Rosie?" She sat at the kitchen table.

Rosemary took several sugar cookies from the cookie jar and handed them to the young girl. "You sure can. So did you enjoy Christmas?" Rosemary asked as she put an aluminum pan of mac and cheese into the oven.

"Yes, I did. I got so many presents. I don't think I've ever gotten that many presents in my life." Sasha munched on a cookie. Rosemary handed her a glass of milk. "Hmm, that's good. I'm going with my dad later today to my Grandmother Nedra's house and to Nana's house tomorrow. I want to see what my cousins got for Christmas. And, I'll get more presents. This is the best Christmas I've ever had."

"I know that. You are a blessed child," Rosemary told the girl.

Sasha nodded. "My best gift was when my daddy came home. " Sasha dunked one of the cookies into the milk and put it into her mouth.

"Good. Every girl needs a daddy in her life," Rosemary said. A flush of guilt coursed through her body. Her own girl, Mariah, never had a father. Rosemary wondered sometimes if that was why Mariah was so gun shy around men. Then her thoughts lightened. Carson proved to be a upstanding Christian man, and his and Mariah's relationship was progressing nicely. *Maybe I'll have me some great-grandbabies in a few years.* She smiled to herself.

"I'm going back to play. Thank you for the cookies, Granny Rosie."

"Okay, baby. Enjoy yourself," Rosemary said. She stirred the greens.

Several hours later, everyone was dressed in their Christmas attire. Rosemary wore a sherry-colored tunic pantsuit. Raquel was dressed in a form-fitting knit skirt and top, with red stiletto heels. Sonyell was clad in a two-piece flowing money-green dress to match Sasha's outfit. Mariah looked stunning in a red cowl-neck sweater and linen trousers, with bronze sandals on her feet and matching jewelry around her neck and on her wrists. Her hair was pulled off her forehead and she wore a multicolored band around her head.

The friends were anxious for the festivities to begin. They assisted Rosemary in the kitchen. Mariah and Sonyell set the dining room table. Sasha put bowls of appetizers on the serving cart as Mariah and Sonyell worked. Raquel prepared a big bowl of punch, her specialty.

Mariah had just taken the silverware from the china cabinet when the doorbell rang. She pushed a lock of hair away from her face and walked to the front door. When she opened the door, Michael greeted her with a kiss on the cheek.

"Merry Christmas, Mari," he said as he pulled off his gloves and stuffed them into his pocket.

Sasha was coming out of the kitchen. She swiftly set a bowl of chips on the cart, and ran to her father. "Daddy," she shouted as she jumped into his arms. "I got so many presents. Come see."

Michael set her down on the floor and took off his jacket as he followed her to the living room. "Nice crib," he told Mariah, as his eyes roamed the surroundings.

"Thank you, it's temporary. This house is too big for one person." She hung up Michael's jacket.

Michael looked handsome. His hair was cut into a low style. His goatee beard looked freshly cut, like he'd just left the barber shop. He wore dark slacks, and a white shirt with a green and red striped vest for the holidays. He had a tiny hoop earring in his ear.

"Don't you look nice," Mariah commented after she closed the closet door.

"Daddy, come on." Sasha pulled at his arm impatiently. She led her dad by the hand and steered him to the tree.

Sonyell walked into the living room from the kitchen. Her eyes lit up when she saw Michael. She joined him and their daughter by the tree and watched Sasha show her father her gifts.

The doorbell sounded again. A few of Mariah's co-workers from Altgeld Garden she had invited to dinner had arrived.

Everyone, with the exception of Rosemary, who was still in the kitchen, was talking and snacking on the appetizers. Raquel's friend Louis had finally arrived. The conversation was animated. The crowd discussed their favorite Christmas carols.

The doorbell rang again. Mariah hopped off the love seat. "That's probably Carson," she said nonchalantly.

She opened the door and Carson was on the other side with his daughters. His hand was full of gifts. "Come in," Mariah said as she held the door open for them to enter the house.

"Merry Christmas," Mariah greeted Carson and his and daughters gushingly.

Ashanti bounded into the house. "Merry Christmas, Miss Mari." She flung her arms around Mariah's waist. Her eyes grew wide as saucers when she caught sight of the tree. "That's a big tree. I've never seen one that big." Her eyes traveled the length of the tree.

"Merry Christmas to you too, sweetie. Did Santa bring you lots of gifts?" Mariah looked at Aaliyah. "How are you, Ali?"

"Hello," the girl responded sullenly. Carson gave his daughter a warning look.

"Carson, why don't you put the gifts under the tree while I take the girls' coats?" Mariah instructed him.

"Sure." Carson walked to the living room and greeted everyone. Then he set the presents under the tree.

Mariah hung up the girls' coats. She walked with them into the living room and introduced the Palmer family to her guests. "There are gifts under the tree for you." She turned to Sasha and said, "Why don't you help Ali and Ashanti find their gifts."

"I will." Sasha jumped up. All three girls walked to the tree. Sasha and Ashanti began talking. Aaliyah looked more animated, and tried not to show how impressed she was by the display.

Mariah waited in the foyer for Carson to return so she could hang up his coat. He returned and took off his coat and handed it to Mariah. He leaned over and pecked her cheek. "How was your morning? It looks like Macy's in there. There is tons of stuff."

"It was good. I got some wonderful gifts from Granny, Sonni, and Rocki. We had a great time last night. Merry Christmas. How was your morning?"

"Mine was fine. Lola brought the girls over a little while ago. I prepared brunch. Then, we ate and opened gifts. They played for a while and then it was time to come here. I must warn you, Aaliyah has a bit of an attitude. She didn't want to come here, but I made her. She has to get used to you being in my life, because I don't plan on letting you go anywhere."

Mariah felt thrilled when she heard Carson say he didn't plan on letting her go anywhere. Then she looked crestfallen. The good feeling deflated as she processed Carson's words about Aaliyah not waiting to come to her house for Christmas. "I know Aaliyah is still getting to know me. We just have to give her more time."

"I agree, and it would be easier if she had a mother who helped her. But we know that isn't going to happen."

"Come on, hon, it's the holiday; let's not let Lola spoil our day." Mariah looked Carson over from top to bottom. His locks had just been done. He wore gray pants with a red shirt with Christmas-patterned suspenders. "Don't you look spiffy." She admired him.

"So do you." He gave Mariah the once-over look.

She shivered. "Come on, let's mingle with the guests. We'll have dinner shortly."

The couple joined the guests in the other room. They sat on the love seat.

"Daddy, look what Miss Mari gave me for Christmas." Ashanti ran up to Carson. She held out her wrist. Mariah had given the younger girl a charm bracelet with several charms on it.

"That nice. Did you thank Miss Mari?" Carson asked his excited daughter.

Ashanti leaned over and threw her arms around Mariah's neck. "Thank you, Miss Mari. I love it and the American Girl Doll, too."

The girl walked back to the tree and returned with her doll. "Look, Daddy."

"Very nice. What did you get, Ali?" he asked his oldest daughter.

"An iPod," Aaliyah replied. "Thank you, Miss Mari. I asked my dad to buy me one, and he didn't, so thank you. I like the charm bracelet and wallet, too."

"Both of you are welcome." Mariah smiled at them.

"We bought you a gift too," Ashanti whispered to Mariah. "It's in the bag that Daddy brought in."

"Thank you very much. So how was your Christmas? Did you get most of what you wanted?"

Ashanti quickly gave Mariah a recap of her Christmas gifts. "Don't you want to open your gift now? I helped Daddy pick one of them," the girl confided to Mariah.

"I'll open it later. It's time for me to bring out the food, so we can eat. I will talk to you later."

"Okay." Ashanti skipped away and peeped under Mariah's tree.

Mariah stood up. Sonyell and Raquel followed suit. They walked to the kitchen and began preparing the food to set on the table.

Not much later, everyone gathered in the dining room, holding hands. Rosemary blessed the food. "Father, God. We thank you allowing us to see another birthday for your Son. Today is the real meaning of Christmas. We thank you for our health, and the food prepared by all the cooks. We thank you for the nourishment of our bodies, through Christ. Amen. Let's eat."

"Amen," everyone replied heartily.

The children went into the kitchen to eat. Sonyell and Michael joined them to prepare their plates.

In the dining room, Carson carved the turkey and ham. The traditional holiday fare was delicious. Everyone dug in and ate to their hearts' content. Raquel's fruit punch was a big hit.

Mariah and Sonyell cleared the table, while Raquel sliced the red velvet, caramel, and chocolate cakes along with sweet potato, lemon, and pumpkin pie.

The doorbell rang. Mariah wiped her hand on a kitchen towel and came out of the kitchen. "I'll get it," she said. As she walked to the door, she thought, *that's probably Cassie. Lord, let her be on her best behavior, the day has been going so well. Please don't let her mess it up.* Mariah opened the door.

Chapter Twenty-three

Mariah's mouth dropped open when she saw Lola standing at her front door. She opened the door slowly. "Lola," she said with false brightness, "what are you doing here?"

"Well, I have a little problem, and I need to speak to Carson. That is if you don't mind," Lola told Mariah quickly. She had an amused look on her face.

"Come inside," Mariah said grudgingly. She stood back to allow Lola entry.

"Carson," Mariah called. "Someone is here to see you."

Carson looked puzzled. He couldn't imagine who could be at Mariah's house wanting to see him. When he caught sight of Lola, he rolled his eyes. "Lola, what you are doing here?" His query echoed Mariah's.

"I have a little problem and I need to see you. Can we talk in private?" she asked Mariah.

Mariah couldn't believe the audacity of Lola. She didn't appear to be overly upset or have any serious problems. In fact Lola was looking around the house appraisingly.

"Why don't you two go upstairs? There is a sitting room to the left of the staircase." Mariah watched Carson grab Lola by the arm and whisk his ex-wife upstairs.

"Who was at the door?" Rosemary asked Mariah when she returned to the living room. "I thought that might be Cassie. She said she was going to come to dinner. She should have been here by now."

"That wasn't Cassie," Mariah answered her grandmother. "Someone stopped by to see Carson." Her smile was forced, a sign of her displeasure of Lola invading her home.

Though the Bose stereo was playing in the living room, raised voices could be heard from upstairs.

"Who is that?" Raquel asked interestedly. She glanced up.

"As I said before a friend of Carson's," Mariah responded through clenched teeth. She looked tense.

Aaliyah walked in the living room. "Did my mom come here?" she asked Mariah innocently. "I told her I didn't feel well and that I wanted to go home. Daddy seemed too busy to take me home so I called my mom."

Carson returned from upstairs, and he fixed Aaliyah with a stern stare. "Did you call your mother?"

"I did," Aaliyah replied sullenly. She rubbed her stomach. "I don't feel well. I want to go."

"You never mentioned you didn't feel well," Carson responded caringly. His voice throbbed with concern. He felt Aaliyah's forehead. "You should have told me. I would have taken you home. You didn't have to call your mother."

"I didn't want to go home," the girl said stubbornly. "I wanted to go back to your house. This is your holiday with us. Not with her." She pointed to Mariah.

"Carson, maybe you should take this conversation to the other room," Mariah suggested.

"You're right," Carson said and led the girl out of the room to the powder room off the foyer. By that time Lola had come back downstairs. She saw the light on in the powder room and walked to it. She put a concerned look on her face. "Oh, *mi hija,* I am so sorry your father was so busy with his new girlfriend that he wouldn't take you home. I cut my dinner short to come get you." She made tsking noises.

"That's not fair, Lola," Carson shot back. "Aaliyah never told me that she didn't feel well. You know I would have taken her home."

"She says her stomach is hurting. Who knows, it could be her appendix. I think it's best we take her home. Go get your sister, so we can go," she told Aaliyah.

Carson felt horrible that he was unaware that his daughter was ill. Aaliyah's eyes were filled with tears. "Okay. You and Shanti can stay at my house tonight. I'm going to tell Mariah we have to go." He looked at his ex-wife. "Give me a minute."

Ashanti came from the rec room upon hearing her mother's voice. "Mommy, you're here. Look at my bracelet that Miss Mari gave me for Christmas."

"That's nice. Carson, get their coats. I'll wait for you in the car." Lola opened the door and walked outside. There was a glint of satisfaction on her face and in her eyes. She felt secure that her mission had been accomplished. She opened her car door and climbed inside.

"Daddy, why do we have to go?" Ashanti tugged at Carson's arm. "I was having fun with Sasha. I don't want to go," she complained. "I like it here. Miss Mariah has a pretty house and all the people are nice."

"Your sister doesn't feel well. So me and your mom decided we should take her home."

"She was feeling fine until she talked to Momma," Ashanti whispered to her father in a confiding tone of voice. "I heard Momma tell Ali to pretend she was sick, so Momma would come get us. I told Ali I didn't want to do that because I was having fun."

Carson felt as if he'd been punched in the solar plexus. He turned to Aaliyah. "Is that true? Did your mother tell you to pretend you were sick?"

Aaliyah's face turned bright red. She fidgeted her hands nervously. She finally nodded.

"Girls, go back and finish whatever you were doing. We're going to stay here. I'm going to go out to talk to your mother." He told Aaliyah sternly, "We'll talk later."

"Goody," Ashanti said with glee. "I'm glad."

Aaliyah shot her sister an evil look and stuck out her tongue. "Momma's going to get you," she warned her sister.

"I didn't do anything but tell the truth. Nana says we should always tell the truth. Remember when she told us the Ten Commandments? Thou shalt not tell a lie. I ain't lying on Jesus' birthday." The little girl skipped back to the living room. She stopped and said to Mariah, "We're staying, Miss Mari. You don't have to look sad." She rushed back to the den to play with Sasha.

Aaliyah slunk back into the living room with her face averted from the guests. She walked quickly back to the den.

Everyone's eyes followed her intently until she was out of sight.

Rosemary shook her head from side to side sadly.

Sonyell commented, "I tell you it's a sad state of affairs when women use their children like that. Apparently the ex–Mrs. Palmer has issues."

"I'll say. That was some baby momma drama on the real," Raquel added. She cackled loudly.

Mariah stood up. Her legs shook. She'd never been more embarrassed in her life. "Excuse me." She fled upstairs to her bedroom.

Finally Carson, fuming, returned to the car alone. Lola looked behind him and asked, "Where are the girls?"

"They are still inside. Ashanti told me that Aaliyah wasn't really ill. And how this was a sick concoction that you cooked up."

"Well, Ashanti misunderstood what she heard. Aaliyah called me and said she wanted to come home and that you forced her to come here." She pointed to Mariah's house.

"She didn't buy into the idea of coming," Carson admitted, "but she came anyway. She was doing fine until you talked her into your harebrained scheme. We are divorced, Lola. We are not getting back together. Mariah is a part of my life and I intend to make sure she stays."

"Why are you with her anyway? It's because of her money, isn't it? I heard that she's Mr. Ellison's daughter. Is that the great attraction? Because she certainly isn't your type," Lola pronounced self-righteously. She tapped her fingers on the steering wheel. She knew that Carson was angry. But she would be darned if she would let another woman have him.

"What goes on between me and Mariah is none of your business," Carson replied. His eyes had narrowed to slits and the vein on the side of his head pulsated. "But, you seem to forget that I'm not broke myself."

"You're hardly in her league," Lola sneered, waving her hand dismissively. Then her expression turned somber. "I want you back, Carson. I still love you and I was a fool to let you go. Please go inside and get the girls so we can go home. Let's talk."

"You must be delusional if you think I'd ever come back to you." Carson rolled his eyes. "We were no good when we were together. You constantly tore me down. Everything was about money to you. I wouldn't have stayed with you as long as I did if it had not been for the girls. And for the record, I love Mariah. L-o-v-e," he spelled out. "I love her for the kind, caring person she is. She is beautiful inside and out, and she's making a difference in the world. I would love her if she was penniless."

"Save it," Lola shouted angrily. "She is not getting her hands on my husband." She shook her fist at Carson. "This is not over; not by a long shot." She threw the car into drive and sped off.

Carson listened to the car screech down the street. His mouth gaped open and he had a stunned expression on his face. Carson couldn't believe what had just happened. He walked back into the house and locked the door. When he walked into the living room it was quiet. Everyone stared at him. He looked for Mariah. He moistened his lips and asked. "Where is Mari?"

Raquel replied gravely as she pointed toward the stairway. "She went upstairs."

Carson ran up the stairs. He found Mariah in her bedroom. Her head dangled between her hands as she sat on the bed.

He knelt down in front of her and removed her hands from her face. "I am so sorry that happened. I knew Lola had issues, I just didn't imagine she would have the nerve to show up here and involve the kids. Please forgive me."

Mariah's face was tearstained. "Lola is one of the very reasons why I never wanted get involved with a man with children. It's not your fault, but you can't control Lola. Therein lies the problem." She moaned. "Maybe we shouldn't see each other for a while and assess what we're doing?"

"If you think I'm going to give Lola that much control over my life, you're wrong. I'm not going anywhere. Mari, I love you."

Mariah's breath caught in her throat. Happiness illuminated her face. Then the happiness faded. "I love you too. But, I don't have the time or energy to get involved in games with your ex."

"I know." Carson's heart was lifted. She loved him too. "I will handle the situation with Lola. Just give me time. I promise it will all work out. Just give us a chance," he pleaded with her.

Mariah hesitated. Then she nodded her head. Carson pulled her up from the bed and crushed her body to his. "We have a good thing going on. I swore I would never get that involved with another woman. Emotionally, Lola took me to the cleaners and back. But, there is something about you"—he tilted her chin up—"that calls me."

"I know. It's like you complete me," Mariah moaned. Carson's lips came down on hers and it was like coming home.

Their bodies stayed entwined for a long minute. "Now let's go back downstairs; you still have guests. Things can only go up from here," Carson said to Mariah gently as he took her hand. They walked to the staircase.

"That will be true if Cassie doesn't put in an appearance," Mariah said grimly. They returned to the living room. Sonyell looked on approvingly. Raquel gazed at her friend, telegraphing the question, are things okay?

Mariah nodded. Then, she and Carson returned to the love seat. Conversation resumed and all was right in their world at least for the moment.

Carson had given Mariah an oversized Coach bag. She quipped, "I think the Coach company made a fortune in this room alone. I love it. When I bought bags for my girls, I thought about buying one for myself, but held off."

"I could tell you wanted one when we went shopping. I went to Carson the next day and bought it," Carson told her. He took another, smaller gift box from his bag and gave it to her.

Mariah quickly opened it. A diamond tennis bracelet was nestled into the box. She exclaimed over it. Carson put it on her wrist.

Mariah gave Carson an ivory chess set and as well as an antique tie pin. He loved both her gifts.

Rosemary asked, "Does anyone want anything else to eat? Mariah bought enough food to feed a small army."

"I think the Bulls are playing today. I wanted to catch the game if that's all right with you," Michael asked Mariah.

"There is another television set in the basement. The kids are using the one on this floor to play Wii. Feel free to use the one downstairs," Mariah told Michael.

The men headed to the basement after Mariah's co-workers departed for home. They thanked Mariah for a great meal and told her they had a great time. After they left, Mariah, Sonyell, Raquel, and Rosemary remained in the living room chatting.

"I can't believe Carson's ex," Raquel began. "She has some nerve." She took off one of her shoes and massaged her foot.

"You're right about that. If Ashanti hadn't told the truth, I probably would have broken up with Carson on the spot," Mariah informed the women. "That was bad enough, but we still have a problem with Ali. She still doesn't care for me."

"Given her mother's actions she may never warm to you," Raquel predicted dourly. "You may have to be content with hi, how ya doing from little Miss Thang."

"I hope not. I guess, like Carson said, we'll have to give it time," Mariah replied dejectedly. She chewed on a hangnail on her finger, a sign that she was nervous.

Sonyell leaned over and held up Mariah's wrist. "I like that bracelet. Carson has good taste. I predict a diamond ring next."

"Yes, it does look nice." Mariah held out her wrist admiringly.

"What did Michael give you?" Raquel asked Sonyell after she returned from the dining room with a slice of potato pie. She stuffed her mouth and sighed. "This pie is to die for."

"Michael gave me the earrings I have on, and this gold bracelet." Sonyell held out her wrist.

"Hmm, I hope he came by the money honestly," Raquel said after she swallowed another piece of pie.

"Actually, he did," Sonyell replied, with a hint of defensiveness in her tone. "And I wish you would stop with the snide comments. Marvin asked Michael to help with chores around his house and he paid Michael. So he earned the money."

Raquel held up her hands. "I'm sorry. I didn't mean that the way it sounded. I just don't want to see you hurt again. You've invested too much time in that man."

"Whatever I've done, it was my own free will. Michael is Sasha's father. It would serve you well to remember that."

"My bad, you're right," Raquel apologized.

"I'm going to go check on the children," Sonyell said. She stood and departed the room.

"That mouth of yours is going to get you in trouble one day." Mariah shook her head at Raquel. She turned to look at Rosemary. "So, Granny, have you heard from Cassie? Is she still coming?"

"She told me she was. Maybe something came up and she couldn't make it," Rosemary said. "She missed a great time. The dinner was lovely, Mariah. You were a great hostess."

"Thank you, Granny. I learned from the best," Mariah praised her grandmother.

"Mrs. Jones's desserts were wonderful. She was so proud that you bought the cakes and pies from her," Rosemary commented.

Mrs. Jones lived in Altgeld Garden and supplemented her income by baking. Her cakes and pies along with homemade ice cream were legendary in the Garden.

"Everything was good. I think I'm going to lie down; I've been up all morning," Rosemary announced, and then headed to a bedroom upstairs.

Sonyell returned to the living room. "The kids are still playing. I think Sasha and Ashanti are becoming fast friends. Aaliyah asked me if she could use the computer to download some tunes to her iPod. I told her that she could. So the kids are doing fine."

"So how do you guys like Louis?" Raquel turned and asked her friends. "I think he's cute. He's been a perfect gentleman. He gave me an expensive bottle of perfume for Christmas."

"He seems all right," Sonyell remarked. "He's your usual type." She shifted her body comfortably on the sofa.

"My thoughts too," Mariah commented. "I'd have to be around him more, but he seemed okay."

"He's a financial planner, making six figures, so I may keep him for a while. At least through New Year's Eve. No one wants to be alone on *that* day. Louis and I are going to dinner and then back to my place. Do y'all have plans for New Year's Eve?" Raquel questioned her friends.

"I'm pretty sure that Michael and I are going to stay home with Sasha." Sonyell told them her plans. "What about you and Carson?" She peered at Mariah.

"We were thinking about going to the city to one of the old-school concerts. We haven't made firm plans; we just know that we have a date for that evening."

"Well, we know you're not going to spend the night with him," Raquel pointed out. "I know it has to be hard for you to be around all that man, and not want to—"

"It's been a challenge," Mariah said quickly, "but I am going to stick to my guns."

"I think you're both nuts, especially Sonyell," Raquel remarked.

Sonyell gritted her teeth. "And that's the reason why I won't have sex with any man with my daughter around."

"Well, when your men start creeping on y'all don't say I didn't warn you. Miss Lola looks like a hot tamale. Mariah, you might want to reconsider your stance," Raquel advised Mariah.

"If Carson and Michael creep then they weren't worth our time anyway," Mariah declared staunchly.

Raquel leaned against the back of the sofa and dozed off.

"We might as well start straightening up," Sonyell suggested. She and Mariah stood up and walked to the dining room.

Mariah and Sonyell peeped in on the kids on their way to kitchen. After verifying everything was under control the friends began cleaning up.

After the Bulls won the game, the men came upstairs and everyone prepared to go home. Rosemary planned to spend another night.

Carson gathered the girls together and told Mariah he would call her in the morning. Mariah told everyone they could come back the following day; she had plenty of leftovers. She turned off the lights after everyone left. The Christmas tree was the only source of light in the room.

She relived over and over in her mind when Carson told her that he loved her. Mariah had never felt so happy in her life. She knew if nothing else, her father's passing had opened up a door for her and Carson to meet. She grudgingly said aloud, "That was indeed a blessing from you, Harold." She set the alarm system. Mariah felt secure in the knowledge that someone in this life loved her, outside of her grandmother and friends. When she walked upstairs her feet hardly touched the floor. Her step was so light it was like she was gliding on air.

Chapter Twenty-four

New Year's Eve 2010 made its appearance amid a brief snowstorm in the Midwest area. Mariah and Carson made plans to usher in 2011 at a stepper's set. Mariah looked ravishing, clad in a black dress with gold accessories, when she opened the door to admit Carson. He looked handsome, dressed in a black tuxedo with a kente cloth vest and tie. He held a red rose in his hand behind his back and presented it to Mariah with a kiss on her cheek.

They traveled to downtown Chicago and supped at Lawry's steakhouse. The couple departed from the restaurant and went to the InterContinental Hotel in downtown Chicago. They sat near the rear of the large balloon-decorated room that was decorated with black, silver, and gold colors. Mariah and Carson sat across from each other at a white clothed table. Mariah gazed about the room, bobbing her head to the beat of the music.

Carson stood. He stretched out his hands and gently pulled Mariah from her chair. He led her to the crowded dance floor. Strobe lights threw sweeping arced colored lights over their bodies.

Carson took her in his arms. They began stepping to the song "My Ship Is Coming In" as it played. Mariah felt at home as his arms encircled her waist. The aroma of Issey Miyake wafted from his body. Carson whispered in her ear, "That song expresses how I feel about you and life."

Mariah pecked his lips. Her eyes were brightly illuminated like there with stars in her eyes. "I feel the same way. This is our song."

They danced as several songs continued to play. Then the couple returned to their seats, and ordered water with slices of lemon.

The song "If This World Were Mine" filled the room. Mariah swayed in her seat and tapped her foot to the beat. Carson held out his hand. The pair returned to the dance floor. Mariah shut her eyes as she placed her arm around Carson's neck and laid her head on his shoulder. She felt perfectly content; being in Carson's arms felt so natural. They danced in perfect sync. She and Carson seemed oblivious to the other couples around them. Carson's arms tightened around her body. Mariah knew that Carson was aware of her as a woman, and he wholeheartedly approved.

Mariah realized at that moment how much she loved Carson. The evening continued to have a fairytale ambience and when midnight rolled around, Carson's lips engulfed Mariah's hungrily. She returned his kiss with the same passion.

Sonyell was right, Mariah thought, smiling. *It is harder to be celibate when you're around that special man.* She realized Carson was the right man. Mariah sensed that Carson would wait for intimacy when the time was right, and only if they were man and wife.

The first day of the New Year, the friends gathered at Sonyell's house to dine. She prepared black eyed peas, mixed greens, chicken, and spare ribs. New Year's resolutions were made. Everyone vowed to report back on who followed through on their resolutions and those who didn't. Aaliyah stayed home with Lola, while

Ashanti tagged along with Carson to hang out with Sasha. The two girls were becoming friends, and called each other BFFs.

Michael had talked to Carson on Christmas day about working with Carson as an apprentice. After checking with Mariah and Sonyell, Carson agreed to hire him.

Sonyell had called Carson and voiced her reservations about Michael working for her best friend's boyfriend. Carson assured Sonyell that the onus would be on him if things didn't work out with Michael. He reiterated that he wouldn't have a problem with letting Michael go if a situation arose that warranted firing. Carson was a firm believer in helping his fellow man. Sometimes his philosophy worked out well, and other times it didn't. Carson knew without his father and Harold Ellison playing pivotal roles in his life, that he wouldn't be the man he was today.

Two weeks later Michael began working for Palmer Construction Corporation. Michael was placed on three-month probation. Carson appointed himself a mentor for Michael, and he provided guidance to Michael in many matters.

Mariah had decided to work from home that wintery January day. Her new house was being painted and she was in and out of the house checking the painter's progress. She planned to move her possessions to the new residence within two weeks. Mariah also called Attorney Cook for an update on her application for the transitional home. He informed her that he had called the mayor's office and the application was still being reviewed.

Mariah checked in with Sonyell and Cierra and all was well. After turning on the television for background noise, Mariah settled in the living room and

resumed reading her father's journal. She had learned
a lot about the man. She found out that he'd endured
a lonely and loveless childhood. He was self-educated
after developing a love for reading. She was anxious to
start the next volume. Her head was in the book when
her telephone rang. She peered at the caller ID unit.
"What's up, hon," she greeted Carson.

"I called your office, and Sonni said you're working
from home. Are you playing hooky today?"

"Partially. The painters are working on the new
house, and I had an ulterior motive for staying home
and it's a good one. I couldn't put down the journal I'm
reading. I finally went to bed around two o'clock this
morning." She yawned. "I wanted to finish up this volume, so I could start the next one."

"That's good," Carson said nervously. "So do you feel
like taking a break? Do you feel like coming out and
having lunch with me?"

"I don't know about that." Mariah peeped out the
window. "It's twenty below zero outside. There's a fire
roaring in my fireplace and I'm still in my jammies. It's
cozy inside. I don't know if I want to brave the hawk
today."

"How about I bring lunch to you? That way you won't
have to brave the elements," Carson said hopefully.

"That sounds like a plan. I have a taste for the grilled
chicken salad from Columbia Gyro, with pink lemon-
ade."

"Got it," Carson said. "I'll see you about eleven-thirty."

They ended the call. Carson returned to work. Mariah's business line rang. She quickly answered the telephone.

At eleven-thirty promptly Carson rang Mariah's
doorbell. After he walked inside, he kissed her cheek.

They exchanged greetings and walked to the kitchen. Carson sat in a chair, while Mariah unpacked the bag of food. She handed Carson his grilled chicken sandwich.

They conversed as they ate.

"So, you're getting to know Mr. Ellison pretty well?" Carson asked Mariah curiously.

"Yes, somewhat, I'd say," Mariah agreed. "In the journals I've read so far, he talks about his childhood. It was pretty dismal."

"Yes, I would agree. He told me about parts of it. He always told me how lucky I was to have a mother and father who loved me."

"Hmm, that's true." Mariah put a dash of salt and pepper on the salad. She daintily cut the chicken strips with a fork and knife.

"I'd like you to go to church with me on Sunday," Carson invited Mariah to his church. "I've gone to your church with you a couple of times. It's time you visited my spiritual home."

"Well, Mr. Palmer," Mariah replied saucily, "I was just waiting for you to invite me. I would love to. It wouldn't be a bad idea for me to find a church to attend in Hammond when the weather is bad. I hate missing church, but Friendship is a nice distance from here."

"Good." Carson smiled. "Morning service starts at ten forty-five and Pastor starts service on time. Do you want to drive or do you want me to pick you up?"

"I'll let you know." Mariah laid her fork down on the table and stared at Carson. "Is something wrong? You have a strange look on your face."

"No, I'm good. Work slows down somewhat during the winter. I have a meeting with a potential client tomorrow. The job would entail inside work, so I'm hoping to win the bid."

"You will," Mariah reassured him. She leaned over and patted his hand. "The quality of your work speaks volumes." She changed the subject. "I need to go to Altgeld one day this week, and work on the budget with Cierra. The fiscal year ends June first. I think I told you that I sat in on a session with her last Wednesday. Cierra is doing a wonderful job. I am happy to say that participation has been up for our teen and parenting sessions."

"That's good," Carson said distantly. His mind was elsewhere.

They continued to talk for a while. Then Carson announced he needed to depart to return to work.

They promised to talk later. Mariah returned to her home office, while Carson decided to make a detour before he returned to his work site. He drove several miles from Mariah's house and decided to stop at his church.

Reverend Cambridge was on the telephone when Carson knocked on his door. The minister gestured for Carson to enter the office. He sat in the chair in front of the minister's desk. A minute or so later, Reverend Cambridge ended his call. He and Carson exchanged hellos, then he asked in a serious tone of voice, "What brings you here today, son? You look troubled."

"Pastor, you're correct, I am somewhat troubled. As you know I've been seeing Mariah Green. And we've developed a great relationship. Sir, I think I've found the one."

Reverend Cambridge's face broke into a smile. "Well, that's good news. Isn't it?"

"It is but I still haven't been quite honest with Mariah. I haven't told her just how well I knew her father. And, how I know what really happened between her mother and father." Carson had a troubled expression on his face. He nervously drummed his fingers on the desk.

Reverend Cambridge nodded his head. "I understand."

"Mariah is reading her father's journals. She hasn't exactly told me how far she is into them. I'm thinking it won't be long before she gets to the part about her conception. Mr. Ellison told me he was quite explicit in his writings. I am not sure how Mariah will respond. Not only have I not been honest, but neither has her grandmother. Mariah is going to be very hurt."

"What do you think can be done to prepare her? I think Brother Ellison's intent was for him to tell Mariah in his own way. Perhaps we should just let things proceed as he planned," Reverend Cambridge counseled Carson.

"A part of me wants to do that, and another part of me wants to shield her from the pain she is going to feel. I am just afraid that she will feel betrayed by her grandmother and me, the people who claim to love her."

"You know, son, that God gives us these tests, and our faith is tested greatly at times. I believe, and this is just my opinion, that Mariah is going to face a test and I pray as I am sure you do also, that by the grace of God she will come through with flying colors. God never promised life would be easy, but He did say He will never leave us alone. That means through the good and bad times."

Carson had a haunted expression on his face. "I know, Pastor, but I feel like I should do something."

"You're aware that I counseled Harold many a time. I suggested he talk to Mariah especially when his health began failing. He felt that divulging to her the circumstances of everything that happened, without her really knowing him, would be too much. Harold hoped by her reading his story, maybe she would be more apt to be more understanding. He was adamant about that."

"I know. Brother Ellison told me the same thing. I guess this is one matter that I'm going to have to let go and let God. Let Him handle this, like He was going to be doing all alone," Carson told Reverend Cambridge.

"Absolutely, God is always in control," Reverend Cambridge announced soberly. Then a smile wreathed his face. "On a happier note when do I get to meet this young lady of yours?" Reverend Cambridge beamed at the young man.

Carson couldn't stop a grin from filling his face. "Soon. I invited her to church Sunday. I have visited her church, and she told me that she would visit mine. So Sunday it is."

"Good. I am most anxious to meet her. You have told me good things about her. And knowing that she is Brother Ellison's daughter, I know she is special."

Carson nodded his head. "That she is."

"So, all signs point to you being in love. When someone puts another's feelings above his own, then that's a good sign. I take it the feeling is reciprocated?" The minister's telephone rang. He allowed the call go to voice mail.

"Yes, it is, Pastor. After what I went through with Lola, I didn't think I would ever fall in love again. And you know Lola, she is making life difficult for me right know. She seems to have a sixth sense and knows when I am involved with a woman. Then she does all in her power to break us up."

Reverend Cambridge chuckled. "That certainly sounds like Lola. But as the Good Book says, no weapon formed against me shall prosper. God has plans in store for Ms. Lola."

"I hope so." Carson bobbed his head. "Mariah has been patient. I have explained Lola's character to her. She has seen her antics firsthand. To make matters worse, Lola has influenced Aaliyah against Mariah, so we are praying and giving Ali time to come to know Mariah. I am hopeful that with time that Ali can see Mariah for the kind, loving woman she is."

"Ali is young. You are doing the right thing by giving her time. Her loyalty is to her mother, and that is normal. Perhaps in time she will accept Mariah as a friend and more if your relationship continues to evolve."

"I hope so, Pastor. Well, I'm going to head back to work and make sure things are okay there. Thank you for your time, Pastor."

"It was no problem. I am always glad to see you and I hope something I've said today has given you comfort. In fact, I'd like to say a prayer for Mariah." Reverend Cambridge stood up.

Carson did the same. He dropped his head and closed his eyes.

"Father God, I ask that you wrap Mariah in your cloak of protection. Help her to see the situation with her father for what it is. We all make mistakes, no one is perfect. Help Mariah to realize that no matter what Harold did or didn't do, he turned his life around. Most importantly, he turned his life over to you. Put love and understanding in Mariah's heart and comfort her when she needs you the most. These blessings I ask in your Son's name. Amen."

Carson thanked Reverend Cambridge and told him that he'd see him on Sunday. The Lord put another mission on Carson's heart as he drove back to work. He made a detour, entered I-94, and headed to Altgeld Garden.

Chapter Twenty-five

Twenty minutes later, Carson knocked on Rosemary's door. She opened the door and was shocked to see Carson in front of her. "Goodness," she said as she brushed her hair back. "I didn't know you were coming here."

"I'm sorry if I interrupted anything, Mrs. Green. I wanted to talk to you if you have time."

"Sure, come on in," Rosemary told him. She stepped back to allow Carson to enter the house.

They walked into the living room. Rosemary sat on the couch and Carson on a chair across from her.

"Is Mariah all right?" Rosemary asked tentatively. Worry lines furrowed her brow.

"I didn't mean to upset you. Mariah is fine. I had lunch with her this afternoon. I won't take up too much of your time. I wanted to talk to you about Mariah's father."

Rosemary seemed to shrink within herself. "What about him?" she croaked out.

"Well, I'm sure Mariah told you I knew her father. In fact he told me about Mariah, her conception, and everything else."

"Why would he tell you something like that?" Rosemary asked. "That information is so personal." A sinking feeling formed in the pit of her stomach. Her hands began trembling. She put them on the side of her body out of sight.

"I agree it is." Carson nodded. "But Mr. Ellison was my mentor and sometimes they share personal information with their mentees. To show they are less than perfect and have made mistakes in the past."

"How much do you know exactly?" Rosemary moaned, clearly alarmed. She put her hand over her chest. She prayed Harold didn't tell Carson about her part in the deception.

"Well, he wasn't graphic or anything, but he did say that you wouldn't let him see or talk to Mariah."

"Under the circumstances, how could I?" Rosemary stated somberly. "Harold Ellison tore apart my family from top to bottom." She snapped her lips shut.

"I know you went through a tough time. The reason I came here"—Carson held out his hand entreatingly—"is to see if there is anything we can do to prepare Mariah for the truth."

"What do you mean?" Rosemary's eyes grew wide as saucers. Her hand flew to her bosom.

"I mean, Mr. Ellison left his journals for Mariah. The journals will tell the truth about what happened. She is going to eventually know that you and I both know what happened."

"Oh, Lord God in heaven." Rosemary's breathing grew shallow. She gasped for air.

Carson gulped. "Are you all right, Mrs. Green? Is there something I can do to help you?"

Rosemary made sucking noises as she tried to breathe. She pointed to the kitchen. Carson sprang from his seat and ran in the kitchen. He spotted her inhaler on the counter, snatched it up, and trotted back to the living room and gave it to Rosemary.

She quickly inhaled the medication. Carson looked on worriedly. Finally her breathing became somewhat regulated. Her forehead was beaded with sweat. "Can you get me water?" she managed to get out to Carson.

He returned a minute later with a glass of water. Rosemary swallowed it down. Carson waited patiently for her to get herself together. Finally, after thirty minutes, her breathing had returned to normal.

"I'm sorry. Sometimes my attacks are triggered due to stressful events. I think that's why I could never talk to Mariah, for fear that I would have a full-blown attack. This one was minor."

"I see," Carson said. He felt miserable for having brought on the asthma attack. He watched Rosemary with a worried look on his face.

"I've had twenty-nine years to tell Mariah the truth. Somehow, even with all that time, I've never been able to tell her. She knows that I am holding something back from her. She has asked me many times what I know and I still can't find the right words." Tears leaked from Rosemary's eyes.

"I almost want to tell her, but I don't think it's my place. Mr. Ellison wanted to tell Mariah his story. My minister thinks I should respect Mr. Ellison's wishes and just be there for her. I know she's going to need both of us." The young man babbled helplessly.

"What exactly did he say in the journal? Do you know?"

"I just know he talked about his childhood. He explained about his decision to go into the army, and how he met your husband. There were entries about his meeting Mrs. Ellison, his marriage to her, your daughter, and of course Mariah," Carson explained.

"Oh, God, what am I going to do?" Rosemary covered her face with her hands and rocked in her seat. Her shoulders shook as she sobbed.

"Mrs. Green, I'm so sorry, I didn't mean to upset you. Maybe I shouldn't have come here today." Carson waited for Rosemary to compose herself.

"You know what scares me the most about all of this? I think Mariah is going to feel I let her down. She has always placed me on a pedestal. I've told her many times that I am a regular person with my good and bad ways. I was all she had and she gave her love to me freely. I just can't find the words. . . ."

"But, when she finds out the truth, she is going to have so many questions, Mrs. Green. Maybe if you don't feel up to talking to her, you can answer the questions. Maybe that's all God wants us to do at this point. My minister says God has this under control, and I guess we will just have to wait on the truth to be revealed."

Rosemary's eyes were red. "I don't know. I am going to have to pray and maybe talk to my own minister. He urged me to tell Mariah the truth many years ago. If I told her what really happened, I feel like I'd tear her world apart and I just couldn't do that to her. I love her too much."

"I know what you mean. I have children of my own, and we try to protect them from the unpleasant parts of life. I guess we'll have to face Mariah's wrath if it comes to that and pray for the Lord to make her strong enough to face what may come."

"I guess so. Like I said, I'll have to pray and talk to Reverend Dudley. I don't know what else I can do." Rosemary shook her head sorrowfully. She felt like her day of reckoning was around the corner and she wasn't quite ready.

"Can I do anything for you? Is there someone I can call? Do you need a doctor?" Carson felt guilty for subjecting Rosemary to his questions.

"No, it's just the shock of knowing that Harold put all of that in his journals. Mariah told me she has been reading them. But she hasn't shared too much about what she's learned. I will be okay. Thank you talking to me, Carson."

"Are you sure? I hate to leave you if you aren't feeling well. I could never forgive myself it something happens to you," he remarked caringly after walking across the room and patting Rosemary's shoulder.

"You're a good man, Carson," Rosemary said. "I know Mariah is not going to take the news well. It comforts me to know that she has you to lean on."

"I don't know about all of that." Carson shook his head. "She'll know I was aware of the truth; she may be upset with me too."

"My girl is not one to hold a grudge. I think with time, she will be okay. At least that's what I pray the outcome will be." Rosemary tried to comfort Carson.

"We have to trust in God she will get through it one way or another," Carson said. He looked at his watch. "I have got to go. I'll call you in a few days to see what you're thinking. If you want to just let events unfold, then I will abide by your wishes."

Rosemary stood up. She and Carson walked to the foyer. After Rosemary opened the door, Carson leaned down and hugged the older woman. "It's going to be okay. God has got this and He doesn't fail. Whatever happens will be a part of His plan."

Rosemary clung to Carson for a minute. "You are absolutely right," she replied. "Everything will go according to His plan."

Carson drove back to Indiana, his heart heavy. He didn't know how fast or slow Mariah was reading the journals. He knew it was only a matter of time before she had the answers to all her questions. Unfortunately, they wouldn't fit into a neat tidy box, like he was sure she hoped they would.

Chapter Twenty-six

Mariah was reading a volume of the journals. She was curled up on the couch in her living room with a cup of hot chocolate on the coffee table. Her eyes were glued to the next entry.

I finished high school today. Most of the kids had parents to cheer them on as they walked across the stage. All I had was the director of the orphanage and Reverend Smith to attend my graduation. I guess that was better than nobody. My guidance counselor, Mr. Price, tried to talk me into going to college. He said I have a natural aptitude for learning and mechanics. I even applied to a few schools and was accepted. But more schooling isn't in the cards for me. I have a hankering in my soul to travel. I've had enough of the South. So I applied to the army and I report for basic training at Fort Bragg, North Carolina in three days. Fresh out of high school to the military, there are worse things a man can do. They army provided me with a bus ticket, my stuff is packed, and I am ready to go. Most people think I'm crazy to enlist with the war going on in Vietnam. Of course I always hear from other boys my age, why would I even consider fighting in the white man's war? But, I haven't quite decided what I want to do with myself. Seeing the world might give me a clearer picture.

In spite of herself, Mariah couldn't help but feel sympathetic for the boy who had become her father. He was raised in an orphanage, never having known his parents, and suffered verbal and physical abuse. She could only imagine what life must have been for him. And it gave her some insight into his mental state. She felt she was coming to know Harold Ellison quite well. Though she still couldn't figure out what Cassie saw in him. Mariah cupped her hand around her chin and kept reading.

Mariah set the journal down on the sofa beside her when her cell phone rang. "Hey, you," she addressed Carson.

"Hey, how are you? What have you been up to?"

"Well, I did a little more work after you left. Then I started reading another one of my father's journals. I'm at the part where he finished high school and joined the army."

"I remember him telling me about that," Carson remarked.

"So, did he like it?"

"He wasn't crazy about being in Vietnam. He said he never got over some of the atrocities he saw committed while he was there. But, I think the army served its purpose. He was able to travel around the world, and found his calling in life. I'll let you continue to read about him. I don't want to give away too much."

"It's certainly fascinating stuff. He's really a good writer. I can picture in my mind a lot of the stuff he talks about."

"Good. I think that's what he was hoping for when he left the journals for you to read. So what do you want to do for dinner? Are you cooking?"

Mariah sucked her teeth. "Are you kidding me? You know how I feel about cooking, especially during the week. What about you? Are you cooking?"

"I could," Carson shot back. "You know between the two of us who the better cook is."

"You're right," Mariah conceded waving her hand. "But you've had more practice than I have. Having children will do that every time."

"Thanks for giving me my props. Oh yeah, I forgot to tell you, Shanti called me last night, and she asked if Sasha could spend Saturday with us. I am taking the girls to Dave & Buster's Saturday evening."

"I am sure Sonni wouldn't have a problem with that. In fact, I'm babysitting Sasha Saturday night to give Michael and Sonni some private time. So tell Shanti I believe Sasha going with you Saturday will be a go. I will check with Sonni first."

"Great. You're welcome to join us if you want to," Carson offered. He sipped from a bottle of water.

"I'll think about it. I may pass this time and spend some time with Granny. We haven't seen each other since Christmas Day, although we've talked."

Carson looked downward when Mariah mentioned Rosemary. He had debated with himself whether to mention that he had gone to see Mariah's grandmother. He decided not to mention it.

"I am so excited about moving into the house next door. It's beginning to shape up, and I feel like it's my house. I've enjoyed staying in the big house, but it never felt like my home. I assume you're going to help me move?" Mariah asked Carson.

"Definitely," Carson said enthusiastically. "I talked to Alex and a couple of guys on my crew and we'll be there bright and early, when you're ready. Are the painters painting the coach house too?"

"Yes. I figured I might as well get everything done at one time. You know I've ordered new furniture and it's stored in the coach house. I donated more furniture to the Salvation Army, and kept some furniture."

"I hear you." Carson looked at his watch. "I need to head out. I'll call you later about dinner. It's supposed to snow steadily throughout the evening. We're supposed to get six inches of snow. If the snow continues, then I'll bring over my snow blower and clear out the snow for you."

"Hmmm, that sounds good. How about I order Chinese as incentive for you?"

"That sounds like a good plan, but you know you don't have to do that." Carson shook his head. "Spending time with you is incentive enough for me."

"I like the sounds of that," Mariah purred. "You've got to go, and I have reading to do. Be careful and I'll see you later."

"You take care," Carson told Mariah tenderly.

Carson entered his office on Kennedy Avenue. He took off his coat and hung it up. Then he sat in the chair at his desk, dialed his voice mail, and checked his phone messages. He jotted the messages on a legal pad.

Carson returned the calls. Then, he called his crew manager to make sure no problems had arisen during his absence. There hadn't been any. Carson swung his chair around and faced the window. He felt so uneasy about the information Mariah was about to uncover. He wished he could take on her hurt, but he knew that he couldn't. He just prayed things would work out the way Mr. Ellison wanted them to. He remembered when Mr. Ellison had first told him about his daughter.

At first Carson had been appalled. He couldn't wrap his brain around what Mr. Ellison had told him. He avoided Mr. Ellison for a few weeks. Finally, he gave up that burden to the Lord, and God instructed Carson not to turn his back on his mentor, everyone makes mistakes, and to have a forgiving spirit. Now, the question was how would Mariah react? That was the $64,000 question, and time would reveal her reaction, sooner rather than later.

Chapter Twenty-seven

Carson had left Mariah's house at eleven o'clock the previous night. The couple shared Chinese food and then watched a basketball game. Carson cleared the snow that had accumulated. Friday morning, at five o'clock, Carson was getting dressed for work when his landline telephone rang. Carson noted that the caller ID unit read Hammond Police Department. Carson snatched up the silver cordless telephone and said, "Hello?"

"Good morning. This is Officer Mark Janokowski from the Hammond PD. I am calling for Carson Palmer?" a male voice inquired.

"This is Carson Palmer, how may I help you?" Carson asked apprehensively.

"Sir, a person who works in the same building as you do reported a possible break-in in your office. We are en route to the premises. Our ETA is five minutes. Can you come to the office ASAP?"

"Yes," Carson answered bleakly. "I am on my way." He grabbed his keys and wallet, threw on his coat and hat, and was on his way. Twenty minutes later, he arrived at his office suite.

Carson gasped when he walked inside his office. The reception area had been trashed. Papers were strewn over the office floor. The locks to his secretary's desk had been picked and the drawers were pulled out. Her personal computer, printer, and telephone had been removed from the desk.

The door to Carson's office was ajar. He walked toward it and bit a curse back when he went inside the room. The locks had been picked on all the file cabinets as well as his desk. His computer equipment, telephone systems, and tools had been stolen. Carson paled when he saw the safe was ajar, and about $3,000 was removed from it.

Carson walked back into the foyer to see if the alarm system had been set. His mouth set into a straight line when Carson saw that it hadn't been set.

Officer Janokowski had followed Carson to the foyer. "That was my next question, if you have an alarm system or a surveillance camera? I see that you have an alarm system. Was it set yesterday?"

"Usually I set it before I leave for the day. My secretary, Janae Hughes, worked late, and stayed longer than I did. In the past, she has always set it before she leaves. I don't have a surveillance camera. I have a meeting set up with my security company this week to install one as a precaution. I had put off getting the camera due to finances. I am now in a position where I could afford one. I guess I was a day late and a dollar short."

The police officer wrote notes on a pad of paper. He asked Carson, "Does anyone else have the pass code to the system?"

Carson closed his eyes. He recited, "Janae of course, my crew manager, and a couple of family members."

"Sir, why don't you take a look around and see what else is missing or destroyed. I'm going to request a couple of crime scene technicians come here and process the scene for evidence."

"I'll do that." Carson walked back into his office. The pictures of his daughters and a couple of snapshots of him and Mariah were upended and on the floor. Carson's chair was turned down on the floor. He placed it upright and set in front of the desk. He slammed his fist on top of the desk and dropped his head in his hands. *How could this happen?* he wondered.

The crime scene technicians arrived within thirty minutes. They began snapping photos and dusting for fingerprints. Carson was irritated at himself for not depositing the receipts from yesterday's clients as well as the petty cash fund. He usually kept no more than a couple of thousand on hand. Several small clients had paid him with cash.

"Thank God for insurance," Carson muttered. He stood up and surveyed both offices to see what else was missing. He couldn't believe it; the thieves had taken food and soft drinks from the dining area. Other various and sundry goods were removed, like Carson's work outfits and boots. He wondered how they had managed to remove all those items from the office without someone hearing a sound. Most of all, he couldn't comprehend why the alarm system hadn't worked.

Carson was talking to Officer Janokowski when Janae walked into the office. She gasped and her knees buckled when she surveyed the scene. Janae dropped the McDonald's bag containing her breakfast to the floor. "My God, Carson. What happened here?"

"Someone broke into the office last night." He pointed to the technicians. "They are processing the scene."

"How did this happen? Everything was fine when I left to go home last night." The young woman moaned.

"Are you sure you set the alarm before you left?" Carson held his breath, awaiting her answer.

"I am positive," Janae replied without hesitation. She walked over to her desk and picked up her chair. "I'm sorry, I need to sit down."

"Is it okay if I speak to Ms. Hughes?" Office Jano-kowski asked Carson. He picked up the McDonald's bag from the floor and laid it on Janae's desk.

"By all means," Carson replied glumly. "I'm going to call my insurance company. I assume they're going to want to come out and make an assessment." He walked back to his office and saw the Rolodex file was missing from the desk. Luckily, the telephone number was programmed into his iPhone. He quickly selected the number and called the company.

The insurance company promised to send a representative out within a couple of hours. Carson sat at his desk and tried to remember who was in and out of the office the previous day. It was payday, so most of the crew had been in the office. Using his phone, he called his parents and then Mariah to bring them up to date on what had occurred.

"Oh, no," Mariah sighed after Carson told her the news. "I am so sorry. Do you have any idea who may have done this?" Mariah felt guilty for immediately thinking of Michael; burglary was part of his old MO. Then she suppressed the thought. Carson had told her many times how well Michael was doing.

"No one comes to mind. The place is completely trashed. Seeing my office like this is a violation. It felt personal."

"What about rival companies, would they do something like that?" Mariah asked.

"I don't think so. The business is going well, but I'm not on a par with the bigger companies. My business thrives mostly on word of mouth. I work with small to midsized companies, and homeowners."

"Do, you need me to come down there? Can I do anything for you? I am just heading to work. I don't have a busy day planned," Mariah offered. She was still in shock by Carson's announcement.

"No, it's just very upsetting to just see the place like this. Janae is a bundle of nerves. So I may just send her home. There's not much she can do here today until the offices are cleaned up."

"You don't have an ex-employee with a grudge against you, do you?" Mariah couldn't help asking Carson.

"No, no one I can think of. I haven't let anyone go since early last year." Carson looked up to see Office Janokowski gesturing for Carson to join him. "Look, babe, I've got to go. I'll call you back."

"Okay. Call me if you need anything."

"Will do." Carson swiped the end call icon and stood up and went to the outer office.

"We were able to get a few good prints. Of course, we'll need fingerprints of you and your staff to do a comparison," the policeman informed Carson.

"Great, maybe we can get to the bottom of this and figure out who did this. If possible can you fingerprint my secretary first? She is awfully upset and I'd like to send her home. In the meantime, I'll call my crew and ask them to come in and we'll proceed from there."

"Yes, we can do Ms. Hughes first." Officer Janokowski called one of the technicians, and they went to over to Janae's desk. Carson joined them.

"After the techs have taken your prints, why don't you go home, Janae?" Carson suggested. "There's nothing you can do today. I'm going to stay and work with the crew to get the office cleaned after the officers and insurance company are done. I'll give you a call later on."

"Thank you, Carson. I can't believe it." Janae looked around the room, dazed. She dropped down heavily in a seat, and waited to be fingerprinted.

Carson returned to his office and called his crew members and asked them to come to the office ASAP.

At Sonyell's house, Sasha was in her bedroom, flipping the pages of her social studies book, cramming for a test that day. Sonyell had taken chicken breasts out of the freezer for dinner. Michael was sitting at the kitchen table finishing a cup of coffee when his cell phone chimed. He answered the phone and listened to Carson. "Say what?" Michael said as his mouth gaped open. "Man, I'm sorry. When did it happen? I'll be there as soon as I can."

Sonyell paused as she put dishes in the sink to look at Michael. His expression was positively dour. "What happened?" she asked after he got off the telephone.

"Someone broke into Carson's office last night. The police are there and he wants all employees to come in to be fingerprinted," Michael informed her looking troubled. He walked to the coat tree and removed his jacket and laid it on the back of a chair. He began gathering his work gear.

"Wow, that's terrible." Sonyell began trembling. She wet her lips and asked, "You didn't have anything to do with that? Did you?" She looked at Michael's eyes. They say the eyes don't lie and she wanted to see what Michael's expressed.

"How could you ask me that?" Michael asked her incredibly. He put his hand on his chest. "Wasn't I here all last night?" Michael put down his work bag and walked to Sonyell. He had a pained expression on his face.

"I don't know . . . I just had to ask." Sonyell dropped her eyes. She then looked back at Michael. "You've been known to do stuff like that before."

"You're right." Michael's eyes glinted with anger. "And, I guess I deserve that question from you. Let me assure you that I had nothing to do with what happened at Carson's office." He sucked his lips. "I just know I am going to be suspect one based on my past."

"Unfortunately you're probably right. I'm going to check on Sasha and see if she's ready to go. I'll take her to school, and then drop you off at Carson's office before I go to work." Sonyell peered at Michael probingly once again and left the room.

Michael could hear Sonyell talking to Sasha urging their daughter to check her backpack. Sonyell was telling the girl to make sure she had everything she needed for school, so that they could go.

Half an hour later, Sonyell had dropped Sasha off at school and had parked her car in Carson's parking lot. She and Michael were unlatching their seat belts when they heard a car horn. They looked up to see Mariah's SUV pull up next to Sonyell's car.

Michael exited the car. He raised his hand halfheartedly to Mariah. His heart beat rapidly. He took a deep breath as he rushed inside the office.

Sonyell got out of her car. She clicked the remote and walked over to Mariah's vehicle. She got inside the passenger side. "Michael told me what happened. I am shocked."

"Me too," Mariah remarked. She left the car running due to the cold weather. "Carson really sounded bummed when I talked to him."

Sonyell looked at Mariah uneasily. "I asked Michael if he had anything to do with the break-in. He said emphatically that he didn't."

"Do you believe him?" Mariah looked back at Sonyell unwaveringly. Her hands clutched the steering wheel tightly.

Sonyell dropped her gaze. She took a deep breath. "I really don't know. He seems to be telling the truth, but I don't really know."

"I understand what you mean. When Carson called me to tell me what happened, my first thought was that Michael had something to do with it. Then I was ashamed, because I was judging Michael."

"Based on his background, he will be judged and probably found guilty. I feel so bad," Sonyell cried. "I wish Carson had never hired him."

"I think we should just let this play out and see what happens. Let's not jump the gun. Maybe Michael is telling the truth. He's been doing so well. Maybe he has turned his life around." Mariah patted her friend's arm.

"You're right. I should at least give him the benefit of the doubt. Although that seems so hard right now." Sonyell brushed away a tear from the corner of her eye.

Mariah turned the car off. "Let's go inside and see what's going on."

As they walked into the building and stamped the snow off their boots, Janae was exiting the building. The women stopped to talk.

"It's awful in there," Janae lamented. She waved her gloved hand in the air. "I feel so sorry for Mr. Palmer. He is devastated. Most of the crew are being questioned and fingerprinted right now."

Mariah and Sonyell looked at each other then back at Janae.

"Do they have any suspects?" Mariah asked quickly.

"The last thing I heard them ask was if Mr. Palmer has any enemies. The police also asked if there are any ex-employees or present employees with criminal backgrounds."

A dart of terror zinged Sonyell's heart. Her and Michael's worst fears had materialized. As Michael predicted, he may indeed become suspect number one.

Sonyell heard Janae babble on as if from a distance. *What if Michael did this?* careened through Sonyell's brain.

Janae finally departed and the two friends pushed the door open to Carson's office and walked inside.

Chapter Twenty-eight

One of the crime scene technicians was packing evidence bags into his black case. Another technician was still fingerprinting a crew member. Officer Janokowski and his partner were taking statements from the men who had already been fingerprinted. Mariah and Sonyell were stunned by the disarray of the office. There wasn't anywhere to sit, so Sonyell walked over to Michael and stood by him. Mariah, meanwhile, went into Carson's office.

He was sitting forlornly at his desk. His chair faced the window; Carson stared aimlessly out of it, seeing nothing. Mariah walked over to him. She bent and wrapped her arms around his shoulders. He held her arms. Then he stood up. Mariah hugged him. Carson set up one of the chairs that lay on its side. Mariah sat in the chair he had placed next to his.

She leaned over, took his hand in hers, and squeezed it. "I know it looks pretty bad now. Once the offices are straightened up it won't seem as bad." She tried to console him.

"I know that, but still I feel violated. I can't believe this has happened," Carson complained.

Mariah nodded. "I understand. Unfortunately breakins happened to me in the Garden at least once a year. So I feel your pain."

"I just can't imagine who would do this. The economy isn't great, but by the grace of God, the company was doing okay. My men make enough money to sup-port their families, so I can't imagine any of them doing this."

"None of them?" Mariah whispered. She wanted to know what Carson was thinking, especially as far as Michael was concerned.

"If you're asking me if I suspect Michael," Carson re-sponded candidly, "then the answer is no. Until I have proof otherwise, that's going to be my position."

"You're simply amazing, Carson, giving him the ben-efit of the doubt," Mariah remarked. "Sonni is here. She's with Michael now. I am ashamed to admit, the two of us are having doubts about Michael's involve-ment."

"It would be easy to do that under the circumstances. He has assured me he had no part in this and I don't want to stereotype him. He's had a hard life. A good part of it was his environment and another part was of his own making. I think deep down inside, Mike is a good guy."

Mariah concurred. "You're right, but this"—she waved her hand around—"is so Michael's MO. It's what he used to do best."

"I hear you." Carson nodded. "He was pretty open about his record. I just had the feeling he was ready for a change. But, if I find out that he played any part in the robbery, I will not hesitate to press charges. I am pretty easygoing. I've helped more than one brother with a record in the past. But, I will not let anyone violate me or mine," Carson said strongly.

"I feel you. I'm the same way. Michael asked me about hiring him before he left prison, but I didn't feel right. Plus, I really didn't have anything for him to do. It's not like he has a great resume. Sonni was initially wary and then pleased when you offered him an apprenticeship. Everything was going well and now this," Mariah stated miserably.

"Thank God I have insurance so the stolen items will be replaced. I made the mistake of not taking a few payments to the bank. That along with my petty cash was taken out of my safe."

"Will the insurance replace that?" Mariah wondered aloud.

"I'm pretty sure they will. I just have to have proof. I will find out from the insurance company. A representative will be here shortly."

"Do you need me to do anything for you? I can stick around and help with the cleanup. After the police finish with Michael, Sonni is going to head back to the office."

Carson's reply was interrupted by shouting from the other office. They sped from the office to find Michael responding angrily to the officer questioning him.

"Whoa, buddy," Carson said pulling Michael's arm. "What's the problem?"

Michael tried to gather himself. "I don't like the way this officer is insinuating that I had something to do with the robbery. He used his laptop computer and pulled up my record. He went from treating me like any other employee to me being the prime suspect." Sparks of anger flew from Michael's eyes. He held his arms tautly at his sides. His hands were curled into fists.

Carson turned to the policeman. "Is that true?"

The policeman held up his arms. "Hey, I'm just doing my job. Your employee has an extensive rap sheet. I had to question him a little bit more intensely than your other employees, based on his record."

"I tried to explain to him," Michael said, pointing to the policeman, "that I've paid my debt, or should I say debts, to society. I have an alibi for last night. Sonni can vouch for me. Isn't that right, Sonni?"

Sonyell was torn. She bit her bottom lip. "I know that when I went to bed and got up this morning, he was at my home, Officer. So I can vouch for his whereabouts," she stammered weakly.

"Was he with you all of last night, ma'am?" the officer asked Sonyell.

"Well, up until I went to bed. We don't, ah, sleep in the same bedroom, so I, ah, don't know that he was in my house all night. I didn't hear any doors opening or closing, so I am assuming he was," Sonyell said unhappily.

"So, she can't completely vouch for your whereabouts," the officer surmised. He turned back to Michael. "Mr. Fletcher, would you mind going down to headquarters to answer more questions for us?"

"This is bull crap," Michael yelled. "And yes, I would mind coming down to the station. I've answered your questions truthfully." He glared at Sonyell. Then he looked back at the officer and asked grimly, "Do I need a lawyer?"

"I don't think that will be necessary at this moment. But, it would be nice if you went to headquarters to answer a few more questions. It doesn't look good that you are refusing to do so. I have your telephone number. I'm sure I'll call you for a few follow-up questions. You are free to go."

Michael glowered angrily at Sonyell. He then stalked out of the office. Sonyell followed him.

"Did you have to be so hard on him?" Carson asked the officer.

"I'm merely doing my job. You know with his record, he automatically becomes a person of interest. I am not saying his is a prime suspect, but his story has to be checked out. We will also compare his fingerprints with the ones we were able to get in both offices."

Carson crossed his arms over his chest. "Problem is that he works here. So you will find his prints in some places in the office."

"We were able to get a few prints off the safe. We'll see how his compare with them. It would behoove you to be wary of the man. If it were me, I would be."

"When you can show me proof positive, I'll react accordingly. Until then, I will take him at his word."

"I hope that works out for you. I will be on my way."

Officer Janokowski walked up. He handed Carson his business card. "We'll be in touch with you soon. I agree with Officer Hutchison; hiring ex-cons is a risky business. I hope the guy didn't lapse into his old habits."

Carson took the card and nodded his head. The police team departed from the office.

The policemen passed by Michael and Sonyell who were huddled in a corner of the entrance of the building talking animatedly. They departed the building.

"You gave me little to no support back there, Sonni. Don't you believe me?" Michael asked her indignantly.

"Of course I do," Sonyell answered reluctantly. "I can't dismiss your past. You've been known to do things like this."

"Sonni, that was in the past. I've been on the straight and narrow because I love you and my daughter. I would never do anything to mess up things between us. I realize I am still in the doghouse, but I would expect you of all people to give me a break. You gave that officer reason to suspect me even more."

"Would you have me lie for you? Is that what you want?" Sonyell reacted angrily. "I don't know what you do when I go to bed. I don't get up in the middle of the night. I just know that you were in the guest room when I got up in the morning."

"I'm supposed to be your man aren't I? Or am I?" Michael asked her ominously.

"Of course you are, but I told you if anything else of a criminal nature occurred that I was done with you. And then this happens? I just don't know." Sonyell's voice trailed off. She raked her fingers through her hair.

"You know what, I think I'd better leave before I do or say something I may regret," Michael said in measured tones. "I am going back to see if I can help Carson. If I can't then I think I'm going to go to my mom's house for a few days. I'm outta here. This is too much." He left Sonyell with her mouth gaped wide.

"Michael," Sonyell said. But Michael kept walking to Carson's office. Sonyell was too embarrassed to return to the office. So she went to her car. She sat for a few minutes waiting for Michael to return. When he didn't, she put the car in drive, and drove to work.

When Michael went inside Carson's office, Mariah excused herself to look for Sonyell. She went to the parking lot and saw that Sonyell's car was gone. She thought, *what the heck is going on?*

She returned to the office. The door to Carson's office was closed. So Mariah busied herself with straightening up the office.

Michael came out thirty minutes later. He looked calmer, but it was obvious he still had an attitude. He told Mariah offhandedly, "I'll see you later." Michael then left the office.

Mariah shook her head and returned to Carson's office. "What just happened? When I went to the parking lot Sonyell had left. Michael looks madder than a wet hen."

"We talked. And for your information, he reassured me again that he had nothing to do with what happened. He is also upset because he feels Sonni didn't support him."

"I understand Sonni's position," Mariah said unwaveringly, ever loyal to her friend. She sat down next to Carson.

"I knew you would. I tried to explain to Michael that he's been judged by his past. I also told him that if he's innocent as he says he is, the evidence would prove it."

"You're right. I guess we're kind of stereotyping Michael. Sonni has just been down this road so many times before that she has all the steps memorized." Mariah shook her head.

"Understandably so, it just takes time for people to realize a person has changed. That's what I explained to Michael. He just has to be patient."

"You really believe him?"

"I do for now. He seemed sincere. We've had many talks. So I just hope for his sake that he is telling the truth."

"For his sake and Sonni's." Mariah waved her hands. "I think when he went to prison this last time she was ready to throw the towel in on their relationship. The only reason she didn't was because of Sasha. She has really missed having a father in her life."

"If I don't know anything else about Michael, I know that he is crazy about his daughter and I don't think he'd do anything to jeopardize his relationship with her."

"I hope so. For a change I am really pulling for Michael," Mariah remarked wonderingly. "Since the police are done, why don't we clean up a little bit? After the police gave me the okay, I straightened up the foyer. The assured me they'll share their findings with the insurance company."

"Good idea," Carson responded. "Thank you and yes, Ms. Green, I would love your help."

Mariah bent over and began picking up items from the floor. Carson looked at Mariah intently, his eyes filled with love. His feelings for Mariah skyrocketed even more. Carson knew that if he were still married to Lola, she would only be concerned about the insurance payout he would receive. She wouldn't deign to help him clean up. Carson realized Mariah was a good woman, he just hoped she felt the same way about him. When all was said and done.

Chapter Twenty-nine

Rosemary, who had not taken a day off work in over five years, called the school district to request a day off. She explained she had personal business to attend to. After she rose wearily from the bed, she showered, dressed, and listened to the morning news as she drank her first cup of coffee for the day.

Afterward, she struggled to get her boots over her feet, put on her down coat, tied a scarf around her neck, and trudged out in the snow to the bus stop. Her friend Alma passed by Rosemary as she waited at the bus stop. Alma pulled over and asked Rosemary if she needed a ride. "I need to be by myself," Rosemary replied. She put her gloved hands inside her pocket.

Alma looked at Rosemary with concern gleaming in her eyes. Though she was loath to do so, Alma respected Rosemary's wishes. "I'll call you later," she simply replied and drove to work. She stared at Rosemary in her rearview mirror until she could no longer see her friend.

The bus was packed with people. Students headed to school, mothers dropped their children off at the babysitters' houses, and men and women headed to work. Rosemary transferred buses at Eighty-seventh Street and before long she walked inside Christian Friendship Church.

Rosemary walked into the sanctuary, and she sat in the back pew. She dropped her head and closed her eyes. She brought her hands together as in prayer. *Why, Lord, why didn't I tell my baby the truth when I had all those chances? Lord, I didn't mean her any harm. If I had it to do over, I would do so many things differently. Help me, Father, I need you now.* She rocked and moaned softly as she sat in her seat. Before long, Rosemary sobbed deeply.

Rosalind was on her way to the ladies' room when she heard sounds from the auditorium. She pulled the door open and peeped in. Her eyes widened when she saw Rosemary. Rosalind rushed back to the office and quickly explained the situation to Reverend Dudley.

The minister looked alarmed and instantly left his office. He sat down on the pew next to Rosemary and put his arm around her shoulder. "Rosemary, is every-thing okay?" the minister asked her kindly.

Rosemary put her face in her hands and bobbed her head up and down. "Pastor, everything is falling apart. I don't know how I'm going to bear it when Mariah finds out the truth. She is going to hate me. I know it." Rosemary began keening anew.

Reverend Dudley sat quietly beside Rosemary until the storm had passed. Rosemary eventually began hic-cupping. He took a handkerchief out of his pocket and passed it to her.

"You know you really don't have to carry this burden alone, don't you? Just turn it over to the Lord, Rose-mary. Let Him guide you."

Rosemary's eyes were swollen. Her voice sounded nasal. "Pastor, I've been praying over this since Mari-ah's father left her that inheritance. And, I still don't know what to do."

"Is it that you don't know? Or you don't want to do what you should?"

Rosemary closed her eyes and sighed. "A little bit of both I guess."

"Why is it so hard for you to trust Mariah to understand what happened?" Reverend Dudley asked Rosemary.

"Because what happened those years ago was so horrendous. Every time I think of the part I played in it, I just want to die." Rosemary began wailing again.

"You didn't do anything out of spite, Rosemary. You did what you thought was best at the time," the minister reminded her.

"I try to tell myself that," Rosemary moaned and swayed in her seat. "When I rehearse in my mind what I want to say to Mariah, no matter how I try to make it sound not too bad, it is. It's the worst thing that ever happened to my family. I feel like I should have done more to prevent it from happening."

"Even when the worst things happen that we can imagine, a murder, a person overdosing on drugs, God is still there to help us each step of the way. I pray you can turn to Him and let Him help you ease your burden. Isaiah 41:10 tells us, 'Fear thou not; for I am with thee, be not dismayed; for I am thy God: I will strengthen thee; yea, I will help you; yea, I will uphold you with the right hand of my righteousness.'"

"I know what you're saying, Pastor. But you don't understand. I can only fix this mess I've created by telling Mariah the truth. To set myself free, I may do harm to the person I love most in this world. And that is so selfish."

"No, I don't think that at all," Reverend Dudley disagreed with Rosemary. "I think God has forgiven you, but you haven't been able to forgive yourself. You have raised a wonderful, compassionate granddaughter. Let it go and wait for Jesus to work it out. I promise you that He will," Reverend Dudley strongly urged Rosemary.

He took Rosemary's trembling hand. "Father, God. I ask that you stop by here today. Please help Sister Green to find peace. Help her to find the right words she needs to talk to her granddaughter. The family secret has been hanging over their heads for so long. By your will, Sister Green will be able to resolve it. Help Sister Green, I implore you in Jesus' name. Amen."

Rosemary wiped her eyes with the handkerchief again. "Thank you, Pastor. I know that you're right. It's time for me to tell Mariah the truth. No matter how it might hurt her or me. I promise. I'm going to think about the way I want to tell her and then I will."

"Trust me, Rosemary, you will feel better in the end. Maybe not immediately, but eventually you will. You will feel like a burden has been lifted. I just urge you not to wait too long."

"I won't," Rosemary promised. "Thank you for seeing me today. I didn't necessarily want to talk to you. I just wanted to be in God's house and listen for His voice to tell me what to do. I believe yours was the voice He wanted me to hear." Rosemary shook her head wearily.

"If you'd like, I can make myself available for support when you talk to Mariah. You don't have to go through the ordeal alone."

Rosemary pondered the suggestion for a minute. "That might not be a bad idea. Let me think on it."

"Take your time but just not too much. Is there anything else I can do for you?"

"No. I guess I will go back home. I actually took the day off work. I haven't taken off for a long time."

"Do you need a ride home? James Stewart will be here in a bit. He's driving the church's van to transport the seniors here today for their monthly luncheon. He can certainly drive you home if you'd like."

"I don't know. . . ." Rosemary replied dubiously. "I'm not really dressed for church."

"I have a better idea. Why don't you help the committee serve lunch? It will take your mind off your troubles. You can work in the kitchen and no one will see you. Then Jim can take you home when he takes the seniors back."

"You know what, Pastor? That might not be a bad idea. I've been lonely since Mariah moved out. Maybe I need something to do like you said. That way I won't focus so much on my troubles."

"Good idea. Let's go downstairs and see what you can do to help."

Rosemary and Reverend Dudley exited the sanctuary and headed to the basement.

Sonyell sat in her office at work. The morning had been a bust. The rest of the day hadn't been productive at all. She had texted Michael numerous times since he'd stormed off. He never responded.

Sonyell tried to convince herself that she was right in the position that she'd taken. Michael had messed up so many times in the past that she couldn't help but be skeptical about his denying he had any part in the robbery.

Mariah had texted her earlier to say that she wouldn't return to the office until later in the afternoon.

Sonyell's cell phone rang, startling her. She snatched it off her desk, praying it was Michael. She wanted to know that he was okay and wasn't doing something foolish or self-destructive. Sonyell was disappointed to see Raquel's number on the caller ID unit.

"Hey, Rocki. What's up?" She greeted her friend dispiritedly.

"Girl, I talked to Mari. She told me what happened at Carson's office. I know you feel like a fool right about now."

"What do you mean?" Sonyell asked her friend, although she knew just what Raquel meant. She just didn't feel like going there with Raquel.

"You and I both know that no one but Michael broke in that office. He's such a loser. Maybe now you'll cut him loose. I know many men who would love the chance to holler at you."

"Don't you think you could be jumping the gun? There isn't any proof that Michael did anything," Sonyell said sulkily.

"Please. That's just a mere formality. Mari told me he took off. If he didn't have anything to do with the robbery then he would have stuck around. I know Sasha wanted her daddy in her life. But, now is a good time for her to learn, life doesn't always work out the way we want."

"I don't know about that. Sasha is only ten years old. Can't she just be a child, a little girl with realistic expectations? Every girl wants her father in her life. I didn't have one, and I always hoped Michael would there for her."

"He certainly can't be there if he's always in the joint can he?" Raquel couldn't resist interjecting.

"You know what? I don't feel like having this conversation with you just now. I have a slight headache." Sonyell rubbed her forehead. "Today has been a tense day. I don't need you adding to the problem."

"I thought I was being a good friend. Friends always tell friends when they are doing something wrong. You went through the bad boy phase. Now it's time for you to grow up, date a man with a little bit more class."

Sonyell could feel her temper rising. "You mean like you do? Some of the men you have dated in the past could be called questionable. But then you certainly subscribe to the theory 'variety is the spice of life' don't you?" she told Raquel snidely.

Raquel's voice was tight. "I am going to let that pass because I know you're upset. I am just voicing my opinion, and you know that your own family feels the same way. Come on now."

Sonyell didn't respond. She closed her eyes and counted to ten.

"A bit touchy aren't you?" Raquel added, "Stay in denial all you want. But you'd better think about what you're going to tell Sasha when you go home this evening. You'll wake up one morning in the future, and all you'll have to show for it is trips to the joint," Raquel went on.

"Good-bye, Rocki, I am hanging up." Sonyell clicked the telephone off, and threw it heavily on her desk. Her chest heaved with anger. Sometimes Raquel got on her last nerve, and today was one of those days. The women had grown up in Altgeld Garden. Raquel was always more of Mariah's friend then Sonyell's. Sonyell learned to tolerate the aggressive, larger-than-life woman. Her tolerance was a bit thin today. Still Raquel had a good point: what was she going to tell Sasha if Michael didn't come home? Sonyell worried as she chewed a hangnail on her baby finger. Life had suddenly become complicated. Sonyell sighed and tried texting Michael again.

Chapter Thirty

Back at Carson's office, the insurance representative had just departed, after filling out an assessment report. Luckily, Carson kept duplicate office files on his laptop computer. So, he had receipts for the stolen property. The insurance rep told Carson that processing would take about thirty days. And that he would be in touch if further information was needed.

Mariah had just returned with lunch. The couple was eating their meal when the office door swung open.

Lola strode into the office. She walked rapidly to Carson. He stood up, totally amazed to find his ex-wife in his office.

Lola threw her arms around Carson's neck. "I heard what happened. I had to come over to offer my sympathy and see what I can do to help."

Carson quickly disengaged her arms, and stepped back. "Uh, thanks. Don't you see Mariah here? It would be nice if you greeted her."

Lola shot a Mariah a look that displayed indifference. "Hello." She turned her attention to Carson. "Is there anything that I can do? I am so glad that you weren't here when the robbery occurred. I shudder to think of what I would have had to tell our daughters if something happened to you."

"Well, you don't have to shudder or anything else. I am fine," Michael told her curtly. He sat back down in his seat. "So, how did you learn the news?"

"Uh, I called your mom this morning. You know I call her every once in a while."

"No, I wasn't aware of that. To my knowledge, you hadn't talked to my mother in years until you stopped by on Christmas Day."

Lola waved her hand. "That just goes to show you how much you know."

"Whatever," Carson said impatiently. "Thanks for stopping by, Lola. Mariah and I are in the middle of lunch. I have some things I need to do. See you later."

Mariah watched the exchange between Carson and Lola with a neutral expression on her face. Inside she felt sweet vindication for Lola's despicable behavior on Christmas. Mariah didn't miss the ugly glares Lola sent her way.

"I guess I'll be on my way. I just wanted to make sure you were okay. I'll call you later," Lola informed Carson.

"I'm pretty sure that I'll still be busy later. So anything you have to say, you can say it now," Carson told her tersely.

"I don't want to discuss family business in front of her," Lola said haughtily. She raised her chin.

"You can. Mariah is my woman, so anything you need to say, you can say in front of her."

Lola's face flushed bright red. "Why, I never. Good-bye." She turned on her heel and walked heavily out of the room.

Mariah burst out laughing. "I'm your woman, am I?"

"And you'd better believe it," Carson told her emphatically.

"Hmmm, I like the sound of that," Mariah preened. "Now you've gotten Lola riled up. She didn't look happy to see me here at all."

"She'd better get used to it," Carson said in an emotionally charged voice. "I don't plan on letting you go."

"You'd better not," Mariah said tapping his arm.

"In the past I allowed Lola to run away a few women. It was a bad precedent. Had I been more assertive then we wouldn't be going through this now. But, maybe I hadn't found the woman worth fighting for until I found you."

Mariah leaned over and kissed him. "Ditto that. I am so blessed that God brought us together when my car broke down." She caressed his cheek. "I really need to head back to the office. I know Sonyell is suffering about Michael's leaving this morning. I have a few business matters to attend to."

The couple rose from their seats and Carson walked her to the outer office. Mariah donned her coat. Carson walked her outside to her car.

"I'll talk to you later. Thanks for coming here. Your being here made me feel better. I appreciate the support." He rubbed her cheek.

"It was my pleasure. Later, babe." Mariah drove to her office on Indianapolis Boulevard.

Carson watched her drive off. He rubbed his hands together and shivered from the cold, then returned to his office. *What a day,* he thought. *I wonder who is responsible for breaking into my office.*

Chapter Thirty-one

After Mariah returned to her office, she found Sonyell in a depressed state of mind. After Sonyell told her about her conversation with Raquel, Mariah sent her friend home for the day. She promised to check on Sonyell later.

At five o'clock, Mariah locked her office and headed to Raquel's House of Beauty, the name Raquel had renamed the beauty salon. Mariah pushed the glass door open. Raquel did a double take when she saw Mariah. She put her hand on her hip and said, "Now, I know you didn't have an appointment today. I would have remembered."

"You're correct. I need to talk to you, when you have a minute." There were three customers waiting to get their hair styled. Mariah greeted them warmly.

Before Mariah took a seat in the waiting area, she walked to the table overflowing with magazines. She picked up the latest issue of *Essence Magazine* and sat in one of the empty seats. She flipped through the pages while she waited on Raquel.

Thirty minutes later, Mariah followed Raquel to her office in the back of the salon.

"What's up, Mari? Do the police have any leads on who broke into Carson's office?"

"Not yet, it's too soon. Investigations take time," Mariah informed her friend.

"We both know who did it. I know that you like Sony-ell, and want to give Michael the benefit of the doubt. A tiger never changes his stripes, and Michael is the tiger in this case."

"Would you stop saying that? There is no proof that Michael was involved. Like you I had my doubts, but at this point it's just speculation."

"See, I knew it," Raquel exclaimed happily. Then her expression sobered. "I guess Sonni told you we had a little spat." Her eyes dropped to her desk.

"A little spat? Sonni was almost a basket case when I got back to the office. Have you ever heard of that saying, 'if you don't have anything good to say, say nothing at all'? You need to implement that saying into your daily life."

"I don't know why. I didn't lie. Sonni stays in a state of denial where Michael is concerned. She's too good for him and has always been."

"Can't you be compassionate?" Mariah implored her friend. "Michael is Sasha's father. You should restrain yourself from those types of comments for that reason if for nothing else. Sonyell is already beating herself up. Michael's behavior has been good since he was released from prison. Carson said he was doing well on the job. There is no indication that he did anything."

"I'd say there are two good reasons why. The number of years he's been in prison, not to mention his juvenile record. He may be Sasha's father, but at the end of the day, he's a convict." Raquel was dogged in her conviction.

"I am sorry to hear you say that." Mariah shook her head sadly. "You've known Sasha since she was born. Imagine how she's going to feel when Sonni talks to her about what happened. Again, I'll ask you, where is your compassion?"

"Sonyell brought this situation upon herself. She never should have gotten mixed up with Michael. I urged her to consider having an abortion when she got pregnant," Raquel said self-righteously.

Mariah fought an urge to wipe that smug expression off Raquel's face. "Like you did, three times before? I swear you use abortions for birth control, like some women use the pill or patch."

Raquel held up her hand. "That was hitting below the belt."

"I know." Mariah crossed her arms over her chest. "Just like you've been doing to Sonyell. We both have loved and supported you over the years. We went to the clinics with you, even though we disagreed with your choices. We fed you, cried with you, and were there for you because that's what friends are for. Not to kick you when you're down."

Raquel looked ashamed. "You're right. I guess I can be so full of myself sometimes."

"Yes, you can. That's why I need to be around to bring you down to earth. Sonni is hurting and she's hurting bad. If you want to be a friend, call her and apologize for the things you've said and go see her. Try to uplift her spirits. Michael has never beaten her. Nor has he disrespected her when he's been on the outside. He's a good father and a nice guy. He's just made bad decisions in the past, like all of us. His decisions landed him in jail. People can change if they want to. Maybe he's finally grown up and he wants to change. We don't have to love Michael but we can like him. At the end of day he's So-nyell's choice."

Raquel covered her mouth with her hand. "Now, I feel like crap," she moaned. "You're right. I may have come on a little strong when I talked to her."

"You think," Mariah replied sarcastically. Her eyebrow rose.

"I will call her and apologize. I'm sorry." Raquel looked dejected.

"You should be. She is at a crossroads with Michael and he knows it. That's why I don't think he did it. I pray that everything works out in Sonni's favor. At any rate it's out of our hands and the truth will prevail."

"Look, that client was my last appointment for the day. Do you want to catch a bite to eat?"

"No, I have a few errands to run before I go home. We'll get together soon."

"We haven't had a chance to really hang out since Christmas. I've missed spending time with you and Sonni."

"We've both been busy with the plans for the transitional home. I've also been shopping, getting ready to move into my new home."

"Oh, I forgot about that. How is it coming along?"

"I should be able to move into it in another week or two." Mariah rose from her seat. "I've got to run. Why don't you stop by Sonni's and apologize to her? I know it will make her feel better. I plan on spending Saturday with Granny. Maybe we can get together Saturday evening. Carson will have his girls this weekend, and he's planning on taking Sasha with them to the skating rink."

"I swear you're sounding more domesticated each time I talk to you."

"Yeah, but it's all good. I am enjoying life."

"Good. I'll go see Sonni and let's plan on spending time together Saturday even if it's at one of our houses."

"Let me know the details. And, Rocki"—she gave her friend an impervious stare—"be nice. I know sometimes that's a foreign concept to you. Be nice to Sonni."

"I will," Rocki assured Mariah fervently. She made a zipping gesture across her face. "My big mouth is on lockdown."

"Good." Mariah walked to Raquel and hugged her. "I'll see you later."

"Okay," Raquel responded. She took her purse out of her desk drawer. Raquel pulled out her mirror, repaired her makeup, and prepared to visit Sonyell. Several minutes later she was on her way to Sonyell's house.

After leaving the hair salon, Mariah decided to head home. The day had been an emotional one. She felt the need to go home and chill out. She called Carson, who said he might stop by to visit later.

Twenty minutes later, Mariah was home. She looked at the stacked boxes strewn around the house and knew that she needed to put a few hours into packing. Yawning, she didn't feel up to the task. Mariah walked into the kitchen, and put a kettle of water on the stove for tea.

She walked into her office and turned on the stereo. Gospel sounds filled the air. Mariah checked voice mail at work. She had received a few calls that required her immediate attention. She sat in her desk chair and returned the calls. When she was done with her tasks, Mariah left her office and went into the living room. She sat on the sofa and leaned her head back against the back of the sofa for a few minutes. Then, she walked to the kitchen and prepared a mug of tea.

Her father's journal was on the cocktail table. She set the mug on the table and picked up the journal and read.

I can't believe I'm really in Asia. Me, Harold Ellison, in a foreign country. Everything about Vietnam is different from America. Someone told me that General

Sherman from the Civil War said war is hell, and he ain't never lied. I thought basic training would prepare me for Vietnam, but training didn't even come close. I am more conscious than ever before of not having family. Most of the GIs write to their family and girls, but I don't have anyone to write to. Sometimes, I scribble in my journal. Some of the guys from my unit back at Fort Bragg are here in 'Nam. I never made friends easily, so I don't really have anyone to talk to. I'm going to try to stop being so standoffish and make some friends. It makes no sense with all the hundreds of men here, I feel so alone. I've got to make a better effort to find a friend, or this tour of Vietnam is going to feel like a lifetime.

Mariah read until her eyelids dropped. She laid the journal down and decided to eat, take a shower, and then read more. Her eyes skimmed the next page, and she saw a name that caused her to blink several times. Her heart rate sped up, causing her breath catch in her throat: *Joseph Green*, her grandfather.

Chapter Thirty-two

Mariah flung down the book, and rubbed her eyes. Initially she thought that she was tired and had misread the name. She rubbed her eyes, and picked up the journal. Her fingers flew from left to right as she reread the entry. Her eyes had not deceived her. She read again Rosemary's husband's first name, Joseph.

Maybe it's another Joseph, was Mariah's initial thought. *It couldn't be Granddaddy, Granny would have told me. This has got to be another Joseph.* She couldn't stop her hands from trembling.

Mariah picked up the journal and quickly skimmed a few pages. Harold had made a few more entries about Joseph. But, he didn't mention any personal information about his newfound friend.

I met a cat named Joseph Green. Everyone calls him Jojo. He's very popular. All the guys seem to like him. He's a real a cool cat. He's from the Midwest. We had guard duty together a couple of nights ago, and met up at mess the following day. He's around my age and doesn't have a big family. He said it was just him and his mother when he was growing up. Another GI, Lee Ferguson, joined the conversation during breakfast, and before you knew it we were talking and feeling more homesick as the conversation went on. Lee is a jovial man, he's tall, built like a tank, but it's all muscle. He said he was given the choice of going to the military or to jail, and he chose the army. Jojo said he worked on an assembly line in a factory. We talked as men do. Who knows, maybe I've found a couple of friends. I know I need to have to someone to talk to who can relate to what's going on here, or I will go crazy.

Mariah skipped a few pages ahead. There wasn't any further mention of Joseph Green. Mariah bit her lip indecisively. She had an urge to call Rosemary and ask her about the information she'd found. She recalled how vehement Rosemary had been, denying she had known Mariah's father.

"I guess it's just one of those coincidences," Mariah said aloud as she shrugged her shoulders. Though her intuition told her that her assumption wasn't true. Mariah laid the journal back on the table. Suddenly, she felt frightened. What if Harold knew Joseph? Did Harold ever meet her family, and most of all, did anything happen between him and Cassie? Mariah's head was awash with questions. She planned to see Rosemary on Saturday, and she hoped her grandmother would have the answers to some of her questions. If Rosemary pulled her "I don't feel well" act, then Mariah planned to press her until she could get answers to questions.

Earlier that evening Raquel left Sonyell's house after repeatedly apologizing for misspeaking earlier. Raquel felt depressed and guilty as she drove home. She could tell that her friend was in a bad way. Raquel wished at times she could be more like Mariah. Her friend always seemed to know the right thing to say and do during a crisis. Raquel bemoaned speaking out of turn. She was so down that Raquel decided to stop at a local bar for a drink before she went home.

She sat in a booth alone in the dim room. She contemplated everything that had transpired during the day. Raquel was deep in thought as she swished the straw around in the glass of her apricot stone sour. She was looking down at the table when she heard a conversation that caused her to slouch down in her seat and listen carefully to the conversation going on in the booth behind her.

"Hey, Esai. I made me some easy money this morning," a drunken male voice bragged.

"What you do, man?" the other man asked the drunken one.

"I trashed an office this morning; my cousin Lola's ex-husband's office. She been trying to get him back but it ain't been working. So she asked me to do a little something, something. She figured that would get his attention off his new woman and back on her."

"That Lola." The other man chuckled. "She something else."

"She is. But cuz got bread and with this recession and all, I needed a little extra something. My wife is pregnant and we don't have much money, so I helped Lola out."

"I hope you was careful," the man warned his friend. "You don't wanna have to be going to jail with your wife pregnant."

The drunken man said in a dismissive tone of voice, "No, this yo' boy. I was careful. Lola gave me all the information I needed to do the job easily. She gave me the code to his alarm system. After I put the digits on the pad, the job was really easy as pie. Easiest money I ever made."

"That's what they all say. But something stupid always happens that gets someone caught."

"Not me," he crowed. "I had on gloves." He lowered his voice. "I even kept some of the computer stuff I took. I figured I could sell it. Lola wanted me to give everything to her so she could dispose of it."

"That sounds like a stupid move to me, keeping the evidence."

"I can use it, man. My wife is having a tough pregnancy. We can't afford her medication sometimes. So this way, I got me a . . . What you call it?" He snapped his fingers. "A nest egg."

Raquel had heard enough. She stood up and walked from the booth to the bar, from the other direction so she wouldn't have to pass the men. "Where's the bathroom?" she asked the bartender.

He pointed to the left side of the large room. Raquel quickly sped to the room.

She took out her cell phone and smiled. When Raquel heard the man mention Lola's name, Raquel edged as close to the booth behind her as she could. She activated the voice recording on her cell phone. She hoped their voices were audible over the music. Raquel wished an opportunity presented itself whereby she could take the men's pictures. Then Raquel felt ashamed because she had been so sure that Michael had participated in the robbery. She figured that she could redeem herself if she could help clear Michael's name. She tucked her cell phone inside her pocket and walked back to the bar and her seat.

She tried to look unconcerned when she returned to her seat. She noticed one of the men eying her suspiciously. Raquel acted like she didn't see the looks the men threw her way. She could hear the men whispering, but she couldn't make out what the men were saying. They began speaking in Spanish. Raquel had a feeling they were speaking about her. She felt a flash of fear. Then, she licked her lips, and stood up. She walked to the booth behind hers, put her hands on her hips, smiled perkily and said, "Gentlemen, can you buy me a drink?"

The men looked at Raquel warily and quickly conducted a conversation in Spanish. Finally the thief turned to Raquel and said, "Yeah, *mami*." The men introduced themselves as Javier and Jose. Jose was interested in finding out if Raquel had overheard any part of their conversation.

Raquel could hold her liquor and drink among the best of them. The older man, Jose, had a thick moustache. He paid close attention to Raquel. It was obvious he was mistrustful of her attention to the younger man. The thief, Javier, thought she was putting the make on him, which Raquel was. But not for the reason he thought, she wanted so badly to take a picture of him.

An hour later, Raquel was about to throw in the towel after enduring constant pawing from Javier. Jose never warmed toward her. Jose's cell phone rang. He answered it and talked briefly. He shut the phone and told Javier, "I've got to go, amigo. That was my wife on the phone. You ready to go?"

"So soon?" Mariah purred as she stroked Javier's arm.

Javier winked at Mariah with a macho swagger. He looked at Jose. "No, Esai. I'm going to stay a little longer. I'll talk to you tomorrow."

Raquel breathed a sigh of relief. If she was lucky, she could get a picture of Javier and get the heck out of Dodge.

"I think you should leave with me," Jose told Javier. "I drove. How are you going to get home?"

"Oh, I can drive him," Raquel chimed in. "It's no problem. I have to leave myself soon. How about one more drink on me?" She beamed at Javier.

"Yeah, I think I'll have one more for the road," Javier told his friend.

Jose stood indecisively for a moment. Then his cell phone rang again shrilly. "That's Maria. I've got to go." He told Javier good-bye, and glanced mistrustfully at Raquel. Then Jose departed.

Raquel unleashed her full feminine wiles on Javier. She flirted with the young man unmercifully. When he left twenty minutes later after Raquel called him a cab, Raquel had his name, address, and telephone number. She'd managed to take Javier's picture without his noticing. He was so drunk that he could barely keep his eyes open.

Raquel was ecstatic. She stood and dropped her cell phone into her purse when she noticed a shadow fall over the table. She looked up to see Jose glaring at her.

"What do you want?" she asked the man snootily.

"I wanted to make sure Javier made it home okay."

"He's a big boy; sure he did," Raquel informed the man as she donned her coat.

"I thought you were going to take him home?" Jose looked down at her.

"I don't think so," Raquel threw out. "He said he was married. Suppose his wife was looking out the window. So no, I didn't. I did call him a cab though."

"You didn't happen to hear us talking did you?"

Raquel looked at him innocently. "Talking about what? I was texting a friend of mine. I don't listen in on other person's conversations."

Jose was silent for a moment as he considered Raquel's words. "If you did hear what we were talking about then I'd advise you to keep it to yourself. Get my drift?"

"I don't know what you're talking about." Raquel fixed her gaze on him unblinkingly. She stood up and pulled her coat about her body. "I've got to go. Excuse me."

Jose stepped aside and fixed Raquel with a piercing gaze. "Don't forget what I said."

"Good-bye," Raquel stepped away from the table and headed to the ladies' room. She locked the outer door and locked herself in a stall. She punched in a number. When Raquel heard the voice mail message, she quickly ended the call. She thought briefly, and dialed another number. When the caller answered the phone she said, "Alex, this is Raquel, can you meet me ASAP at the Copper Penny Bar and Grill on 170th and Kennedy? It's a matter of life and death."

Alex listened to Raquel in amazement; then he said, "I'm on my way."

Chapter Thirty-three

After Raquel left Sonyell's house, Sonyell prepared dinner for herself and Sasha. Sonyell picked at her dinner, her appetite all but gone. Sasha's expression was stricken as she watched her mother simply go through the motions. By eight o'clock that evening, Sasha was in bed. Sonyell had given her daughter a sanitized version of the day's earlier events.

The little girl was shattered with fear. She imagined demons were following her father. Sonyell lay on her bed with her hand over her brow. She sat up and picked up her cell phone from her side, and tried calling Michael's number once again. She had called him off and on during the day and as before the call was routed to voice mail.

She clicked off her phone when she heard a key turn in the front door. The door was opened and then closed. Sasha sprang from her bed and ran to her father. Michael caught his daughter in his arms. Sasha sobbed.

"Baby girl, it's going to be okay, I promise." Michael tried to comfort the girl.

Sasha raised her tearstained face to her father's and asked, "Daddy, did you do it?"

Michael held his daughter in his arms and walked to the sofa. They both sat down. "I swear on all that is near and dear to me, and that includes you, that I had nothing to do with what happened at Carson's office."

Sasha replied firmly, "I believe you, Daddy."

Michael held Sasha in his arms. "Why don't you go back to bed? Before you know it, it will be time for you to get up and go to school."

Sasha cried hysterically, "I don't want to go to bed. I want to stay with you." It was as if the young girl sensed her father was about to leave for good.

Sonyell, who had watched the painful exchange from the room entrance, walked inside the room. She told her daughter in a stern voice, "Sasha, do as your father told you. Go to bed. You've seen him and he's all right."

Sasha reached over and hugged Michael again. Then she rose and went to her bedroom.

Sonyell stood at the room entrance with her hands on her hips. "Where have you been? I've been calling you all day."

"I needed some space to do some thinking," Michael responded carefully. "I think it's time for me to move on."

"What do you mean?" Sonyell asked in a troubled tone of voice. Her body began shaking.

"I think it's time for me to go. I have done some dumb things in my life, I admit it. But I felt like you should have supported me when I told you I had nothing to do with what happened to Carson."

Sonyell waved her hand indifferently. Then she took a deep breath and exhaled. "I tried to believe in you, Michael, but all those stunts you'd pulled in the past came roaring into my head. I'm sorry you feel that way. I told you that I'd need time to try to get over the past."

"Well, you don't need any more time. I'm out of here," he said, jutting his chin upward.

"What do you mean?" Sonyell asked in a shocked tone of voice.

"Just what I said. If you can't believe in me, then I don't need to be here," he told her aggressively. Anger simmered in his voice.

"I . . . I don't know what to say," Sonyell stammered. "Maybe you shouldn't be so hasty." She rubbed her forehead.

"Sonni, I think we need to just end this. You're different. I don't know, maybe you outgrew me?" Michael rubbed his eyes tiredly.

"Don't you think we should discuss this first? There is more than just you and me involved. What about Sasha?" Sonyell pointed toward Sasha's bedroom.

"I will always be there for my girl. I'm glad you had my baby. But, we're not good. While I was in prison paying my debt to society, you outgrew me. I don't want to hold you down. You've got your house, a good job, and I have nothing."

Michael spread his arm out. "I contribute but I know it's not a lot. I'm trying to learn to be a better person, Sasha's father, your man. I talk to Carson, I see him around Mariah, and I don't think I have it in me. I waited too late." Michael's shoulders slumped.

Sonyell put her hand over her mouth. Initially, she felt devastated. Then she thought perhaps there was some truth in what Michael said.

She cleared her throat. "Maybe you're right. Perhaps we have run our course. I don't know. . . ." Her legs felt weak. She stumbled into the chair.

"I know I'm right," Michael whispered. He walked out of the living room into his bedroom.

Sonyell sat in stunned silence. She dropped her head into her hands and sobbed softly. The parting had not occurred the way she'd envisioned for her and Michael.

Finally, she stood and walked into the spare bedroom. Michael was packing his meager possessions.

His gym bag lay on the bed, the dresser drawer was open, and he was stuffing his meager possessions into it.

"What are you going to do about your job? Where will you go?"' Sonyell asked him as she looked around the room sadly.

"Marvin is outside waiting for me. I'm going to stay with him and Ashley until I decide what I'm going to do." Michael opened the closet door and removed a couple of shirts. He folded them and put them into his bag.

"You should at least talk to Carson before you decide to make a drastic change. You know he took a chance bringing you aboard his company."

"I plan to. I know he took a chance on me. You act like I brought nothing to the table. I was a good worker and I enjoyed the work. It's too bad you couldn't believe in me, and realize that I have changed my ways."

"Maybe," Sonyell said thoughtfully. "Even if things don't work out for us, you still owe it to yourself and Carson to continue learning a trade. Especially in this economy."

"I probably will stay with Carson," Michael said. He took toiletries off the dresser and scooped them into the bag. He picked up the bag and said, "I'll be back over the weekend to get the rest of my stuff."

"What about Sasha?" Sonyell asked in a strangled tone of voice.

"I will be back to see her and I will explain to her why I'm leaving."

"I don't know why you think she'd understand when I don't myself," Sonyell murmured.

"Trust me, I got this. Oops, I forgot, you have trust issues. Look, I've got to go, Marvin is waiting."

"Can you just leave? What about the police investigation?" Sonyell asked stalling for time. She held out her open hands.

"The officer has my number. I had nothing to do with the robbery; if they try to pin this on me because of my record, then I'll fight that battle when I get to it." Michael brushed past Sonyell as he exited the room.

He walked to the front door and opened it. "Tell Sasha I'll talk to her tomorrow." With that Michael was gone.

Sonyell felt bereaved, like she'd lost her best friend. Her body slid to the floor. Tears leaked from her eyes as she sobbed quietly.

She sat on the floor near the door for a long time until the telephone rang. Sonyell didn't bother to answer it. She let the call go to voice mail. A few minutes later, the telephone rang again.

At Mariah's house the telephone rang also. She was still reading the journal, trying to figure out if Jojo, as Harold referred to his friend Joseph, was actually her grandfather.

Finally, in desperation, the young woman skipped to the back of the book. She read the following words. Her heart felt like it was going to burst out of her chest.

My best buddy in the world is gone. My heart is heavy. We had a skirmish with the 'Nam soldiers yesterday. Jojo was a few miles away from where I was fighting. When the battle was over, Lee came by later that evening to tell me that Jojo was missing. There were heavy fatalities among our men. I felt like my whole family, mother, father, sister, and brother had died. I kept the hope for a long time that Jojo would return, but as the days went on, he didn't. We knew he had been captured, or he was dead. I realized more than likely I wouldn't see my friend again in this lifetime. I don't care how long it's going to take me, when I leave this godforsaken place, full of death and despair, I am going to see Jojo's family. I know he's married and has a daughter, and I am going to do everything I can to help his wife. Jojo was like a brother to me. I promised him if anything ever happened to him that I would go see Rosie. By the power vested in me, I will see and take care of his family.

At first, Mariah was dumbfounded. She just sat on the sofa in a daze. She reread the entry. That's when she realized that her life as she knew it had changed drastically, and for the worse. Granny did know her father. Mariah couldn't figure out why Rosemary would lie to her over something so important. She had many questions and only one person could give her the answers. Her eyes gazed around the room with thoughts going a mile a minute in her mind. She sat that way until the telephone rang. Carson's number appeared on caller ID. She clicked on her cell phone, and answered it lethargically.

"Mari, what's wrong?" Carson asked her anxiously.

Mariah wet her lips. "Carson, my granny lied to me. She did know my father."

"How do you know?" Carson asked the question, although he knew why.

"I read it in my journal. He was in Vietnam with my grandfather. All this time, Granny knew and she lied to me. I don't understand why she would do that. If she lied about this, what else has she lied about?"

"Are you sure?" Carson asked stalling for time.

"I'm positive. I feel betrayed. If she knew him why didn't she let him come around me? The only reason I can think of is that he raped Cassie. Nothing else makes any sense."

"I'm going to come over there," Carson promised.

"For what?" Mariah's voice rose hysterically. "I am probably the product of a rape. God, I feel so dirty."

"Sit tight. I'm on my way." Carson clicked off his phone.

Mariah turned off the light in the living room. She sat enveloped in the darkness waiting for Carson to return her life to normalcy. She needed his help to escape the nightmare that engulfed and held firmly to her soul.

Chapter Thirty-four

Carson pulled into Mariah's driveway and Raquel pulled in behind him. Alex was with her. Carson exited his car and waited for them to do the same. After greeting the pair, he asked, "What are you doing here?"

"I have some good news for you. I can't wait to tell you and Mariah about my night," Raquel boasted. The trio walked up the steps.

"God knows I can use some good news right about now," Carson remarked agitatedly. He had no idea what he was going to say to Mariah. "Look, this might not be a good time to visit Mariah. She's learned some shocking news."

"Like what?" Raquel asked. She cocked her head to the side.

"I'm not at liberty to say. Can't you wait and tell us your news in the morning?"

"Well, actually it's about you. I found out who robbed your office," Raquel told Carson smugly.

"Really?" Carson raised his eyebrow. Raquel held his interest.

"Yes, really. I overheard a conversation in a bar tonight." She pulled out her cell phone. "And I recorded it. You'll never guess who was behind this."

"I really need to talk to Mari, Raquel. Can this wait until the morning?"

"You should listen to her, man," Alex urged his friend. "This is the real deal."

"I understand, but I really need to get to Mari. Raquel, I promise I'll talk to you first thing in the morning. Would you guys just leave? Mari and I need to talk." His voice cracked. Carson's lips were a thin slash.

"Humph, talk about ungrateful." Raquel snorted. "If that's what you want, sure. I'll call you in the morning." She looked at Alex. "I can tell when I'm not wanted. Let's go."

Raquel and Alex returned to the car. Seconds later they pulled out of the driveway.

Carson rang the doorbell. It seemed to take Mariah forever to answer the door. Carson was about to use the key Mariah had given him for emergencies, when she finally opened the door.

"You look like death warmed over," Carson told her after he entered the house. They sat on the sofa. He took her cold hands in his.

"I feel numb," Mariah whispered. "I should have known nothing good would come of associating with Harold Ellison. I know something bad happened. That's why Granny pretended she didn't know him. He probably raped Cassie. I know it in my heart. That would explain why she's addicted to drugs."

"Now, babe, don't get ahead of yourself. You don't really know what happened. I think you need to talk to your grandmother."

Mariah pulled her hands away from Carson. "What do you mean? Of course I know something bad happened. It's obvious from the way my grandmother has been acting. She didn't want to move here with me. She said she didn't know Harold Ellison and she did."

"Did you read that?" Carson asked. He was in a quandary because he knew the truth and he wanted to tell Mariah so badly.

"I didn't. But I know that's what the journal is going to say if I keep reading." She looked at him with new eyes. "Do you know what happened, Carson? If you do, then you need to tell me."

"I, ah, I can't say, Mari," he managed to say. His face looked grim and Carson was so torn between a promise he had made to a man who was like a father to him, and the woman he loved. When Harold confided in Carson, he made him promise the information would stay between the two men. Later, Harold relented and told Carson that he could talk to Reverend Cambridge if he needed someone to talk to after he was gone.

"Can't or won't say?" she pressed him. Mariah felt doubly betrayed. She couldn't believe Carson wouldn't help her.

"I made a promise to Mr. Ellison," he said helplessly with his hand held out. "I think it's best you keep reading or talk to your grandmother."

"You know what? I thought we were a couple and I could talk to you about anything. If you feel like you can't talk to me about this because of a promise you made to a man who was probably a rapist, then I think you should go."

"Mari, you're being hasty," Carson said cajolingly. "I will be there for you. I love you. I'm conflicted because I know Mr. Ellison wanted you to learn what happened in his own way. He didn't know we would ever meet. I promised him I wouldn't share what happened with anyone except Reverend Cambridge. As much as I want to I can't interfere with his wishes."

"I can't believe you," Mariah shouted. She glared at him. "You know what? Go." She pointed to the door. "Just go."

"I don't want to leave you here in this state of mind. I'm not going anywhere," Carson said vehemently.

"You can scream, yell, or whatever you want to do. I'm not going."

Mariah gritted her teeth. "Do what you want. I'm going to bed." She snatched the journal off the table and raced up the stairs. She slammed the door shut.

What a day, Carson thought. *When it rains it pours. But like the Father says, weeping endureth for a night, but joy will come in the morning. I hope that's true, because we definitely need joy.* He bowed his head. "Father, we need you here tonight. Mariah is hurting. She's forgotten to lean on you. Comfort her Lord, and bring her peace, in the Savior's name. Amen."

Carson closed his eyes and leaned against the back of the sofa. His cell phone chirped. He looked at it, clicked it on, and said, "What's up, Alex? I thought I told you and Rocki I'd talk to you in the morning."

"Man, I know you said that. But Rocki is right. What she had to tell you, you need to hear right away."

"For some reason unknown to me, you and Rocki seem to think you know what's best for me," Carson complained. Then he glanced upstairs. He knew Mariah wouldn't be returning downstairs anytime soon. "Go ahead, tell me what happened."

Alex filled Carson in on what had transpired earlier. Carson was thunderstruck. When Alex finished talking all Carson could say was, "Tell me you didn't just tell me that Lola set up the robbery. I know I heard you wrong."

"No, you heard me right. The beauty is that Rocki managed to record Javier bragging about robbing you. Can you believe Lola involved her own cousin? After we left you, Rocki and I went to police headquarters and gave the information to the police. They plan to pay a visit to Javier immediately. I didn't think Javier had it in him to do something like that."

"You know what? He came to me and asked me if I could help him out, a few weeks before the robbery. He was probably casing my office then so he could rob me. I can't believe it." Carson felt dazed. He opened and closed his eyes a couple of times.

"Believe it, brother man. I heard the recording myself," Alex informed him.

"And, he said Lola put him up to it?" Carson felt totally disheartened.

"Yep, he said that too. You know Lola, she can be manipulative. She's been tripping hard since you got together with Mari."

"I know but to stoop that low is foul. I had a feeling the police were going to try to pin the robbery on Michael. Thank God the evidence points to his innocence. So something good came out of Rocki's discovery. We know some police are capable of changing circumstances so they can close a case."

"You're right it could have gone bad for Michael. What are you going to do about Lola? Your babies' momma could end up in jail." Alex snickered at the thought.

"I don't know. The matter could be out of my hands. If Lola pulled a stunt like this, then maybe I need to reassess her having joint custody of the girls. This is really going to be a problem."

"Yeah, you're right about that. Who would have thought your ex-wife would become a con." Alex snickered.

"That's not funny," Carson complained. "Since Raquel has Javier on tape, her goose is cooked. Trust me when I tell you that she is not going to walk away without getting her hands dirty, one way or another," Carson promised his friend.

"So what's up with Mariah? Is everything okay?"

"At this point things are tense between us. She's reading the journals. Remember I told you that Mr. Ellison left a bunch of them. I knew there was a chance her finding out the truth could affect our relationship. I just hope she can cope with everything that happened. Right now, she's in a bad way." Carson yawned. "Look, I've got to go. I'll holler at you in the A.M."

"You do that, bro. I'll talk to you tomorrow."

The men ended the call.

Carson seethed with anger. "Father, forgive me. I just want to run to Lola's house and confront her. Knowing Lola like I know her, she will just deny, deny, deny. Help me to do the right thing for the girls, because they come first. But I can't let them stay with someone so unstable. Lord, help me to do the right thing."

Several hours later, Carson hadn't heard a peep from Mariah. He pulled his jacket around his shoulders and went to sleep.

Upstairs, Mariah continued to read. Finally, she fell asleep with the journal clutched in her hand.

When she awakened the next morning, the aroma of coffee wafted through the air. She felt aggrieved that Carson was still in her house. Mariah hurriedly showered and dressed. The first order of business for her was to talk to Rosemary.

She pulled her hair back, twisted a headband around her hair, and ran downstairs. "You're still here." She scowled at Carson. He sat at the kitchen table with a mug of coffee in front of him, and another cup across from him.

"Good morning to you too," he commented. "Look, I don't like to argue. I'm sorry you feel the way you do. I think you should keep reading the journals and see what Mr. Ellison has to say."

"Mr. Ellison can kiss my butt. I'm going to see Granny. She knows a lot more than what she has let on. Today she is going to answer my questions. I won't take no for an answer." Mariah looked stony. Carson knew that Rosemary was in for a tough time.

"I would counsel you to go easy on your grandmother. She was doing what she thought was best at the time. We all make mistakes. Try to be like Christ and forgive."

Mariah's eyes widened. "You're right, all of us make mistakes. I've asked my grandmother point blank about my father for years. So she had plenty of time to come up with an explanation after all this time."

"Okay, just try to keep an open mind. Can you do that?"

"I can't make any promises," Mariah told him truthfully. "I'm headed to Chicago, so lock the door on your way out."

"I will." Carson stood up and tried to hold her in his arms, but Mariah pulled away.

"Good-bye, Carson," she told him. Then, she walked to the closet, put on her coat, and proceeded to leave the house.

Mariah's thoughts were all over the page as she drove to Altgeld Garden. She rehearsed in her mind what she would say to Rosemary. Using side streets to avoid rush hour traffic, and speeding, Mariah arrived at Rosemary's house twenty minutes later.

Rosemary was locking her front door when Mariah pulled up. When she turned around, Mariah was pulling into a parking spot. Mariah exited the car and rushed to Rosemary's door. "Granny, I need to talk to you and I need to talk to you now."

Rosemary's stomach dropped to her feet. Her day of reckoning had arrived and there was no turning back.

Chapter Thirty-five

After the women went inside Rosemary's house, she asked Mariah weakly, "Are you hungry? I can make you breakfast." She set her purse on the kitchen table.

"No, I'm not hungry. But, I do have questions for you," Mariah informed her grandmother. She took a journal out of her purse.

"Oh, that," Rosemary said. She sat tensely on a kitchen chair and faced Mariah. She could see her granddaughter was distraught. Tendrils of hair stuck out of the headband around Mariah's head. Dark circles enclosed the young woman's eyes. Mariah's complexion looked ashen, like she hadn't slept all night. The sparkle had gone out of Mariah's spirit.

Rosemary closed her eyes and prayed for the Lord to help her. The confrontation with Mariah was nothing like she'd imagined. She knew her granddaughter was feeling hurt, and instead of alleviating the pain, Rosemary was going to add to it.

"I've been reading Harold Ellison's journals, and imagine my surprise when I came upon an entry of his about being in Vietnam and his good friend Jojo. Jojo was Granddaddy wasn't he?"

At first, Rosemary couldn't say anything. She numbly nodded her head.

"So all these years, you knew who my father was. You knew he lived in Hammond and you never told me? Why, Granny?"

Rosemary fidgeted in her seat, and blindly groped the plastic tablecloth. "I didn't know how to tell you, Mariah. For so many years, I've tried to tell you in my mind, but I couldn't ever get the words out."

"Why? Did he rape Cassie? Is that the reason why? If that's the case, I can understand your not telling me." Mariah's hand fluttered to her chest. "But I'm a woman now. I know bad things happen in life."

"If only it were that simple," Rosemary moaned as her eyes filled with tears. "I went crazy after Joseph was declared MIA. I had lost my reason for living, and I shut down. Cassie was always moody. She suffered terribly after we got the word about Joseph. Cassie needed me to lean on. But, I couldn't help her, I couldn't help myself. Luckily, Alma was around to help me pick up the pieces. There is no excuse for me shutting everyone out, but I did."

Mariah patted Rosemary's hand. "I understand, you had lost the love of your life."

Rosemary dipped her head. "I was just going through the motions when Harold came to visit me. He helped me get over my depression . . ." Rosemary faltered.

"I would think so. From his writing he was fond of Granddaddy. Harold wrote he was like a brother to him."

"That was true and things went wrong. They were so good for a while and then they went terribly wrong." Rosemary sighed.

"What do you mean? Oh, you mean, when he raped Cassie, don't you? I figured that must be what happened." Mariah tried to console her grandmother.

Rosemary seemed to shrink in her seat. Her eyes dropped to the table and she closed her eyes. "No, Harold didn't rape Cassie. He wasn't that type of man. I really don't know any other way to tell you the truth of the matter. I love you, Mari; I always have from the moment I laid eyes on you. I just wasn't thinking clearly back then and I made the situation more difficult than it had to be. I didn't want you to go through life possibly being disrespected because of mistakes I made." Rosemary's breathing became labored. She looked into Mariah's eyes; her own eyes were teary. "Cassie is not your mother. I am."

Mariah felt as if the world had flipped upside down. It was quiet in the room; the only sound was the tick-tock of the clock. Mariah drew her body tight and held herself rigidly. She said in a thin, reedy voice, "What did you say?" She peered at her grandmother with eyes as wide as saucers, stunned, as if she'd never seen Rosemary before.

"I said I'm your mother," Rosemary croaked out. She dropped her gaze to the table.

"But, I thought . . . Oh no, you were with Harold?"

"Yes," Rosemary whispered. "I had an affair with Harold. He helped fill the void that Joseph's absence left."

"Granny, how could you?" Mariah cried. "I don't believe you. You denied me as your child, and perpetrated the lie that I was Cassie's child. Why?" the young woman asked hysterically. Tears streamed from her eyes.

"It was the most stupid thing I've ever done. Everybody knew Joseph was MIA. How was I going to explain having a baby? What if Joseph came back?" Rosemary tried to explain.

"So, what? Things like that have happened before especially here in the Garden. It wasn't the worst thing that could have happened."

"It was back then. But when I look at things now, I should have just claimed you as my baby, and let the chips fall where they may."

"How did Cassie get involved?" Mariah asked. Like the pieces of a puzzle fitting together, the truth explained Cassie's treatment of Mariah.

"I begged Cassie to say she was the one pregnant. One day, Harold and I were careless, Cassie came home early. She went crazy, and she's never been the same since then. I knew she loved me and would do anything for me. She didn't want to go along with the lie, but I begged her to and eventually she did."

"This is so ugly and sordid. No wonder Cassie hates me. I am a double reminder to her of your infidelity and having to claim me as her child. Granny, you could have handled the situation differently."

Rosemary's ears clogged. Her chest felt tight, she couldn't catch her breath. "I'm sorry, Mari. I never meant to hurt you." She gasped. Rosemary keeled over and fell from the chair.

Mariah jumped out of her seat and ran over to Rosemary. She knelt on the floor and patted Rosemary's face, which was turning gray. Mariah ran her hand over Rosemary's chest. She quickly began administering CPR. Five minutes later, Mariah felt exhausted. She stood on shaky legs and called 911. She then ran to the front door and opened it. She returned to Rosemary and cradled her grandmother's head in her lap. Mariah waited for the ambulance to arrive.

Back at Mariah's office, Sonyell dialed Mariah's cell phone number and was routed to voice mail. Sonyell became worried. She called Mariah five minutes later with the same results. Feeling desperate Sonyell found Carson's number in her contact list. She quickly selected his number and pressed send.

"Carson, how are you?" She waited for him to reply. "I hate to bother you, but I can't find Mari. I've called her several times this morning and she isn't answering.

"She went to visit her grandmother," Carson answered. "You know she's been reading her father's journals, and she stumbled upon some upsetting information. She went to confront her grandmother about the information."

"Oh, my. I hope everything went okay. How long ago was that?"

"About an hour and a half ago. She was very upset. So I'm not surprised she isn't answering. Try her again later," Carson advised Sonyell.

"Will do. What's happening with you? Is there any news about the break-in, or is it too soon?" Sonyell asked.

"Actually, there is news. I talked to Office Janokowski this morning," Carson replied morosely.

"Was it good news?" Sonyell asked as her heart raced inside her chest. Her hand tightened on the pencil she held. She nearly broke it.

"Yes and no. Michael was cleared. It seems my ex, Lola, paid her cousin to break into my office," Carson informed Sonyell.

"That's horrible. Though, I'm glad Michael wasn't involved." Sonyell felt giddy with relief for a moment. Then, her mood changed abruptly when she remembered Michael's departure.

"I never thought he was, really. He was really on his grind. He was a hard worker. Michael was doing a good job."

"Carson," Sonyell said in a strangled voice, "I think I messed up." She told Carson what had happened the previous night.

"Give him time, he'll be all right. He's upset that you didn't believe in him." Carson tried to console Sonyell.

"Carson, hold on for a minute. Mari is calling me. "

Carson waited until Sonyell returned to the call. "That was Mari," Sonyell said frantically. "Granny has become ill. Mariah called an ambulance and they're taking her to St. Margaret-Mary Hospital in Hammond. I'm going to go there now."

"I'll head over too. I'll see you there," Carson said.

They ended the call and rushed to the hospital. Carson drummed his fingers on the steering wheel as he waited at a railroad crossing. He impatiently waited for a long freight train to pass.

Carson arrived first with Sonyell on his heels. When they entered the waiting room, they found Mariah sitting alone. Her head was bowed. Carson sat on one side of Mariah and Sonyell on the other. "Is she all right?" Sonyell asked.

"I don't know. . . ." Mariah's eyes were swimming in tears. "I think she had a heart attack. She just fell out. I feel so guilty. I was so mean to her." Mariah sobbed.

"She'll be all right." Sonyell put her arm around Mariah's shoulders.

Carson grabbed her hand and held it.

"She told me the most incredible story." Mariah sobbed. "Granny is my mother. She's not my grandmother. I don't even know who I am, and worse I don't know who Rosemary Green is."

Sonyell looked floored. She fell back in her seat. "Say what?"

"Granny is my mother, not Cassie." Mariah pursed her lips together tightly.

"What did you say? I can't believe what I just heard you say," Sonyell cried. She shook her head in disbelief. "What happened?"

"She said something about being lonely and getting involved with my father. He fought in the war with my grandfather. I actually saw red; before I knew it, I snapped on Granny, and that's when she fell out." Mariah dabbed at her eyes. "All those years, I thought she used illness as a way to avoid unpleasantness and she really was sick. What if she dies?" Mariah whispered as her eyes filled with tears.

"Stop saying that," Sonyell admonished her friend. "Granny is not going to die."

"I'll see if there is any news," Carson said. He then stood up and went to the nurses' station. He returned a few minutes later. "There still isn't any news yet. The nurse said the doctor should be out soon." He sat back down and took Mariah's hand.

"Is there anything I can do? Do you need me to call someone?" he asked Mariah.

"I'd like you to call Reverend Dudley and ask him to come here," Mariah answered. She still didn't look good. Carson was worried about her.

Sonyell took her BlackBerry out of her purse and unlocked it. She scrolled through her contact list and handed the phone to Carson. "This is his number."

Carson stood up and walked to hallway and called Reverend Dudley. When Carson returned to the waiting area, he informed the women that Reverend Dudley was on his way.

After an eternity the nurse called Mariah's name. When the trio walked to the nurses' station, the nurse told Mariah that she could see Rosemary. She informed Mariah of Rosemary's room number and told her that the doctor was available to talk to her.

Mariah's legs shook so badly when she stood up. Carson put his arm around her waist and drew her into his body. He hugged her tightly. Then he and Mariah walked to the patient area. Sonyell waited and wiped a tear from her eye. She wished she could call Michael. But that wasn't an option now. With her cell phone still in her hand, Sonyell sighed audibly. Then she called Raquel.

Chapter Thirty-six

"Ms. Green." The doctor extended his hand. "My name is Dr. Morrison." He wore a white jacket over green scrubs. A stethoscope dangled from his neck. His brown face was wreathed in wireframe glasses and had a nerdy, intelligent look about him.

Mariah cut him off. "How is my grandmother?" She couldn't call Rosemary "mother," not yet.

"She is stable for now. I understand you performed CPR. Doing so probably saved her life. Mrs. Green suffered a heart attack. We are running tests. I'll have a better idea of the severity of damage to her heart when we get the test results back."

"Is she conscious? Can I see her?" Mariah asked apprehensively. She had a worried look on her face.

"She's been in and out. Yes, you can go see her. Don't be alarmed by all the equipment and try not to stay too long and tire her out."

"Thank you. Please keep us posted," Carson interjected.

"If you have any questions, feel free to ask. I will be in and around the area. One of the nurses can locate me if needed." Dr. Morrison made his exit.

"You all right?" Carson asked Mariah. He looked at her with a concerned, caring look.

"As all right as I'm ever going to be." Mariah nodded. She inhaled deeply and then exhaled, trying not to hyperventilate.

She and Carson walked to Rosemary's room. They found Rosemary surrounded by many machines and an IV was attached to her arm. Mariah's heart rate slowed. Rosemary looked so small and frail. Her eyes were shut and her breathing raspy. Mariah moaned and her knees felt like they were going to give out.

Carson put his arm around Mariah's waist. They walked over to the bed. Mariah looked at her grandmother and sobbed. "Granny, I am so sorry. Please forgive me." Mariah's knees buckled. She would have fallen had Carson not tightened his grip around her body.

For the next ten minutes per the doctor's instructions, Mariah just stood next to the bed. She clutched Rosemary's hand like it was a lifeline. The nurse entered the area, and told Mariah that time had elapsed. She informed Mariah that she could return within an hour. Mariah nodded and bent over to kiss Rosemary's cheek. Rosemary opened her eyes and choked out, "Find Cassie. Bring her to me?" She turned her head slightly and closed her eyes.

Mariah's hands flew to her mouth. Carson led her out of the room. "Do you think she's going to make it?" Mariah asked Carson worriedly as they walked to the waiting area.

"Babe, I don't know. We'll have to wait and see." Carson pushed open the door. They returned to their seats. Reverend Dudley and Raquel arrived thirty minutes later.

Raquel's eyes were red. It was apparent she had been crying. She hugged Mariah and Carson.

"Reverend Dudley, thank you for coming so quickly. I appreciate it," Mariah told her minister.

"You knew I would come. How is Rosemary doing?" he asked in a grave tone of voice.

"The doctor said she's stable, but she's not out of the woods yet. The next twenty-four hours are critical," Mariah informed Reverend Dudley.

"Jesus is always in control, so don't despair."

"I know. . . ." Mariah gulped. "She just looks so ill. For all her ailments, I've never seen Granny look so sick." Tears sprung into her eyes. She clumsily brushed them away and sniffed. Sonyell passed her a tissue.

"You've got to stay strong for Rosemary. When our way seems dim, God shines His light to remind us of His omnipotent power. Stay focused and most of all, keep the faith. Shall we pray?"

Heads bowed and hands clasped together as everyone stood in a circle as Reverend Dudley prayed, "Father, God, we ask that you stop by this hospital today, and lay your healing hands on Sister Rosemary. We know that there is no sorrow that you can't heal. When all seems lost, you step right in. Help Mariah to stay strong and to keep the faith as you work your miraculous powers. Bless the doctors, nurses, and other hospital personnel as they care for our sister and the other ailing people in the hospital today. These blessings I ask in your Son's name. Amen."

"Amen," the circle replied and sat back in their seats.

"Has anyone been in touch with Cassie? I imagine she'd want to know about her mother." Reverend Dudley looked at Mariah.

"Granny just asked me to try to find her." Mariah's lips trembled. "I don't know if that's a good sign."

"It's not up to you to try to interpret signs right now," Reverend Dudley told Mariah gently. "Stand on your faith and stay prayerful."

"I will," Mariah promised halfheartedly. "Pastor, can I talk to you in private?" she asked Reverend Dudley.

"Of course." He and Mariah walked out of the nearest exit to the outside of the building.

The minister looked at Mariah questioningly.

Mariah bowed her head. "My father left a series of journals and I've been reading them. I was especially surprised to find my grandfather's name in some of the entries, since I've asked my grandmother if she knew my father and she told me no."

Reverend Dudley judged by the tortured expression on Mariah's face and her monotone voice that she'd stumbled upon her family secret.

"At first, I thought my father raped my mother, and I rushed over to confront Granny about it. Then, she told me the truth; that she's my mother and she had an affair with my father." Mariah rubbed her arms as if she were cold. Her body trembled. "I lost my temper, I yelled at her, and then she had the heart attack. If Granny doesn't make it, I will never be able to forgive myself."

Reverend Dudley put his arm across Mariah's shoulders. "I am so sorry that you learned the information the way you did. Rosemary confided in me her dilemma a few years after you two joined church. I urged her to tell you, but she wasn't quite ready. I know the news was devastating to you, but God had a reason for the way you learned the information. You said your father left journals?"

Mariah bobbed her head. Her throat was so tight with grief that she didn't trust herself to speak.

"Then maybe this is how God intended you to learn the information, from your father's point of view. I already know Rosemary's thoughts and she was misguided. She compounded one mistake with another. God intended for you to be born. He has great plans for you. Rosemary's heart was weak. She could have had the heart attack at any time. I don't want you blaming yourself for what happened."

"I feel like it's my fault," Mariah lamented. "If I hadn't lost my temper and just spoke to her in a normal tone of voice, perhaps she wouldn't be lying in the hospital fighting for her life today," Mariah cried, as her eyes leaked tears again.

"You don't know that for sure; something else may have triggered the attack. I want you to pray over the matter. When I began counseling Rosemary, she'd talk about how she felt her family was cursed, and I likened that to the Israelites, who felt they were cursed. I suggested she meditate on Nehemiah 13:2, which reads, 'Because they met not the children of Israel with bread and water, but hired Halaam against them, that he should curse them; howbeit that our God turned the curse into a blessing.'

"The hardest thing for people, and that includes Christians, is to forgive themselves. I know when this crisis passes, and you have time to reflect on all that has happened, you will see that the situation wasn't what you imagined at all. Your father actually played a role in your life, and he was a blessing from the Father," Reverend Dudley said wisely as he patted Mariah's shoulder.

"I will," Mariah vowed. "Pastor, will you pray for my granny?" She looked at the minister hopefully.

"Of course I will. Let's see if they'll let us go back and see her for a few minutes."

Reverend Dudley and Mariah returned to the waiting area. Reverend Dudley spoke to the duty nurse and she agreed to let Reverend Dudley go back to Rosemary's room to pray. The pair returned to the waiting area shortly, and Reverend Dudley departed. He informed Mariah that he and his wife would return to the hospital later in the evening.

As Reverend Dudley was walking out, Michael entered the hospital. He quickly strolled to the group of friends and told Mariah he was sorry to hear about her grandmother.

Sonyell was pleased to see Michael, and proud of him. *Maybe,* she thought, *he has really changed.*

Mariah informed Sonyell and Raquel that they could go and peep on Granny during the next short visit. Mariah looked up and saw Alma walking toward them with a concerned look on her face.

"I heard about Rosie," she told Mariah after embracing her. "If there is anything I can do, please let me know. Rosie is like a sister to me." Alma choked up.

"I will. If you could keep us updated as to what the doctor is doing and her progress that would be great," Mariah told her grandmother's best friend.

Alma exited the waiting room and after telling Mariah she would keep her posted.

"So is there anything we can do?" Michael asked. He peeped at Sonyell then fixed his gaze on Mariah.

"Actually there is something you and Carson can do." She glanced at Carson and then back to Michael. "If you don't mind that is. Granny asked for Cassie." Mariah tugged on a lock of hair. "I have no idea where she might be. But, if you and Carson can go to the Garden and see if you can find anything out, that would be one less thing I'd have to worry about."

Raquel looked at Michael. "Do you remember what Cassie looks like? Do you need me to go with you?"

Michael nodded. "I remember her vaguely. All I have to do is ask around for her. I know where to go and who to ask where she might be. I still have some associates in the Garden." He stuck his hands in his jacket pockets. "We'll see what we can do."

Carson nodded and stood up. "God willing, we will find her." He leaned over and kissed Mariah's cheek. "Try not to worry. We'll be back as soon as we can." Carson and Michael exited the hospital.

"I have to admit both men are stepping up to the plate." Raquel watched the men's retreating backs. "I always told you Carson was a keeper and perhaps I was a little hard on Michael." Raquel looked abashed.

"So was I," Sonyell remarked sadly. "Michael broke up with me," she announced.

"He had some nerve. He'll never find a woman as good as you," Raquel roared, as she pounded the side of the chair. "I take back all I said."

"No, he had a good reason, although I think my reason for not trusting him was valid. I guess we'll just have to wait and see how the situation plays out," Sonyell said airily.

"Girl, you know Michael love him some Sonni. He'll be back," Mariah predicted. She looked around and lowered her voice. "I feel guilty as sin about what happened today. Granny getting sick was my fault. I lost it when Granny told me that she's not my grandmother, she's my mother." Mariah's voice cracked when she said "mother."

"Come again? What did you say?" Raquel asked, clearly astonished. She was sitting on the edge of her seat and she nearly fell out of the chair. Her eyes widened.

"Y'all heard me right. Granny is my mother." Mariah's brow wrinkled with incredulity. She was still trying to process the news she'd learned earlier that day.

"On the real, I'd rather have Granny for a mother than Cassie any day." Raquel swiveled her head on her neck, and snapped her fingers twice.

"I'm with Rocki on that one. That explains Cassie's behavior to you all these years. It was sibling rivalry." Sonyell shook her head and glanced at her two friends, then back to Mariah.

"It was a little bit more than sibling rivalry. Granny perpetrated a lie, a big one. I took the news badly. And look where Granny ended up," Mariah cried. She began sniffling and placed her hands over her eyes.

"You couldn't help reacting the way you did. I probably would have acted worse. Still, the truth is out now. Once Granny regains her strength, you can find out what really happened. I'm sure she doesn't blame you for her attack, Mari, and you shouldn't either." Raquel tried to find words of comfort for Mariah. She threw her arm around Mariah's shoulders.

"For once, our friend is showing good sense," Sonyell teased Raquel. "Seriously, though, Rocki is right. Stop focusing on the negative and pray for Granny. Let's pray she has a speedy recovery."

"I'll try but it's so hard." Mariah closed her eyes and looked upward.

"It's tough now, but things will get better. You don't have to face this crisis alone. We're here with you. Girl, we ain't going nowhere," Raquel informed Mariah.

The two friends sat vigil with Mariah.

The young women silently prayed that Rosemary would recover from her attack. They were also hoping that Carson and Michael would be able to find Cassie.

Mariah and her friends took turns visiting Rosemary. The women were ever conscious that Mariah's grandmother was in for the fight of her life.

Chapter Thirty-seven

Carson and Michael had gone to several crack houses and had yet to find Cassie. Carson had called Mariah several times for updates on Rosemary's condition.

"Let's check a couple of more places. If we don't have any luck, then I suggest we come back tomorrow," Carson told Michael as the afternoon began rolling into the evening.

"Okay. I told a couple of my old buddies to keep an eye out for Cassie. Eventually someone will find her," Michael agreed as his eyes scanned the streets.

"How you holding up? I'm sorry the police rode you so hard." Carson glanced in his rearview mirror and changed lanes. He put on his turn signal.

"I'm good. I guess what happened is to be expected when you have a record. I am an ex-felon and I guess that tag will follow me the rest of my life." Michael sighed.

"It will, but only if you let it. There are other tags you already and can wear. How about father, employee, friend, and son? Don't get caught up in the negativity," Carson informed Michael.

"That's easy for you to say; you don't have a record," Michael glumly told Carson. He glanced at the clock on the dashboard of the car.

"You're right, I don't, but I have friends who did and they were able to turn their lives around. You are on the right track, just stay steady on course." Carson made a left turn on a street.

"Man, I don't know. I broke it off with Sonni last night. I had planned on resigning from the job and staying with my mom until I got my head together. Luckily you wouldn't take no for an answer when we talked this morning. You just told me to take a few days off." Michael didn't look at Carson. He peeped in the rearview mirror.

"You went through a rough patch. Now, what possessed you to break up with Sonni? You didn't mention that," Carson said. He glanced at Michael. Then he looked at the road ahead of him.

"I been thinking a lot lately. I realized that I ain't ever going to be able to measure up to what Sonni had and what she has accomplished. While I was wasting time doing stupid, she was doing her. The new Sonni has left me behind."

"Did she tell you that? Or are you using that as a shield?' "Carson threw in. "Relationships are hard. If the woman is worth it, you do what you gotta do. Mariah is not too pleased with me right now. She feels like I betrayed her."

"Sometimes I think you just can't please a woman, no matter how hard you try," Michael complained. He shifted in the seat.

"Some women are harder to please than others. But again, if she's worth having, then love and cherish her, and treat her like the queen she is," Carson advised Michael.

"That's easy for you to say. You're educated, have your own money and your own business." Michael held up two fingers like quotation marks. "You're what the sistas would call a keeper."

"If you weren't a keeper, do you think Sonni would have waited for you, and invited you to share her home? Don't sell yourself short." Carson turned, and headed south on another street.

"She probably only let me stay there because of Sasha. I tell you I'm going to miss my baby girl. She's a good kid. I admit Sonni did a good job raising her."

"She is. And, she needs you especially now. I've had many problems with my ex, and Mari hasn't been happy about the situation. After Lola's last stunt masterminding the robbery, I am considering petitioning the court for custody of the girls. When we began hanging out, Mari told me about her rule about not dating men with children. She didn't have a problem with me having joint custody, but full custody is another ballgame. I don't know how Mari is going to feel about that."

"She'll come around. Anyone with eyes could see you two are in love. I know I love Sonni, always have, since she was a skinny girl in the fifth grade. Shoot, she still skinny, but I love her, man. I just don't think I'm good enough for her." Michael dropped his head.

"Again, don't sell yourself short. Sonni saw and felt something. It hasn't gone away that quickly."

Michael's cell phone sounded. He clicked it on. "Sup, man. She where? Okay, me and my boy are going to go there now. Good lookout. Peace out." He turned to Carson. "That was one of my associates. He said Cassie was seen going to a crack house near the back of the Garden a few hours ago. I know the place. Let's go there now." He gave Carson directions.

Ten minutes later they arrived to a dilapidated building. Carson parked the car.

Michael told Carson offhandedly, "I can go in myself. You don't have to if you don't want to. There's no telling what we might see in there."

"No, I'll go with you," Carson said. He turned the truck off.

The men exited Carson's truck, walked to the door, and banged on it.

A man opened the door. His eyes lit up when he saw Michael. "Big Mike, whatcha doing here? I know you ain't on that stuff." He stepped aside so the men could enter the town house.

"Naw, man." Michael squinted as his eyes adjusted to the dimness of the unlit room. "I'm looking for Mari's mother, Cassie. You know Miss Rosemary's daughter. Is she here?"

"Yeah, she came here a few hours ago. She upstairs in the back bedroom with her man Frog." He pointed to the back of the house.

"Thanks, man." Michael and Carson walked upstairs and to the second bedroom. The men burst into the room. Cassie and Frog had nodded out. Their bodies were slumped as they sat on the side of a dingy bedspread.

"Cassie," Michael said. He repeated her name louder. Cassie didn't respond. He walked to the bed and gently slapped her face.

"What?" Cassie asked with a glazed look on her face. She shielded her eyes with her hand and said, "Oh, you Sonni's man. Whatcha doing here?"

"Your momma's sick. She at the hospital. She asked Mari to find you and for you to come to the hospital."

Cassie tried to stand up, but kept falling backward into the bed. It was a minute before she was finally able to sit erect. "Whatcha mean my momma sick? What's wrong with her?"

"She had a heart attack. Miss Rosemary is very sick and she wants to see you. Can you pull yourself together enough so we can go?" Michael asked her.

"Who dat?" Cassie pointed at Carson accusingly. "He ain't the law is he?"

"Naw, he a friend of Mari. You straight? Can you make it to the hospital?"

"Yeah, I gots to go see 'bout my momma." She turned to Frog, and elbowed him until he came out of his stupor. "I gots to go," she told the man. Her voice was slurred. "My momma sick. These dudes gonna take me to see her."

Frog scratched the matted hair on the side of his head. "'Kay, handle yo' business. You got some paper I can hold 'til you get back?" he looked up at Cassie and asked hopefully. His eyes were narrow slits and reddened.

"You crazy. I ain't got nothing. I be back later." Cassie stood up. She picked her jacket up off the floor and put it on. She staggered slightly as she followed Michael and Carson out of the room.

The three departed the crack house and walked to Carson's truck. The men sat in the front seat and Cassie in the back. The stench from Cassie's body was so horrendous that Carson and Michael immediately cracked their windows.

No one spoke as Carson drove. Carson glanced at the back seat through his rearview mirror. Cassie's head lolled against the headrest. Spittle dripped from her mouth. She had nodded off.

Carson looked at Michael and glanced again in the rearview mirror. "I'm not trying to be funny or nothing, but I'm not sure about her going to the hospital like she is. She smells and looks a mess."

"I hear you." Michael threw up his hands slightly. "But what can we do? Miss Rosemary is critical. We don't know what might happen. I think we should take her and hope for the best."

"I don't know if they will let her inside the emergency room looking like that. Why don't we stop at my sister Tiffany's house and try to clean her up? Tiffany is thin like Cassie. I'll call Tiffany and tell her we're coming."

Michael nodded. "Hey you the boss. Whatever you say."

Carson quickly activated his Bluetooth device and called Tiffany. She wasn't crazy about the idea but agreed to Carson's suggestion.

When they arrived at Tiffany's apartment, the men roused Cassie. She was kicking and screaming. She finally calmed down when Carson told her he didn't think the hospital personnel would allow her to see Rosemary if she didn't bathe and change clothes.

Tiffany graciously showed Cassie to the bathroom. She laid a change of clothing for Cassie on her bed in her spare bedroom.

"If I were you," Michael told Tiffany after Cassie was in the shower, "I'd remove any valuables before she gets to the bedroom. She's a junkie, and she may take anything not glued down."

A horrified expression crossed Tiffany's face. "Carson, you know you owe me big time for this." She folded her arms across her chest, and glared at her brother.

"I know, I got this." Carson tried to pacify his sister. "Mari's grandmother is critical and this is her only child. So Michael and I are doing what we can to adhere to Mari's grandmother's wishes." Carson didn't want to air Mariah's secret about her grandmother being her mother to anyone.

Carson, Michael, and Tiffany watched the news. Finally they could hear Cassie exiting the bathroom. Tiffany hopped off the love seat and showed Cassie to the bedroom.

Forty minutes after they arrived at Tiffany's house, the trio departed for the hospital. They stood at Tiffany's front door.

Tiffany looked at Cassie and told her in a gentle tone of voice, "I'll keep your mother in my prayers."

"Thank you," Cassie mumbled. "Can we go now?" she asked Carson. She put her trembling hands inside her jacket pockets.

"Tell Mari if she needs anything to let me know," Tiffany informed Carson. She quickly hugged him goodbye.

"I will. I'll talk to you later." Several minutes later, Carson was on his way to St. Margaret-Mary Hospital.

Cassie fidgeted in the back seat the closer they got to the hospital. "So, is my momma going to be okay? I know heart attacks ain't good. She didn't have a bad one did she?" Cassie cut her eye at Carson.

"It was bad enough. You'll see when we get there." Carson pulled up in front of the emergency room entrance. "I should be back in about an hour. Tell Mari to call me if she needs me," he informed Michael.

"I will," Michael replied. He got out of the truck, and waited for Cassie to exit the truck.

Cassie suddenly looked frightened. Carson waved before he pulled away from the hospital entrance.

Michael and Cassie silently walked inside the hospital. Cassie trembled like a leaf in a strong wind as she walked by his side.

Carson was ticked off as he drove away from the hospital. Every time he thought about what his ex-wife had done, Carson became angry all over. He headed north on Calumet Avenue to Whiting.

Lola happened to be looking out her bedroom window of her condo, when she saw Carson pull into the parking lot. She was thrilled. She ran to her bedroom and hurriedly pulled off her sweat suit. Lola rushed and put on a sexy negligee. She tousled her hair as she walked to the door after the doorbell rang.

Lola took her time walking to the foyer to the intercom. She pressed a button and asked, "Who is it?"

"It's me," Carson answered brusquely.

Lola pressed another button to allow Carson entry to the building. She waited for him by the door. Lola opened the door and smiled until she saw the cold look on Carson's face.

"What's wrong?" she asked as Carson pushed past her, and stalked into the apartment.

Carson walked to the middle of the living room and turned to face Lola.

She tried to hug her ex-husband, but Carson pushed her away. "Hmm." Lola batted her eyes at Carson. "I know you're still upset about the break-in. I was just so happy nothing happened to you. Thank God it happened at night. People are so crazy. They'll break in your house during the day, while you're there." She gave Carson a knowing look. "It's probably someone associated with your new girlfriend. I swear, Carson, I don't know what you see in her," Lola babbled nervously.

"Stop playing, Lola, I know what you did," he said through gritted teeth. His hands folded into fists.

"I don't know what you're talking about," Lola retorted. She stepped back. Her heart thudded rapidly in her chest.

"Cut the act. I know your cousin Javier was involved in the robbery. He's probably already been picked up by the police. There is no doubt in my mind that he's going to sing like a bird." Carson enunciated each word carefully.

"I don't care what Javier says, I was not involved. I'd be a fool to try something stupid like that. What reason

would I have to pay someone to break into your office?"
She cut her words off and put her hand over her mouth.
"I can explain. . . ."

"Do tell," Carson said furiously. He tapped his foot
impatiently. He had never hit a woman or even wanted
to. At that moment Lola tried his patience extremely.

"*Mi amor,* I did it for us. I hope you didn't think I
was going to stand by and let some other woman have
you," Lola yelled. "You're mine and that's never going
to change. I should never have given you the divorce."
She shook her head violently.

"Lola, when will you get it through your head that
you don't own or have me? I am my own person." Carson pointed his finger at his chest. "The marriage ran
its course, and at the end life was a nightmare for both
of us. The only good thing that came out of the marriage was Aaliyah and Ashanti. I will always take care
of and be there for them. I suggest you call a criminal
lawyer because Javier will give you up, especially if he
can cut a deal. And, secondly, you'll need to call your
lawyer because I'm going to apply for full custody of
the girls."

"But, Carson, I love you," Lola protested as she
pulled at his arm. "I did it for us. I wanted you to open
your eyes and see her for the person she is. She's nothing, she's from the gutter. The only thing that woman,"
Lola said venomously, "has going for her is her daddy's
money. I have money too. Please, Carson, let us get
back together for the girls. I need you and they do too."

Carson pushed Lola away from him. "That woman,
as you call Mariah, you're not fit to wipe her feet. I
wouldn't get back with you if someone paid me a billion
dollars. Why can't you understand we're over?" Carson
made a slashing motion across his throat.

"*No*," Lola shouted and stamped her foot. "I will never let you go."

Her doorbell chimed. Lola ignored it. She continued trying to plead her case to Carson.

There was a loud banging at the front door. Lola ignored it, but the sounds continued. She cursed in Spanish, walked to the front door, and flung it open. Her face whitened when she saw who was on the other side. She tried to shield her half-naked body.

"Hello, Mrs. Palmer. My name is Officer Janokowski from the Hammond PD." The detective flashed his badge. "This is my partner, Officer Linton," he introduced the female officer. "I need to talk to you about the break-in that occurred at your ex-husband's office. You might want to put on some clothes. Officer Linton will go with you." He nodded at Carson.

Lola was knocked for a loop. Her hand fluttered to her chest. Her legs felt weak as overcooked spaghetti.

"It's good to see you're on the case." Carson smiled. He looked at his ex-wife and said, "Think about what I said. I'll talk to you later. Oh, I'll pick the girls up from the afterschool program. You may be tied up for a while." Then Carson departed the apartment.

When he returned to the truck, Carson's body throbbed with anger at Lola's audacity. He told himself to calm down as he headed to his daughter's school. He decided to take them to his parents' house and return to the hospital. Carson wondered how Mariah was coping with Cassie. He said a quick prayer and hoped all was going well and that Rosemary's condition had improved.

Chapter Thirty-eight

At the hospital, Sonyell escorted Cassie back to Rosemary's room. When Cassie entered the area and saw her mother lying in the bed, with tubes in her arms, and machines humming, her step faltered. Mariah was standing next to the bed holding Rosemary's hand and talking to her softly.

Cassie thought she'd never seen her mother look so pale. She stood motionlessly near the door and watched the rise and fall of Rosemary's chest to make sure she was still alive.

Cassie walked over to the bed and rudely bumped Mariah aside. "Momma," she yelled in a scratchy voice. "Momma, can you hear me?" She ran her hands across the white sheet covering her mother's body.

Mariah interrupted Cassie, and said firmly, "She needs her rest. Try not to disturb her."

"Don't tell me what to do." Cassie's chin shot up. "She's my mother, not yours. She's always concerned about you and your feelings. Can I just be with my mother for a minute without you telling me what to do?"

Mariah bit her lip. She wanted to tell Cassie to cut the crap, that she knew that Rosemary was her mother too. She realized now was not the time or place. "Sure, but try to be mindful of her condition. She had a bad attack. She's not out of the woods yet."

"Did I ask you?" Cassie retorted as she looked back at Mariah. "I ain't gonna do nothing to hurt Momma.

I love her." Cassie looked like a little girl as she looked down at her mother. She wasn't sure what to do with her hands; she patted Rosemary's arm.

Rosemary opened her eyes. She smiled and then grimaced, as if in pain. "Both my girls are together, praise God." Then she closed her eyes, turned her head, and promptly fell asleep.

"It's the medication," Mariah explained. "She's been in and out. We can only stay with her for ten minutes. I'll be back in the waiting area."

"Thank you," Cassie said and frowned at Mariah's back. She turned back to Rosemary. "Momma, I'm sorry. I hope I ain't the cause of you being here. I promise, Momma, if you get better, I'ma try to get myself together. I ain't said this in a long time, but I love you." She put her head on Rosemary's bosom and cried.

Cassie refused to leave her mother's side, until the nurse came into the room to inform her that time was up. Cassie got lost trying to find the waiting room. When she finally located it, she kept her swollen eyes averted from Mariah, Sonyell, Raquel, and Michael. Cassie sat away from them on the other side of the room.

Michael stood up. "She can have my seat if she wants. I'm going to tell her she can sit with y'all."

"Michael, no." Mariah shook her head before he could leave. "I don't know if I can cope with Cassie and with Granny being so ill. Maybe she should stay where she is."

"I think your grandmother would want the two of you together right now," Sonyell declared. "I know Cassie is not the easiest person in the world to be around. Couldn't you put up with her for a little while?" She looked at Mariah encouragingly. Raquel nodded in agreement.

"I guess. If she gets on my last nerve, then you're going to have to deal with her," Mariah told Sonyell.

Michael walked over to Cassie. He sat next to her and began talking.

"Okay. We got you. Do you want coffee or anything?" Raquel asked. "I need to stretch my legs." She stood up, and waited to see if Mariah wanted anything. Mariah said that she didn't and Rocki departed the room.

Mariah's gaze fell on Michael and Cassie. "I wonder what Michael is saying to Cassie." She turned toward Sonyell.

"Probably the same thing I said to you. How the two of you need to come together for Granny," Sonyell quipped. Her tone became serious. "I have a feeling it's going to be a long night. I need to run and get Sasha from day care. I'm going to take her to my mother's house and then I'll come back."

"Okay." Mariah's grabbed Sonyell's hand. "Please hurry back. I couldn't bear it if something bad was to happen to Granny. Rocki is okay and all, but in a crisis, I'd rather have you here than her."

"I know, girl. I'll be back as soon as I can." She looked at her watch. "I should be back in about an hour. Keep the faith, Granny will be fine." She stood up and headed to the exit.

Michael caught up with her before she reached the door. "Where are you going?"

"I'm going to pick up Sasha from school, take her to my mom's, and then come back."

"I can stay with her. You could drop us off at your house, I'll stay with her. She's going to be worried sick. It's best that one of us stay with her."

Sonyell hesitated then she nodded her head. "Okay. Then I can get back here sooner."

As Mariah looked at the couple departing together, a little smile crossed her lips. She turned her left to see Cassie sitting in the seat next to hers.

"Michael told me to be nice. I know Momma would want me to. I guess it ain't gonna kill me to sit by you," Cassie announced curtly. She looked up at the television screen perched on a stand in the left corner of the room.

Mariah simply bobbed her head up and down. She looked at her watch and discovered she had forty minutes before she could go back and see Rosemary again.

Raquel returned with a cup of coffee. She handed it to Mariah. "Do you want anything?" she asked Cassie, who shook her head.

"Where's Sonni?" Raquel asked Mariah after she took the vacant seat on Mariah's other side.

"She and Michael went to pick up Sasha," Mariah leaned over and told her.

"Hmmm." Raquel narrowed her eyes and shook her head. "I knew they wasn't over."

Carson and Sonyell returned at the same time, about an hour later. Mariah and Cassie took turns checking on Rosemary. Her condition was the same; it hadn't worsened. She would be moved from the emergency room to Cardiac ICU was soon as a bed was available.

By nine o'clock that evening, Cassie was becoming edgy. She became short-tempered, and was clawing at her arms like she had the measles or chicken pox. Everyone noticed her behavior.

"I think I'd better take her home," Carson told Mariah. "She's getting worse. I'll come back if you'd like."

"No, you go on home. I know you need to talk to your girls. I'll call you if anything changes. Carson, thank you for being here with me." She took his hand, and held it tightly. "Your being here makes my heart glad."

"No problem, love. I know you would do the same if it were me." Carson squeezed Mariah's hand lightly. "I love you and I'll do what I can to help."

"I love you too." Mariah became choked with emotion. "I'll see if Cassie is ready to go and walk you to your truck."

She nudged Cassie's arm and whispered, "Are you ready to go? Carson says he'll take you home."

Cassie looked relieved. She jumped out of her seat. "Yeah, I'm ready. I'ma just go see Momma. I'ma tell her I'll be back tomorrow."

"That's good," Mariah said approvingly. "I'm going to spend the night at the hospital. I should be here when you come back." She watched Cassie rush to Rosemary's room.

Cassie returned to the waiting room several minutes later. Mariah and Carson were standing near the exit. Mariah waved Cassie over.

"Bye," Cassie told Sonyell and Raquel. She nearly ran to the exit door.

"Take care. See you tomorrow," Sonyell told her.

As the trio walked to Carson's truck, Mariah said, "Cassie, I know you don't have a phone. How do I get in touch with you, if something were to happen?"

Cassie answered, "I can give you a number. It's to the lady who owns the building I stay in. You can leave a message with her and she can get it to me."

Mariah took her cell phone out of her purse. "Give me the number and I'll program it in my phone."

Cassie recited the number. They arrived at the truck.

"Thanks for coming, Cassie," Mariah said as Carson opened the truck door for Cassie. "I'll call you if anything changes."

"She's my momma," Cassie said dramatically. "Where else would I be?"

"Okay." Mariah held up her hands in surrender. "I'm sorry. What time do you think you'll be here tomorrow?"

"Look, I don't know. I gotta try and find a ride. I'll be here when I get here." She looked at Carson impatiently. "I'm ready if you are." She clawed at her arm again. "This place makes me nervous. Bye, Mari."

Carson gave Mariah a comforting look. He held two finger nears his ear, and mouthed, "I'll call you," before he and Cassie departed.

Mariah returned to her friends and sat in the chair between Sonyell and Raquel. "If you need to go home, I'll understand," she informed them.

"We ain't going nowhere." Raquel thumped her hand on the side of the chair. "We'll sleep here in the waiting room tonight. We are not leaving you alone."

"What did I do to deserve such good friends?" Mariah's voice cracked. "You know I love both of you; thank you for staying with me. If you could just stay until they transfer Granny to a room, I can take it from there."

Raquel turned to Sonyell. "I think this girl is hard of hearing." She put her hand near her ear and said to Mariah, "Didn't you hear me say we were staying with you no matter how long it takes?"

"You know," Sonyell said with a deadpan expression, "she's slow sometimes. We're going to forgive her today. I heard you. You're right; we're going to stay all night."

Mariah reached over and hugged Sonyell, then Raquel. "Again, thanks."

The women talked to pass the time, and Raquel made a food run. They were in and out of Rosemary's emergency room. Finally, the older woman was taken to the Cardiac Intensive Care Unit at 10:00 P.M. After she was settled into her room, the nurse informed Mariah she couldn't stay in the room with Rosemary, since she was in intensive care, but that the three women were more than welcome to bunk in the waiting room.

Mariah called Carson and he told her the girls were at his house. He told her again to stand on faith, and to call him if she needed to talk regardless of the time. When Mariah finished talking to Carson, she went to the ladies' room. She splashed cold water on her face. She looked fatigued. She closed her eyes, "Father, thank you for allowing my Granny to live one more day. Lord, please take care of her. I can't imagine life without her. Thank you for my sisters, Sonni and Rocki. I don't know where I'd be without them. They are my rocks in the storm. And, Father, thank you for bringing Carson into my life. In the midst of his problems, he took time to take care of me. Lord, help me to be kinder to Cassie. I know that's what Granny would want. These blessings, I ask in Jesus' name. Amen."

Mariah felt strengthened. She realized that she wasn't alone. God had sent angels to her in her time of need. Most of all, the Father was there for her to lean on whenever she needed to. The old song "Jesus on the Mainline" came to mind. He was available twenty-four seven. Mariah inhaled deeply, and exhaled. Then, she departed to check on her grandmother.

Chapter Thirty-nine

Two weeks later, Rosemary was released from the hospital. The heart attack she'd suffered was severe. She was put on a new regimen of medication, and a new diet. The cardiologist informed Rosemary that she couldn't return to work for at least three months. Mariah was hoping her grandmother wouldn't ever return to work. She planned to care for Rosemary, as Rosemary had cared for her as a child. The physician emphasized the importance of rest. If Rosemary's condition continued to improve, then she could resume normal activities within six months.

A week after Rosemary's heart attack, Sonyell and Raquel supervised the move from Mariah's father's house to her new one. The spare bedroom was prepared for Rosemary's recuperation.

Rosemary initially insisted on going home. But after talking to her doctor, she realized Mariah's house was the best place for her to be. Cassie didn't return to the hospital for a couple of days after Rosemary's attack. It was obvious to everyone when she did reappear that she had binged.

Rosemary became troubled. She begged Cassie to consider entering a rehabilitation facility. Mariah didn't want her grandmother to suffer a setback, so she found a highly recommended facility in Arizona. Cassie couldn't refuse her mother's pleas for her to go for treatment due to Rosemary's health issues.

A week later when Mariah and Carson went to pick up Cassie to take her to the airport for her flight to Arizona, Cassie was a no-show. Mariah had to bite her tongue, and refrain from saying to Rosemary, "I told you so."

Rosemary again implored her daughter to go to Arizona for treatment. Three days later, Sonyell and Michael drove Cassie to O'Hare Airport. That time Cassie was on the nonstop flight to Phoenix.

Carson picked up Rosemary and Mariah from the hospital the day Rosemary was released. He drove them to Mariah's new home. He didn't stay long since he had a hearing for custody of his daughters that afternoon. He told Mariah he'd come by later.

"Well, Granny, I guess it's you and me again," Mariah told her grandmother after Rosemary had settled into bed in the guest bedroom. "See, you couldn't get rid of me that easily." She pulled the peach floral comforter over her grandmother's shoulders.

"I guess you're right, this time," Rosemary admitted. "Don't get the idea that my stay here is permanent. As soon as I'm back on my feet, I'm going home," Rosemary insisted.

"No, you're not," Mariah shot back. "The coach house is ready for you to move into. I don't think you should live alone. I have a perfectly good house out back waiting for you."

"I'll think about it." Rosemary smiled. Secretly, she enjoyed being pampered by Mariah.

"It's not up for discussion," Mariah chided her grandmother. "Are you hungry? Can I get you anything?"

"I think it's time for my medication. You can bring me a glass of water."

"Fine, I'll be right back." Mariah left the room and went to the bathroom and returned with a paper cup of water. She sat at the reclining chair near the bed.

"I like what I saw of the house. It looks real good," Rosemary commented after she set the cup on the nightstand.

"Luckily, most of the work was done. The house was painted and new carpeting was installed. All that was left was to move furniture from the old house to here. Carson, Michael, and Alex handled that part with ease."

"Carson is a great young man. I am glad God put him in your path. If anything had happened to me you would have been in good hands," Rosemary commented. She shifted her body slightly. She glanced around the room. The bedroom set was oak. There was a wall-mounted television. Mariah had put her clothes in the closet. The room had an attached bathroom.

"Nothing was going to happen to you. It wasn't your time." Mariah held up her hand.

"I know you want to talk about me and Harold and what happened. Just give me a little time, if you don't mind. I need to get clear in my head as to what I want to say to you."

"That's fine. I plan to continue reading his journals. I'd like to hear his side too, if you don't mind."

"Now that everything is out in the open, I think you should," Rosemary said magnanimously. "I realize I handled the situation incorrectly. It was just a different era back then. I hope you can find it in your heart to forgive me." Rosemary looked ashamed.

"Consider it done. I'm going to fix you lunch. I'll be back in a sec." Mariah left the room and went downstairs to the kitchen.

She smiled admiringly at the furnishings in the house. She loved her new place.

That morning Mariah had received a letter from the Hammond Planning Commission asking her to come in for a meeting. Mariah was hopeful her dreams would eventually come to fruition.

***

After Rosemary had eaten lunch and was asleep, Mariah returned to her bedroom and picked up a journal and continued reading. She was engrossed in the entries when her telephone rang.

"Hi, babe," she greeted Carson. "How did the hearing go?"

"It went well. I now have sole custody of the girls. Luckily, I didn't have any problems. As soon as I got wind that Lola was going to be charged in connection with the robbery at my office, I called my lawyer. He prepared the necessary paperwork."

"That's good. What's happening with Lola?"

"It looks like she'll get off with probation. She's spent all of a night in jail. The next day her father posted bail. I heard that Lola was ranting and raving like a madwoman. Her cousin, Javier, confessed she was the mastermind behind the break-in."

"I don't want to speak ill of your ex, but what a shame. It's obvious she's still in love with you," Mariah remarked as she shook her head.

"In her mind she is. In reality Lola just hates to lose. She has always been overly competitive. When she realized I was serious about you, her competitive nature went haywire."

"And that is why, Mr. Palmer, I don't like to deal with men with children: too much baby momma drama," Mariah responded.

"I'd like to think all exes are not like Lola; she's the exception to the rule."

"Why is it we never hear about them, I wonder?" Mariah commented cattily.

"Why you ask? Because the media shoves drama down our throats. Look, at all the reality shows. Most of them are full of drama or so I hear," Carson answered firmly.

"You could have a point there. So, are you up to being a single parent? I don't envy you that task."

"Whether I am or not, I've got to get ready fast. Although, I think I am. It helped that Lola and I shared joint custody. So now, the challenge begins, taking care of my daughters every day."

"Do you think you'll ever split custody with Lola again?" Mariah couldn't prevent herself from asking. She knew that her relationship with Carson had changed the minute he told her that he had taken the girls from Lola. She was aware that Carson spending more time with his daughters would leave less time for her.

"I'll cross that bridge when and if I have to. As part of her probation Lola will have to see a psychologist. I will have to wait for a clean bill of health from the doctor. If that occurs, then and only then would I consider joint custody with her again," Carson answered truthfully.

"So where does leave us?" Mariah asked. This was one of those times she wished that life stood still and never changed. She loved Carson dearly. But due to Lola's drama and his having full custody of his daughters, she didn't think they would have time to take their relationship to the next level. Mariah wasn't quite ready for marriage. But she couldn't imagine life without Carson.

"Things will change to a certain degree, that's true," Carson admitted. "But life always changes, Mari. Nothing stays the same. I care for you, and by that I mean I love you deeply. I just ask that you continue what we have and see where life takes us. I have plenty of family, that village it takes to raise children. And, my family will always be there to step in when needed and that time will be spent with you.

"I think we have that once-in-a-lifetime relationship that people dream of. God has blessed us. He will see us through any storms we may encounter. He was already on the case when Rocki went to the bar, and heard Javier bragging. So I suggest we stay on the status quo and see where life leads us. I already know where it will, if a certain businesswoman is willing to take a chance and follow her heart."

Mariah exhaled loudly. "You're right, I'll have to be patient. I will put in the time to see where the relationship and God leads us."

"That's all I ask," Carson responded, clearly relieved. "So how are things going with your grandmother?"

"Pretty good. She tried to make a stand for independence about moving back to the Garden and I told her that I wasn't having it. The only place she could move is to the coach house."

"How did she feel about that?" Carson chuckled.

"I think she's ready to stay here now that her secrets are out in the open."

"Good. She should enjoy the fruits of your labor. Are you nervous about the meeting with the planning committee?"

"Nope. Not really. That meeting is one step closer to the transition home being a reality. Sonni and I are already on it. We'd already anticipated some of their questions. Sonni has put together a very compelling PowerPoint presentation. I meant to ask you, how do Ali and Ashanti feel about staying with you?"

"I couldn't tell them what had really gone down with Lola. So I simply told them that their mother is tired and needs a rest and that they're going to hang out with me for a while. Ali was upset as I knew she would be. I feel like Lola was becoming too much of a negative influence on her anyway. Shanti is fine with the new living arrangement. So we'll work through it."

"One of my church members is a psychologist. If you think they need to talk to someone let me know. Zora has a great reputation," Mariah offered.

"I will keep that in mind." Carson looked up to see a computer technician at his door. "Say, I've got to run. My computer system is being installed today. I didn't need to upgrade, but with the check from the robbery, I decided why not. It won't hurt."

"Good idea. I'll talk to you later. I'm going to look over my notes for the presentation, and read more journals. Talk at you later."

"If you need me to run any errands let me know. I'll see you later," Carson informed Mariah.

The call was ended. Mariah checked on Rosemary and then she went to her bedroom. She sat on the chaise longue. She turned on the nightstand light and picked up a journal and read:

After I got out of the service, I went to Chicago to pay my respects to Rosemary Green. I still couldn't believe that Jojo hadn't ever been found. It was like he'd disappeared off the face of the earth. I miss my friend. Rosemary was still grieving for her husband. I always knew she and Jojo shared a special love. All he talked about was Rosie, as he called her, you couldn't shut him up. I envied him for finding that special woman. I had saved up my money from the service, Uncle Sam saw to our every need, so I have a nice little nest egg saved. When I met Rosemary, she was sad like I knew she would be. Rosemary is a spunky woman. I offered her part of my money, and tried to explain that's what Jojo would have wanted, but she would have none of it.

Cassie was a sullen young woman. It was obvious that she was still missing her Daddy. I tried to engage her in conversation, but her answers were always

*short, monotonic. Sometimes I think she resented me,
because I am still alive and Jojo's whereabouts are
unknown. I think if she gives me time to get to know
me, she might feel different, but maybe not.*

Mariah skimmed over entries regarding Harold's
employment and was drawn to the ones that mentioned her grandmother.

*I know Rosemary doesn't make much money, so
I leave little amounts of money at her house. I want
to help her, but she still doesn't want to take money
from me. So I leave it on the bottom shelf of the cocktail table where she'll find it. I go see her once a week,
usually on the weekends. We talk about Jojo and Vietnam. It's not a subject that I really want to talk about.
When I think of 'Nam, I feel horrified. It was a terrible
place to be. We killed people, even children, and that
will haunt me the rest of my days.*

Another entry dated six months later read:

*I have come to care deeply for Rosemary. I love her
but she still clings to the notion that Jojo will come
home one day. I coaxed her into going to dinner with
me. I had never seen her dressed in anything except
work clothes, a dress or skirt and blouse. She dressed
up, her thick hair was down, and she had on makeup.
I was enthralled with her closeness, and the scent of
her perfume. I knew she was feeling lonely. I hoped I
wasn't taking advantage of her since we ended up at
a motel making love. Rosie felt so guilty afterward. I
told her that I love her, and want to take care of her
and Cassie. Rosie told me in no uncertain terms that
that wasn't going to happen. She still loved Jojo and
she would wait for him as long as it took. She told me
I was wasting my time with her and that I should find
someone who was free to love me. I disagreed, but I
will give her time to see things my way. When I took*

Rosie home, she told me she didn't want to see me again. I told her I'd see her Friday and I plan to.

Mariah shut the journal. Thoughts swirled through her head. She was shocked to read about that side of her grandmother. Rosemary was tightlipped about the past. She only shared good times about Joseph. Realistically, Mariah realized that her birth was a secret, one that would be hard for Rosemary to explain. Mariah had about five journals in her room and she skipped to the one predating her birth.

I am beginning to make headway with Rosie. We kind of got careless after going to the movies. I brought her home, kissed her, and then there was a ruckus from the kitchen. Cassie began screaming hysterically. She ran over to me and began pounding me with her fists. Rosie pulled her off me, and held Cassie's arms. She asked me to leave and never come back. I went back a week later. I sat in my car around the corner from Rosie's house and waited for Cassie to leave for school. Well, I saw Cassie leave, but she didn't go to school, she met a boy, they left, and she never got on the bus to go to school. I walked to Rosie's house. She was quite upset when she opened the door and saw me standing there. I again tried to convince her to marry me. We had a good thing going on. Rosemary was adamant that she was going to wait for Jojo.

We continued to meet each other secretly. Cassie was giving her the blues. She missed curfew, started skipping school, and Rosemary had lost what little control she had over her daughter. Then, I met Rosemary one Friday night and I could tell immediately that she was upset. After she got inside my car, she told me the words that would change my life. That she was pregnant with my child.

Chapter Forty

After Mariah read those words, her breathing became shallow. Her eyes teared. Mariah's hands became clammy, and she couldn't read another journal for two days. When she picked up the journal the next time, Mariah had to force herself to read.

I am happy about becoming a father. Being an orphan with no family, knowing I would have a child is a dream come true. I just know Rosie will marry me after she calms down. I know she could have Jojo declared legally dead since enough time had elapsed. Instead I was in for a rude awakening. Rosemary again insisted that I leave and told me she never wanted to see me again. I went back for a solid month and she never opened the door.

I am heartbroken and at odds. One of my army buddies, Walter Stinson, moved to Hammond, Indiana. He had used his G.I. loan to start a business and asked me if I wanted to work with him. I decided to move to Hammond. It wasn't far from Chicago and especially from the Garden. I could check on Rosie from time to time. I sent her cash and keep hoping and praying she would have a change of heart. She didn't. I went to see her around the time the baby should have been born. She let me inside the house, and told me coldly that she had a miscarriage. I didn't believe her, and then I heard a baby cry from upstairs. I flew upstairs like a bat out of hell to Rosie's bedroom. Nothing. Then I went to Cassie's bedroom and saw a bassinet. By the time Rosie came upstairs. I asked her about the baby. She told me Cassie had gotten pregnant and the baby was Cassie's. I know in my heart, Rosie is lying. I told her I understood how she felt about Jojo, but please don't make me deny my child. I picked up the child, saw it was a girl, and fell in love for the second time in my life.

Rosie went downstairs and waited for me to come back down. She told me that I couldn't see her or the child ever again and to go on and live my life.

I'm not too ashamed to say that I begged Rosie and even cried for her not to deny me my child. Her mind was made up and I couldn't change it. All I could do was make sure my child was taken care of financially. I didn't think I'd ever love again. Everybody I had ever loved was taken away from me, even my child.

Mariah read the next entries; Harold talked about meeting his wife Dorothy two years after his breakup with her grandmother. How his business with Walter was booming. Harold was ready to settle down and raise a family, but alas that was not to be.

Dottie and I have been married for five years and she hasn't been able to have a baby. We went to the doctor and found out that she's unable to bear children. I felt as low as I did the day Rosie told me to leave and not come back. I don't love Dottie with the intensity that I loved Rosie. But, we have a good life. She is an excellent wife and I will stand by her, though she offered to give me a divorce. She knows how much I want children. I joined a church in Hammond, and after that I

*turned my life over to God and became saved.
I've done well financially and I've vowed to help
children, especially males. I feel like I can make a
difference in the world.*

*At times I think I'll go crazy following Rosie's
wishes. I sneak to the Garden for glimpses of my
daughter. What a fine young woman she's grown
into. I went to her eighth grade graduation. I sent
Rosie an extra check to cover expenses. God, I
wish I could tell her who I am, but I know I can't.
I will cherish and love her from afar.*

*I paid for Mariah's high school expenses and
even paid for her and her friends to go on their
class trip to Cancun. I would see her and two girls
who appeared to be her best friends from time
to time. I sent Rosie a hefty check for Mariah to
attend college. I was disappointed that Mariah
didn't want to attend a four-year college. I had
been putting money aside for that since the day
she was born. But, it's her choice as to schooling,
not mine. I am so proud of my girl.*

Mariah's heart rate increased when she read her father's first entry about Carson.

*I met a young man at the Boys & Girls Club
today named Carson Palmer. He's a little misguided right now because his father has a drinking problem. Carson has a good head on his
shoulders. He has a knack for the construction
business. I'm going to encourage him to go to college and get his degree. When he finishes, I'll help
him finance his own business.*

Though she knew she shouldn't, Mariah put down the current journal and picked up the last one. She quickly read the last few entries.

My Dottie is gone, I am all alone. Carson comes by to check on me regularly. I have prostate cancer and I know my time on earth grows short. I have had a wonderful life; my only regret is that I didn't meet my daughter. I plan to leave all my money to her. I have read in the newspapers about her accomplishments in the Garden. Rosie did a good job raising her. I don't know how Rosie pulled it off, but apparently her plan that Cassie become Mariah's mother worked. Mariah is my mother's name. So I know Rosie didn't forget me completely. I will go to meet my Maker soon, knowing I have been a blessed man. I have talked to Carson about Mariah. I hope those two meet one day. I would love to have had him for a son-in-law. I have told Carson if he ever meets my daughter, not to talk to her about my relationship with Rosie. I know it's a long shot those two meeting. But, you never know what God has planned. I want my daughter to get to know me from my journals.

I am beginning to feel weak; I know the end is not far off. I will see my Dottie again, and maybe my parents I never knew. I will still be able to keep an eye on my girl from heaven. I am ready to be with the King.

The last entry read:

Mariah, I loved you. I was never able to tell the world you were mine. You've had a special place in my heart since Rosemary told me she was pregnant. I am not upset with Rosie. I understand why she did what she did. Don't hold it against her. She was trying to protect you. It was a different time when you were born. Take care of her as I would have. Love, your father, Harold Ellison.

Mariah put down the journal. Tears spilled from her eyes. She cried for the man she'd never known. God had blessed her with a father and she just didn't know it. Mariah was too aware that she had received many blessings from the fathers, her earthly and heavenly one.

A few weeks later Mariah went into Rosemary's room. Her grandmother was up watching a soap opera on the television. Mariah sat in a chair next to the bed. "Granny, I've read Harold's story. It is truly heartbreaking and I only have one question for you. How did you get away with Cassie being pregnant and not you?" The young woman's eyes shone with a bright intensity.

Rosemary turned to her granddaughter and explained. "Cassie made it a little easy for me. Unknown to me she had already dropped out of high school. I was always thick and my pregnancy showed in my behind, not my midsection. So no one really knew I was pregnant, just that I had put on a little weight. I managed to talk Cassie into staying in the house, at least until I gave birth. When we went out she had a pillow stuffed down her pants."

Rosemary lay back against the pillows and closed her eyes, as if reliving her daughter's birth date. "Alma is a nurse and at that time she worked in a doctor's office and not at the hospital, where she works now. When I went into labor, she came over and helped me with the delivery. She cut the cord, cleaned you off, and placed you in my arms. Alma and Cassie took care of me.

"To convince Cassie to say you were her baby and not mine, I explained how I couldn't bring shame upon the family and most of all, upon her father. We never stopped hoping that one day Joseph would return home," Rosemary said sadly, "but he didn't.

"The doctor Alma worked for came to my house and helped us do the birth certificate. We took it downtown to the Department of Vital Records. That's what happened." Rosemary opened her eyes.

"Did you ever love my father?" Mariah couldn't help but ask. She sat on the edge of her seat.

"I loved Harold in my own way. He was not the love of my life, Joseph was," Rosemary proclaimed.

"If Granddaddy had been declared dead and not MIA, do you think you would have married Harold?"

"Maybe," Rosemary allowed. "I knew he was a good man and that Harold was headed places much like you." Rosemary smiled. "I loved him. But I couldn't risk hurting Joseph, if by a miracle he came home."

"Fair enough," Mariah said. "That's all I wanted to know. Thank you, Granny. I haven't wrapped my head completely around you the fact that you're my mother yet. I love you, I always will. I wish things had turned out differently and I'd grown up with my father."

"I wish I had allowed that to happen especially since Harold didn't have children except you. I think he forgave me. I just hope you will." Rosemary's eyes filled with tears. She reached for Mariah.

Mariah rose from her chair and sat on the bed next to Rosemary. The two women hugged each other, and stayed that way for a long time, each mourning the loss of two special men.

Epilogue

The opening of the transitional house was scheduled to open on June 19, 2012. A little less than two years after Mariah talked to Attorney Cook about her inheritance. Mariah and Sonyell had worked nonstop over the past few days to ensure the event would go smoothly. Hammond dignitaries would be on hand for the event. It was rumored the governor of Indiana would attend.

The sun was shining, peeping from the thick, downy clouds, a hint that the day would be a triumph.

Mariah stood in her bedroom in front of her dresser. She put a pair of earrings in her ears. She stood back and admired her red power suit with a white silk blouse. She was dressed for success. Mariah put perfume on her wrist and patted her hair one final time. She closed her eyes in prayer. "Father, thank you for the many blessings you have bestowed upon me. The journey to today wasn't an easy one. I had a few setbacks. But, with your help I've weathered the storm. Thank you for keeping my mother safe. Her health has improved, as well as my and Cassie's relationship. Thank you for my friends who have been there with me every step of the way. Most of all, thank for sending me a good man. Carson was right, I just had to stand on faith and that included my relationship with him. Father, you have never failed me. Bless the house we are opening today, and the people who are going to occupy it. Father, I love and praise you." Mariah raised her arms upward.

A few minutes later Mariah went to fetch Rosemary and Cassie from the coach house. The older woman looked younger and quite attractive. Her health was on the upswing and with the releasing of her secrets, Rosemary looked years younger.

Cassie had completed her treatment after a few relapses; so far she'd been clean for six months. She and Rosemary received counseling with Zora and their relationship had improved. Cassie had put on a few pounds, Raquel had hooked up her hair, and she bore little resemblance to the drug addict she'd been a year ago. Cassie wore a black dress, and looked quite presentable.

After the women exited the house, Mariah locked the door and put her keys inside her purse, when they heard the shrill beep, beep of a horn. Carson was pulling his Cadillac into Mariah's driveway. He and his daughters hurriedly exited the vehicle.

Ashanti ran to Mariah and hugged her waist. "Miss Mari, this is so exciting. You are a celebrity," the young girl gushed. She took Mariah's hand.

"Oh, I wouldn't say all that." Mariah smiled modestly. She looked at Aaliyah. "How are you today?"

"Good," Aaliyah replied. Her eyes were set on the television trucks parked in front of Green-Ellison House. "I'm with Shanti. This is exciting. Are we going to be on television?"

"I'd say it's a good chance," Mariah answered. She turned to Carson. He looked handsome as always in a dark suit, and white shirt.

He bent down and asked her, "Are you ready for today?"

"As ready as I am going to be." Mariah sighed. "For real, I'm just as excited as the girls. My dream is coming true."

"You should be proud and excited rolled into one. I am proud of you."

"Thank you, Mr. Palmer," Mariah replied with a huge smile on her face. She took his hand and the group walked across the street.

Flashbulbs greeted them when they walked in the house. Local newspapers covered the story. Rocki headed their way with Sonyell, Michael, and Sasha behind her.

The friends hugged and kissed. Everyone offered congratulations to Mariah. They walked inside the house. Mariah took the dignitaries on a tour of the home. Mrs. Palmer and Granny were now in business partnership with each other. They shared ownership of Mrs. Palmer's catering company. The women served light refreshments.

When the tour ended the director of Green-Ellison House introduced the first occupants of the house. Eight mothers and daughters tearfully thanked Mariah for the opportunity to get their lives together.

Carson and Michael talked when there was a lull in the festivities.

"You and Sonni seem to be doing okay. I guess you two managed to settle your differences," Carson commented to his employee.

"We're still a work in progress." Michael nodded with a twinkle in his eyes. "But, I think we're going to be okay." He whispered, "Hey, boss man, I may need a raise. I plan to ask Sonni to marry me real soon, and this time I think she's gonna to say yes."

"You got it. We'll talk on Monday." Carson held out his hand. He and Michael clasped hands.

"So when you and Mari going do the thing?" Michael queried his boss.

"Soon I hope. I was waiting on her to finish doing her thing with the home. I plan on popping the question soon. I think she's ready too." Carson's eyes followed Mariah, while Michael's were trained on Sonyell.

Everyone took a seat. Reverend Dudley read scripture and prayed for the success of the transitional home. Then, Hammond dignitaries made speeches.

When they were done, it was Mariah's turn to speak. She walked to the podium, and adjusted the microphone. "Praise God, from whom all blessings flow. Today has been a dream come true for me. I've always had a burning desire to help people. Everyone needs help now and again. The Bible teaches us to love our neighbor as ourselves. This project of love was the result of hard work of many people. There are a few people in attendance that I'd like to give thanks to. First and foremost are my lifelong friends, Sonni and Rocki. I love my sisters from another mother. I'd like to thank the Hammond Planning Committee, for making suggestions where needed. I'd like to thank the mayor for giving the green light to implement the program.

"I have to give a shout-out to my mother." She smiled at Rosemary, who blew her a kiss. "She molded me into the woman I am today. I also have to thank my friend, Mr. Carson Palmer. He lent me an ear to bounce many ideas off of. He was responsible for the renovations to the house. All of this"—Mariah's arm swept the air— "would not have occurred without the blessings from the fathers. My biological one, Harold Green, and my heavenly one." She pointed upward.

The audience applauded loudly. Mariah finished her speech and basked in the afterglow of a job well done, and the love of family and friends, especially Carson.

She and Sonyell knew their men planned on popping the question soon, and like Sonyell, Mariah's answer would be *yes*.

Mariah looked up and smiled. She knew her father was up in heaven, blowing kisses her way. While the other Father said, "Good and faithful servant, well done!"

Readers' Discussion Guide

1. Should Rosemary have told Mariah about her conception when Mariah became older?

2. How difficult is it for a parent to admit parental secrets to a child?

3. Did you feel Rosemary was responsible for Cassie's emotional problems? Did you understand Rosemary's reasons for the deception?

4. Do you feel like Rosemary was a bad mother?

5. Did Mariah idolize her grandmother?

6. Should Carson have confessed to Mariah he knew the truth of her conception or abided by her father's wishes as he did?

7. Should Mariah's father had overridden Rosemary's wishes and told Mariah that he was her father?

8. Do you feel Mariah remained rooted even after inheriting millions of dollars? Would you gift a house to your closest friends if you could afford to?

9. Was Raquel a true friend to Mariah, even though their philosophies on life were different?

10. Did Carson initially allow Lola too much leeway in his life after their divorce?

11. What did you think about Lola using her children to scheme to win Carson back?

12. Did you feel Cassie was a bad person or just misguided?

13. Who was your favorite character?

14. Who was your least favorite character?

15. Do you think if a family member knows a secret about another family member that they should tell that person? Why or why not?

16. Do you think Mariah emotionally distanced herself from meaningful relationships with men because of her unresolved issues with her father?

17. What do you think of celibacy in a relationship? Is it possible or not?

About The Author

Michelle Larks is an Illinoisan native. She was born and raised in the Windy City, Chicago, and currently resides in a western suburb. Michelle was educated in the Chicago public school system and attended the University of Illinois at Chicago.

Michelle has written eleven books since 2003. The titles include *A Myriad of Emotions, Crisis Mode, Mirrored Images.* (in e-book format) and *Who's Your Daddy.* Michelle contributed to two anthologies, *Blended Families* and *The Midnight Clear.*

Urban Christian Books published: *Keeping Misery Company, The Legacies, 'Til Debt Do Us Part, Faith, Couples Therapy,* and *Letting Misery Go,* the sequel to *Keeping Misery Company.*

Michelle is married and the mother of two adult daughters.

UC HIS GLORY BOOK CLUB!

www.uchisglorybookclub.net

UC His Glory Book Club is the spirit-inspired brain-child of Joylynn Jossel, Author and Acquisitions Editor of Urban Christian, and Kendra Norman-Bellamy, Author for Urban Christian. This is an online book club that hosts authors of Urban Christian. We welcome as members all men and women who have a passion for reading Christian-based fiction.

UC His Glory Book Club pledges our commitment to provide support, positive feedback, encouragement, and a forum whereby members can openly discuss and review the literary works of Urban Christian authors.

There is no membership fee associated with UC His Glory Book Club; however, we do ask that you support the authors through purchasing, encouraging, providing book reviews, and of course, your prayers. We also ask that you respect our beliefs and follow the guidelines of the book club. We hope to receive your valuable input, opinions, and reviews that build up, rather than tear down our authors.

What We Believe:

—We believe that Jesus is the Christ, Son of the Living God.

—We believe the Bible is the true, living Word of God.

—We believe all Urban Christian authors should use their God-given writing abilities to honor God and share the message of the written word God has given to each of them uniquely.

—We believe in supporting Urban Christian authors in their literary endeavors by reading, purchasing and sharing their titles with our online community.

—We believe that in everything we do in our literary arena should be done in a manner that will lead to God being glorified and honored.

—We look forward to the online fellowship with you. Please visit us often at *www.uchisglorybookclub.net*.

Many Blessing to You!
Shelia E. Lipsey,
President, UC His Glory Book Club

ORDER FORM
URBAN BOOKS, LLC
78 E. Industry Ct
Deer Park, NY 11729

Name:(please print):_____

Address: _____

City/State: _____

Zip: _____

QTY	TITLES	PRICE

Shipping and handling-add $3.50 for 1st book, then $1.75 for each additional book.
Please send a check payable to:
Urban Books, LLC
Please allow 4-6 weeks for delivery

ORDER FORM
URBAN BOOKS, LLC
78 E. Industry Ct
Deer Park, NY 11729

Name: (please print): _____

Address: _____

City/State: _____

Zip: _____

QTY	TITLES	PRICE
	3:57 A.M Timing Is Everything	$14.95
	A Man's Worth	$14.95
	A Woman's Worth	$14.95
	Abundant Rain	$14.95
	After The Feeling	$14.95
	Amaryllis	$14.95
	An Inconvenient Friend	$14.95
	Battle of Jericho	$14.95
	Be Careful What You Pray For	$14.95
	Beautiful Ugly	$14.95
	Been There Prayed That:	$14.95
	Before Redemption	$14.95

Shipping and handling-add $3.50 for 1st book, then $1.75 for each additional book.

Please send a check payable to:

Urban Books, LLC

Please allow 4-6 weeks for delivery

ORDER FORM
URBAN BOOKS, LLC
78 E. Industry Ct
Deer Park, NY 11729

Name: (please print): _____

Address: _____

City/State: _____

Zip: _____

QTY	TITLES	PRICE
	By the Grace of God	$14.95
	Confessions Of A preachers Wife	$14.95
	Dance Into Destiny	$14.95
	Deliver Me From My Enemies	$14.95
	Desperate Decisions	$14.95
	Divorcing the Devil	$14.95
	Faith	$14.95
	First Comes Love	$14.95
	Flaws and All	$14.95
	Forgiven	$14.95
	Former Rain	$14.95
	Forsaken	$14.95

Shipping and handling-add $3.50 for 1st book, then $1.75 for each additional book.

Please send a check payable to:

Urban Books, LLC

Please allow 4-6 weeks for delivery

ORDER FORM
URBAN BOOKS, LLC
78 E. Industry Ct
Deer Park, NY 11729

Name: (please print): _____

Address: _____

City/State: _____

Zip: _____

QTY	TITLES	PRICE
	From Sinner To Saint	$14.95
	From The Extreme	$14.95
	God Is In Love With You	$14.95
	God Speaks To Me	$14.95
	Grace And Mercy	$14.95
	Guilty Of Love	$14.95
	Happily Ever Now	$14.95
	Heaven Bound	$14.95
	His Grace His Mercy	$14.95
	His Woman His Wife His Widow	$14.95
	Illusions	$14.95
	In Green Pastures	$14.95

Shipping and handling-add $3.50 for 1st book, then $1.75 for each additional book.

Please send a check payable to:

Urban Books, LLC

Please allow 4-6 weeks for delivery

ORDER FORM
URBAN BOOKS, LLC
78 E. Industry Ct
Deer Park, NY 11729

Name:(please print):_____

Address: _____

City/State: _____

Zip: _____

QTY	TITLES	PRICE
	Into Each Life	$14.95
	Keep Your enemies Closer	$14.95
	Keeping Misery Company	$14.95
	Latter Rain	$14.95
	Living Consequences	$14.95
	Living Right On Wrong Street	$14.95
	Losing It	$14.95
	Love Honor Stray	$14.95
	Marriage Mayhem	$14.95
	Me, Myself and Him	$14.95
	Murder Through The Grapevine	$14.95
	My Father's House	$14.95

Shipping and handling-add $3.50 for 1st book, then $1.75 for each additional book.
Please send a check payable to:
Urban Books, LLC
Please allow 4-6 weeks for delivery

ORDER FORM
URBAN BOOKS, LLC
78 E. Industry Ct
Deer Park, NY 11729

Name: (please print):_____

Address: _____

City/State: _____

Zip: _____

QTY	TITLES	PRICE
	My Mother's Child	$14.95
	My Son's Ex Wife	$14.95
	My Son's Wife	$14.95
	My Soul Cries Out	$14.95
	Not Guilty Of Love	$14.95
	Prodigal	$14.95
	Rain Storm	$14.95
	Redemption Lake	$14.95
	Right Package, Wrong Baggage	$14.95
	Sacrifice The One	$14.95
	Secret Sisterhood	$14.95
	Secrets And Lies	$14.95

Shipping and handling-add $3.50 for 1st book, then $1.75 for each additional book.
Please send a check payable to:
Urban Books, LLC
Please allow 4-6 weeks for delivery

ORDER FORM
URBAN BOOKS, LLC
78 E. Industry Ct
Deer Park, NY 11729

Name: (please print): _____

Address: _____

City/State: _____

Zip: _____

QTY	TITLES	PRICE
	Selling My soul	$14.95
	She Who Finds A Husband	$14.95
	Sheena's Dream	$14.95
	Sinsatiable	$14.95
	Someone To Love Me	$14.95
	Something On The Inside	$14.95
	Song Of Solomon	$14.95
	Soon After	$14.95
	Soon And Very Soon	$14.95
	Soul Confession	$14.95
	Still Guilty	$14.95

Shipping and handling-add $3.50 for 1st book, then $1.75 for each additional book.
Please send a check payable to:
Urban Books, LLC
Please allow 4-6 weeks for delivery

ORDER FORM
URBAN BOOKS, LLC
78 E. Industry Ct
Deer Park, NY 11729

Name:(please print):_____

Address: _____

City/State: _____

Zip: _____

QTY	TITLES	PRICE

Shipping and handling-add $3.50 for 1ˢᵗ book, then $1.75 for each additional book.
Please send a check payable to:
      Urban Books, LLC
Please allow 4-6 weeks for delivery